BETRAYED

THE TAELLANETH - BOOK 3

VANESSA NELSON

BETRAYED

The Taellaneth - Book 3

Vanessa Nelson

For more information about Vanessa Nelson or her books visit: http://www.taellaneth.com

Cover design by Lou Harper at CoverAffairs.com

For my fellow alumni of the online self-editing course Autumn 2014 and our fabulous tutors

It's hard to believe the course was so long ago!
Your sharp insights, wisdom and humour have helped me more than you can know
No green socks in this story, though!

CONTENTS

CHAPTER ONE

T he air was saturated with the heady scent of spring, fresh green and citrus cut through with the coolness of water. The burner was turned as low as Arrow could manage, the pot simmering gently, mixture almost the right shade of green. Almost. Almost.

Even as she reached for the handle to take the pot off the heat, the colour shifted in a blink from forest green to mud brown, the scent of growing replaced by a stink Arrow had no reference for.

"Oh, fur and fang," she said to the uncaring air, borrowing a favourite phrase of the 'kin, and ducked under the workbench, tucking her legs and arms underneath its shelter, covering her head with her hands.

Above her the pot exploded silently, the brown, sticky, stinking stuff spattering every surface. An impossible volume from such a small vessel. It coated the large workspace. The wooden bench. The concrete floor. The pale, painted walls. The plasterboard lining the ceiling, high overhead. The skylights. The side of the vehicle parked several feet away.

Pieces of the pot, a hardened ceramic that had been extremely expensive, clattered to the floor next to Arrow's feet. She took a moment to be glad she had worn socks today.

Breathing in the fumes, she tried to find something else to be grateful for as her eyes watered with the smell. All the cupboard doors were closed, the open shelves covered with heavy duty tarpaulin. Cleaning up was going to be easier. This time. After the first two attempts had resulted in similar explosions, noxious stuff spread all over her workspace, coating her few precious books, and her, she had learned to be cautious. Numerous attempts later, and she felt she was making progress. At least she had a routine for cleaning now.

When the bits of pot had settled, she cautiously crept out from under the bench, wrinkling her nose, then coughing on the fumes as she straightened. The words of the cleaning spell stuck in her throat and she had to cough some more before she could send the spell out. She made a mental note to pre-prepare a household cleansing spell for next time.

Silver magic rose around her, cutting through the stench and spiralling out across all the surfaces, the magic finding its way into every crevice that the potion had gone, leaving pure, clear surfaces behind. The cleansing spell gathered the noxious remnants into a tight ball in the room's fireplace, then set that alight, burning fast and hot, until there was only another handful of ash to add to the pile already in the grate.

With the surfaces clear, she sent another flare of magic up to the ceiling to open the skylights, letting out the remnants of the smell and letting in some fresh air, carrying the faintest scent of spring.

Worst of the damage taken care of, she bundled the bits of pot into a waste bag and padded across the floor to the large waste bin in the corner. The bits of pot clinked together and clashed with their brethren as they hit the other bags already there.

Arrow sighed, looking at the number of bags in the bin, each one a failed attempt. She turned back to the workspace and shook her head slightly. It was so clean it was almost sparkling. No evidence of the explosion or further failure.

She had run out of ceramic pots now, the half dozen the shifkin had provided all now in the waste bin along with at least three metal containers. She was not using metal pots again. The explosion sharpened metal into knife-like shards. She still had a bandage on one arm covering a cut that had come too close to an artery for comfort.

About a month had passed since the rogue magician had been defeated in the Taellaneth. An Erith lord thought long dead but in fact melded with a *surjusi*, a malevolent spirit from another realm. Between them, the Erith and *surjusi* had been powerful, skilled in forbidden magic, leaving a trail of dead behind and gathering support for their hatred of the Erith among disaffected humans. Defeating them had come at a cost. Erith, human and shifkin lives had been lost in the rogue's quest for revenge and power.

Arrow had held the rogue down in the middle of the Taellaneth's most powerful spells, sent the *surjusi* back to its realm. And been summarily dismissed, the Erith wanting no more to do with her after her oath-service to them had been completed.

The shifkin had given her shelter. The building around her that hummed with layers of warding, space enough for an entire cadre of White Guard and more besides, and all for her personal use, although she spent most of her time in the workspace. Released from the Erith's restrictions, she could use her magic freely for the first time in her life and even the simplest spells brought their own delight, the course of power running through her, shaping to her will.

The weeks spent here had been more than pleasant. No one had tried to kill her. She had her own space. The 'kin had also provided her with a vehicle to use. And, although they gave her work, it was not enough to fill her time. It was a completely new experience to have time for herself, time that was not taken up with chores.

Chores that had previously taken days under the Erith's restriction on the use of her magic, could now be done in moments. She could clean the entire building, all the crockery and utensils she had used, all her clothing, and her person if she wanted to, with a few simple cleansing spells, and for several days had cleaned everything apart from herself every morning and night, just because she could, and taking long, hot showers or long baths filled with scented bubbles, delighting in being clean and having a never-ending supply of hot water.

It was strange to be able to do as she pleased and she was still experimenting, the freedom a heady experience and daunting at the same time. Curiosity often took her out into the city. Despite her Erith heritage, she could pass for human as long as she kept her ears covered and was careful not to let the power show in her eyes. So, she explored the human world. Visited art galleries and museums. Pretended to read human books in cafes whilst listening to the human conversations around her, fascinated by the variety and complexity.

As far as she could tell, the human city of Lix continued much as before, most humans ignorant of the threat that had been so narrowly defeated.

The weeks that had passed were not long enough for everything to be completely back to normal, of course. Residue of unclean magic clung in places the rogue had used for his spellworking. The shifkin had learned that they were highly sensitive to the aftermath of unclean magic and *surjusi* impressions on the world. It would not harm them, but they found the traces unpleasant, and some were close to shifkin territory. Zachary Farraway, the shifkin Prime, had asked Arrow to come up with a way of cleaning areas that had been tainted, or had battle magic performed on them.

It seemed a simple enough task. There were several cleansing spells, some specifically designed to remove *surjusi* taint and cleanse areas where forbidden magic had been used. It should be straightforward to make a potion, but was not, as the shards of pot in the waste bin proved. Arrow was running out of ideas and increasingly frustrated by her failures. She could cleanse each area, naturally. But that would take time, and would need her to be physically at each site for quite a while with 'kin escort. The sites were on human land and the 'kin did not wish to disturb the humans more than they had to or raise awkward questions among the human authorities about why the 'kin had access to an Erith-trained mage. Besides, they had other requests for her, too. Having a pre-prepared potion that anyone could use, quickly and discreetly, would be worth it. If she could get it right.

The building's wards flared for a moment, cutting through her thoughts, announcing a visitor. Welcoming the interruption, Arrow made her way to the front door.

The newly-installed, human-made spy camera, an upgrade that the 'kin were making to all their buildings, showed her a dark vehicle parked at the roadside, and a tall male walking along the short path to the front door. She froze, hand half-raised to the door handle, stomach turning itself into a knot. She knew this Erith, and was not at all sure she wanted to see him.

Kester vo Halsfeld. Youngest member of the Taellan. Trained warrior. The only Erith ever to kiss her. Her mind slid around the possibilities of why he was here and refused to calm as she forced herself to open the door, and locked her spine to overcome the impulse to bow.

"My lord."

"Arrow." He inclined his head, a polite greeting that somehow made her conscious of her tangled hair, and the cheap human clothing she wore.

"You wished to see me?" She could not think of any other reason for him to be here, but it still seemed unlikely.

"I did." There was a trace of what might have been laughter in his voice. She could not read his expression.

"Come in." She stepped back and had a momentary sense of dislocation as he came into the building, the wards recognising him as a previous visitor. He moved with the fluidity of a trained Erith warrior. She felt graceless and clumsy by comparison.

Not knowing quite what to do with her uninvited guest, she went back to the workroom. He followed without comment.

She retreated to the other side of the workbench and faced him across its bright, clean surface, curious as to why he was here and slightly puzzled. He was looking even more polished than normal, a sharp contrast to her own person. She did not think she had any remnants of potion on her but despite careful washing, she often found bits of herb in her hair as she had a habit of shoving her hair back when she was working, and her fingers were stained, ink difficult to remove with soap and water alone. The 'kin seemed to find the dishevelled look amusing, not caring what she looked like, but she doubted an Erith lord would share their relaxed attitude.

"You seem settled here," he observed, looking around the space, mouth twitching in what might have been a smile as he saw the tarpaulin draped over the shelving. Arrow followed his gaze around the space, wondering what he saw. With the cupboards closed and shelving hidden, he could not see the rows of ingredients she had collected, or the dozens of vials of potions and pre-prepared spells she had created. Even if the cupboard doors had been open and shelves in view, he would not have been able to see the backpack that she had recently bought and started to carefully stock, one item at a time. Things she would need for her travels. A pack big enough to carry essentials and small enough that she could, in fact, carry it. She carefully did not look in that direction. Her plans were still forming and she did not wish to share them.

"A recent cleansing?" he asked, and that was definitely a smile in his voice. Arrow's skin heated.

"A new spell," she said, then closed her mouth against further explanation. She no longer answered to the Erith. And having this Erith in her workspace was making her uneasy, particularly as she did not know what he wanted. A month of working with the 'kin, and she preferred a direct approach, so asked, "How may I serve?" It was a traditional Erith request from servant to master, words familiar on her tongue after so many years' service. His face tightened in response and she frowned inwardly, wondering how she had offended him.

"You have not returned to the Taellaneth," he observed.

"I am banished from the Taellaneth," she reminded him, brows lifting.

"I would have preferred to speak with you there," he said stiffly, back straight. There was nothing in his manner apart from proper Erith outrage, but Arrow's cheeks scorched. Last time she had seen this particular Erith lord had been un-settling to say the least.

"You could have requested my presence," she reminded him. None of the rest of the Taellan would have dreamt of seeking her out. A touch of colour along his high cheekbones drew her attention. "Unless you did not wish the other Taellan to know, of course. What is it, my lord?" She had been sent on enough sensitive errands by Erith lords and ladies over the years that she thought she now recognised the signs. She expected to be sent to one of the higher quality human retail establishments to procure items considered contraband within Erith bor-ders. The ban on human items was upheld particularly within the Taellaneth, the heart of Erith government and the Erith's showpiece closest to the human world. Chocolate or coffee were always popular human items, no matter how the more tradition-bound Erith might disapprove.

Instead, he reached into a pocket and drew out a long, slender, flat box. It was Erith made, beautifully crafted of nearly translucent pale wood, a House symbol on its front. Not the Halsfeld House. A crest she did not know. The box was old, humming with quiet magic. A family heirloom. He made a small bow, and passed the box across the surface of the workbench, setting it carefully and precisely near her hands. She felt her brows lift further. She had only seen one of these before in her life, carried with great ceremony by a messenger within the Taellaneth grounds, but knew what it was.

"A first courtship gift?" She was more than surprised, but kept her voice even. "And who would you like me to deliver it to, my lord?" Among the Erith, courtship could be a tortuously elaborate process. The first gift was normally delivered via intermediaries following a series of delicate conversations and negotiations between the hapless parties' families. A brief bit of rapid thinking and she concluded that, with his birth House disbanded, this lord might not wish his brother by *vestrait* to act for him. Using a neutral third party made sense, although she could easily think of at least a half-dozen better candidates for the task.

"I have delivered it," he said, voice tight. She frowned, seeing the colour still high in his face.

"Yes, to me, but who is it intended for, my lord? Perhaps the Lady Suranne, or Lady Aen, or Lady Missel?" All daughters of Taellan Houses, and among the few eligible ladies that she had met. Also among the few eligible ladies who did visit the Taellaneth from time to time, and who she might reasonably be expected to reach. If she were not exiled. Her brows drew together. He seemed to have missed that important point.

"For none of them." His face was stiff now, voice clipped. He seemed angry.

She frowned, looking down at the courtship gift so carefully placed in front of her.

"You will need to give me a destination, my lord," she told him, bending under the counter to fetch a clean, plain square of cloth from one of the boxes there. Careful not to touch the immeasurably precious object, she gathered it into the cloth and wrapped it, focusing on making the folds as neat and precise as possible. Whoever the lady was, she would doubtless appreciate some care having been taken over the gift, and that a half-breed's hands had not touched it. Most Erith reacted with disgust at her heritage. Placing the wrapped box back on the counter she glanced up and took an involuntary step back, fingers twitching in the first rune of a defensive spell in automatic reflex.

Kester vo Halsfeld's eyes blazed pure amber, lips thinned to white, face taut. He was almost entirely still apart from rapid, shallow breathing. She swallowed, hard, not recognising the stranger in front of her.

"You think to insult me?" he hissed.

"By no means, my lord," she began.

"Stop calling me that." The sharp words snapped off the glass skylights and echoed back into the room.

"Of course, *svegraen*." She bowed her head, realising she was falling into the learned habits for dealing with enraged shifkin, but, exiled from the Erith and autonomous from them for the first time in her life, she had no precedent or pattern for dealing with an enraged Erith warrior.

"You consider my gift beneath you?" His voice was low, furious.

Her mouth opened, no sound emerging for a moment.

"Beneath ... by no means," she started, stopping again when he gripped the side of the bench with white-knuckled hands and bent forward slightly, amber eyes holding her own. She could not look away for five long heartbeats, mouth dry.

"Then you find me unworthy?"

"I ... what?" Arrow blinked, utterly confused.

"Not the gift but the giver," he ground out.

Blinking again, she looked from the wrapped box up to the furious Erith lord. None of her extensive knowledge of Erith magic, or 'kin protocol, was helping her to understand. But something in Erith manners snagged her attention, made her recall the very careful and precise placing of the box in front of her hands.

"W-who is this meant f-for, my lord?" she asked, her own voice strange to her, a high pitched squeal.

"Now you mock me." His voice was a bare sound. With a movement so rapid that she stumbled back in reflex, not wanting all that fury so close to her, one hand snaked out, caught the wrapped box, and in the same movement he turned on his heel and left, boot heels striking the floor in a hard staccato. A moment later the front door slammed, hard enough to make her jump, and the building's wards twitch in response to his exit.

Arrow found she had backed against the shelving unit, the slight rattle of bottles a counterpoint to her trembling. She slid down the shelves as her knees gave out, tarpaulin coming with her, landing in a heap around her. She ended up on the cold concrete floor, useless tears standing in her eyes as she looked at the now empty doorway. She tucked her hands under her arms, drawing her knees up. She was still not entirely certain what had happened, playing and replaying the scene over in her head.

When her feet and the tip of her nose had lost feeling, she blinked again, releasing a pair of hot tears down her cheeks. Nausea gripped her. She had reviewed the possible permutations of the lord's behaviour, and the meaning carried by that slender box, and was now wondering if she had imagined the entire thing. If she had, then she had a far more creative imagination than she had given herself credit for. However it was an easier conclusion than the other.

If the events had been real, and not some odd, fanciful imagining, then she thought that it was possible, barely, that a lord of the Erith, a Taellan, had presented her, an unNamed mixed-breed, with a courtship gift. Blood drained from her face and she shivered. There was no advantage to him in such an odd action, and considerable chance of disgrace.

Of course, she thought, tilting her head as a new option occurred to her, it was also possible that courtship was not his intent. Did lords woo their mistresses with gifts? A crease fractured her brow as she considered that, stomach lurching and the chill working its way all the way through to her core. Too many years spent in invisible, silent attendance at Taellan meetings had given her a fair idea how many Erith lords regarded their mistresses. She had no wish to be anyone's plaything. Her chest ached, and more tears formed, at the realisation that Kester vo Halsfeld might have so little care for her that he would offer her a position of such social disgrace. It was a higher place than most Erith would consider she deserved, she knew, but it still hurt. Whatever else she might be, she was an Academy graduate, in theory of equal standing to any Erith lord. In theory. Despite their great difference in station, she had believed the youngest Taellan to have integrity, a rare quality among the Erith's rulers and something which she admired. And he had kissed her. Once. In front of others. A secretly-longed for moment, something she had never imagined possible even in her most vivid imaginings.

A harsh, painful sound tore the silence apart and she stilled, shocked that she could make such a sound or that it was possible to feel so much pain without being wounded. Broken ribs had not hurt this much.

A shiver of the building's wards brought her to her feet, limbs not working as smoothly as they should. She was about to have more visitors.

She scrubbed her face with her hands and went to the door.

Tamara's wide smile loosened some of the ice inside her. One of the warmest-natured people Arrow had ever met, it was impossible not to respond to that smile, Tamara's generous nature a sharp contrast to her mate's stern demeanour. Matthias Farraway was absent, though, no doubt on some duties for his father, the shifkin Prime.

Arrow's lips curved in response, fractures coursing through her as Tamara's smile faded to a slight frown. The 'kin tilted her head, looking her up and down.

"You look like you've had a hell of a day. Want to help me catch some bad guys?"

"Let me get my coat." Arrow turned to go back into the building.

"Boots would help too, and your bag of tricks."

CHAPTER TWO

A rrow tried, and failed, to keep up. Tamara ran like the graceful predator she was, even in human form, flowing effortlessly around yet another corner into a narrow alleyway between buildings only to immediately fling herself sideways, striking the wall, the flat crack of a gun firing making Arrow pause before following Tamara's headlong flight into the alleyway. The shifkin had much faster reflexes. And Arrow had damped her wards down, not wanting to draw attention in Lix. A routine pick up, Tamara had said. Someone the Lix muster wanted to question. Should be fun, Tamara had said.

From the broad grin on Tamara's face, at least one of them thought this was fun.

Arrow's lungs were burning with effort, pulse thudding in her ears, legs wobbling slightly with the unexpected exercise. They must have run six blocks through the city after this surprisingly fleet-of-foot, foolish human.

The human in question was above them now, still trying to escape, climbing a metal ladder attached to the run-down red brick building that formed one side of the alley. He paused about one storey up, turning. There was a dark blot in his hand. Weapon.

"Get his gun, would you?" Tamara was not even breathing hard.

The human fired again, missing even though Tamara was standing still, just in front of Arrow. A shield for the mage. Arrow could not think of that now. She needed only a few moments to recite the necessary spell, sending a targeted, concussive shock into the human's arm. As soon as Arrow released her spell, a tight fist-sized ball of silver power lifting her hair as it passed, Tamara was moving to the ladder. The human squealed as the spell struck. Pain and anger combined. He dropped the gun. It fell into Tamara's waiting hand and she kept moving.

Seeing a determined shifkin chasing him still, he turned to the ladder, rising faster than Arrow would have expected. Tamara followed.

Arrow went after them, hoping the ladder would hold their combined weight. It creaked ominously under her boots and she moved a little faster, legs and arms aching by the time she reached the top. She had not realised she was so unfit. Or perhaps Erith-trained mages were simply not meant to keep up with shifkin.

Thankfully this building was only four storeys high. The last one had been eight. Or perhaps ten. She could not recall. It had been an external staircase that time. A lot of stairs, Tamara's face lit with joy at the chase.

Arrow paused at the top of the ladder, breath coming in noisy gasps, sweat trickling down her back under her leather coat. Apparently leather was not sensible to wear when chasing people. She would need to remember that. She took a moment to assess the roof before moving on. It should have been flat and featureless, but was littered with packing crates, cardboard boxes and a few chairs as well as a strong smell of human alcohol. But no Tamara. At least not visible.

The quiet, furious sounds of a struggle drew her attention to the largest pile of packing crates and she forced her aching legs up onto the roof, gathering her wards as she cautiously crept around the side of the crates.

Tamara had their quarry neatly tied up, ropes around his ankles and wrists and a makeshift gag of some sort stuffed into his mouth. Part of his shirt, Arrow thought, seeing torn fabric.

"There you are." Tamara was cheerful, showing no sign she had been running. Arrow wanted to collapse onto the nearest chair and not move for a while.

"This is definitely the one?"

"The one and only." Tamara got to her feet and gave the human what she might have intended to be a slight nudge, but her toe sent the human sliding over the roof surface. "Thought he could cheat the muster."

"Very foolish."

"We need to get him back to the muster house for questioning." Tamara casually lifted the man by his belt. A very painful process, judging by the human's bulging eyes and squeals behind the gag. She set him across her shoulder, his head bumping against her back, and looked around. "There we go." There was a doorway to the roof that Arrow had not spotted before. Tamara set off, her pace not hindered at all by the additional person she was carrying, Arrow following, trying to keep her breathing under control as much as possible, taking stock of the various crates and boxes they walked past. She stopped, seeing something that looked familiar, reading the labels more carefully.

"These are stolen goods," she noticed. The shifkin had access to the human law enforcement bulletins, and Zachary had made sure that Arrow was copied into them. He thought she might find it interesting. Or so he said. She did find it interesting. She had not known how much crime humans were capable of. The packing crates they were walking between had featured on several news bulletins.

"So they are." Tamara looked around, lips twitching. "There's a huge finder's fee for some of this stuff." She pulled out her mobile phone and sent a quick text. "Some of the muster will be along soon to take inventory."

The journey back to the muster house was uneventful. If one discounted the stares and mutters from the humans they passed, all giving Tamara and her wriggling burden a wide berth. A few humans, brave or incredibly foolish, Arrow was not sure which, tentatively approached her, enquiring in high-pitched voices as to what authority she had for manhandling the human. Tamara answered them all with the same easy grin and short response: the human had tried to deceive the muster.

"I am not sure that frightening humans is quite the thing to do," Arrow observed.

Tamara chuckled. "No, it's not really. But we're known as fair trading partners. Fair runs both ways."

"Tamara," Arrow began, more hesitantly. The 'kin turned, mischief back in her face. Arrow sighed. "You should not stand in front of bullets."

"I've got body armour. You don't. Besides. This idiot couldn't hit the side of a building." Tamara gave Arrow a sunny grin and continued on her way.

"I have wards," Arrow protested, shaking her head slightly.

"Give me body armour any day," Tamara answered over her shoulder.

Arrow hoped that Matthias would not find out about that particular moment. Arrow's own heart skipped a bit, remembering Tamara standing, straight and still, as the human pointed a gun at them. It was true that the bullet would most likely do more damage to Arrow than to Tamara, even without body armour. But it was doubtful that Matthias would see it that way. Tamara and Matthias were equally protective of each other and Arrow did not want to get in the way.

After a month of working for the shifkin, the muster house was a familiar place. A large, red brick building, in immaculate repair, it sat at the edges of the city, close to the open land that the 'kin claimed as their own. Despite the 'kin's nature as master predators, Arrow always found the building to be a peaceful place. Polished wooden floors, pale painted walls and minimal decoration, everything was kept clean and neat. The Lix pack was fairly small, as far as Arrow could tell. Perhaps thirty 'kin in all.

There were always about half a dozen 'kin in the house. A few greeted her as she followed Tamara through the double doors and she returned the greetings with an unfeigned smile. The 'kin accepted her. They did not judge her mixed heritage. They did not call her names, or harm her. It was not a home, in the way a human would say it, but it was a place she felt comfortable.

Tamara dropped the human in the muster leader's office. Actually dropped him. Simply let him go so he fell onto the wooden floor with a thump that made Arrow wince in sympathy, the human unable to break his fall thanks to the ropes. From the expression on the muster leader's face, he and his enforcer had plans to make the human's stay even more uncomfortable. They would not seriously wound, or even kill, the human. Arrow knew that. The shifkin held to the treaties they had with the humans. The human wriggling on the floor did not appear to know that.

Tamara closed the door behind them as they left. Like all 'kin buildings, the walls and doors were soundproofed, so Arrow could not hear anything more from the room.

"Told you it would be fun," Tamara said.

"It was most interesting," Arrow answered. Tamara's grin took over her whole face.

"You're useful to have around. Come on, there's hot pies and beer somewhere in here. I can smell them."

Arrow blinked, both at the odd combination of refreshment and at the casually-thrown invitation. For all that the 'kin welcomed her, she had never been included in a social engagement before today. Tamara turning up unannounced at her door earlier in the day had been unusual, but Arrow suspected that Tamara had not needed any help and that she was, instead, a little bored. Matthias was in Hallveran, assisting the local muster in settling the city after the recent disturbance and had, apparently, refused to take Tamara with him.

Tamara was a few paces ahead, following her nose to some combination of smells Arrow had not detected. They were in the main part of the muster house and it was oddly deserted, which set Arrow's skin prickling, defensive wards shimmering, reacting to possible danger. She drew a breath, keeping her wards close to her and invisible. It was a necessary discipline in the human world. Humans were exceptionally good at sensing threats, even when they could not identify the source.

There was no sinister threat. Just an angry 'kin male standing a short distance away in the entrance hall to the building, silhouetted against daylight. Matthias was dressed head to toe in close-fitting black. He might not be openly carrying weapons, but his scowl alone was enough to make Arrow stop and stay very still, not wanting that scowl turned on her. Her stomach twisted. She had seen enough angry males for one day.

Ahead, Arrow saw Tamara check in her stride, apparently surprised to see her mate. Arrow knew that was a lie. Tamara would have been able to sense Matthias' presence a long time before she saw him, with the innate 'kin magic she possessed.

"Matt! How lovely!" Her voice was light, airy even, but Arrow took an involuntary step back at the bite under the words. The last thing she wanted was to step into the middle of an argument between mates.

"Tamara." Matthias' growl raised the hairs on Arrow's neck even though his anger was not aimed at her.

"So glum," Tamara teased, teeth flashing in a parody of a smile. Arrow edged a few more paces away, wondering if she could quietly make her exit.

"Arrow." Matthias' voice had changed, becoming a polite acknowledgement. "Did you enjoy the day?"

"It was interesting. Although I do not particularly like running, I find." Arrow said honestly, keeping her voice steady despite a healthy fear that Matthias might ask about bullets. Tamara was behaving oddly. Matthias even more so.

"We were heading for pies and beer." There was nothing in that statement that should have been a challenge, but something in Tamara's tone and posture made it the opening to combat. Arrow opened her mouth to deny any such arrangement, wanting no part of their conflict, and closed it with a snap when Matthias looked down at his mate, white bracketing his mouth.

"Beer?" There was weight behind that one word that would have made any sane person pause.

"Alright." Tamara's shoulders stooped a fraction. So little that if she had not been looking for cues, Arrow would have missed it. "Maybe not beer. But definitely pie."

Arrow's attention sharpened. There had been something different about Tamara. A slight shift in her personal scent, a slight thickening of her waist, an aversion to coffee when they had taken a break earlier, which Arrow did not understand. And now no beer. The puzzle pieces snapped together in Arrow's head, finally, and she wanted to leave even more than ever. They had been shot at, and she had been too far behind Matthias' mate to help. Even worse, Tamara had stood in front of her whilst the human fired.

"I'll get you pie," Matthias promised. And nothing in those words should have made Arrow feel she was intruding on a private moment, but her face heated and she wished very much to be elsewhere, Matthias' fury vanishing into intensely personal, gentle warmth.

"Sure you're not too busy?" Tamara was not finished with her challenge.

"Pa is dealing with it."

Tamara stilled for a moment, then all the fight went out of her. Arrow drew a slow, careful breath. The shifkin Prime was dealing with business he had assigned to his son, allowing his son to travel to be with his mate. The Prime was cunning and determined in the protection of his people. And that included looking after them, even when they behaved badly.

"Oh."

The word hung between them for what seemed an age, Arrow's feet twitching in her boots, wanting to move.

"Arrow, are you staying?" Matthias lifted his eyes briefly from his mate's face and Arrow caught the edge of the heat in his gaze before his expression shifted back to polite inquiry.

"No, thank you. There are things I need to deal with at the workspace." Even after a month she could not call it home, the human word for places they stayed. And it was not a residence, the Erith word. It was the place she slept and worked, so she called it the workspace, even in her mind.

"We can give you a lift," Tamara offered, head turning from Matthias. Her body was curved into her mate's, aligned so that, even a foot apart, they stood firmly as a couple. All the anger and combat had vanished.

"I like to walk," Arrow answered honestly. Shifkin could smell a lie as easily as she could read magic. "And it is not far. Good day to you both."

She checked her impulse to bow, still close to the surface. Too many years among the Erith and too short a time outside their ungentle care for the habit to have left her.

She was not sure that Tamara and Matthias noticed, too caught up in whatever wordless communication was passing between them. Arrow glanced back, just once, before they were out of sight and they were still standing, barely touching. A pair about to become three. Or possibly more. Multiple births were possible.

Arrow's chest hurt. Sorrow and loneliness and longing combined. There had never been a moment when she had stood so close to another person that they made up her entire world, with no barriers between them. Had never been a place where she fitted so completely as Tamara and Matthias fitted together. She thought she had set aside that wish, for now, but the awkward visit from Kester earlier, that she still did not understand, and the 'kin pair brought it back, a sharp, bitter twist under her breastbone. She turned away with a sting in her eyes, glad of the walk to settle her mind and distract her.

———ell———

Night fell as she walked slowly back to the workspace, the warmth of an unexpectedly sunny day vanishing into the dark, making Arrow wish she had put on a warmer coat. Or remembered her gloves at least, walking with her hands shoved into her pockets, the street lights casting everything into orange and yellow tones.

The workspace was shadowed, set back from the road and the city's lights, the thick wards around the building just visible at the edge of Arrow's vision. There was a vehicle outside the building, carefully parked just outside the perimeter wards, a tall figure standing beside it, breath visible in the chill air. Arrow's stomach tightened at the unmistakable shimmer of Erith magic, the wards around the vehicle amber in contrast to the silver of her own magic. She was torn between fervently wishing it was not Kester, not wanting to see him ever again, and hoping it might be, wanting to know what had happened that morning.

The flavour of magic was wrong. Not Kester. Disappointment and relief chased through her. She slowed her approach, freeing her hands and gathering a coil of magic, wondering what business any Erith had with her now. There were a few Erith living in Lix, oddities among their race, preferring the human world with its technology over the slower paced, tradition-bound life among their own kind. But she did not think that the person waiting for her was one of the Erith in Lix. The vehicle's wards bore the familiar trace of the Taellaneth's chief mechanic, the work haphazard and sloppy. The mechanic and his crew loved the vehicles under their charge with the sort of single-minded focus that Neith vo Sena reserved for his horses, but were second rate magicians on their best days.

A tall warrior straightened from the shadows of the vehicle, one she knew. The knot inside loosened. Kallish nuin Falsen would not hurt her. It was a core-deep belief. And Kallish was, perhaps, something of a friend.

"Greetings, *svegraen*." Her voice was a little rusty, but served.

"Greetings, mage. You are well?"

Arrow almost replied that she felt as though she had been broken and put back together wrong, a lump of hurt in her throat she had to swallow before she could answer. She side-stepped the question.

"Would you like to come in? I can make coffee."

"Coffee would be welcome. And are there perhaps cookies?" The human word sounded odd from the warrior's lips, drawing a tiny smile to Arrow's stiff face.

"The shifkin are excellent hosts, *svegraen*. There is a selection." One of the 'kin was a master baker and Arrow was the frequent, happy recipient of boxes of baked goods.

She closed the door behind Kallish and kept herself busy preparing coffee and laying biscuits on a plate at the end of the workbench, trying not to think about the earlier confrontation in this spot as she pulled stools over for them to use.

The warrior took a careful sip of the coffee, closing her eyes a moment.

"At first taste, I could not believe anyone would voluntarily consume this liquid in the quantities the humans appear to. However, I now find it quite pleasant."

"Like Erith tea," Arrow suggested, nudging the plate of cookies closer to the warrior, and passing her a napkin. The warrior thanked her and made her way through three cookies and half a mug of coffee in companionable silence.

"Were you working?" The warrior looked around the spotlessly clean room and the one set of shelves revealed by the fallen tarpaulin.

"I was this morning. I have been out with the 'kin."

"You have been busy, I see," the warrior said, eyeing the rows of full jars and vials on the shelves she could see.

"You did not come by, in uniform, simply to drink coffee and eat cookies, *svegraen*. How may I serve?" The echo of her own earlier words, the phrase so familiar to her tongue, held her still a moment until the warrior's frown snagged Arrow's attention. "Have I said something wrong, *svegraen*?"

"You are a servant no longer, mage," Kallish pointed out.

"Force of habit." Arrow shrugged a shoulder, a very human gesture, not meeting Kallish's too-penetrating dark eyes.

"You still consider yourself a servant?"

"I believe that most Erith consider me such," Arrow hedged.

"Many of the Taellan, perhaps," Kallish agreed easily, "but not among the White Guard."

It seemed to be a day for incomprehensible conversations. At least Kallish was not furious. Arrow took a sip of coffee, hands clasped around the mug, warmth seeping back into her limbs.

"I do not know what I am," she said at length, giving the warrior bare honesty.

Kallish's gaze held more understanding than she had expected. "Little wonder."

The trace of warmth, as unexpected as the comprehension, brought the unwelcome threat of further tears. She could not remember the last day she had cried so much. Arrow blinked tears away rapidly, swallowing more coffee.

"What do you need of me, *svegraen*?" The different question received a slight tip of the warrior's head, and tiny smile.

"I am sent by the Preceptor."

"How is he?"

The Preceptor had been seriously injured by the rogue magician, tainted with *surjusi*, and left for dead, opening his wounds again in the effort to defeat the rogue. The rogue had been unmasked as Preceptor Evellan's younger brother, thought dead in the last *surjusi* incursion into the heartland. When Arrow had last seen the Preceptor, he had been lying on the blood-stained floor of the Taellaneth Receiving Hall under close attention of several healers.

"Healing slowly." Kallish's mouth quirked again in another smile, eyes dancing. "He is a poor patient, by all accounts. Only the Lady Vailla can be near him for long. He is not impatient with her."

"Vailla has a way." Arrow returned the smile.

"A delightful child," Kallish said, reminding her how very old this warrior was, without a trace of grey in her dark hair.

"Is my presence requested?" Arrow straightened, understanding now why Kallish was here. She was not greatly surprised. The Preceptor had his own way of dealing with things.

"Tomorrow around midday, if that suits," Kallish hesitated a moment, eyes assessing Arrow's clothing. Arrow's eyes lit with humour. She had not paid much attention to what she was wearing when Tamara came to fetch her earlier.

"I have better clothing, never fear. I am not very tidy when working," she added, holding out one arm, freely spattered with vivid colours from various herbs and ingredients she had used. Laundry only made it worse, seeming to set the colours in.

They talked a while longer while the warrior had another mug of coffee, and more cookies, exchanging news. The political unrest in Hallveran following the destruction of the city's biggest human gang by the shifkin, the gang having made the grave mistake of bringing their guns to shifkin territory. The progress of healing and repairing after the rogue magician's attack on the Taellaneth. Orlis' presence at the Academy, apparently to assist the Preceptor but, in Kallish' judgement, more likely assisting Vailla to keep Evellan resting as long as possible. The silence from Evellan's deputy, Seivella, also recovering slowly from her wounds. The speculation among the Taellan and Erith as to what the shifkin Prime might do next, with the knowledge that an Erith rogue magician had been responsible for his mate's death.

It was not the lightest of conversations. The Erith had sustained losses and more than one House was in mourning. Relations with the shifkin were in a state of change and no one quite knew where things might fall.

Still, the rogue had been defeated and, as Kallish pointed out with typical bluntness, the loss of life had been limited.

Closing the door behind the warrior, Arrow yawned hugely and sought her rest with a lighter heart than she would have believed possible a bare hour before.

CHAPTER THREE

The next day the warriors posted as gate guards opened the pedestrian gate for her with quick attention, and one, the junior by his braids, inclined his head to her in a mark of respect. She nearly stumbled as she crossed the threshold to the Taellaneth. She could count on her fingers the number of times any Erith had bowed to her. The gate guard, no matter who was on duty, more commonly appeared as though they would dearly love to keep her out of the Taellaneth altogether.

She did not have long to consider the odd behaviour, senses overwhelmed by the Taellaneth. After any absence, no matter how long, the rich scents and familiar hum of magic against her skin always took her by surprise. The last time she had left here, after the rogue magician had been defeated and the *surjusi* banished, she had thought she would never return, exiled by the Taellan.

Now, her whole being sang with the knowledge she was back on familiar ground. For years, under the restrictions of the oath spells, she had been furious at herself that her every sense seemed to crave the Erith lands, a large part of her finding peace in the scents and underlying magic within the Taellaneth, at the same time as the Erith themselves despised her. Over the years, she had chosen to not waste energy on anger at something she could not change and instead simply accept that some part of her, perhaps the Erith in her, found comfort in the magic that saturated Erith lands and which could be hard to find in human territory.

The struggle rose up again, a great knot of tension inside loosening in response to the familiar magic around her even as her chest hurt with the knowledge that she was in exile, and, after this visit was over, she may never return. She had tried several times before to memorise the sensations of being in the Taellaneth, knowing that one day she might be banished for good and wanting to keep some part of the place with her. Her memory was usually highly accurate. Not quite perfect, but very close to it. And yet, no matter how hard she tried, she had never quite got the memory of the Taellaneth right.

As well as the familiar sensations, there was a familiar face. Orlis, journeyman mage and Gilean's companion, was waiting for her about twenty paces inside the gates with a broad, warm smile and such open delight that she could not help smiling back.

"Greetings, mage." He did not bow, thankfully.

"Greetings, journeyman. Are you to be my escort?"

"If you please. The Preceptor is still within his residence. If you will come with me." He waved a hand and Arrow, amused at the formality which contrasted with his travel-worn clothing and tangled red hair, let him guide her along paths that were almost certainly more familiar to her than to him.

"You appear well rested," he commented after they were out of earshot of the gate guards.

"Thank you, yes. It has been pleasant to pass some time without anyone trying to kill me," she said lightly. He laughed, bright hair dancing as he skipped ahead, turning to face her while walking backwards.

"It is indeed. I have missed you, Arrow. Everyone here is so proper it is stifling."

She bit her lip, holding in a laugh. The Taellaneth was the show piece of the Erith and nothing less than perfection would do, from the grounds around them to the behaviour of the servants under the Steward's keen eye. Behind the walls of the Taellan's residences, or within the Academy's dormitories, Arrow was sure that less formality was observed. Outside those private spaces, everyone conducted themselves with absolute propriety. It was stifling. And a sharp contrast from the way the humans and shifkin lived or, Arrow thought, the way Orlis was used to living.

Orlis was more used to travelling Erith lands in company with Gilean vo Presien, the pair of them sleeping out of doors as often as indoors, and getting up to whatever mischief they could. Or so she thought, based on Gilean's correspondence with Evellan.

Orlis had more news, though.

"The White Guard have been furious about something for the past several days."

"Indeed?" Curiosity piqued, she tilted her head, inviting him to continue.

"I am not certain what. They do not gossip at all." His heartfelt disappointment drew an open smile from her. The journeyman had a nose for information, and seemed to have a knack for getting people to talk to him.

"That may be a good thing. Some of their secrets are dangerous." The White Guard, like the Taellaneth servants, were privy to secrets and conversations right to the highest levels of Erith government. And, like the Taellaneth servants, were sworn to secrecy and famously reluctant to talk.

"True. But it is so frustrating. The students know nothing, even the well-connected ones, although they are most curious about what has happened to the lady."

"Seivella is missing? Again?" Arrow checked her stride, heart speeding up. The lady, although not the most powerful mage among the Erith, was cunning and dangerous.

"No, of course not. The guard have her, but it is not widely known or discussed."

Arrow's pulse slowed and she started walking again. In truth, it was not clear how dangerous the lady really was. Seivella had conspired with the rogue magician, and had nearly died for it, the rogue not pleased with her service. The rogue, unmasked, had been revealed as Lord Nuallan, the lady's former betrothed and Evellan's brother, caught by the last incursion of *surjusi* into Erith lands when the House had been burned with him inside. Thought to have been dead many years, he had in fact melded with a *surjusi*, and then persuaded Seivella to silence and secrecy while planning his revenge on the Erith, Evellan inevitably drawn in.

Last Arrow had heard, and thanks to Kallish's visit she was very up to date with news, no one had managed to question either Seivella or Evellan about the extent of their involvement, or their knowledge of what Nuallan had planned. For all that Arrow wanted to believe that neither of them, particularly Evellan, had truly meant harm to the Erith, there were still questions to be asked and answered. It seemed that the lady was still confined whilst the Preceptor had been allowed back to his own residence. A reflection, perhaps, of the regard which most Erith had for the Preceptor. Or the influence of Vailla vel Falsen, Evellan's betrothed, who had a habit of getting just exactly what she wanted.

And there was more Orlis had to tell, she sensed. The light tone and laugh of earlier was fading. Something was worrying him.

Whatever else Orlis might have said was cut off as Arrow spied Vailla coming towards them up the short path from the Preceptor's residence. There were tired shadows under the lady's eyes, but her smile was bright as she greeted Arrow.

"Thank you," Vailla said, enveloping Arrow in a fierce hug.

Arrow returned the gesture with an awkward pat on the lady's back, immediately wary. One of Vailla's favourite tricks when they had been at the Academy together had been to act as though someone had already agreed to whatever favour she was about to ask.

"For what, precisely, my lady?"

"For saving my Evellan," Vailla brushed a stray tear away with a careless gesture, smiling, "you were the only one who could."

"It was not me alone." Arrow felt faintly ashamed of her suspicions. It seemed the lady was sincere in her thanks. Still, Arrow did not let her guard down. Vailla was as dangerous in her own way as Seivella.

"Mostly you," Orlis corrected, exchanging brief nods and smiles with the lady.

"He is waiting for you," Vailla told Arrow. "Please try not to keep him too long. He is not as strong as he believes."

"My lady." Arrow bowed slightly.

"And, for the sake of reason, stop being so formal, Arrow! And do visit when you can. I should love to hear what you have been about in the years since I knew you."

"Vailla." Arrow hoped her smile did not seem false, thinking that she would not be telling the lady even a quarter of everything that had happened in the intervening years. Vailla was no fool, but she had been brought up in, and still lived, a sheltered, privileged life.

Vailla seemed satisfied and continued on her way.

"You and the lady were friends?"

"Almost, perhaps." Arrow knocked on the door to the Preceptor's residence, not meeting Orlis' inquisitive gaze. "A long time ago."

ele

"Come in, Arrow." The Preceptor's voice, projected with a thread of his magic, accompanied the door opening. "I am in the study." The thread of magic curling around the door, coated with the familiar shadows that accompanied Evellan everywhere, seemed thinner than normal.

Following his direction, Arrow made her way through the residence to the Preceptor's private study, the room she had visited on her only previous visit. It was considerably tidier than when she had seen it last, with the addition of a long chaise by the window, where the Preceptor was reclining, in what Arrow thought might be a dressing robe. It was certainly the least formal attire she had ever seen him wear.

"I will bring some tea," Orlis said and left the room, footsteps fading rapidly.

"A good heart that one, even if he talks more than breathes," Lord Evellan commented, setting aside the book he had been reading, and giving Arrow his full attention. "Exile appears to agree with you, at least."

"Thank you, my lord. You are looking better, too." When she had last seen him, in the Taellaneth's Receiving Hall after Nuallan had been defeated, he had been badly injured, bleeding from a stomach wound and Arrow had not been sure he would survive. Although he was alive, thanks to the skill of the Erith healers, his face was shadowed and he seemed somehow diminished. Vulnerable.

With that thought, Arrow realised how much her perception of Evellan had been coloured by her early experiences of him, the seemingly giant, imposing figure who had stared down at her from a height when Nassaran had brought her to the Academy, and the implacable figure, shadows gathered around him, who had not hesitated or wavered as he spoke the oath spells to bind her to the Taellan's service, not pausing once as she screamed under the magic's bite. Evellan was the highest authority on all matters of Erith magic. His position carried power among the Erith. His word carried equal weight to the Taellan and Lord Whintnath, something that many Taellan resented.

Implacable, and yet Arrow did not hate him. The oath spells had kept her alive long enough to learn. And, unlike many other Erith, Evellan had never been deliberately cruel. Demanding, yes, pushing her to work harder and try harder, as he pushed all senior students. He was no genial mentor. She had seen him be kind to others, and the softness in his eyes when he spoke of Vailla showed he had a heart. He had rarely shown any warmth to her. It mattered little. She had considered the rewards to be worth it. Working magic was a stronger pull on her being than even the Taellaneth.

And her instincts pushed her to trust him. Mostly.

"Do sit, and forgive me if I do not get up."

"Thank you." Arrow took one of a pair of straight-backed chairs that looked like they were part of a dining set, brought in to serve Evellan's guests. The only other chair normally in the room was the great, carved chair behind the desk and she could easily imagine that the Preceptor would not want anyone else settling behind his desk. "I am sorry that matters ended so badly with Lord Nuallan," she said, feeling that something was required.

"There was no possibility of a happy ending for that." He would not meet her eyes, fussing with a fold of his collar. "And it could have been much worse."

"The other Erith who were possessed and survived. Are they healing?"

"Most of them. One or two still in a healing sleep. The healers expect them to recover in time."

"I see." She stood up on reflex as Orlis came back into the room, carrying a large, heavy tray, and busied herself with assisting Orlis to clear a space for the tray and then organise servings for each of them, Orlis staying at the Preceptor's gesture.

"Vailla will be back soon, so we do not have much time. I need your services, Arrow," he told her bluntly, when they had taken their first sips of tea.

She was not obliged to serve, she reminded herself, biting back the immediate acknowledgement. She straightened further, holding the tea cup carefully, very aware of the delicate china in her calloused hands.

"For what task, my lord?"

"Gilean is missing." Orlis' voice was quiet, all his vivacity gone. This was what he had been wanting to tell her outside, Arrow realised. The most important news.

"For several days now," Evellan confirmed to Arrow's lifted brow. "Her Majesty contacted me personally with a request for aid." His eyes strayed to the communication orb on his desk. He shifted on the chaise, colour rising in his face. "I cannot go," he said bitterly. "But you can."

"Go? Go where, my lord?"

"The Palace, of course. Where else?"

"I cannot go to the heartland." The Taelleisis. Loosely translated from ancient Erith, it meant the heart of the world. The Taellaneth had been created to be the mind of the Erith, to govern through the hands of the world, the Taellan, but the Taelleisis was where the Erith came from. The precious heartland.

A wash of old bitterness gripped her. Made useful by the oath spells, her access to Erith lands had been severely restricted. It took effort to hold herself quite still, to not close her fingers around the cup, to keep her voice steady.

"You have never been, you mean." Orlis frowned.

"No, I mean I cannot go. Even if I were not an exile, the Taellan passed an edict to forbid my presence any further into the Erith lands than the Taellaneth grounds and the far borders where required." That last addendum had stung Seggerat, she knew, forced to make the concession to allow her access to the Erith's administrative complex and the lands that lay between the Taellaneth and Lix.

"Edict?" Orlis' surprise almost made Arrow smile. A formal edict was a rare thing. Made only by a near-unanimous decision of the Taellan, it required a similar majority, or the Queen's formal word, to overturn.

"A pox on them. I had forgotten." Evellan drew a breath, harsh and loud, drawing Arrow's attention. She did not remember that his lungs had been damaged, but it was possible she had missed it among everything else. He thought for a moment, brow creased, pale tint around his mouth which might have been irritation or pain. "It is not like Gilean to vanish like this. There appeared to have been a struggle in his rooms. Some blood was found. Her Majesty is convinced some harm has come to him and that magic is involved." The Erith Queen's instincts were famed among the Taellan, and had rarely been wrong, from what Arrow knew. Those instincts had led to the lasting peace with humans and 'kin, however much some of the older Erith still craved war with their long-time enemies.

"My lord." She could not continue for a moment. She had always wanted to see the Erith heartlands, even once, tormented for years by Academy students who, on learning that she was banned, would then tell her stories of the heartland that made it sound the most wondrous place in existence, with power laced in the air, magical creatures commonplace, and an astounding natural beauty which, they said, far outstripped the Taellaneth. With each new intake of students there was a new wave of the fashion of disdain for the Taellaneth and the Academy generally. Arrow wanted to see for herself. She was honest enough to admit, in her own mind, that she partly wanted to prove to herself that the students' stories were more imagination than reality, and partly simply curious about what was so special about the Erith heartland that Seggerat had used his influence to secure the edict barring her from entry.

But. She was barred from the heartland, the edict specifying the punishment for breaching the order was death. Not worth the risk, in her view. And, more than that, she was no longer bound to the Erith's service. A month in the human world and she was enjoying exploring her new freedom. Freedom to act. Freedom to choose. And the ability to choose, to say no, was powerful. There were a host of others more capable than she was of tracking down a war mage.

"My lord. This is not a task for me. Perhaps Kallish nuin Falsen and her cadre?"

"No, no. Too noisy. Too clumsy." Clumsy was the last word Arrow would use for the warrior. And she thought a cadre of White Guard was likely to attract far less attention than she would. If Seggerat was to be believed, she was anathema to most Erith, likely to provoke their immediate disgust.

"My presence in the Palace would likely cause a riot. Hardly quiet." Arrow heard the bitterness in her voice, unable to suppress it, and took a sip of tea, the flavours of the Erith rich on her tongue after so long in the human world. Orlis' mouth twisted as though he wanted to disagree, but could not.

"Riot! Of course!" Evellan sat up quickly, then winced, white showing around his mouth, and sank back onto the cushions. "Orlis, writing paper, ink, my seal."

"At once, my lord."

Orlis moved about the room with no hesitation, clearly familiar with the Preceptor's space and used to the request, and in short order was holding paper steady on a writing board over the Preceptor's knees, Evellan scowling at the parchment as if it had personally offended him. Orlis' expression was blank, for once, and all Arrow could see was that the Preceptor was writing a few lines in large handwriting, bold and strong despite his injuries.

There was no point in pressing Evellan for answers. He would tell her when he was ready and not a moment before, so she finished her tea and the morning scone that Orlis had provided, a rare treat that tasted far better fresh than two days old and grudgingly handed to her, the Taellaneth's chief cook despising waste more than her.

At length the Preceptor was done, placing a large amount of wax and ribbon at the foot of his note and impressing his seal, infusing it with power. The effort cost him and he sank back with a gasp, breathing lightly for a few moments before beckoning Arrow across. She rose, ingrained habit of obedience to his wishes taking her to his side before she really knew what she was doing.

"You are now an Inquirer," he told her, words interspersed with shallow, harsh breaths.

Shock held her still and she almost asked him to repeat himself, except that he had sounded perfectly lucid. And determined. There was a set to his mouth and jaw she recognised.

An Inquirer Extraordinary, appointed by one of the triumvirate of power among the Erith for a specific mission, had power to open doors even the Taellan could not, second only to the Queen for the duration of their mission. And whatever he might have done, Evellan was still head of the Academy, head of one of the triumvirate. Stunned to silence, she waited as he gathered himself before continuing. "Go. In my place. Find Gilean."

"No." The word was out, flat and implacable, before she quite knew what she was saying. She did not take the parchment held out to her. "The Erith have no more call on me. You have no more call on me. My service is done. Over. There are others capable of finding Gilean."

"You would let pride stop you from helping?" Evellan was furious, white around his mouth.

"I have no pride where the Erith are concerned." Her voice was still flat. Better than tears. Better than the fury she could feel coursing through her. She had been used by the Erith once too often. "You have no call on me," she reminded him.

"We can pay you." His lip curled, showing what he thought of that. A mercenary.

"No." She straightened her spine. "Find someone else. I am sorry." She addressed that last to Orlis, who looked stricken. "Good day to you."

And she turned, ignoring the incoherent outburst from Evellan and Orlis' quiet plea, and left, going out of the residence and back along the path towards the gates.

There was a lead weight in her chest. She had the right to refuse. She had the ability to choose. She was not bound to the Erith. And yet. Some instinct was telling her that it was a mistake to refuse. That the Erith might need her, after all.

It did not matter. She thought of the workspace. Of the maps and plans barely formed. Of the backpack tucked away. Of the quiet acceptance by the 'kin. A contrast to the sneers she was used to from the Erith. She had, as she had told the Preceptor, done her service. All her dues were paid.

Rapid footsteps behind her made her turn quickly, wards flaring for a moment before she recognised Orlis.

He stopped, slightly out of breath, just outside the range of her wards, his eyes travelling over them.

"You think you are in danger here?"

"Always among the Erith," she answered. She would be foolish beyond belief to ever forget that. The misaligned fingers of her hand clenched in memory and she forced them open.

"Something is very wrong," Orlis told her bluntly. "Gilean was acting oddly when he was here. And why was he here? He normally sends letters."

"Orlis," Arrow began, exasperated.

"No. Listen. Something is wrong. Gilean is missing. It is not like him." Orlis ran both hands through his hair, struggling for words. That caught Arrow's attention more than anything he had said. Orlis was never at a loss for words. He took a few paces away and turned back. "Gilean was worried. He did not tell me why he was here. He always tells me. We-" He broke off, shook his head, and Arrow saw the sheen of tears in his eyes. "We argued about it before."

More than a mere argument, Arrow guessed, from the tension in Orlis' body and the way he would not meet her eyes. Gilean, a war mage used to keeping secrets. Orlis, a curious, lively mind who revelled in information. A dangerous companion for a war mage, she thought. But clearly Gilean considered it worth the risk.

"So now he tells me. Even if he cannot tell me everything, he tells me there is something. But not this time. He refused. Whatever it was he thought it was more important than-" His voice choked and a tear fell, catching the light.

More important than me. Arrow had no difficulty in filling in the unsaid words. Still, she hesitated. This was no business of hers. And yet. A war mage did not scare easily, and was even harder to capture.

She moved a fraction, more fully facing Orlis, and caught his attention away from whatever inner fury he was dealing with.

"So you think whatever it was that brought him here, to the Taellaneth, has caused him harm?"

"Yes."

"And now you want me to find Gilean?"

"Yes."

That one word seemed to be all he could manage.

Arrow shoved her hands in her coat pockets, a human gesture that would have earned her instant reprimand in the Taellan's service. Hidden from view, her fingers clenched. One misaligned hand. One perfect. Perfect thanks to Orlis' healing. The sorry mess of broken bones he had applied his skill to. Saving her life, perhaps. As he had done when he healed a bullet wound before that. A mage without use of her hands was all but defenceless, left with only her voice to craft spells, a voice that could all too easily be stopped. And a mage bleeding to death was no use at all.

She let out a long breath. Orlis had healed her as a matter of course. He was asking for nothing in return for the healing, freely given. Any pull of obligation she felt was hers alone. The first person she had met who had mixed heritage. Someone who had accepted her immediately, with open curiosity.

Invisible hands, Gilean's and Orlis', pressed each shoulder. A personal plea from Orlis. A graver plea from Gilean. Something had worried a war mage enough to bring him to the Taellaneth, a place he had not visited in Arrow's lifetime, and to conceal his reasoning from his life companion, at the risk to that relationship.

And underneath that, she had to be honest with herself, was the opportunity to visit the heartland. To see for herself the fabled home of the Erith. And to avoid a death sentence, with the Preceptor's orders giving her access.

Even with the decision made, she stood for long moments, apprehension, obligation and curiosity warring within her. Going to the heart of the Erith was dangerous. The Erith were dangerous. And yet she would go.

"I will need your help." The words were dragged out of her.

"Yes." That word again, the tone completely different. To her shock, and discomfort, Orlis took a few steps forward and flung his arms around her, enveloping her in a hug that threatened to break ribs, her lungs full of the warm scent of burnt amber, Erith magic, and a richer hint of something green, Orlis' personal scent.

She self-consciously straightened her coat when he released her.

"I will need the parchment."

"Here." He pulled it out of his satchel, the once-pristine surface slightly creased, ribbons tangled until he straightened them before holding it out.

She took it, forcing herself to read slowly, absorbing each word. Even so she had to read it three times to be certain. By that time each word was impressed on her mind. The missive stated simply that the Preceptor had appointed the mage known as Arrow as an Inquirer Extraordinary to investigate the whereabouts of Gilean vo Presien and to seek justice for any harm done to Gilean. All under Erith law were to aid her. She was authorised to pursue anyone who had caused harm or detained the war mage and to deal such punishment as she considered necessary.

Her hand shook slightly, ribbons fluttering where they hung from the bottom of the page, eyes going back to the blunt statement requiring aid. That one line on its own was a significant gift of power.

"That should work." Orlis' voice was full of satisfaction as he unashamedly read over her shoulder. His grief and worry had faded, eyes bright with determination, jaw set.

"Providing the Preceptor's authority is recognised." Arrow's voice was faint, mind beginning to consider the magnitude of the authority she had been granted. The last Inquirer Extraordinary, appointed more than a hundred years before, by no less a person than the Queen, had arrested one of the Taellan. She read the words again, knowing she was putting off action, struggling to take it all in. The Preceptor had made her an oath-bound servant and now an Inquirer Extraordinary. An enormous change.

And yet she was under no illusions. It was not trust but desperation that had led the Preceptor to change her status so drastically. If Gilean had not been the subject of the order, it would be Gilean standing with this parchment in his hands, she was quite sure. The Preceptor considered her useful, a tool he had deployed in the past. The order was simply to make her more efficient at the task.

And still she had accepted the order. Not for Evellan, but for Orlis and for herself.

She would, as she had told him, need Orlis' help. An assistant, and a guide in the maze that was the Palace. Not to mention the heartland. Her heart skipped. Not even in her most outrageous day-dreaming had she imagined being permitted into the heartland, let alone the Palace itself.

"His authority has not been revoked. If that was going to happen, it would have been done already," Orlis said, voice full of certainty, cutting through her spiralling thoughts. Arrow had to take his word for it as he was far more familiar with the Palace and its politics. "We will need transport and, well, new clothes for you."

Arrow looked down at herself and her lips twitched, trying to imagine the reaction of the Erith to a mixed-blood, exiled, unNamed mage wandering the heartland in human clothes.

"I will need copies of this, too."

"Go speak to the Archivists," Orlis told her, "and I will arrange everything else."

Before Arrow quite knew what he was doing, or what he had meant by everything else, he was gone, strides quick and purposeful.

Chapter Four

—— · ——

Securing the Archivists' assistance in copying the Preceptor's order was far easier than Arrow had expected, even with the Archivists' curiosity and their offer of tea. They made copies as they pelted her with questions. Orlis returned, as if by magic, as she was leaving the Archives, the journeyman carrying a travel sack and a bundle of clothes which he handed to her before pushing her into a disused study room and telling her to change.

Changing out of her human made clothing, Arrow realised that the items handed to her were the clothes she had been given when she had been under the watchful eye of Kallish and her cadre. Erith made clothing, beautifully fashioned, finer than anything else she owned. Narrow-legged trousers long enough to mostly disguise her human-made boots and a soft over-tunic that allowed her freedom of movement. It should pass unnoticed among the Erith at the Palace.

Stomach tight with nerves at the thought of visiting the heart of the Erith, she followed Orlis out of the Archives and towards the Academy, mind turning to the next practical question, that of how to get to the Palace. The Taellaneth had horse-drawn carriages she should be able to commandeer. She had no clear idea of how long a journey it would be to the Palace, but suspected several days, even with famed Erith horses. Time enough, she hoped, to adjust to her new status, prepare for the heartland, and to ask Orlis for information. That decided in her own mind, she then noticed that Orlis was not leading her towards the stables but deeper into the Academy.

"Where are we going? The heartland is the other way."

"Mirror travel," Orlis told her briefly. He glanced across, a shadow on his face for a moment. "The relay was already being opened. We are just taking advantage."

Arrow's feet checked, and her mouth opened in protest before she snapped her jaw shut. It was not what she would have chosen, but it was practical.

Orlis led the way to the Preceptor's study in the Academy building. A third of White Guard were already present, standing watch around the Preceptor's vast sheet of mirrorglass, three of the teaching staff working together to hold the connection stable to a stone room at the other side, another robed mage visible.

"We are nearly ready," the seniormost Teaching Master said, strain of holding the magic evident in his rigid posture.

"My apologies. I was delayed." Kester vo Halsfeld entered the room, a travel sack of his own on his back, dressed formally, and with a band of deep purple silk around one arm. Arrow flinched back, unable to stop herself, the memory of his rigid fury and her own absolute confusion too vivid. Thankfully, no one was paying her any attention.

"It is quite alright," the Teaching Mistress said, her voice softening as she went on, "we were all so sorry to hear about Teresea. She was a gentle soul."

"Yes, she was. Thank you." Kester's face was tight and closed, eyes barely touching Arrow as he looked around the room. "Good day to you." He stepped forward into the portal, appearing a moment later beside the mage in the stone chamber.

The teaching staff turned to Arrow next, one of the master's faces tightening in disapproval, an expression she was heartily familiar with.

"You go next," Arrow told Orlis, palms prickling, feet twitching with the urge to run. She hated mirror travel. He lifted a brow in surprise but stepped through without hesitation or protest. Arrow gave her thanks to those gathered, both as a courtesy and a further moment's delay, took a deep breath, and stepped forward.

And was torn apart, mixed up and put back together again, body not quite sure the reassembly had been done right, foot sliding away from a wobbling surface as she reached the stone chamber on the other side.

She staggered, feet not finding any purchase on the floor, eyes refusing to tell her which way was up or down, stomach twisting. Dimly she heard Orlis' voice. Some sort of query.

Something solid smacked against her side and she put a hand out. Cold. Rough. Stone. A wall. Relief made her even more dizzy for a moment and she leant against the wall, breathing shallow and too rapid. Nothing was stable. Nothing was up or down. What she could see made no sense. Random colours and shapes. The only real thing in the world was the wall, stone cool against her forehead and palms, wall bearing her weight as of no consequence.

Orlis' voice repeated a query, concern cutting through the distortion and nausea.

She could not understand the words but guessed the question. "Mirror travel." Her voice was thin and too high.

"Try this," he suggested, voice closer to her and much clearer.

A small object appeared before her face, eyes blurring then clearing a moment to show her a small flask, stopper out. She breathed in, pungent odour blurring everything again. She slid down the wall to a heap, spinning worse, stomach twisting, closing her eyes, fist against her mouth to stop being sick. The darkness behind her eyelids helped a fraction.

"Perhaps not."

She thought he stepped back, sound of his boots loud on the stone floor, rustling in his satchel abrasive in her ears, then the soft sound of cloth told her he was kneeling beside her. She risked opening her eyes and found another flask, a little larger, held out. More cautiously, she sniffed the open top and almost wept with relief at the familiar scent of Erith tea. A few sips and her stomach settled enough that she was no longer in danger of throwing up.

"Thank you." She handed the flask back and glanced up to find that they had an audience. There was the mage who had held the mirror open, Kester vo Halsfeld and a third of White Guard. Very highly ranked warriors, by their braiding. Heat surged up her face and the tips of her ears burned under her hair. All Erith that she knew of could step through mirrors without any ill effect. She normally managed to stay upright at least.

"You are the mage, Arrow?" the leader of the third asked. His face and voice did not betray much expression, but Arrow was used to reading the Taellan and her face burned again at the disbelief.

"I am. Greetings, *svegraen*." She managed to get to her feet with assistance from the wall, and then bow without her head falling off. She considered that an extraordinary achievement.

"I am Miach." He did not elaborate, but did not need to. Arrow's knees wobbled and she nearly slid down the wall again. There was only one Miach. Head of the Queen's own guard, a position he had held for longer than she could remember at present. Since well before the last incursion, a hundred years before. In the way of the Erith, he appeared ageless with unlined pale skin and pitch-black hair confined in elaborate braids, his uniform pristine. "We have had trouble here. The lady asks if you would investigate."

"What kind of trouble?" Arrow heard her voice ask, before she realised how stupid a question it was. The purple band on Kester's arm, and the purple braids on the warriors' uniforms, the colour of Erith mourning, gave their own clues.

"Lady Teresea vel Fentraisal died earlier."

"I am sorry to hear that." Arrow made another instinctive bow, Court manners folding around her like a familiar coat.

"The circumstances were unusual."

"And your lady wishes me to investigate?" The effects of mirror travel were still with her, as once again she only realised after she had spoken how crass the question was. Miach's lady was none other than the Queen herself.

"She would welcome your assistance. You have investigated such matters before."

"Something like," Arrow hedged. Other deaths, yes. Sent by the Taellan as a disposable tool, often not expected to return. She had never investigated of her own will, and never the death of a prominent Erith in the Palace at the heart of all Erith. And not when she had travelled from all that was familiar to the Erith's heartland and was still not quite sure which way was up or down.

"We need to find Gilean," Orlis objected, jaw and mouth set.

"We do," Arrow agreed, turning her head to Miach and finding the warrior as grim-faced as Orlis.

"His room has been preserved. Those on watch have orders to let you both in."

Arrow hesitated, torn between the Preceptor's orders and the Queen's command. Expressed as a request, it was nonetheless a command. It did not take long to decide which to follow first. This was the Palace, where the Queen's word was law.

"I will go to Gilean's rooms," Orlis offered, following her line of thought more easily than she had. "I will not touch anything," he added, in response to her evident hesitation. "We will meet later."

"Yes." Arrow took a step forward and wobbled, stomach and head still not reconciled after the mirror travel, putting a hand back on the wall for a moment.

"Come." Miach gestured to the doorway. "The fresh air will help."

She followed them in silence, steps small and uncertain, wishing as fiercely as she ever had before that she was invisible. None of these competent Erith would have reacted so badly to mirror travel, she was sure.

ele

Her embarrassment was forgotten, sliding away like smoke as soon as they stepped through the door from the stone room, through the thick tangle of wards that protected the relay room, and out into the heartland.

Magic saturated the air and the earth, twining around her, a seductive call to her senses. There was so much magic she could smell it, the trace of burnt amber, rich and thick as caramelised sugar on her tongue. Power fizzed against her skin, raising static in her unruly hair which crackled around her head. Her wards sparked in a silver cascade, eyes shimmering in reaction, every nerve ending waking up. Some long-dormant part of her roused, an empty part that she had not been aware of before, fulfilled and filled by the presence of the heartland's magic within her. There were echoes of the Taellaneth here, the sense of place that she felt when returning, multiplied a hundred fold. For the first time in her life she felt more Erith than outsider. She was light as air. A great laugh gathered inside, wanting to be let out.

Biting her lip to hold in the laugh was second nature, the slight sting widening her awareness and reminding her of the people nearby. She closed her eyes, breathing slowly, trying to find her balance, searching for the inner quiet that allowed her to perform magic.

As she reached for calm, there was a brush of something other against her wards. She tensed, her wards hardening, before she recognised the presence as carrying the essence of the heartland. Exuberant, more powerful than anything she had sensed in her life before, the great spirit of the Erith heartland swirled around her in the second world, too vast to look at directly, seemingly delighted by her presence. A bubble of invisible laughter surrounded her, echoing her own, a trace across her face, a bright counterpoint to the shadow world, all seasons all at once, with a trace of clear water, heat of summer air, trace of frost, scent of green.

She swayed on her feet in the first world, overwhelmed, and the presence withdrew a fraction, enough for her to find her balance and open her eyes, blazing silver.

"Apologies." Miach's voice was far away. He sounded sincere. "I forgot that you had not been to the heartland before. And arriving through a mirror. It must be a shock."

The words floated in her ears, sounds meaningless, taking an age to make sense. She could not form anything to answer for several moments, still searching for calm, her heart now racing for another reason. Her control was fractured, her defences compromised. The words might not have made sense initially, but they reminded her that she was among the Erith, an inherently dangerous place.

"Arrow, are you alright?" Orlis asked.

"Perfectly fine, thank you." She gathered her wards in tight, wriggled her toes to remind her feet that they were on solid ground, damped down her power, closing her eyes briefly before opening them, restored to their normal grey with sparks of silver the only sign of the heartland's effect a small smile tugging her mouth, a smile she could not hold back. "My apologies."

Miach's faint, answering smile surprised her and he shook his head at some unknown thought. In contrast, Orlis was frowning.

"I am not sure I should leave you," he said.

"You should go," Arrow contradicted. "We will get more done that way."

"No harm will come to the mage under my care." Miach's promise was sincere, the weight of it almost visible in the air. This was the heartland, Arrow reminded herself. Words, which carried weight anywhere they were spoken, were even more powerful here.

Still, Orlis hesitated a moment more before bowing his head and heading off with quick strides, tension betrayed in the set of his shoulders.

"A fine young man," Miach observed, "and will be better still when he learns some patience."

Arrow bit back a smile at the assessment, partially agreeing. Patience was not one of Orlis' stronger qualities. And yet, there was something endearing about his open curiosity, and she had nothing but sympathy for his concern about Gilean.

She said nothing, a long ago learned habit among the Erith, letting Miach and his third guide her away from the mirror relay. Kester was silent, still, a faint line between his brows betraying some emotion she could not read. And did not try to. The youngest Taellan was a mystery she did not have time to solve today, her chest still echoing with the pain of their last encounter.

After the overwhelming introduction to the Erith heartland's power, the sight of the Palace itself was almost an anti-climax and Arrow was able to keep her feet, and her wits, as they walked.

The Taellaneth, naturally, had many paintings and tapestries showing the Palace which Arrow had found fascinating, intrigued by its contrasting architecture and beauty. However she discovered that even the Erith's master craftsmen had only managed pale copies of the reality.

The Palace was not one building, rather it was a massive complex of buildings, added to over the centuries as different monarchs and their consorts added their own style. Barely half of the buildings were fully occupied, from what Arrow knew, and there were some that had never been used. The older, more tradition-bound Erith might like to say that their population had been decimated by the wars with the shifkin, lamenting the empty buildings of the Palace complex, but even most of the Taellan would admit that the Erith had never been a populous race, not like the humans. The Palace was not expanded for lack of capacity but to satisfy its monarchs and the Erith's desire for beautiful things.

Seen with her own eyes, the buildings were extraordinary, constructed with the same skill and attention to detail that the craftsmen had brought to bear in the Taellaneth, and made in dizzying variety. Arrow suspected it could take many days to map the whole extent of them, let alone the insides. There were low, single storey buildings of dark grey stone, tall, narrow buildings of blond stone that gleamed in the light, structures two and three storeys high made of a mix of cream and red bricks arranged in elaborate patterns, and, nestled among the others, Arrow could see an enormous structure, larger than the Taellaneth main building, with several domed roofs in bright colours, deep azure, shimmering gold and pure crimson, that must be the heart of the Palace. Beyond the main building were tall towers, dark stone rising into the sky. Arrow tipped her head back to see the height of them and nearly lost her footing as she realised that some of the towers did not appear to end, rising into the sky and disappearing into the blue.

Catching her balance, she felt heat rising in her face again. None of her companions appeared to have noticed her staring, or perhaps they were used to newcomers or recent arrivals falling over their own feet as they tried to take in every sight.

Dragging her attention closer to the ground, Arrow realised that, in true Erith manner, the buildings were set far apart with gardens between, the air saturated with the scent of herbs including the citrus notes that went into Erith tea, medicinal herbs a tart undertone. Even if she had been blindfolded and her magic stripped away, all it would take would be a single breath to know it was impossible to be anywhere else but on Erith lands.

The walkways were raked gravel, familiar underfoot after so many years treading the paths at the Taellaneth and finally grounded Arrow back to reality.

"Can you tell me what happened, *svegraen*?" she asked Miach's shoulder. He and Kester were matching strides just ahead of her.

He hesitated, checking in his stride before glancing over his shoulder, face serious. "I would rather show you and let you draw your own conclusions."

She nodded, frowning slightly when he turned away again. Now her brain was finally working again, she wondered with some apprehension what circumstances would lead the Queen to ask an unknown, exiled mage to investigate a death in the Palace, particularly when she had an experienced investigator close to hand. Miach's dedication to his duty and his sharp mind, as well-honed as his weapons skills, were legendary among the White Guard. Highly unlikely that so competent a warrior would need outside assistance.

CHAPTER FIVE

— ∘ —

The path that they were following led to the enormous building at the heart of the Palace, the building growing larger and even more impressive as they approached. Its pale stone walls were carved with complex symbols of the Erith, windows spelled so that the interior was slightly blurred. From what Arrow could see, the building had several arms extending out from a centre dominated by the glittering gold dome, which vanished from sight as they walked into the shadow of the building.

Miach led them to the end of one of the short arms and a pair of closed doors, clearly a secondary entrance. One of Miach's third stepped ahead and opened a door. They entered a high-ceilinged single storey arm of the main building to a wide, straight corridor that Arrow thought might lead, eventually, to the gold dome. This part of the building was brightly lit by overhead skylights, the walls on either side hung with portraits, painted faces watching the visitors as they passed.

"I thought you might be interested in this," Miach said, moving a little further down the hallway of faces, stopping at one of the smaller portraits. "The Lady Alisemea."

Arrow felt her limbs stiffen but moved obediently after him, looking up at the portrait. It was as finely executed as all the others in this long hallway, showing an Erith lady seated by a window, turned as though the artist had called her attention from the outside so her face was partly cast in shadow. She had wide-open, deep blue eyes and creamy pale skin and, unusually for the Erith, blond hair that gleamed even in paint. Like many of the paintings along the hallway, the artist had not painted in the amber of her magic, the clues to her heritage in the lines of her face and the fantastical landscape beyond the window.

"Your mother," Miach prompted, clearly expecting more from her than her silent stare. Beside her she could feel Kester stiffen, as though he had only just made the connection.

"Yes." Arrow heard her voice clear and even and for one brief moment was glad of her service with the Erith which had taught her to keep calm on the outside, whatever turmoil was on the inside. Seeing the face, with no warning, was a shock and, apart from that, she could not track the feelings running through her. She wondered, as she looked at the painting, what she was supposed to feel. Apart from Gesser, who had taken great delight in telling her how far the lady had fallen from grace, no one had spoken the name directly to her. She had pieced together the details from what others said around her, the Erith often speaking over her head as though she did not exist. Once a great lady among the Erith, Alisemea's name was no longer spoken, excised along with Arrow's lineage.

Looking at the painted face, Arrow felt no kinship or connection. This polished and posed lady was as much a stranger as all the other faces on display. She did not look anything like the face Arrow saw reflected back at her from time to time. It was impossible to reconcile this beautiful, composed, young Erith lady, wearing her finery with confidence and familiarity, with the knowledge that this same woman had defied her House and her father, leaving as her legacy a mixed-blood, Nameless, outcast daughter.

"You have seen her likeness before?" the warrior persisted, clearly expecting more from her, puzzled frown drawing his brows together.

"No." Arrow turned from the painting to face him. Watching that painted face hurt somewhere deep inside, a place long dormant. She needed time to adjust, to settle those feelings down again, and she was not safe here, or anywhere among the Erith. "There are no images of her in the Taellaneth or in her former House."

"She was considered a great beauty," Miach said, eyes travelling past her shoulder to the painted face. A shadow crossed his face. "She was a favourite of my lady."

Arrow was speechless for a moment. It was more information than anyone had given her for years, and jarred with the taunts that Gesser had used. And now that she thought of that, she wondered why Alisemea's portrait was here, in this gallery, on open display at the Palace.

"I know nothing substantive about her," Arrow clarified, aware of Kester's close interest, and some curious glances from Miach's third.

"Surely your grandfather must have spoken of her?" And most surely a sign of how disturbed the warrior was, that he would ask such an open question. The Erith did not normally pry so openly.

"Seggerat vo Regersfel rarely spoke to me beyond the Taellan's commands." Arrow was proud that her voice did not shake, did not betray her shock that he would raise the matter or the renewed shame she felt. Within the Taellaneth her blood relations were never openly mentioned and she had been taught, many times, that her heritage was shameful.

"But your other grandfather?" Miach persisted. He seemed genuinely confused.

"I have never met Serran vo Liathius," she answered, skin itching under the intense scrutiny. The painted faces stared down at her, casting their judgement alongside the warrior's disbelief, unease reflected in the faces of his third. She did not turn to look at Kester, glad for a moment that Orlis was not here with his incessant curiosity. She might now carry the order making her an Inquisitor Extraordinary, but among the Erith she had always been an outcast, even before her exile, her impure heritage setting her apart forever. The respite in the human world and among the 'kin made the renewed scrutiny and reminder sting all the more.

She discovered that the respite had also given her some confidence and assurance as to her ability to survive beyond Erith borders. Most importantly, she had had enough of being observed and found wanting by the Erith. She moved a step away, nodding towards the end of the corridor. "May we proceed, *svegraen*?"

Still frowning, to Arrow's relief the warrior did not say any more, his lips closed in a firm line which suggested many thoughts unspoken. They continued along the corridor to its end, a set of double doors which were simply burnished wood, the lack of any decoration making them stand out next to the fine paintings and ornately patterned floor. Two of Miach's third moved forward and took a door each, opening them to release a blinding wave of sunlight into the corridor that had seemed bright enough a moment before.

Arrow moved, not caring about the audience for a moment, drawn forward by the familiar scent of parchment and ink and the hum of magic which fizzed against her skin. Without warning she was faced with one of the wonders of the Erith, jaw slack as she stopped in the doorway, feet simply freezing of their own accord.

There was only one place in the world that this could be, at the heart of the Erith Palace. The library. Tael ab Niasseren, or in the common tongue, Niasseren's Folly.

She tipped her head up to see the domed ceiling, impossibly high above, a vast array of stained glass painted with fantastical Erith creatures. The several stories' height from the floor to the ceiling was full of a series of elaborate bookshelves floating in the air. For a moment she just stared, captivated by the sight. The large bookshelves, taller than an Erith lord and almost twice as wide as they were tall, travelled in slow, serene grace through the air. It might be fashionable among the Erith to disdain the room, calling it Niassaren's Folly, but Erith travelled to the Palace just to see this one room, bypassing the many other wonders the Palace contained. To anyone magic-blind, it was a truly amazing sight. As it were, even through her awe, the complex web of spells holding the bookshelves in the air teased her second sight.

"Hopelessly impractical, of course," Miach said, the appreciation in his face belying his caustic words, "and it is nearly impossible to find anything for the courtiers move shelves at will to suit themselves and their various research projects. They rarely return things to the proper shelves."

Arrow suppressed a smile, reminded of the Archivists. She could all too easily imagine the Palace courtiers destroying any sense of order in the shelves.

Despite its vast size, the library was almost empty. In the distance, Arrow could see what must be the main entrance, a far larger set of double doors with what looked like a third of White Guard on watch. Not far from them, a pair of sombrely clad Erith, who Arrow guessed to be librarians, were working at a set of shelves that they had temporarily called to the ground.

"You, there." A noble Erith, dressed in elaborate, embroidered robes and trailing scent in an almost visible wake behind him, strode up, angular face flushed with fury, ears twitching under his elaborate braids. There was a considerable amount of grey in his brown hair, Arrow saw, and his outrage and age placed him immediately in her mind, even before Miach spoke. One of the Queen's relatives, his name was mentioned often in Taellan meetings, and rarely with any favour.

"Lord vo Lianen." The warrior made the most perfunctory bow Arrow had ever seen, so swift if she had blinked she would have missed it.

"This is an outrage," the elder lord hissed, glare darting momentarily to Arrow, then immediately away as though the mere glance had scorched his eyes.

"The Lady Arrow's assignment has been endorsed by Her Majesty herself," Miach said, hands folded behind him, "who has been most troubled by recent events. Would you contradict our sovereign's will?" The voice was mild, but the words were as sharp as steel.

"It is an outrage."

"You are entitled to your views, my lord," the warrior was still mild, "but I suggest you direct them to Her Majesty's ears. I have my commands."

"Outrageous," the lord spluttered and flounced away. Arrow watched with interest. She had never seen anyone, Erith, shifkin or human, truly flounce before, but it was the only word she could think of to adequately describe Queris vo Lianen's progress as he made his way across the room to the main entrance. The lord's disgust settled her at last, something deeply familiar among all this strangeness, reminding her of who and what she was, and why she was here.

"The scene of the incident, *svegraen*?" she prompted when they had both been staring at the lord's retreating back for a long moment.

"Over here. The scene was secured."

They rounded a pair of bookshelves hanging in mid-air and found two thirds of a cadre of White Guard, wearing elaborate Court uniforms, insignia on their sleeves showing them to be the Queen's personal guard, holding a plain ward around them and whatever was behind them. The rest of Miach's cadre, Arrow guessed, and wondered who was watching the Queen.

"How long after the incident did you set up your wards, *svegraen*?" Arrow asked, peeking behind him. The wards they had established were strong enough to shimmer in the first world, impenetrable.

"Too long," Miach answered, clearly displeased, "for it was not immediately clear that this was anything other than a terrible mishap." He glanced past Arrow's shoulder. "We should have been more thorough." He checked a moment, hesitation out of character and drawing Arrow's attention before he spoke, eyes on Kester. "Had we known, we would not have moved the lady from here."

"Why would you suspect anything amiss in the library?" Kester asked, sounding quite sincere. The lady had been his relative, Arrow remembered, and wondered, far too late, whether she should have offered any words of condolence.

She was distracted as Miach stepped to one side and waved a hand. The rest of his cadre stepped back as well, a co-ordinated, easy movement, and the wards moved with them, still containing the scene but moving back with the warriors so that the destruction was clear. As they moved back, the sweet, unmistakable scent of Erith death filled the air, constricting Arrow's throat and drawing unwanted tears to her eyes. She would never get used to that scent.

She took a long breath in, coating her lungs in the scent, and let the pain fade as she breathed out. A calming technique taught at the Academy.

With the sorrow of Erith death set aside, she could focus on the scene.

Three of the floating bookshelves had fallen, breaking against each other, spilling precious books and parchments across the polished, patterned floor. In the centre of the chaos was a hollowed-out spot which was spattered with blood. Old enough to have mostly dried. Fresh enough that the slightly bitter tang was still present in the air, even to Arrow's dull senses. The hollow had been disturbed, parchments torn and books in pieces, but it was still very obviously the impression left by a body, initially defended by personal wards then crushed by the shelves.

Arrow glanced up at the floating shelves high above and could all too easily imagine the terror of one of them falling.

"We believe the lady felt no pain," Miach said quietly, "which is the only blessing in all of this. What aid may we provide, mage?"

"Has such a thing ever happened before?"

"Never. The librarians and Palace ward keepers renew the spells frequently." The warrior glanced up, face tight. "All the other shelves have been checked. There is no other disturbance."

Arrow thought about that for a while, eyes following the gentle course of the bookshelves high above, each with its own unique rune pattern at either end, enabling them to be called down. The whole library had seemed like a fairy story when she had first heard of it, a conceit of Niasseren, long-dead Consort of another Queen, who had wanted something to occupy his time. Arrow had wondered how the thing had survived, for the power needed to maintain such elaborate spells would drain most mages. A very short time in the heartland and she knew there was power enough here to charge a dozen such libraries many times over, and for as long as there was a sun and moon, and never be a danger of draining the magic well under them.

Added to which, the Palace ward keepers, who were responsible for maintaining all the wards and spells around the Palace, were among the most skilled of Erith mages, undertaking many years of training before they were entitled to call themselves a ward keeper.

"Do you know what happened?" she asked and saw the faintest glimmer of something in his face. Approval. Speculation. Something she could not read.

"Not yet." He maintained his parade rest.

"It may take a while," she warned him, sliding her bag from her shoulder, moving to put it on the ground, then handing it to the junior cadre member who stepped forward.

"We will wait," Miach told her, with no hint of impatience.

The whole cadre melted back further, maintaining their plain wards as a perimeter. Even if Lord vo Lianen had lingered in the room, he would not be able to see past those wards. She stepped forward, drawing a breath in. She truly hoped that the lady had not seen the bookshelves falling, had been unaware of anything untoward. The result was the same, but it seemed better to hope she had not suffered.

The world in second sight was a mass of power and spells that caught her breath, the sheer strength of the heartland's magic almost too much to bear, even indoors. It took a few moments of steady breathing until she found her balance again and managed to separate out the layers, disregarding the heartland to focus instead on the spellwork in the room. The level of skill demonstrated here, the Palace ward keepers' work, was extraordinary, the protections around the library and the other bookshelves beautifully crafted.

The spells around the fallen bookshelves which had kept them above the ground were torn into shreds, broken runes waving aimlessly in the air as she looked. Deliberately broken. There had been nothing subtle about this attack. But there had been a considerable amount of skill, she thought, seeing the many layers of protections and counter-spells woven into the levitation spells. Whoever had designed these impractical bookshelves had been well aware of the risk so much unwieldy weight posed and had provided protection against accidents. It was not simply a case of cutting one set of runes, or unleashing a snap of mage fire. To bring these shelves down had taken a focused, determined, and complex attack.

Interested, despite the grim spattering of blood at her feet, Arrow bent to look more closely at the broken runes, calling a spark of power to enhance her sight. The runes had been cut through. Not cleanly enough for a blade, but perhaps a very slender thrust of mage fire. She cupped one of the trails in her palm, bringing it closer to her face to examine it further. She opened her second sight fully, murmuring a further spell to allow her to see in more detail, and turned the fragile thread between her fingers for long moments, seeing fragmented runes of spellwork, before she caught the tiniest trace of another signature. Mage fire had indeed been used, so finely crafted it was nearly invisible.

"What do you see?" Miach asked, breaking her concentration. Whatever was on her face must have broken his discipline.

"Magic," she answered, picking up more of the broken runes. "Is there a reader in the Palace?" she asked, wondering if the magician's trace might be familiar to someone else. Readers were as specialised as the ward keepers, capable of parsing a magician's signature from traces too small for other magicians. They were also rare, but Arrow knew that there was at least one in the Palace.

There was a short, odd silence, and a sharp intake of breath. Dimming her second sight she looked up to find Kester and Miach looking at her with grim expressions.

"Have I said something amiss?"

"The lady was a reader," Miach confirmed. "One of the most accurate ever born."

"I did not know." Arrow felt her ears heat. She probably should have known that. She ducked her head. "My apologies."

"You have found a trace?" Kester asked, checking himself before he could move.

"I have," she confirmed. "A moment, if you please." She opened her second sight again and recorded the impressions of the spell runes. Despite the wards the cadre had placed, the trace was degrading quickly. Burrowing into the second world she found the unravel command buried within the mage fire. A clever, skilled magician had done this. She sighed, memories of her last encounter with a clever, skilled and ruthless magician all too clear.

Dropping the fragmented threads, she knelt amid the chaos, careful to not cause further damage, and examined the broken spells, destroyed shelves and ruined books with her second sight engaged.

"There is a book missing," she noted absently, cataloguing the shelves' contents.

"Where?" Miach's voice sounded close by her ear.

She stiffened slightly, not having heard him move.

"Here," she pointed, "this is not a series, but there is a gap in the residue. Something was removed from under the lady's body." She blinked, dimming her second sight again, and looked up at him. "I would assume that that was before anyone raised the alarm."

"Indeed," he was grim. "This place has been under constant watch since the lady was found. Partly to ensure that no one else suffered the same accident."

"This was no accident," she told him, coming to her feet. He nodded, unsurprised. "The Palace has wards against battle magic, and alarms," she noted. She had seen the whole building covered with beautifully crafted wards as they walked towards it. "Were any of them tripped?"

"Not one." There were lines about the warrior's mouth now, weariness and sorrow. "Battle magic was used?"

"A blade of mage fire cut through the spells supporting the shelves. It was fine work. Very fine work," Arrow told him, conscious that the cadre were maintaining a ward preventing her words from carrying beyond the group. He drew a sharp, shocked breath.

"That must have been thinner than a sword blade." Kester was fascinated despite the circumstances.

"About the width of a *kri-syang*," Arrow confirmed. The silver blades used by mages in their spellwork, slender and short enough to wear along a mage's forearm.

"No war mage would achieve that precision," Miach objected.

"I did not say a war mage," Arrow pointed out, "just that mage fire was used."

"Who else would use mage fire?" Kester asked, curious.

"A better question," Miach spoke before Arrow could answer, "is who could learn such a spell, and such skill with it?"

"The teaching is widely available to senior students," Arrow told him, casting her mind back to her Academy training. "So, that means anyone who has been a student at the Academy beyond the initial required learning. Or anyone who has had access to the Archives. The Archivists are careful, but books on mage fire are not in the restricted section."

"The skill?" Kester prompted.

"A great deal of power to bend the spell to the caster's will." She stopped, lips closing for a moment, before going on. "Normally that would drain most mages. But the heartland is saturated with magic. The draw would be nothing. Unnoticed. And the mage has had hours and hours of practice." She crouched in the chaos again, something catching her attention.

"Could you do it?" Kester asked, curious.

She paused, tilting her head in thought, silver flaring in her eyes.

"If there was need enough," she answered at length, "but this was not done out of need, but out of clear intent to harm the lady."

"She was deliberately killed," Miach stated the conclusion.

"Without doubt."

"I had hoped that was not the case." The warrior's already grim face settled in stern lines. He beckoned to his second and issued a series of commands in a low voice. Unable to catch the orders with her inferior hearing, Arrow turned her attention back to the scene before her. There was something amiss, something out of place other than the missing book and the grim depression where the lady had fallen.

It took her a long moment, overlaying her first and second sight, before she realised that the blood stain was the wrong shape.

"Was the lady severely wounded, *svegraen*?"

"She was dead, mage."

"Pardon. I meant, did her body bear many wounds?"

"A head wound that the physician determined as the cause of her death. Other than that she had sustained many broken bones, but not other open wounds."

"There is too much blood for just one person," Kester noted, kneeling beside Arrow with a fluid movement.

"Can we separate the two?"

"In time, yes," Arrow confirmed, "but I will need to obtain the lady's essence first to separate her blood. Is her body still preserved?"

"Yes. Awaiting Kester's arrival to conduct the rite."

With a start she remembered, again, that the warrior kneeling beside her was here for as grim a purpose as she was, to conduct the last rites for his relative.

"My apologies, *svegraen*," she said, not quite meeting his eyes, "may I examine the lady's remains?"

"If it helps to catch her killer, of course." Kester rose, brief expression of something like revulsion crossing his face before it resumed its impassive expression. The brief glimpse of something else hurt more than it should. Far more than Lord vo Lianen's earlier disgust.

"*Svegraen*." She forced her attention away, turning to Miach. "Would it be possible to restore the stasis over this area?" She took her bag back with a nod of thanks.

"Of course," Miach nodded to the leader of the second third, then turned back to them, "I will take you to the lady's remains."

CHAPTER SIX

—•—

The Erith had a long history of fighting, with the shifkin and amongst themselves, so Arrow was not surprised to find that the Palace had an entire suite of rooms devoted to laying out the dead in preparation for the final rites. As a happier counterpoint, she knew that the vast complex of buildings also contained a large, purpose-built infirmary that would treat any Erith citizen who came to the door.

The rooms for the dead were underground, entrance a short distance from the main building. The doorway was a small, stone building that contained nothing more on the surface than stone steps going down. A cool breeze, the temperature underground more or less constant because of the vast earth around them, brushed Arrow's face as she followed Kester and Miach's shoulders down the plain steps. The rest of Miach's third stayed above ground, keeping watch.

The walls were lined with unadorned white stone, niches in the walls holding fat, bright candles that provided light and a gentle fragrance to counter the sweet scent of death. Preparation rooms for the dead opened from a central, wide corridor, and none of the rooms had doors. Through the doorways Arrow glimpsed empty stone beds, raised to waist height, and one or two occupied beds, the dead covered by large sheets of cloth that had been dyed deep purple. Physician's apprentices, their status clear from their pale robes, moved on noiseless feet, one greeting Miach with a slight bow and guiding them to the appropriate door in silence before returning to another room along the way. There was another body there, Arrow knew, the scent of death carrying even to her blunt nose, waiting for the apprentices to prepare it for the rites.

Hot tears burned her eyes at the scent, an automatic reaction she did not think any amount of time, or death, would cure her of. There was something about that unique scent of Erith death that twisted her being, sorrow rising in its wake.

She paused at the doorway, Miach waiting with her, allowing Kester to pay his respects before she violated the lady's corpse.

Kester's face did not show any emotion as he looked down at one of his last few blood relatives. A kin woman of the House he had held before Juinis vo Halsfeld had wed Kester's sister and appropriated their House.

With her face and body frozen in death, Arrow could not tell anything about the lady's character. The lady had been laid out for her death rites, an elaborate headdress covering the wound, her features still and calm, hands folded across her stomach.

Movement from the corridor drew all their attention, the apprentice bowing slightly, skin paling as he was faced with the Queen's first guard and a high-status lord. His eyes skipped over Arrow, dismissing her.

"Your pardon, *svegraen*. The master had asked me to set the lady's clothing aside, in case it was needed." He bowed again, a package in plain linen cloth offered on his flat palms.

"Has the clothing been cleaned?"

"No, *svegraen*. The master was very clear about that." The apprentice, eyes downcast, folded his hands in his sleeves as Kester took the bundle. Arrow wondered what the Palace's master physician, in charge of the dead as well as the living, had seen that caused him to take such precautions, or if he was just naturally cautious.

"Convey my thanks to the master, and I would speak with him later," Kester told the apprentice, who bowed and left. "Arrow, do what you need to do."

He left the room, clothing still in hand, back stiff.

Arrow waited until he was out of sight before she moved to the lady's side, the scent of death overwhelming. The lady was covered with a purple cloth, her folded hands resting on the fabric, which bore not a single crease, her head and neck bare to viewing. Seen more closely, her face was serene in death, pale skin bearing the faint trace of lines that Arrow guessed would have been laughter in life, evidence of her long life. A subtle gloss of cosmetics had been applied, covering the unique pallor of death. Thanks to the headdress there were no wounds visible. If she was not so still, she might be sleeping. Arrow hesitated, hands clenching slightly at her sides.

"The apprentices will be able to restore her appearance, if you need to remove the cosmetics and headdress," Miach offered from his post by the door. She glanced up, silver in her eyes catching the light. His mouth twisted, "This is not the first suspicious death I have investigated."

"I am sorry," she said sincerely. "Do you wish to observe?"

"Yes. My lady requires a thorough report." The warrior took a step to the side, back to the wall, and stood at parade rest.

It was hardly the first time she had worked under scrutiny. Arrow turned her attention back to the lady, pulling on a pair of fine gloves. The gloves were human-made, of pure silk, and woven through with the finest magic she could make to avoid leaving any mark on whatever she touched. The Erith did not like her touching things where it could be avoided, and using natural materials should be less offensive to the Erith than the latex gloves humans would use for such tasks.

A clean cloth, coated with a small spell, removed the lady's cosmetics, revealing nothing new. The faint lines were clearer, that was all. And definitely put there by laughter. Arrow breathed through a moment of sorrow that such obvious joy in life was gone. Few of the Erith she knew had laughter lines.

The headdress came away more easily than she expected, light in her hands, revealing a terrible wound, somehow all the worse for the fact it had been cleaned, leaving it pale and bloodless, the lady's abundant, dark hair clipped away around the edges. She put the headdress down.

Forcing herself to concentrate she took stock of the placing and shape of the wound, realising two things. First, that the lady would have died almost at once, and second, "This was not caused by the bookshelf."

"What?" Miach came forward rapidly.

"It is the wrong shape entirely for the corner, or even shelf. See." Arrow called a spark of power, providing a more powerful light, and they bent over the lady's misshapen head.

"That was a heavy blow." Miach's voice had deepened. "So she was struck first."

"And then the shelves pulled down on top of her." Arrow glanced down the length of the lady's body. Now she was looking for it, even with the sheet covering the lady it was clear there were bones broken, her limbs not quite straight.

"And a second person was involved."

"A second person was certainly wounded," Arrow agreed.

"No body or soul stone was found." The head of the Queen's personal guard was grim. "If you will excuse me, lady mage, I need to ensure a search is begun. Quickly and quietly."

"Of course, *svegraen.*" Arrow was almost too distracted by the wound in front of her to notice the address he gave her, frowning a moment after his back when her mind caught up with her ears.

Left alone in the cool, dim space with the lady's body, Arrow took a moment to send a silent prayer to the lady's spirit, still trapped on this plane as her body was not yet gone, before opening her second sight and all her senses.

The lady's essence was vivid even in death, the sharp, lemon scent of a mind honed over centuries together with the warm, burned amber smell Arrow associated with powerful Erith mages. Miach had said that the lady had been a reader. He had not mentioned how powerful a mage she had been. Powerful enough to match at least Lady Seivella, and perhaps even Evellan.

Arrow stood with her hands on the lady's shoulders, feeling the cool of death even through the gloves, gathering in the impression of the lady's essence, for long moments until she was quite satisfied that the job was done. Sending another silent prayer for the lady she drew back into the first world and opened her eyes, startled a moment to find Kester standing inside the door, his hands still full of the lady's clothing. He was just outside her personal wards so she had not heard or felt him come into the room. She wondered briefly how he had known to stand there. He was watching her with an intent look she could not read. Or, rather, watching her hands, the white of the gloves a sharp contrast to her dark clothing.

"Do you have what you need?"

"Yes, *svegraen.*" She put the lady's headdress more or less back in place, thankful that the warrior could not see the full extent of the wound from where he stood, and took a step back from the body. "Lord Miach is organising a search for a possible second body," she added, when he remained silent.

"I see." He took a step forward, bringing himself to the edge of her personal wards and lifted the clothing slightly. "I thought you should examine this."

"Did you find anything?"

"Nothing of note, but my spell work is quite blunt."

"Perhaps if we could lay the clothing out?"

"There is an empty room next door." He indicated direction with a tilt of his head, heading out, expecting her to follow which she did, frowning again, wondering what had changed. Despite Teresea's death he seemed relaxed, the sharp edge to his movements gone. She followed his straight back into the corridor, seeing the apprentice watchful nearby, satisfied that the lady would remain undisturbed until Kester was ready to perform the final rite.

Without prompting, Kester laid the clothing out on an empty stone bed. The lady's clothing was finely made, as suited her station in life, full of the scent she favoured and her essence, and something foreign that tugged at Arrow's senses. She slid back into the second world, puzzling over the unexpected traces.

"What have you found?"

"Someone else." With her sight enhanced by magic, Arrow examined the faintest shadows on the lady's clothing. "She held a book here," she used a gloved finger to outline the shadow, "and was held by the arm here, in a firm grip. Some of the threads in the sleeve are broken. It was close to her death. There was no bruising on her body." The lady's arms, pale and bare, had not shown any marks.

"A book?" Kester was sceptical.

"The missing one from the shelves?" Arrow speculated. "And the one gripping her arm was not the same one who brought the shelves down."

"More than one person involved." Miach's voice cut through the room, grim. "Do you have the lady's trace?"

"Yes. We should go back to the library," Arrow agreed, coming back into the first world and stripping off her gloves, tucking them back into the satchel, noticing Kester's eyes following the movement.

——ele——

Kester took his leave of Miach, saying he wanted to speak with the head physician. Miach and his third escorted Arrow back to the library, approaching its main entrance this time. They found a crowd gathered, every one finely dressed in the bright colours favoured by the Erith. Palace courtiers and the highest nobility, Arrow realised, from the quality of the clothing and the way they were confidently seeking entry despite the entire cadre of White Guard barring the door. The White Guard seemed unimpressed, holding their ground with implacable courtesy despite the darkening tone of some of the gathered nobility and several pieces of parchment being waved in their faces, perilously close to giving them paper cuts in a few cases. Arrow took in the scene with curiosity, wondering if she would recognise any of the names of those gathered from overheard Taellan reports and discussions over the years.

The gathered crowd paid very little attention to Miach and his third, though there were resentful mutters as the cadre on watch parted without question to let them through, and a few sharp looks sent in Arrow's direction, another set of muttering rising up. News of her presence in the Palace would be spread quickly. Assuming that any of the Erith there knew who she was, she reminded herself, hearing puzzlement in some of the murmurs. Her presence had been a continuous sore for the Erith within the Taellaneth. However, it was possible that Erith within the heartland had no knowledge of her at all. It was a curious thought and one she wished she had more time to explore, this idea of being anonymous, just one face in a crowd, rather than an unwelcome presence.

Miach exchanged words with the cadre leader as he passed, lips tightening into a thin line as his third opened the library doors, surrounded Arrow and escorted her back into the library.

"Some sort of game," Miach said, letting out a weary breath as the doors closed behind them, "and the next clue is in here. Apparently."

It made as little sense to her as many things the Erith nobility did, so she ignored it, turning her attention instead to this new perspective of the library, now completely empty apart from White Guard, with the floating bookcases serene high above. It felt different and for a moment she thought it was the different view of the interior. She paused, realising that was not the change, drawing the immediate attention of the warriors.

"Someone else has been in here," she told them. An almost-familiar trace in the air. Not a magician she knew. "I think they are gone. But there is so much magic here it is hard to tell." An understatement. The entire library blazed in second sight, the hum of the heartland's magic fizzing against her skin, a distraction she could ill afford.

"Search," Miach commanded. The two thirds of his cadre who had remained in the library moved, Erith steel hissing out of scabbards, the sound lost in the vast room, faint shimmer of ward spells rising and forming a net between them as they spread out.

Miach and his third continued on their way back to the scene, Arrow nearly tripping over a discarded book as they approached. Ears burning at her clumsy feet, she looked down and stilled. The book had fallen, perhaps by accident, so that its title was clearly visible. *On the Capture of Mages.* A fanciful work, the Preceptor had often claimed, but with a small following of people who believed that things like iron bars and certain herbs would hinder a mage's power.

"That is new," Miach observed, amber points rising in his eyes. He was more powerful a mage than most warriors, Arrow noted absently, most of her attention still on the book.

"Someone having a joke?" his second asked.

"Doubtful." Arrow knelt by the book. "There are only supposed to be a dozen of these in existence, and none in this library. The Archives have two copies."

"Does it work?" Miach asked, crouching nearby, eyes direct as he looked at her. She lifted a brow. "Or does someone believe it works?"

"Apparently there are those who believe it works." Arrow put on the gloves again, checking second sight to make sure there were no spells on the book before picking it up carefully and opening its front leaf finding a handwritten inscription, ink slightly faded from time. *Property of Alisemea vel Regersfel.* Her face tightened. The partly shadowed face from the portrait rose in her mind's eye. Was that painted stranger someone to believe in the capture of mages?

"The lady was not a powerful mage, but she was a keen scholar," Miach observed, face and voice tight, doubtless not believing in coincidence any more than Arrow did.

Arrow's mouth was in a flat line, unease twisting her inside. Years of little to no mention of her mother and in the space of one day she had seen a portrait of her for the first time, and held an item the lady had owned. If she wanted, she could take her gloves off and see if she could feel the lady's presence. It was possible, even after all the years since Alisemea's death, and even though Arrow was no reader.

Arrow handed the book to Miach. "I am sure this belongs elsewhere."

She rose to her feet and, not wanting to discuss it further, trusting the warriors to search the rest of the room, went on to the scene, looking again at the spread of blood. Too much blood for one person, yet even with her blunt senses the death scent was not strong enough for two.

Stripping off the gloves, she set her bag aside and sank to her knees next to the blood pool, parchment crackling under her weight, steadying her wards and personal defences, swallowing her instinctive revulsion, before she reached forward and put her bare hand onto the blood pool, sliding into second sight.

With the lady's essence clear in her mind it was a matter of moments to separate out the two different pools of blood. The lady had lost most of her lifeblood on this floor, her heart pumping even as her head was split open. Arrow sent a tiny pulse of power through the lady's blood, marking it in second sight, and focused on the other blood. Much smaller in volume. A grave wound, which would weaken any Erith enough that they would require a healer's urgent attention. The blood was smeared, as though the person had struggled to gain their feet and leave, the trace unfamiliar. They had got up, though, and leant against one of the fallen bookcases for a moment before leaving.

Arrow murmured a cleansing spell as she took her hand out of the blood, magic cleaning her skin far more thoroughly than soap and water, then rose, still in the second world, careful to step around the blood, and went to the edge of the bookcase, seeing the handprint there and, more, a tiny scrap of cloth.

"What have you found?" Miach was impatient, she thought. And worried. A violent, deliberate death in the Palace had dangerous repercussions.

"The second person slid as they got to their feet, and put their hand here." She demonstrated, holding her own skin carefully away from the surface. "They snagged their sleeve. A bit of cloth."

"Too small to be useful," Miach said, disappointed.

"Vivid colours," Arrow disagreed.

"It looks plain."

"Second sight." She came back to the first world to find that the little scrap of cloth was indeed plain in first sight. Miach was focused on the cloth with single-minded intensity.

"Imbued with magic."

"Possibly. Or it is possible the wearer was cast with a spell." Arrow tilted her head, considering the spellwork she could see in second sight. "Glamour or concealment."

"Would you know them again?"

"No." She ducked her eyes from the flare of amber in his. "The essence is not complete." The short silence between them was weighted with the knowledge that the one person who could have read the essence, from either the small scrap of cloth or the blood pool, had been killed here. "This other person would have needed urgent care, though. How many healers are in the Palace?"

"A dozen. Twenty, perhaps," Miach's eyes flickered as he considered that. "Enquiries will be made. What sort of wound?"

"I cannot tell. A lot of blood. There is no trace of blood elsewhere on the bookshelf so a separate blow. Possibly a bladed weapon."

"Miach!"

The cry from across the room drew their immediate attention, Miach striding away, Arrow pausing to gather the bit of cloth in one of her gloves, tucking into a pocket, before following.

The rest of his cadre were gathered about one of the servants' doors to the library, the door standing ajar, wooden panels dented, lock twisted.

"Nothing else here but this," the leader of the second third reported.

"The exit for our wounded?" Miach speculated.

Arrow doubted it. The door had been forcibly ripped open, although curiously the wards remained inert and intact, as though they had not recognised a threat.

That required both physical and magical strength. Very few Erith could maintain that kind of focus while wounded.

But there had been two people present at the lady's death. The one who had gripped her arm. Perhaps the one who was wounded, and left the scrap of cloth behind. And the unknown mage who had killed her with a heavy blow to her skull, then used mage fire to sever some of the library's levitation spells, trying to disguise murder as an accident. It was possible the two had been working together, and the unknown mage had helped his conspirator out of the room.

She listened as the cadre debated among themselves, coming to the same conclusion she had. Her input was not sought, or needed, the cadre clearly used to working together and piecing together incomplete information.

One part of her mind following the conversation, which contained a series of names and terms she did not know, she could not help glancing around the library again, feeling a guilty thrill. She was in the library of Niasseren, however grim the circumstances. A place where anyone was free to learn. Perhaps even exiled, mixed-blood mages, now that she was here.

The lazy, seemingly random course of the bookshelves above caught her attention again. There must be a design, for the Erith would not tolerate anything else. Even if the design only came to pass once in a hundred years, there would still be a design. She wondered if there was a pattern visible from the centre of the room, if someone lay on their back, staring up. Tipping her head back she could see only meaningless gaps between the shelves, the wooden structures themselves not forming any pattern she knew.

There was the faintest trace of amber at the edge of her vision, some event in the second world powerful enough that it was visible, however briefly, in the first world. Turning, she saw one of the great bookshelves change its course, sweeping down from the heights towards her, a dark mass gaining speed as it fell.

A cry of warning, a wordless sound. Wards flared, silver blinding, no time to flee. A bare moment to think and she poured power into her wards, raising all her defences.

The mass of shelf struck her wards with a force that had her sliding back on the polished floor, wooden shelves splintering, parchment and books spilling out, the tangled weave of the bookcase's spells fragmenting against her wards, scraping against her senses.

Arrow's wards dimmed a fraction, reaction to the impact, before flaring again.

The book case fell with a thump that shook the floor.

The sheen of Erith magic, deep amber of a group of powerful magicians, overlaid her silver, less than a heartbeat after the shelf hit the ground, Miach's cadre reacting with admirable speed to the attack. Too slow, if she had not been there and seen the danger.

"Are you alright?" Miach asked. He sounded calm.

"Perfectly fine, thank you."

"Someone just tried to kill us." His voice was edged and she glanced across, finding him watching her with a lifted brow, disbelieving.

"Not the first time." She released the full force of her wards, silver dying in the first world, and stepped forward to the fallen bookcase. "Much more crude," she noted, second sight engaged. "Someone simply cut the spells and gave it a shove towards us. A powerful shove."

"Same person who killed the lady?"

"Possible." She was not convinced, enhancing her sight to examine the broken spell threads. "Certainly the same person who broke the door. Not the same person who was wounded."

"Two conspirators." Miach's voice was deep, rich with emotion she could not follow.

"When was the last time there was an unexplained death inside the Palace?"

"Almost a decade." His back was to her, the tightly woven spells of his personal wards clear in second sight. Looking at something else. She dimmed her second sight and rose to stand beside him.

Above them, the rest of the library's bookshelves spun slowly in their predetermined courses, the pattern still invisible to her.

"They all need to come down," he said, still in that heavy voice. "A watch set until that is done, and the library closed until further notice."

"It will be done." The leader of the second third acknowledged, and padded silently away across the room, her third a close cluster amid the growing chaos.

"The library has never been closed?" Arrow asked, cued by the feeling in Miach's voice. A tone normally reserved for disasters.

"Not once in the seven hundred years of its existence."

"It is a favourite of our lady's," one of Miach's third offered.

Arrow drew a sharp breath. Teresea, a favourite of the Queen's, killed in a room that was also a favourite. A room that was now closed. Even from her place outside the intrigue of Erith politics, Arrow knew that the Queen was vulnerable to opposition. Having the library closed was a potent symbol that the lady could not protect her own House, a serious weakness among the Erith.

"Can you track the conspirators?"

"Sorry. No. There are too many other traces. Too much active magic." That was an understatement. The library was alive with spellwork. It would require a highly skilled tracker, or a reader, to follow the lead.

Miach absorbed that in silence. Arrow tried not to squirm, wishing she had more to offer, and knowing that her day was not yet done. She had not been sent here to investigate Teresea's death but Gilean's disappearance.

"We should take you to Orlis. There are rooms for you there." Miach moved, reluctance clear in his clipped strides across the floor. Arrow, following in his wake, took one final glance up at the Folly of Niasseren, perhaps the last time the bookshelves would be airborne.

CHAPTER SEVEN

— : —

Miach handed her to his junior third, who accepted their charge with the same competence they had shown in the library, forming a loose escort around her and guiding her through the Palace. Arrow was lost in moments, the vast complex of the Palace buildings swallowing her up, the fizz of the heartland's magic against her skin unsettling. Everything was new. Nothing was familiar. She did not belong here. But she was used to not belonging and knew that she would eventually get used to the abundance of magic.

Passing through yet another heavily scented garden, Arrow glanced up at the nearest windows and saw a few faces looking out, openly curious. And worried. She wondered what kinds of stories were travelling about this place, a city-sized set of buildings.

Eventually, when the sky was darkening to night, her feet were aching and her stomach was reminding her it had been hours since she had eaten, they arrived at the entrance to a large building which reminded her strongly of the Academy dormitories. Plainly built, several storeys high, it resonated with magic.

"Quarters for visiting magicians," the senior warrior said, stopping a few paces from the door. "The warriors' quarters are over there." He nodded to a relatively close building, which even at this distance Arrow could see was decorated with stylised weapons. "If you have need of us, they will know where to find us. Good hunting, mage."

"Good hunting, *svegraen*." Arrow made a small bow as the third left, only realising when they had gone that she had never asked for any of their names. Too late, for now.

Turning, she stepped across the threshold, the wards of the building prickling across her skin, testing her. Apparently the keepers of this building were quite serious in only allowing magically-trained Erith inside. It seemed juvenile. She bore the scrutiny with a slight shrug, confident in her wards.

Once the prickle of magic faded she found herself in a large entrance hall, a wide wooden staircase ahead of her leading up to the building's upper stories, a dimly lit corridor to one side leading deeper into the building and an open doorway to the other side showing a large room that seemed to be a refectory, full of long tables, plain chairs and benches, a number of Erith sitting in small clusters, idly talking or playing dice. She imagined that the warriors' refectory held a similar sight, only with more weapons and a more uniform dress code. A few of the magicians glanced at the door, attention snagging on her presence, and the slight sheen of silver to her wards which would be vivid in the second world if any cared to look. They were mostly dressed in rich fabrics as befitted Palace courtiers, a couple in well-worn travel clothes similar to Orlis. Wondering if any of the magicians would know where the journeyman was, she moved towards the refectory, pausing as she heard footsteps above.

Orlis was scrambling down the stairs, hair even more tangled than earlier, face pale, eyes sparking amber.

"There you are. You have been ages."

"There was much to do. What have you learned?"

"Come." He turned and ran up the stairs to the first landing, hopping impatiently from one foot to another until Arrow joined him before striding along the corridor to the door at the end where a third of White Guard were on duty, the amber sheen of their wards rippling uneasily against the building's defences.

Stepping past the warriors with a quiet greeting, Arrow stopped inside the door. She had been expecting a single room, a combined bedroom and study, similar to the Academy's dormitories, and instead found a suite. The door from the corridor opened onto a small, comfortable room with soft chairs and a fireplace, with another two doors on one side, both open. One showed a study, the other a bedroom. Orlis was hovering in the doorway to the bedroom, eyes flickering around the sitting area and study.

"Well, what do you think?"

Arrow thought that the Academy's dormitories might have been built in the style of this place, but she was certain that the Academy's students were not given quarters quite this fine. Used to the finery of the Taellaneth and the occasional glimpses of the Taellan's residences, she looked past the elegant furnishing and craftsmanship, engaging her second sight as she took a careful walk through the rooms. It did not take long to realise that although these might be designated as Gilean's rooms, Orlis was here as often as Gilean, and neither of them were here often. The rooms bore little deep impression of either mage.

"There was a struggle," she said at last. "Two or three people came in through the door. Gilean was at his desk in the study. It seems that he was overpowered and taken." Although how any intruder managed to get through the first room and into Gilean's study before he had time to raise a defence was a mystery. Gilean was a war mage and, more than that, experienced in dealing with danger. He and Orlis would be dead several times over if he did not have good instincts and quick reactions.

"That is what I thought, too." Orlis sank onto one of the chairs in the first room, tension drained out of him.

"What was he working on?"

"A letter to Evellan."

"Is it still here? No, stay there, I will go."

The half-written letter was on the desk, ink smudged where the pen had been dragged across the page, falling on the rug, ink stain spreading. Arrow leant over, noticing that the mage's writing was much better when he was settled at a desk compared to his usual scrawl to the Preceptor.

"Do they have a code?" she asked Orlis, frowning over the odd phrasing.

"Not that I know of." He was at her shoulder, leaning over with her. "Why?"

"I have read a number of Gilean's letters to the Preceptor over the years. Lord Evellan claims he cannot read the writing. But this is odd."

Orlis' mouth tightened, pulse beating rapidly in his throat.

"We will find him," Arrow said, putting as much conviction as she could into her voice.

"Yes."

They re-read the unfinished letter together. Gilean had apparently been to visit a farmer a day's ride from the Palace, commenting that the flowers were in full bloom. There was something about a cows' milk spoiling. The letter also referenced an unusual weather pattern, the design of a lady's shoe and a flock of geese the mage had seen several days before.

"It is odd," Orlis agreed.

"Gilean seemed troubled when he was at the Taellaneth. You said he did not tell you, but can you guess why?"

"No. The only thing is he wanted to speak to Evellan but never got the chance. Evellan was too sick and under guard for days. Then Gilean left, told me to stay and assist Evellan."

"Nothing more?"

"No. No letter for Evellan, no message for him or Seivella." Orlis went back to the sitting area and sank into a chair again, dragging his hand through his hair. "He has never left me like that before. He would always tell me."

Arrow settled on the edge of a chair nearby, turning the information over in her mind, distracted by her hollow middle. It had been a long, difficult day. Tea with Evellan and the Archivists were a distant memory.

"Is there anyone Gilean would confide in?"

The sour look Orlis sent her made her bite back a smile, despite the circumstances.

"Besides you and Evellan, I mean. Anyone in the Palace? Anyone who might have seen him or know what was bothering him?"

"No." Orlis looked thoughtful. "He is very private. But he is also well known."

"So it should be possible to trace his movements?" Arrow lifted a brow at Orlis. He sat up straighter, expression darkening.

"Why did I not think of that?"

Arrow thought that was an excellent question, with an obvious answer. "You are very pale. When did you last eat?"

"Eat? Arrow, Gilean is missing."

"Yes. And you are not thinking clearly," Arrow told him, more bluntly than she had intended. He glared up at her, jaw set in a stubborn line. "I assume the refectory has food?"

Orlis said nothing, white lines bracketing his mouth. Arrow waited a moment. He looked like he would sit there all night.

She smothered a sigh. She was out of place here in the heartland, more so than the Taellaneth which at least had become familiar, and worn out from all the changes and revelations of the day. They both needed a pause.

"I am hungry, too, and it would be nice to have a familiar face for company," she said quietly. His resistance melted, glitter in his eyes fading and he rose silently, leading her out of the room, past the warriors, and down the stairs to the refectory.

The food was excellent, among the best Arrow had ever tasted, perhaps influenced by the magic that saturated the land, and there was a seeming never ending supply, the kitchens here clearly accustomed to the demands of magicians.

Orlis and Arrow had settled at a vacant table near one of the windows but were not alone for long. As with the Academy, people seemed to gravitate towards Orlis and their meal was interrupted by a series of well-wishers, expressing concern about Gilean's absence, and wanting to know any news from the Academy. Orlis revived a little under the attention and the food, Arrow quietly observing the various conversations, the whole setup reminding her more and more of the Academy. Very little stayed secret at the Academy for long, and it seemed the same was true here.

Arrow herself received almost no attention, a few sideways glances but no overt stares or questions. Perhaps they already knew who she was. Or perhaps, she thought, an echo of her earlier realisation, they did not know who she was and it did not matter to them. The idea was still a new one, turning over in the back of her mind, and one she still did not have time to explore, the many unanswered questions from the lady's death and Gilean's disappearance needing her attention first.

It was late before they got to bed, Arrow allocated a more modest room on the floor above Gilean's. She did not mind. The bed was comfortable and, more importantly, there were strong wards to guard her sleep.

CHAPTER EIGHT

M iach was waiting in the magician's refectory the next morning, settled on one of the wooden chairs, drinking tea as though he was not isolated amid a gathering of glaring magicians, most eyes reflecting amber in the light that streamed through the tall, slender windows. Arrow could not help thinking that if it had been Kallish there, the warrior would have had her knives out on the table before her, sharpening each one with close attention. Miach simply sat, unchallenged.

"Good morning, *svegraen*." Arrow stopped on the opposite side of the table, lips twitching as the magicians turned their hostile gazes to her. They might not appear to care who she was, but they did care about the violation of their space by a warrior, it seemed.

"Good morning, mage. I trust you slept well?"

"Well enough."

Miach waved a hand to the chair opposite and she settled, unsurprised when one of the refectory staff appeared with a large mug of Erith tea and plate of breakfast for her. As with the Academy refectory, diners were expected to gather their own food, but the Queen's first guard had a way of getting people to do what he wanted.

"Is there news?" Her eyebrows lifted slightly as she sipped the tea. The mix was slightly different here, the citrus accents stronger.

"Regrettably not. Ah, good morning, Orlis."

"Miach." Orlis settled beside Arrow, more rumpled than he had been the night before. He made a low sound of acknowledgement when a mug and plate were put in front of him, scrubbing his face with his hands.

"You did not sleep," Arrow observed. Erith did not need as much sleep as humans normally, but he was under stress, eyes reddened.

"A little," he shrugged off her concern. "I decided to retrace his steps," he continued, shoulders straightening, jaw setting with a sense of purpose.

"That seems sensible." Arrow agreed.

With at least a dozen pairs of ears trained on them, they finished their meals in silence before Miach nodded to Arrow.

"The lady wishes to see you."

"Now?" Arrow's voice was too high. She quickly glanced down at her clothing.

"Now." Miach's mouth twitched, reading her dismay with ease. "She does not require formality at this hour."

"Go," Orlis waved her away, "it may be hours before I know anything."

Apprehension clutching her stomach, glad that Miach had waited until she had finished her meal before telling her what waited for her, Arrow followed the warrior out into the morning sunlight, leaving Orlis to whatever investigations he had in mind.

Miach led her along another winding route that had her hopelessly lost within a few turns, heading for the older parts of the Palace where time and weather had turned the stone pale, wearing the decorations to rounded edges and indistinct features. Arrow nearly lost her footing trying to make out a particularly impressive set of gargoyles above a stone archway. The stone faces laughed as she passed under them, entering what appeared at first glance to be a wild meadow, a vast field of scented grass scattered through with wild flowers. The crunch of gravel underfoot gave lie to the wildness. There were other Erith here, a half dozen or so, strolling along the narrow paths amid the grass.

"The Queen's current favourite garden," Miach said as though that explained everything. Arrow could not hide her frown as he glanced across and his face twitched as though he were hiding a smile. "She often walks here in the mornings."

Arrow's confusion cleared at once and she paid more attention to the courtiers as they made their way at a steady pace around the meadow. Despite the hour, all were beautifully dressed and their eyes flitted around, keeping a watch over who was nearby, the apparent ease of their postures another lie.

"Her Majesty has not been here today?" The courtiers' alertness reminded Arrow of warriors before battle. Her stomach twisted again. She had little appetite for politics.

"Not for several days." Miach's voice held a note Arrow could not trace. Sorrow, perhaps. Perhaps anger. Then the warrior sighed. Ahead of them, bearing down the wider gravel path that led from the building to the meadow, was a group of five or six finely dressed Erith, among them Queris vo Lianen. "Priath is dangerous," the warrior said in a low, urgent voice. "He has missed the opportunity of being Taellan more than once and is bitter for it."

There was no time to acknowledge the warning as they reached the group, who did not stand aside to let them pass, instead blocking Miach's path.

"Well, look, here is the Queen's most obedient hound," Queris sneered, high colour rising, confident among the other nobles. A soft ripple of amusement coursed through the group.

"Did you want something?" Miach asked, back straight, apparently at ease.

"News of our Queen would be welcome." The soft voice raised every warning instinct Arrow possessed. Outwardly the lord was unremarkable, almost plain by Erith standards, with ghost white skin and pitch black hair tied in an elaborate knot, clothing bright shades that should have clashed but did not, in the way of the Erith. And yet that voice held her frozen for a moment. Seggerat's silky tone was a pale imitation of the quiet menace held in that voice. Assessing the age of the Erith in front of her, Arrow wondered who had copied the other.

"What would you know?" Miach seemed unaffected by the voice or the chill that had crept through Arrow. But the Queen's first guard had been playing Court politics for many times Arrow's lifetime. Dangerous, he had said. Not in any magical sense, for the man barely had any amber in his eyes. That meant little, Arrow reminded herself. Seggerat possessed little magic either, and was a force to be reckoned with.

"Is she well?" The voice had lost some of its impact, menace reined in. The lord's expression remained politely attentive, with not a hint of disquiet at Miach's lack of courtesy.

"Her Majesty is hale," Miach returned, "and I must attend her. Good day to you." He made a shallow bow and a lord at the edge of the group moved slightly, stepping out of his way, letting Arrow and the warrior past.

"Do give her my best wishes." The voice followed them.

None of the courtiers had addressed her directly, Arrow realised, or betrayed any great curiosity about her. She kept her outward calm, years of practice attending the Taellan coming to her aid.

Miach kept his strides deliberately even, not showing anything other than the normal alertness of a warrior on duty as he followed the path to the shallow steps outside the building, up the stairs to a set of glass panelled doors that were closed, designating this a private entrance to the building.

The doors were opened by a pair of White Guard stationed inside, senior warriors by their braids, and there was no time to ask Miach about Priath as Arrow realised she had just been shown into the Queen's own quarters, with as little ceremony as entering the refectory that morning.

Miach exchanged a few words with the guard and then led her up a shallow flight of stairs.

"He is far more dangerous than the Queen acknowledges," he said abruptly.

Arrow thought about the chill voice and the sense of foreboding the lord carried with him, and about the fact that the Queen had ordered the Taellaneth and Academy built far from the Palace, with a large posting of White Guard in support. Arrow had always believed that the presence of such an important part of the Erith government so close to human lands was a potent display of power that the humans could not ignore, and allowed the Queen's servants to keep a close eye on the other races. Now, Arrow realised that the Taellaneth's position served another, vital purpose. It was distant from the heartlands, requiring time or significant amounts of magical power to travel between the two. The Taellaneth was out of the influence of Palace politics. And dangerous individuals.

Arrow wondered if Miach had spent any time in the Taellaneth and opened her mouth to share her insight with him, closing her jaw quickly as they arrived at another pair of double doors, this pair made of wood carved with extraordinary Erith creatures. The doors were opened from the outside by another pair of White Guard, with as little ceremony as the doors below. All the warriors remained outside, Miach waving her forward to her first audience with the Erith's life monarch.

The room was a wide rectangle, lit by a series of large windows along one of the long walls showing a nearly uninterrupted view of the meadow, wild grass and flowers interspersed with the bright colours of the Palace courtiers. Inside the room was curiously still, surfaces gleaming with polish, internal walls hung with mirrorglass and some of the finest paintings Arrow had ever seen. She had no time to stare, her attention drawn to the one other occupant of the room, a finely dressed Erith lady on one of the low settles near a fireplace that would comfortably hold an entire third of White Guard, the stone surround carved with ornate plants and flowers.

"There you are." The voice sent a shock through Arrow, the sound light and bright, full of life.

Arrow made a hasty bow, remembering her manners at last, and was met by a soft laugh.

"None of that. Come, sit. Yes, there. No, no more bowing. These are my rooms and I will not have it." The voice seemed wrong, Arrow realised, another jolt running through her. Too vivid for this still room, or the delicate lady who spoke.

"Your Majesty." Arrow checked her impulse to bow again and sat carefully where the Queen had indicated, a high-backed settle opposite the Queen that, Arrow quickly discovered, was as hard as the benches used by servants around the Taellaneth, despite its elegant appearance. The fire between them was unlit, laid ready for use, the hearth and grate spotlessly clean. There was a reading stand a little distance behind the Queen, bearing a large volume of botanical reference. Sat opposite the Queen, Arrow could see the open page and an almost-familiar purple flower.

"They are quite uncomfortable, but the best place to sit for the light this time of day," the Queen continued, with a nod of her head to the settle.

Arrow could not think of any appropriate response to that, mind scattering in a dozen different directions. This was the Erith's Queen, yet she had furniture she disliked in her room. The lady before her seemed far too frail to belong to that voice, which promised exuberance and life. And too sad to speak with so much joy in the sound.

Freyella, the Erith's Queen, was delicately boned, with large, deep brown eyes shot through with amber sparks even at rest, and hair that might once have been as dark as her eyes but was now completely silver, lines of age and laughter across her face. Under expertly applied cosmetics, her face was pale, the lines of her neck and collar bone cast in sharp relief at her neckline, and she had smudges under her eyes that no amount of powder or paste would hide. Sitting in the middle of the astonishing beauty the Erith could create, the Queen seemed small to Arrow's eyes, not the woman who had forced her people to peace with the shifkin or insisted that the heart of her government take place outside the Palace, against the counsel and wishes of the collected Erith nobility.

Then the lady smiled, warmth at odds with the shadows under her eyes and the pallor of her skin, and Arrow's breath checked. The lady contained as much exuberance as the heartland's magic.

"I have long wanted to meet you, Arrow."

"Thank you, Your Majesty." Arrow could not entirely hide a frown at that thought, wondering what the Queen could want with her.

"Your mother was a great favourite. Such a charming young woman. Quite beautiful, of course, but stubborn." A light laugh. "I think you are more like her than your appearance might suggest."

Arrow felt heat coursing up her face and into her hair. No one would ever think her beautiful, among the Erith. Stubborn, yes. It was a basic requirement for survival.

"And powerful, too." The Queen's voice remained light, and Arrow tensed inwardly, the stark contrasts of the Queen beginning to draw together. Arrow wondered how many Erith were fooled by the Queen's outward appearance and the vibrant voice, forgetting that under that polished surface there was a woman accustomed to rule, to navigating her way through the tortured civility of Erith public life and the tangled interests of the Palace's inhabitants. Arrow could imagine that light voice ordering an assassination without changing tone and suppressed a shiver. The most powerful Erith alive. It would not do to show weakness.

Between one breath and the next, Arrow checked her internal defences and wards. All intact. The power in her veins stirred, reacting to her unease.

The Queen gave Arrow another smile, one that seemed to reach her eyes. "That must be from your father. And grandfather. None of Seggerat's House ever had power worth mentioning."

"Not magical power, no," Arrow agreed, something about the Queen's manner drawing a more unguarded response than she would normally make. This woman was truly dangerous. Arrow was very glad to be sitting down. None of the Erith at the Taellaneth would speak of her heritage and here was the Queen casually discussing her family background as though they were talking of the weather. It was unsettling.

"Oh. Seggerat and his ambition. At least he has the ability to match it. And Serran had no ambition, but too much ability to let him be still for any time at all." The Queen's voice held sorrow now, unfeigned. She was famed for having her favourites through the Court. A woman who liked exceptional people, so Arrow had heard. And Serran had been exceptional in many ways.

"You miss him still," Arrow heard herself say and was met by a soft, sad laugh.

"I miss all of them. All the bright stars. Thomshairaen. Serran. Alisemea. And now Teresea. Too many others to count."

To her horror, the Queen blinked and wiped away a tear. Arrow sat rigid, wondering what she should do or say. She was ill-equipped to offer comfort.

"But we were talking about you. And your power. Miach was most impressed. He says that not one in a hundred magicians would have spotted the things you did."

"He is kind to say so."

"He is rarely kind." The Queen's voice shaded to acid and Arrow bit her lip to hold in an unexpected smile. "Infuriating, more like. And thinks he is in charge."

"A common trait among the White Guard," Arrow answered, thinking of Kallish.

"So true." The note of acid was still there, gone in a moment. "And you will find who did this to my dear friend? And what has happened to Gilean? And you will see that it is set right?"

"I will do everything I can." The words, carefully measured in her mind, slipped out into the air laced with a trace of power that she had not intended. Perhaps it was the Queen's presence. Perhaps it was the presence of the heartland's magic bubbling against her senses even in this quiet room. Whatever the cause, the words carried more weight than she had planned. A magician's promise. The vow hung in the air, a binding as sure as the oath spells she had carried for so many years.

"Good." The Queen accepted Arrow's assurance with quiet grace. Perhaps she frequently received magician's vows. The highest power among the Erith then visibly shook herself, lips turning up in a smile that might well have been genuine. "Now, I do not think anyone has told you about your mother. Let me."

And so the Queen told Arrow story after story about her mother. From how Alisemea had smuggled a baby wildcat into her bedroom as a child, believing she could tame the creature, to how she had set fire to her father's ceremonial robes when he would not let her go riding in a storm, to how, as a young woman, she had disappeared for a few days, scaring everyone around her, and come back with a distant, dreaming look on her face and announced that she was wed.

Listening to the stories of a woman she would never know, Arrow struggled to reconcile the wilful woman described to the perfect, painted lady in the gallery. Struggled, too, to keep her composure as a hollow grew in her chest. These were the kinds of memories held within families, the shared history that bound fractious Houses together. Not the kind of disclosures she expected from a monarch to an exile.

It was clear from the Queen's stories that Seggerat had adored his youngest child. She had been a spoiled favourite, indulged and treasured. Until she met Serran's son.

The Queen's face shadowed at length and she fell silent for so long that Arrow wondered if she had missed some signal of dismissal, and that she should now leave.

As Arrow straightened further, preparing to request permission to leave, the Queen opened her mouth to speak, interrupted by a quiet knock at the door and an unfamiliar warrior entering the room, not waiting for permission. One of the Queen's own guard. Only Miach and his people would be so free in the Queen's presence, Arrow was quite sure.

"Your pardon, my lady. Your appointment."

"Of course. Thank you." The Queen rose and Arrow followed her. "You must come and see me again."

Taking that for her dismissal, Arrow bowed and left the room.

CHAPTER NINE

A part from the pair of warriors guarding the Queen's door, there was no one in sight. Miach had left, doubtless with a dozen things requiring his attention. She paused on the stair landing, disoriented, her every sense telling her she was among the Erith and yet nothing was familiar to her eyes, ears or mind.

The Erith's Queen, the highest authority the Erith recognised, had talked to her as if she were a whole person, not the abomination that Seggerat called her, and not the exile that she was, by the Taellan's order. And she had been given an insight into her mother. A faceless figure until the day before, now a series of puzzle pieces in Arrow's mind, none of the pieces fitting together. The privileged daughter of an ancient, powerful House. A favourite of the Queen. A young woman who had defied her family and House to throw her lot in with Serran's son.

A quiet noise nearby snapped her focus back to the here and now, senses coming alert with old, ingrained instinct.

There was no threat here, only an unsubtle movement from one of the warriors, a shuffle of feet to draw her attention. Arrow realised she had been standing staring into space for too long.

"The main entrance is down the stairs and along to the left," the warrior said.

"Pardon? Oh. Thank you." Her attention might be back into the right place, her speech certainly was not.

The warrior's face softened into what might have been a smile and he nodded. She wondered how many people came out of an audience with the Queen completely disoriented. She returned the nod and went down the stairs, following the directions until she came to a large pair of double doors with a whole third of warriors on watch, all wearing the braid of the Queen's own guard. The trip down the stairs had reminded her that she had no idea where she was in relation to where she needed to be. She made a slight bow, Court manners ingrained, to catch their attention.

"Your pardon, *svegraen*, I need to return to the magician's dormitories. Where might I find directions?"

"If you go to the main building of the Palace and ask one of the pages, they will take you." The youngest, by her braids, responded, no hint of impatience in her tone. It also sounded very practised. Arrow's estimate of the number of people who left the Queen's presence disoriented rose.

"My thanks. The main building?" She felt her ears burning as she asked. It seemed the sort of thing any Erith would know. The warrior simply stepped forward, went through the door with her and pointed the way with perfect courtesy. Arrow made her thanks and went on her way, ears still burning. She was not used to being so lost. The entire Taellaneth, from the main building to its extensive grounds, were so familiar that she could navigate blindfolded if needed. And almost everywhere she had been in the human or shifkin world there had been a map. The last time she had been so lost had been in shifkin territory, trekking across Farraway Mountain, and for most of that journey she had been too exhausted to really notice.

With the double questions of Gilean's disappearance and Teresea's death to solve, Arrow suspected she might be in the Palace some days. A prospect which would have seemed impossible a handful of days before, and an exciting mystery. Now she was here it was another matter. She needed to be able to find her way without guidance. There were memory spells that could help and nothing, now that the oath spells were gone, to stop her from using them. Her back straightened slightly, eyes shading to silver for a moment as she set her will to creating a mental map.

The main building was approached from this side by a wide walkway of rose quartz gravel, the stones making almost no noise under her feet, the path leading to an enormous pair of glass panelled doors set in rose stone that reflected the colour of the walkway, the doorway twice as tall and twice as wide as it needed to be. The doors were open wide, in Erith tradition, to signal welcome, a third of White Guard keeping a casual watch, positioned here and there around the entrance, somehow managing to blend in. Above the extravagant doors, the glass sparkling with ward spells, the main building rose. Within its shadow Arrow felt for a moment as small as one of the pieces of gravel underfoot. It was the single biggest building she had ever seen, set here in the heartland as a blunt testament to Erith power and skill. Twisting her neck to look up, she caught a glimpse of several more floors above ground level, and a haphazard array of architectural styles reflecting the centuries it had been in use. The library, as large as that was, was a small fraction of the whole building. Her mind could not hold the concept of its sheer size and her curiosity spiked instead, wondering what purpose all those rooms served in the middle of the city-sized array of other buildings scattered around.

She made her way from quiet quartz up stone steps, smoothed from centuries of use, to soundless, handmade carpeting, abruptly aware of her human-made boots tramping across the ancient Erith work. Impossible that Miach had failed to see her boots, and yet he had said nothing. So, a little piece of the human world was touching the heartland of the Erith. She could not help a small smile at the thought of how furious that would make Seggerat and Eshan, particularly when they realised that neither of them had the power to give her orders. The Preceptor's appointment and the Queen's request took priority.

The smile vanished as she remembered the promise she had given to the Queen. To do everything that she could to find out what had happened to Teresea and Gilean. A heavier, wider promise than the undertaking of the Inquirer writ provided by the Preceptor. A greater promise than she had intended. But the words had been spoken, the promise made and she would not go back on her word, even if she could. Someone had killed Teresea and possibly destroyed Niasseren's library at the same time. Something had happened to Gilean, serious enough that a skilled war mage had not been able to resist.

A babble of chattering ahead drew her attention. There was a large group of brightly dressed Erith strolling along the corridor towards her, taking up the entire available width. They were caught up in their own concerns, not paying any attention to Arrow, dark clothing probably marking her as a servant in their minds. Every one of the group, all of them strangers, was moving with the absolute assurance of Erith nobility who knew they were entitled to be there, steps light and carefree.

All at once Arrow was conscious of her borrowed clothes, tangled hair and the human-made boots she had found so amusing moments before. She was alone among strange Erith, with only her magic to defend her. Even with her wards, modified and reinforced since she had left the Taellaneth, there was an itch between her shoulder blades. She had also had enough of strangers for the moment. There was a small, unlit side corridor nearby and she stepped into it, moving into shadows where she would not be easily seen, stomach uneasy, eyes prickling with the unexpectedly sharp sting of not belonging. Foolish. She had never belonged.

Safe and alone in the dark, she wiped a tear from her face, what might have been a sob firmly lodged in her throat. The chattering group went past the end of the corridor, a waft of perfume reaching her, a scent she did not think she had come across before. It was another reminder of how strange everything was around her, and how vulnerable she was. Among the Erith, in the Erith heartland. For all that the Queen had seemed happy to see her, the monarch had ruled for many times Arrow's lifetime and, outside the Queen's vibrant presence, Arrow found herself doubting the warmth she had been shown. Too used to condemnation and disgust from the Erith, it was hard to believe that their Queen could accept her so easily.

Perhaps she could stay in the dark for a while. She was hidden. No one knew where she was. A little time to gather her composure would be welcome. A much longer time to unpick all the revelations since her arrival here would be even more welcome. Unlikely, though. Orlis would be looking for her before long, she was sure, and the weight of the promise given to the Queen lay across her shoulders.

She brushed another tear away, blinking rapidly to hold back more, annoyed at her lack of control. Being told stories about her mother had opened a void inside that she had never known existed, a void that was filling with old hurt that she would never meet the woman and avid curiosity to know more. What had driven Alisemea, younger than Arrow was now, to throw her lot in with Serran's half-breed son, breaking faith with House Regersfel and infuriating Seggerat? And how had her parents died? They had died soon after Arrow was born. A matter of months, she had been told, and not by natural causes. No one would tell her more, and the Queen, grieving for her most recently lost friend, had not mentioned Alisemea's death.

Arrow found more tears on her face and brushed them away, hard enough that her skin felt raw. She could not hide forever, however tempting it might be. Besides, she had no idea where this corridor led. It might be full of people in a few moments, or deserted for hours.

Still she hesitated, not wanting to move. She was not ready for more strangers just yet. She had a momentary, unexpected, wish to be back at the Taellaneth. Familiar territory with people she knew, however hostile they might be.

Too much too quickly, she thought, closing her eyes. Answers to a dozen questions she had never dared to speak, and many more questions to take their place. And a pair of mysteries to solve with no real idea where to start.

Nothing would be resolved here. She forced her feet to move, the slight breeze of another opening nearby catching her cheek. There must be another corridor opening. Any Erith would be able to see it, but, without enhancing her sight, she could not. She hesitated, considering the enhancement, and a trace of something other crossed her senses. Her wards flared, every single one, blinding her, the sword at her back blazing silver. Something other. Something that should not be here. *Surjusi.*

It was a matter of moments to enhance her sight, sword springing eagerly to her hand as she moved carefully along the corridor. She must be mistaken. There was no possible way that there could be a *surjusi* loose in the Palace and the ward keepers not know.

She lost track of time and direction as she searched and failed to find that trace again. There was nothing. So much so that she began to wonder if she had imagined it. But her wards and sword had reacted on their own, without her command, which meant there had been something there. She just could not prove it. Or find it.

Frustrated and conscious of time passing, she shoved the sword back into its scabbard and mentally reviewed the finding spells she knew. She was completely lost.

The rustle of cloth in the dark told her she was not alone. She turned towards the sound. A hard grip landed across her mouth and jaw, smooth and cool.

The faint scent of leather. Fingers clamping, bruising. Band around her middle, trapping her arms by her sides. A stranger's arm. Trapped. Jerked up. Off her feet. Hauled backwards. Wordless sound muffled. Lip split under pressure, sharp sting, blood in her mouth. The rapid rhythm of footsteps, bearing her weight with ease. Further into the dark. Turn and turn again. Truly lost. Again. She struggled, kicked. A harsh grunt. The hold tightened. Ribs bruised.

"You are not welcome." A stranger's voice. Male.

Kicked again, as hard as she could. Another sound of pain, grip closed in. More blood in her mouth, the creak of bone at her ribs.

"Stop interfering."

Almost full dark to her stupid eyes, even with enhanced vision. Faint wash of silver from her own power. Just enough to make out the plain dark cloth of the sleeves holding her. No House insignia, or any trace to show one had been removed. The faintest scent of a spice she knew. Erith. She struggled harder. Her captor swore, and moved, too quickly to follow, releasing her and throwing her backward. She slammed into a hard, upright surface. Wall. Breath gone. Knees did not work. On the ground. Thick carpet underneath. Curled up in instinct, too many years the brunt of Gesser's fury. Impact of a hard boot to her back rather than her face. Another kick and she slid across carpet, into the wall again. Breath returning, she gathered her power, silver crackling as her wards formed.

Another kick, blow landing through her wards, and a grip on her arm that wrenched her shoulder joint, dragging her away from the wall.

"Leave this place. And do not return."

Wards fizzed, silver sparks giving a little light. Trying to see her attacker's face, Arrow almost missed the heavy fist that punched out of the gloom, turning her head a fraction too late, taking the blow across one cheek, momentarily blind with pain before the sound of rustling cloth told her that her attacker had left.

She lay still, breathing hard, mind scrabbling to make sense of what had happened. Beatings she was familiar with. This was different. Her wards had failed. They were rebuilding now, settling around her with familiar warmth, the sword at her back waking up, spells shivering against her senses. But they had not stopped a stranger from seizing her, or landing several blows.

Her back ached, a hard knot of pain below her ribs, a higher, sharper note under one shoulder blade, a line of pain across her back where a kick had shoved the scabbard into her, fine points of agony in her shoulder joint, her face pulsing with each heartbeat.

Faint voices brought her to her knees and then to her feet. There were Erith around. Showing weakness was unwise. She swayed on her feet, lightheaded, points of pain merging into one mass of discomfort. Gathering her power she pushed some healing through her body, then had to rest against the wall, breathing too fast, prickle of sweat across her face. When she could stand straight she spent a few moments constructing a small glamour to hide the bruise she could feel along one side of her face. Just enough to get her through the Palace without questioning.

That done, she turned her focus to the scene, pulling more power to enhance her sight further. Her attacker had been careful not to leave any trace. The faintest trace of the medicinal herb, which every Erith had access to. Commonly used for headaches. The anonymous, dark cloth. The leather gloves. All items which any Erith could access.

The only thing she could be sure of was the determination to see her gone. To remove her interference.

Her breath was loud in the quiet space, betraying her presence. Another faint burst of laughter, closer than before, and she stirred. Time to move.

She was glad of the dark as her first few steps were shaky, feet going in different directions as she went towards the sound of voices and laughter, correctly guessing that was the main corridor.

Finding a page and making her way to the magician's dormitories took a frustratingly long time, the various aches taking up residence in her body meaning she had to focus on moving normally, not betraying the soreness. Gesser had liked to use a stick, not wanting to sully his hands with her. She supposed she should be grateful in an odd way for the practice of walking normally while every muscle ached.

CHAPTER TEN

At length she reached the magicians' building, the page who had escorted her accepting her thanks with a shallow, solemn bow, leaving her without a word, travelling away at a far faster walk than she had managed, his straight spine and upturned nose suggesting he had more important matters to attend to. Arrow did not care. Even the slow, steady pace she had managed was difficult, muscles cramping in waves, every footfall sending a jolt of pain across her back. She had pretended to be interested in everything around her, to give her the excuse of the slow walk, and the effort had been exhausting.

Her head was ringing with echo of the blow across her cheek, the occasional stabbing pain behind her eye, growing worse as she had walked, making it impossible for her to focus on healing herself. That pain would fade, she knew, but it would be a while before she could use focused magic.

The idea of lying down in a quiet room had formed somewhere on the walk and that was all she wanted to do, to rest for a bit and to examine her wards for the flaw that had allowed someone to break through them so easily. Her mind, sluggish with pain, was working on possible explanations for why lying down for a while was necessary. She could not tell the Erith she had been attacked. Could not reveal that vulnerability.

As the page left she realised that her defences were already badly compromised. She had been focusing so intently on keeping moving forward and not showing weakness that she had not noticed Orlis, waiting outside the building. Her wards flared a moment, silver catching in the sunlight, a display of unease and lack of control, reacting to the lurch of her stomach and the prickle across her skin that warned of danger. Even from Orlis.

The journeyman had not noticed. He was almost dancing from foot to foot in impatience, both their bags at his feet. Arrow checked in her slow pace, muscles cramping in protest, dismayed again as she wondered if the simple wards on her bag had failed. No one should have been able to open her bag. The wards were intact in second sight, her heart rate slowing a little as she realised Orlis must simply have picked the bag up, ignoring the bite of defensive wards. Magicians were trained to focus through pain, after all.

"Finally!" He threw his hands up, fading trace of silver along one arm showing where her wards must have woken. "Where have you been? Never mind. Come, we need to leave."

"Where are we going?" Arrow held her ground. Lying down was what she wanted to do. Or perhaps soak in a hot bath. A sharp pinch across her lower back had her hissing in a breath. Healing potion, then bath, then bed. Perfect. Orlis did not notice.

"Gilean." Orlis seemed shocked by her question. "He was a day's ride from here not that long ago. The last place he was seen. Some farm. We are going to follow his path."

"A day's ride?" Arrow's whole being seized in rejection of the idea, her mind coming up with easy objections. "We do not have horses. And-"

"I have arranged horses," Orlis cut off her words. "Come on." He handed her bag to her, silver wards flaring angrily at his touch, not noticing her wince as she took the weight of the bag, striding away along a path formed of bark chippings that curled around the side of the magician's building.

She watched his back for a moment, truly tempted to ignore his demand and go inside. Healing potion. Bath. Bed. The words slid through her mind with a seductive pull. But. There was Gilean's absence, the war mage perhaps taken with violence. And Orlis was too disturbed to be rational.

So, she settled the bag over her shoulder, bit back a cry of pain and set it on the other shoulder instead, forcing her body to move after Orlis. Bath and bed were out of the question for the moment, but there were healing potions in her bag. Her fingers fumbled with the straps as she tried to follow Orlis and get a bottle out without dropping the bag. She paused, nearly losing sight of his bright hair, and swallowed the potion in two hasty gulps. The bare tingle of magic through her body told her that she was more badly damaged than she had thought. Not just surface bruising, then. She was no healer, to be able to read the path of magic through her body, but she wondered if there was internal damage. Bleeding, perhaps, as she did not feel the ache of broken bones. The strongest healing potion she could conjure was barely touching the aches of her muscles, spreading lukewarm healing through her lower back and stomach. Internal bleeding, then.

Her throat closed in cold fear. Attacked out of nowhere. An attacker who had slid through her wards as if they did not exist. She shivered, wondering if she should follow Orlis. With a potential flaw in her wards and her whole body feeling like a single, freshly formed bruise, she was not sure she could defend herself let alone assist in finding Gilean.

There were more healing potions in her bag, and for a moment she considered taking another one. Stern warnings from the Potions Master at the Academy rang in her head. Something odd happened to a magician who swallowed back too much of their own power too fast. She could not remember the specifics just now, but she did remember the forbidding tone. Deciding she needed what little of her wits remained, she left the other potions untouched and hoped that the worst was over.

Orlis was out of sight now, too far ahead for her to call him back, so she kept walking. The potion settled to a distracting itch as it got to work, muscles barely eased enough that she could keep moving. Perhaps she could sleep on a horse. Or at least find some calm to pull some power from the heartland for more healing.

Arrow did not remember much about leaving the Palace, almost her entire concentration taken up with moving as normally as she could and not betraying how badly injured she was, how vulnerable she was among the Erith. She remembered Orlis' dismay as he learned she did not know how to ride, something she might have found comical on another day. She remembered the odd sensation of sitting on top of a horse for the first time, her body stretched, muscles pulling, the rocking motion as the horse moved, the scent of the creature, warm and soothing, filling her lungs, creak of leather and soft sounds of the horse's great hooves meeting the ground.

The horse's long strides were smooth and even, and every one of them sent a fresh wave of pain through her body, nerve endings in her back protesting even the bare movement of cloth against her skin. Badly damaged indeed.

She came back to herself with a start as they rode through the bounds of the Palace wards, the static of the powerful wards raising her hair into wild curls as they passed.

Immediately beyond the wards was a wide expanse of rough grass. A tactical stretch of land, Arrow guessed, so that the White Guard would have early warning of anyone approaching. Beyond the rough grass lay woodland, the wide earth road continuing at an easy curve through the large, broad-leafed trees. Her breath caught at the sparks of magic dancing among the branches and leaves. The heartland's magic, visible here in the first world. Her breath caught again a moment later as the slight numbness left by the healing potion wore off with no warning.

Movement nearby. Another horse and rider. Erith. Her wards flared a moment before she drew them back, catching Orlis' attention before he recognised the rider.

"Kester." The greeting was flat.

"Orlis." Kester drew his horse to a halt nearby, sending a sharp glance over Arrow before returning his attention to the journeyman. The warrior was perfectly comfortable on a horse, Arrow noticed. She felt graceless and clumsy in contrast once more, even without the pain cascading across her back.

"Where are you going?" Orlis' chin was set, tone still rude.

"I am coming with you," Kester answered, voice pleasant, ignoring the hostility. "Gilean is my friend, and anything that can overpower him is likely to be dangerous."

It was clear that Orlis had not thought about that, so eager to follow Gilean's trail. His shoulders slumped a moment.

"Very well. But you will need to keep up."

Arrow opened her mouth in silent protest at the idea of moving faster. She had used the distraction of their conversation to begin drawing on the heartland's magic again, a tiny thread of healing that was slowly repairing the damage. Head first, so that she could regain her focus. Any faster movement of the horse and she would lose that small bit of healing. Not to mention fall off the horse.

"Orlis, you are being a brat," Kester said baldly, startling Arrow out of her misery. "Arrow looks like she has never ridden a horse before."

Heat scorched across her face at his accurate assessment. She had reminded Orlis that servants do not ride, and yet most Erith did, in fact, learn to ride from a very young age. And use weapons. And doubtless would have been able to defend themselves easily against an unseen attacker, even if the attacker did breach their wards. But she was not Erith. No one had thought it necessary to teach her how to ride a horse. Or how to defend herself from physical attack.

Old, familiar anger lit inside. Not worthy of the sort of education Erith took for granted. But useful to them.

Here, now, in the heartland, because she was useful to them.

Here because an Erith lady was dead, killed by skilled magic, and a war mage was missing. And the Erith, who had dismissed or ignored her most of her life, now needed her help.

A small, tight smile crossed her face as Kester and Orlis rode on ahead. She was useful. That had currency. And if she could not, yet, defend herself from physical attack, there were measures she could take. Body armour. A cadre of White Guard. Her nose wrinkled at the idea. She was too used to working alone. White Guard tended to follow their own rules of conduct. Still, they could be useful.

The ringing in her head finally faded, leaving her mind clear. Another small smile, this one darker-edged. She had the Preceptor's writ in her bag. The Queen's command. Resources to draw on besides her own. And she had survived oath-service to the Erith, constrained by those oaths. Not helpless. Not by a long way.

When the river of pain across her back had finally gone, ache reduced to a bearable level, she surrendered the heartland's power with some regret, and with thanks. The well of power all around her could have healed her several times over in the mere blink of an eye, but that would have drawn some notice.

She stretched, arching her back, hissing as the barely healed muscle protested. The dragging warmth inside was gone, whatever internal damage there had been mended. She was still sore. But she had use of her limbs, and her mind. And now her head was clear she wondered if an attacker who freely walked the halls of the Palace might already be known to the Erith. There were two Erith riding ahead of her. Well, one Erith, she amended, and one mostly-Erith, who was accepted by them. And Orlis had a knack for gathering information.

"*Svegraen*, mage," she called, drawing the immediate attention of the pair ahead of her, engaged in a good natured discussion about some sporting event.

They slowed their horses, coming to ride alongside her, Orlis' eyes narrowing. He had been too distracted earlier to pay attention to her.

"When did you put on the glamour? And why does it just show your own face?"

"It seemed prudent," she answered, opening her second sight a fraction and sending her senses out. There were no other Erith nearby that she could sense.

"You are injured?" Kester asked, brows lifting. She could not read his expression. It might have been simple surprise. It might have been something more.

"I was attacked in the Palace," she told them, and released the glamour she had held over her appearance. The sharp indrawn breaths on either side confirmed the glamour had been necessary. She reached a hand up and touched the side of her face, grimacing as she found the skin hot and swollen, grimacing again as the movement made the bruises ache. She wondered how bad the damage had been before the makeshift healing she had managed.

"Orlis. A healing," Kester commanded.

"Not now," Arrow contradicted. "The worst of it is mended."

"Not much I can do on horseback anyway. The horses get spooked," Orlis explained. His eyes narrowed on Arrow's face. "But I do have something to help with the swelling and bruising." The journeyman rifled through his satchel for a moment and handed a vial across to Arrow.

"Thank you." The potion was faintly bitter, full of Orlis' magic, and sent a savage, healing itch across her face that had her hissing a breath through her teeth. Her head spun with the combined effect of three lots of magic inside her before the itching descended through her body, making her twitch under her clothes until it settled to a bearable point that she could ignore.

"What happened?" Kester asked as she handed the empty vial back to Orlis.

She told them about the attacker who had breached her wards as though they were not there, and the message he had so brutally delivered. Both faces were grim when she finished.

"What did Miach say?"

"I have not spoken with him."

"He would want to know," Kester insisted.

"I did not know where he was. He took me to the Queen's chambers and was not there when I left."

"You saw the Queen?"

"Patience, young mage," Kester's voice was firm, "one thing at a time. Miach was at the rites." The funeral rites for Lady Teresea vel Fentraisal, he meant.

Arrow had not realised they were taking place that day and wondered briefly if she should have attended them, dismissing the idea as quickly as it occurred. She had not known the lady, and her presence was more likely to offend the Erith. Perhaps more interesting was the realisation that the Queen had not attended the rites, despite claiming Teresea as a friend. Arrow had no more time to think as Kester was continuing.

"He was delayed when the rites ended. A lot of courtiers wanting to know where the Queen was." By the tightening of Kester's face, it was a question he had asked himself, too.

"How was the Queen?"

"She seemed well," Arrow answered slowly, thinking back to her meeting with the Erith's monarch.

"Well? What does that mean?"

"I have never seen her before," Arrow reminded him. Orlis' scowl took over his whole face before he nodded.

"I keep forgetting you have not been here before." He shook his head slightly. "There have been a lot of nasty rumours about her health and well being. And Miach is not talking to anyone."

"He is very loyal," Arrow remarked.

"And not very trusting," Kester added with a ghost of a smile.

"But he would still want to know about the attack," Orlis pressed.

"So, it is not common?" Arrow asked, part genuine curiosity, partly needing to know.

"Someone roaming the Palace corridors who can break through a mage's wards and inflict damage?" Orlis' voice was as high as his eyebrows. "No. Not common. Your personal wards are some of the strongest I have ever seen and if someone can break through those, well ... Miach would have the entire White Guard scouring the Palace for such a person. No courtier would leave their rooms until they were caught."

"Interesting." Arrow turned the new information over in her mind. "But is someone who can break through wards unknown?"

"I have never heard of such a thing," Orlis told her, eyes narrowing as he thought, "although a ward keeper would be able to dismantle any ward, given enough time."

"This was not a dismantling."

Both Kester and Orlis had more questions, few of which she could answer although she surprised herself at the details she remembered when they prompted her. She had not been able to see anything about her attacker. He had not been wearing any House insignia or carrying weapons as far as she could tell. Taller than her, but only slightly.

Eventually the questions ran out and they rode in silence for a few moments, Arrow finding the steady rocking of the horse soothing now that every movement did not cause pain.

"What do you need?" The quiet question from Kester saved her from making the request that had been turning in her mind.

"Some body armour would be wise, I think." She tried, and failed, for a light tone, trying to make it a joke. Trying, too, to ignore the sudden, shaky feeling as speaking the words aloud made the threat more real. She had rarely required body armour before.

"Yes. A cadre?"

"The Preceptor did not want to send a cadre," Orlis said. "He thought they would be too noisy. Too visible."

"When it was only Gilean, yes," Kester began.

"Armour for now." Arrow broke through the brewing argument. "And I will take care to only be in public spaces when alone."

"Or always have someone with you." Orlis' jaw was set again.

Arrow made a non-committal sound that drew a sharp glance from both of them. To her surprise, neither of them pressed the matter, simply exchanged looks she could not fully interpret. For the first time, Arrow wished that Kallish nuin Falsen was here. The warrior had a quiet, competent manner that made her a peaceful companion. Unlike Orlis, who could never be quiet for long. Or Kester, riding nearby and simply by his presence stirring up flickers of memories too new and too raw. She did not want to be his mistress. She was not sure what she wanted, but not that.

The short space of quiet was broken by Orlis, naturally.

"What did you talk about? The Queen," he added, impatiently, at Arrow's puzzled expression.

"She told me about Lady Alisemea." Arrow heard her own voice flat and hoped that Orlis would leave the matter alone. The void inside was still there, demanding attention, wanting to be filled with more stories, more knowledge. A woman who had been nothing but a name a few days before now had a face and the tentative edges of personality forming in Arrow's mind.

"Orlis." Kester interrupted before the journeyman could utter any of the dozen questions so obviously forming on his lips. "Ride ahead and check which way we need to go at the crossroads."

The journeyman opened his mouth to protest, took another look at the warrior's face, swallowed, and rode ahead in silence.

Arrow shifted in her seat, not really sure of Kester's purpose, mind full of the stories the Queen had told her about a woman she would never meet.

"Here." He steered his horse slightly closer to her and stretched, a pot of White Guard healing salve balanced on the palm of his hand. "It should help with the bruising."

"Thank you." She took the pot, careful not to touch his skin, and managed, somehow, to keep her position on the horse and smear some of the salve across the bruised side of her face, the familiar fresh mint scent of the salve loosening the last knot between her shoulders.

Kester shook his head when she would have handed the pot back, and they rode on in silence until the rapid pattern of hoofbeats ahead indicated Orlis' return.

The journeyman merely pointed out the correct turn at the crossroads now coming into view, casting a sharp glance at Arrow before riding ahead in silence, tension clear in his back.

Worried about Gilean, Arrow knew, and half opened her mouth to call him back and distract him, thinking he might want to know more about her visit with the Queen. But she found she did not want to share the stories that the Queen had told her, and, body heavy with the aftermath of healing, still sore, could think of nothing else of interest to say. Even as she tried to think of something, Kester rode ahead until he was alongside the mage and the pair struck up an apparently friendly conversation. With their attention elsewhere she allowed her shoulders to slump slightly, and arched her back slightly, muscles easing, grateful for the small amount of privacy.

Now that they were out of the Palace grounds and the bruises across her body had settled down, she had time to be amazed that she was in the Taelleisis. The Erith heartland. And not in chains. Her one prior visit to Erith lands beyond the Taellaneth had been for the Trials and her graduation, and there had been no time to look around.

She tipped her head back to see the sky, a clear blue carrying the last of winter's bite as the world turned into spring, a few clouds scattered here and there, even the air saturated with magic. The trees around them were larger, more regal versions of the trees in the Taellaneth and every leaf and branch carried sparks of the heartland's magic. A few more years, she thought, and the Taellaneth would more closely resemble this place. Once the trees there had been given more time to settle, to send their roots deeper and draw up the world's power. For now, the Taellaneth's magnificent gardens were a pale imitation of the heartland. It was no wonder that few of the Taellan stayed very long in their residences, preferring to return to the Palace or their Houses when they were not required for Taellan business. Arrow thought that if she had the option to freely travel between the heartland and Taellaneth, she would also spend more time here.

Not that she would get the chance. She was here on specific orders. Once she left, the borders would be closed to her again.

A lump stuck in her throat and she blinked away stupid tears, casting a quick glance ahead to make sure her weakness had not been spotted. It was foolish to be upset by something she could not change and had no control over. The Erith would never welcome her into their lands. Once she was done with her missions, to find Gilean and discover what had happened to Teresea, she would return to the human world, to the haphazard employment of the shifkin, and her barely-formed plans for what she wanted to do with her freedom.

CHAPTER ELEVEN

—·—

I n late afternoon, by Arrow's reckoning, they were still riding through the forest, the horses never seeming to tire from their walk, still striding forward and looking about with interest, curved ears twitching in different directions as things in the trees around them caught their attention. Kester and Orlis had spent much of the afternoon in easy silence, which had surprised Arrow, used to the journeyman's constant conversation. The conversation ahead and the silence had given her time to settle her own mind a little, relaxed further by the easy sway of the horse beneath her and the constant hum of the heartland's magic all around. She chose not to think about the fact that she would likely never be here again. That hurt more than the attack had done. She was here now.

Kester and Orlis both slowed their horses a little, until her horse caught up with them and she was riding between them.

"Bruising looks better," Orlis commented. "Salve?"

"Yes." She resisted the urge to touch her face, not wanting to wake the bruising again.

"We will reach a waystation soon," Kester said, "and stop for the night."

She was not sure when that had been decided, but Orlis did not object.

"Should I use another glamour?" she asked. She was faintly sore from head to toe, not entirely sure what was the aftermath of the attack and what was the effect of riding a horse.

"It might be wise."

She focused a moment, called the spell to mind, and spoke the necessary words, a brief tingle of magic across her face, stinging against the bruise, telling her that the glamour was in place.

"Is the farm far from here?" She thought to ask, as a low building appeared between the trees ahead.

"Not far. We could make it before dark," Orlis told her, "but Gilean often stopped at waystations so there may be news here."

"If he came this way," Kester added, something in his tone telling Arrow he had already made that observation more than once.

Orlis shrugged a shoulder, mouth turning down in an expression Arrow could only describe as sulky.

"There is doubt?" she asked, wanting to know.

"It is not clear when he was last here," Orlis admitted, reluctance clear. "Very few people I spoke to could remember the dates. This just seemed the most recent."

"Well, we will learn soon enough," Kester said easily, effectively ending the conversation.

The waystation, when they reached it, was by far the most humble Erith public building Arrow had seen. Seen more clearly, it was also not particularly low or small, simply dwarfed by the ancient forest around it. Built from wood, it was a two storey structure shaped like a large box, with plain windows and no decoration at all. There was a long, rectangular structure, of similar construction, to one side that she identified after a few moments as stables.

Humble or not, the place was steeped in Erith magic, the wards sparking in Arrow's sight as they rode up, powerful magic woven in.

"Are there many predators in this place?" she asked, startled by the spellwork.

"Occasionally," Kester lifted a brow, "why?"

"The building has some of the strongest defensive wards I have ever seen. Even next to the Palace."

"A lot of Palace courtiers stop here on their way to and from the Palace." Orlis' lip curled.

"The owners pride themselves on providing a comfortable rest," Kester added, lips twitching in response to Orlis' sideways glance. "A lot of the courtiers consider this wild territory."

Arrow blinked, looking around and casting her senses out a moment. It seemed very tame to her. But the waystation was the only structure within range of her senses and she could, perhaps, understand how a courtier used to the vast sprawl of Palace buildings and constant bustle of other Erith might find the apparently endless stretch of woodland to be intimidating.

Getting off the horse required a moment of standing, head resting against the horse's side, before she was able to move away on her own feet. Her legs had grown new aches in the afternoon's ride and returning to the ground had woken the bruising across her back.

"Hot baths, I think." She thought Kester was hiding a smile and lowered her eyes quickly. She was sure she was highly amusing, not used to the experience of riding, and bit her lip to hold back a moan as she shouldered her satchel, careful to put it onto her less injured shoulder. She might be mostly healed, but there was no point in making things worse again.

There was no time for more conversation as the waystation's hosts arrived, a surprisingly young Erith couple. Not all Erith, Arrow realised after a bare moment. The woman was wholly Erith but the man had something else in his lineage. Not human, but something.

She was too distracted by the building, the layers and layers of warding, to focus much on the discussion that took place around her, allowing herself to be shown to a small room furnished with a single bed and nightstand, and a second door that opened onto a small bathroom complete with a full-sized bath tub. And taps. She had not thought that indoor plumbing would be widely available in the heartland and spent a moment blinking at the sight before she realised that Orlis was trying to get her attention.

"You have time to bathe before the meal. Do you need healing?"

She thought a moment and shook her head.

"A bath will help."

He frowned slightly then held out another small vial.

"First time on horseback. This should ease some of the ache. Let me know if you need more."

"Thank you."

The bath was an extraordinary luxury. Arrow could have stayed there for the rest of the evening, but her growling stomach forced her out eventually. She cast a quick cleaning spell over her clothes before putting them back on, still feeling a frisson of delight that she was able to use such common household spells without restriction, the oath spells completely gone. Orlis' potion chased away the last of the aches, although she left her glamour in place, knowing that the bruising would take more time to fade.

She paid more attention to the building on the way down the flight of shallow stairs to the main entranceway. For all its plainness, the building was beautifully crafted. And old. Now that she had got used to the strength of the wards, she could sense the age of the place. Whoever had built the place had built it to last. The stairs did not creak at all, floorboards steady under her boots, window glass clear, letting in the very last of the daylight and the first glimmer of stars.

She followed the sound of voices to an open doorway, finding a haphazard arrangement of tables and chairs in a large, low ceilinged room with an enormous fireplace opposite the door. The hosts were standing behind a waist-height wooden structure she thought was a workbench at first but soon realised must be a bar, large jugs set at one end and a set of shelves behind it holding a variety of bottles, a wooden stand at one end holding a large barrel.

Stepping into the room, she looked about with open curiosity. The layout was not that different from human bars she had passed through, although the materials were very different and the unlabelled bottles, she suspected, held drinks far more potent than would be legal in the human world. Erith bodies, and shifkin for that matter, could handle alcohol far better than humans.

There were a few other Erith in the room. The hosts were chatting quietly with a medium height male in the plain clothing of a workman, and three Erith nobles sat at another table, the two ladies staring around the room with displeased expressions while their male companion sipped from a large metal drinking vessel.

Orlis and Kester were settled at a table near the wall, Kester with his back to the wall and a clear view of the room, Orlis to one side. The table was covered with closed dishes, and three plates with eating utensils set beside them.

Taking her place opposite Orlis, Arrow breathed in the scent of food.

"The food here is very good," Orlis told her the moment she sat down.

"I am sorry if you were waiting," she answered, having little attention for anything apart from the food.

"Can you ..." Kester made a brief motion with his fingers, part of the runes for a confusion spell.

Arrow dug in a pocket, producing a short piece of chalk and sketched the spell on the table surface, faint sheen of silver showing the spell active.

"The hosts are reliable," Kester told her, "but I do not know the others."

"Can we eat now?" Orlis asked, voice plaintive.

Nothing more was said as the dishes were opened and nearly all the contents consumed, Arrow pausing frequently as unfamiliar flavours hit her tongue. Orlis had been right. The food was good.

Once most of the food was eaten, the three sat back and only then did Arrow spot the beaker of plain water at her elbow. She took a sip and watched her companions for a moment. Kester had not asked her to disguise their eating. They had news, or something they wished to discuss.

"Gilean has not been here for months," Kester said without warning. "The hosts were surprised he had been seen in the area."

"If he had been nearby, he would have called in," Orlis added, face grim.

"Was your information good?" Arrow asked.

"Several people said they had seen him travelling in this direction."

"After the struggle in his room?"

Orlis scowled at her, amber sparks rising in his eyes.

"The struggle suggests he may have been injured," Arrow reminded him, "so was he injured when people saw him riding this way?"

"I ... did not think to ask." Orlis' anger vanished into irritation.

"You have investigated matters before," Kester noted.

"Several times." Arrow did not look at him, staring at the dark windows. The Taellan had sent her on several tasks over the years which had required her to find people, or investigate things that had happened. Kester vo Halsfeld had been in the room for many of the reports she had given to the Taellan on her return.

"Well, what should we do, then?" Orlis' voice held a hard note of challenge, amber back in his eyes.

"You said several people saw him riding away from the Palace in this direction. And that he was seen at a farm near here? Then we should continue on to the farm," Arrow suggested. "He may not have come to this waystation if he was in a hurry."

"And how do we find out if this was before or after the struggle?"

"Check dates," Arrow answered promptly, drawing another scowl from Orlis, "and ask the people who saw him leave if he was injured at the time, or appeared so."

"No one remembered dates," Orlis grumbled, "I did ask."

"Very few people remember dates, but they may remember by reference to events. Was there a ..." she hesitated to use the word party as it seemed too undignified for Erith nobility.

"There have been several musical recitals," Kester put in, "and a few receptions hosted by different Houses."

"Yes. Ask whether it was before or after those. And about injuries."

"He would try to disguise any injury," Orlis objected, sitting up straight, glaring at her.

"Then was anything different about him that day. Was he more stiff in the saddle," Arrow speculated, remembering the pain of the ride here.

Orlis' mood darkened, amber sparks flaring in his eyes. Arrow spread her hands in a pacifying gesture.

"Most times enquiries are very unexciting. Lots of questions. Often really dull questions. But they yield information. Little bits at a time. And most puzzles can be solved by asking the right question."

"The farm is not far from here," Kester put in, voice calm, "we can go there tomorrow morning and be back to the Palace by nightfall if need be."

"Very well." Orlis rose from the table and stalked away, the confusion spell disappearing as he moved.

"He is worried," Kester said as quietly as possible.

"Yes." Arrow agreed, then hid a yawn behind her hand. As she stumbled to apologise, he bit his lip against a smile and then hid a yawn of his own. It was a surprisingly peaceful end to the day.

The waystation was near silent in the middle of the night, just the faint sounds of an old, well maintained building. The gentle creak of a wall. The brush of wind against a window. The wards quiet all around, and yet something had woken her. No sense of danger, just a tug at her sense that suggested something worth exploring. There was a bite of chill in the air that had not been there when she went to bed. She got dressed in the dark, years of practice coming to her aid, moving quickly despite sore muscles, and paused at the door of her room, opening it a crack, the lock turning quietly.

The corridor outside was dimly lit to her eyes, adequate for Erith. She paused to enhance her sight, then stepped out. No one. A brush of chill air, carrying the scent of the outdoors, crossed her cheek and she turned to follow it, along the corridor, past several other closed doors, to a door at the end which was open a fraction, letting in the outside air.

Curiosity drew her through the door and up the stairs she found behind it, treads of plain wood coated with some kind of heavy varnish that her boots could grip.

The roof of the waystation opened out before her, a pitched roof design with a wide, flat area near the stairs. Even the tallest points of the roof were lower than the canopies of many of the trees around, but still high enough that the night sky shone, seemingly close enough to touch, stars glinting in the bottomless black.

The waystation's host was settled on one of a pair of chairs placed on the flat area, leaning back, what looked like a pottery mug held against his stomach, face turned up to the sky.

"Do join me," he said, voice soft but carrying in the still night. "Although I did not bring another mug."

"That is alright. I did not mean to disturb you."

"You are not. Come and sit." The tone made it an invitation, not an order. He glanced across with a small smile. "I run a waystation. I enjoy company."

The sky above was reason enough to stay, but the host was also only partly Erith, only the second she had spoken with after Orlis. Arrow's feet moved before her mind caught up with her and she settled in the other chair, finding it piled with blankets, ready to ward off the chill.

"It is beautiful." She tipped her head back and was overwhelmed for a moment by the spread of stars above, mind immediately trying to make familiar patterns out of them. None of the stars were in the right place compared to those above the Taellaneth. She was completely out of place, far from everything familiar. And safe. The old building's wards were settled, ancient. The host nearby was not threatening.

"Yes. The lights of heaven."

"Caphaisan," Arrow identified his other species. Distantly related to the Erith. Very distantly, according to most Erith. An elusive and not numerous race, they preferred the dark.

"My grandfather. Apparently my grandmother was worth coming out into the light." The easy way he said it spoke of many years' affection and knowledge.

"He lives among the Erith?" The question was out before she could stop it. "I beg pardon. That was rude."

"Natural curiosity." He was laughing, the sound soft and warm.

That was another feature of the Caphaisan. They might prefer the dark, but they welcomed anyone who cared to visit into their homes. Arrow had long thought that they were one of the races she would like to meet. The Erith despised them for their lack of magical skill or battle prowess, but left them alone as the Caphaisan could venture deep into the ground without worry, bringing back treasures that the Erith prized and which the Caphaisan then traded with the Erith. And other races.

"Grandfather is dancing in the heavens. Some twenty years now."

"I am sorry."

"So am I. So is everyone who knew him. He had a long and full life, even in the light."

They sat in silence a few more moments, surprisingly comfortable. Arrow's mind was still trying to make sense of the stars. To be quiet, still and unthreatened among the Erith was a rare treat. And one she would not have had if she had stayed in her bed.

"You left the door open for me," she said after a while. Oddly the thought did not irritate her.

"There are few of us. The mixed bloods. And Seggerat has had you confined to the Taellaneth your whole life. I thought you may not have met many others."

"You thought right." Arrow closed her lips before anger could spill out. This peaceful night was no place for her old anger or bitterness. "Orlis is the only one I had met before. Before him I did not know that there were any others like me."

A soft laugh, no mockery in it. "There is no one like you. Trained mage. Most powerful one he has ever met, according to Orlis."

"He talks too much."

"Often," he agreed easily, taking no offence at the bite in her words. "But often for good cause."

A small pause. Arrow stayed silent, sensing he had more to say.

"And none of us are as well connected as you. Claiming kinship to two of the oldest Houses."

Arrow could not help the laugh that escaped, a hard sound. "They do not acknowledge me."

"Serran would, if he were still here."

"You knew Serran." It was not a question. The waystation had a plentiful bar and, even on a quiet evening, several other people to talk to. Serran was as famous for his love of drink and conversation as he was for his magical abilities.

"His was a sad loss." The host laughed. "And not just for my bar takings. He had a way of cutting to the heart of a matter, not caring who he offended on the way."

"You knew him well."

"Quite well. He was friends with grandfather." No need to say which one. Serran had always been curious about the other races, travelling outside the Erith heartland to meet them. "He would have been proud of you."

Arrow breathed lightly, the notion that any relative of hers would be proud of her sending a sharp pain through her chest. No one had been proud of her. She had passed the tests required of her to graduate as a war mage and the Preceptor had simply nodded, as though he had been expecting it. She had defeated *surjusi* and the Erith had accepted her efforts as their due and complained about the mess.

"Serran did not fit well into the Erith nobility." He kept talking as if he had not noticed her indrawn breath or stillness. "As much as he was a favourite of the Queen, he was also an irritant. One of the few people who dared to openly oppose her will. Just before he disappeared, they had a furious argument. No one knows what about, but the Queen was angry enough that she did not send anyone to look for Serran for many days after he vanished. And by then it was too late. Gone without a trace. Swallowed up by his magic, some say."

"You seem to know much." And had painted an image of her grandfather far more vivid and real than the snippets of information she had gathered over the years. And had given another insight into the Erith Queen. So furious, all those years ago, she had not sent after one of her favourites. And now one of her favourites was dead and another missing, and, in the middle of the Erith Court, the Queen had charged Serran's granddaughter to find the truth. Another twist of pain. Growing up in the Taellaneth, her heritage had been a source of shame and derision, that such famous Houses should produce her, of all things. In the Court, things were different. Just how different she did not know. Yet. And did not wish to find out. She wanted to go back to the quiet workspace the shifkin had provided, to plans for her future. Away from the Erith.

Another soft laugh from the host drew her attention. "People talk. Even the Erith who pride themselves on holding their secrets. And waystations are meeting points for all sorts of odd combinations. A lot of talk. A host is invisible to most Erith."

"Like servants." It was not a fair comparison, but it fitted.

"Indeed. House retainers and the like would never talk outside their House. But they forget to put wards up. And the rivalries between the Houses run deep. There are arguments."

"People talk too much when they are angry. Or drunk." Arrow nodded, eyes catching on something almost familiar in the sky.

There was another silence.

"We are looking for Gilean," Arrow said at last, "as I believe Orlis told you."

"He was last here before mid-winter. But my lady thought she saw his horse running past perhaps twenty or thirty days ago. Difficult to be sure. Perhaps a little over thirty."

Before his disappearance. Before the struggle in his rooms.

"Would he always stop here?"

"Not always. With Orlis, yes. That young one loves company as much as breathing and Gilean knows it. On his own, Gilean would stop when it was convenient. If he was in a hurry, no."

Arrow absorbed the information in silence. A running horse. In a hurry, then.

"Did your lady think the horse had been running long?" It was a question in the dark, Arrow knowing little about horses, but it seemed a sensible thing to ask.

"Not long. It was not sweating, running freely with a spring in its stride. If she had to guess, she thinks he had started his journey not far from here and was heading back to the Palace."

Thirty days ago. Or a little more. Arrow's heart skipped, remembering where she had been. Had it only been that short time ago? The easy pace of life in the human world, among the shifkin, had distorted her sense of time. About that time, Gilean had appeared at the Academy, warding a room where a *surjusi* had possessed a spoiled Erith. He had not explained his appearance, or disappearance, to anyone, as far as Arrow knew, beyond wanting to speak with Evellan. But the Preceptor had been gravely injured, and there had been a fight. Not long after, Gilean had left the Academy, leaving Orlis to care for Evellan.

"What is nearby?" she asked. What could Gilean have found that sent him running back to the Palace and then to find his old friend Evellan. Something he wanted to discuss with Evellan in person, not via a communication disk or through letter. Something dangerous, then. Dangerous enough that a war mage, one of the Queen's favourites, had disappeared in the Palace, with violence.

"A lot of forest. It would not be easy to hide much in that. The forest itself would know and it would be easy for any tracker to find it. There is the flower farm not far away." The host paused, tone shifting slightly as though he had just realised something. "We have not seen the farmer for a while. Butris. A good man. Trusted by the Palace."

Arrow's mind tried to understand what a flower farm might be, having only seen flowers in carefully tended gardens before. The farm, then. How flowers could be dangerous she did not know.

"Whatever you find, you will be welcome here at any time." The host rose, and stretched, easy in his movements as any Erith warrior. Not a simple host. Naturally not. Too near the Palace. Too many high ranking Erith passing through. Arrow wondered how closely he kept in contact with Miach. Or perhaps even the Queen. She did not ask the question, as it would be rude. He had given her the information he thought she should have, and the invitation extended was quite genuine. He bowed slightly. "Now I should get to bed. Stay as long as you wish."

With that little fuss, he walked away, disappearing into the building, leaving Arrow with a head full of clues and the unknown skies above.

CHAPTER TWELVE

— • —

They left the waystation early, Orlis having woken them just before first light, hammering on Arrow's door until she opened it, woken from a confusing dream filled with people she knew wearing the wrong faces. He had woken Kester first, so Arrow was behind and had no time to give her breakfast the attention it deserved before Orlis had almost dragged her out of the waystation and onto her horse.

She woke up properly as they passed the waystation's wards, the heartland's magic coursing through her, every sense sharpening, taking in the fresh bite of early spring against her face, the ice of winter still in the air. The great trees, their tops far overhead, and the shrubs closer to the ground all showed the first signs of green growth, full of rustling life as the small group rode along the path. Arrow caught glimpses of four legged, furred tree creatures scampering through the trees as they rode. Like and not like the squirrels found in the human worlds, these creatures had vibrant auburn fur that shimmered now and then with the amber of Erith magic.

Despite Orlis' rush to leave the waystation, they were riding at the same sedate pace of the day before, and in the same formation, with Kester and Orlis ahead. Arrow was grateful for the steady pace. She was sure that if Kester and Orlis had been travelling alone, they would be riding much faster, and was tempted to suggest that they ride on without her, sure that Orlis, at least, would want to do so. Even as she thought to suggest that, the trees ahead of them thinned showing open ground ahead. Her horse's ears pricked and his head lifted, snorting out a breath as some new scent caught his attention. The abrupt movement reminded her that her body was still healing, bruising across her back tightening in protest.

The bruising on her face was nearly gone, a shadow across one cheek that would be gone by nightfall.

They rode out of the woodlands to a series of large fields, neatly bordered by wooden fences, each field full of flowers that she mostly did not recognise, Kester and Orlis slowing their horses until they were grouped together.

"Decorative blooms," Kester told her.

"So many." She turned slightly, tracing the patchwork of fields that stretched as far as she could see, the bright shades reminding her of the Taellan in their finery.

"The Palace is as large as a city, and the courtiers very fond of cut flowers."

Arrow remembered the great displays of cut flowers in the Taellaneth, fussed over by the Steward and his staff, each carefully woven with preservation spells. Even with preservation spells, the flowers did eventually fade and Arrow remembered the Steward complaining, at length, that no magician had been able to create a preservation spell that kept the scent as long as the flowers.

"It seems extravagant," Arrow said, turning again, almost unable to believe her own eyes. A farm for flowers. She had never imagined such a thing, having assumed that the flowers in the Taellaneth came from the extensive gardens. Not from somewhere like this. Dozens of fields. Purples and blues and reds and yellows and oranges. Each colour available in a range of hues. She could see shocking pink and, a short distance away, a softer, paler shade. And all to supply the courtiers' whim. She liked the Queen's meadow far better.

"It keeps the farmer and the courtiers happy," Kester answered, shrugging one shoulder.

"And does this farmer have cows?"

"Cows?"

"Red spotted cows."

Kester blinked at her, then his eyes narrowed. "Is that a joke?"

"I do not think so. Gilean had left an unfinished letter in his rooms. There was reference to a farmer with a cow whose milk had spoiled. And I recall he wrote to the Preceptor about red spotted cows."

"So he did." Kester's face was grim, doubtless recalling the letter, too. "Orlis, can you see any cows?"

Orlis looked ahead, power rising in his eyes for a moment before he blinked, turning to them. "There are a few large beasts, possibly cows, behind the residence."

They were riding in a narrow, grassy lane between fields now, having to travel in single file, Kester in the lead, one hand on a weapon hilt. Difficult to imagine there was danger here, Arrow thought, and was immediately wary. There was always danger among the Erith. The rich scents of the flowers rose around them, a heady mix from deep, rich tastes that were almost edible to fresher, more frivolous smells that teased her nose. The field next to them was full of bright yellow flowers, huge heads turned towards them. Beyond that was a field of purple, an odd patch of slightly different shade in the midst catching Arrow's eyes for a moment.

Ahead of them, tucked in the middle of the patchwork, was a modest-sized residence built of red brick, accompanied by several large wooden outbuildings and a few fields of plain grass.

The lane ended at an open expanse of grass around the residence, large trees here and there providing shade. It was an idyllic scene, and yet Arrow's shoulder blades prickled with unease and the sense of being watched.

Orlis rode ahead and got off his horse with more grace than Arrow had yet to manage, knocking loudly on the closed door.

The closed door. The quiet fields. The scent of flowers.

"Something is wrong." Arrow got down from her horse and winced as her muscles protested. On reflex, using a fingertip to draw, she sketched a quick rune for protection across the horse's shoulder, silver sparks making him snort, but, Erith bred and trained, he remained still, ears flicking back and forth.

Kester was on his feet, too, readying his weapons.

"No one home," Orlis said as he came back to them.

"The flowers are ready to harvest. No farmer would leave them." Kester's voice was calm, at odds with his keen gaze, eyes flickering across their surroundings, taking everything in, and with his stance, the apparently relaxed poise of a warrior ready for battle, feet apart, knees relaxed, hands casually resting near weapons.

"The cows are restless," Orlis observed. "Though none of them have red spots." He was much less calm than Kester. Worried, Arrow thought.

They moved ahead in silence, going round the corner of the residence, the cows, all a creamy brown colour, greeting them with loud noises of protest as they came into view.

"No one has tended them for a while," Kester observed. Arrow glanced across and saw only cows, staring back at her with dark eyes, a few ears twitching.

There were three large wooden barns behind the residence, long and low, the narrow ends, with wide wooden doors, pointing towards the house. The doors of the barn nearest to them were open, showing nothing but shadows behind them.

They moved towards the open doors, Kester slightly ahead, Arrow raising her wards so that silver formed around the group.

As they stepped from sunlight to shadow they all stopped for a moment, a familiar sweet scent rising to meet them. Erith death. And cutting through it, a scratching sound that raised the hair on Arrow's neck.

The gloom of the barn stretched out before them, odd shapes making no sense to her eyes.

"Light," Kester suggested.

Arrow reached for her bag, only then realising that she had left it on the horse. The sword across her back pulsed in readiness, waiting for her command. She dug through her pockets and found a piece of chalk, crushed it in her fingers and blew, sending silver sparks out before them, spreading through the barn, giving her, finally, enough light to see by.

Wooden racks were suspended from the ceiling, reminding her strongly of the Taellaneth laundry's drying room, except these racks were hung with a range of flowers, blooms pointing down, stalks held on the wooden beams. A faint trace of amber laced through the flowers. A low-level preservation spell, she guessed. Nothing harmful.

About halfway down the barn the racks had been disturbed, a large gap in the neatly ordered rows, flowers scattered over the packed earth floor underneath a crumpled pile of cloth. Kester went forward, swords out, movements silent on the bare earth, Arrow following, not silent at all, with Orlis her shadow, the journeyman's breathing rapid and harsh.

The cloth was dark, perhaps that of a war mage's cloak. Orlis tripped against Arrow's heels, wrenching the barely-healed muscles in her back as she fought to stay upright. He did not apologise, surging ahead of her, going past Kester to kneel by the pool of cloth, tugging it to one side.

The cloth gave with reluctance, resolving into the shoulder of a plain cloth tunic, worn by an unfamiliar Erith, body turning towards them as Orlis tugged, expression distorted in his final cry. The hilt of a knife protruded from his chest.

"Facing his attacker," Kester noted, not relaxing, eyes darting around them.

As he spoke the scratching sound came again, closer this time.

"*Rallestran*?" Arrow strained, trying to see through the gloom. There were other small Erith predators, but that particular sound was familiar.

"Sounds like." Kester was grim. "They should not be here. This place is warded."

"The wards were down," Arrow said absently, most of her attention on calling more power, extending her wards.

"Down?"

"We did not pass through any wards at the perimeter," Orlis confirmed, straightening.

Kester had not noticed, Arrow realised, his attention on looking for a more physical threat, but both magicians had spotted the absence of active wards at once.

Orlis' eyes lit with amber as he stared into the gloom around them. "We need to get the vermin outside. This scene needs to be preserved."

"Agreed."

The only sure way to kill the *rallestran* was mage fire, which would destroy the evidence. Arrow drew a breath, readying herself. *Rallestran* were cowards, but could not resist a chase.

"Run." She turned as she spoke and began running back towards the door and the light, not surprised when both Kester and Orlis outpaced her after only two or three strides. She lengthened her strides, blinking away tears as her injuries stung, the healing weakening as she abused her muscles, and made it to the doors of the barn just as the first creature sprang at her, trying to latch on to her calf. Her wards flared, silver burning the creature, and she kept going until she was standing with Kester and Orlis, turning to face the barn, breathing hard, speaking the necessary spell as quickly as she could, calling mage fire to her hands. No time for the *kri-syang*, or calling on the heartland's power. All the mage fire would need to come from her own resources.

The dark opening of the doorway shivered as a mass of creatures spilled out of the building, bodies swarming towards them. Arrow released mage fire, silver light scorching across the first wave of creatures, and the next, and the next. Beside her she was dimly aware of Kester's swords flashing and the deeper amber of Orlis' power as he used smaller bursts of mage fire, catching those *rallestran* that made it past her fire.

She was sweating and trembling by the time the creatures were all dead, the ground between her and the barn littered with charred remains, stench of burning flesh overriding everything else.

Sure they were all gone, she released her fire, limbs shaking with effort, the well of silver inside dimmed to a small pool. Drawing in a breath, she choked on the stench, turning away, stumbling into a large soft leaved shrub and throwing up onto the ground underneath.

"Here." Kester handed her a flask and she took it, shivering as she knelt on the dirt under the shrub. She was freezing cold, teeth chattering. The grey weight of so much death pressed on her and she swallowed, hard, against more nausea before rinsing her mouth. Erith tea. It chased away the foul taste and the stench for a moment.

"I will call Miach," Orlis announced, digging a communication disk from his bag.

"He will want to know about a death so close to the Palace," Kester answered Arrow's puzzled expression.

"Of course." She forced herself back to her feet, kicking dirt over her sickness, and tried to hand the flask back to Kester.

"Keep it. Come, we should take a better look."

She wrapped her arms around herself for warmth and, now she had a moment, called some of the heartland's magic to chase away the chill of death and try to ease the renewed ache through her body. The bright warmth of the heartland curled around her, more than she had asked for, steadying her steps as she followed Kester into the barn, silver sparks of light still active, past bunches of preserved flowers, to the body.

"He knew his attacker," Arrow observed. "Was taken by surprise." The expression on the man's face was horror and shock combined. There had been no time for him to defend against the knife.

"The attacker knew what he was doing," Kester said, kneeling by the corpse. "A single thrust upwards, piercing the heart."

"Trained in weapons, then." Arrow made a slow circuit around the body, keeping close watch on where she put her feet. "A tracker may find more, but I cannot see any other footprints."

"We are trained to leave no trace."

"A warrior?" Arrow looked up, dismay clenching her stomach, nausea churning again. The Erith's elite did not murder. It was one of the many codes of honour that bound a warrior's conduct.

"Perhaps." Kester was still looking at the body, bowed shoulders only sign of his feelings. "Or perhaps someone who has had some training but not passed the Trials."

"There must be a number of those."

"Many. And many at the Palace."

A shadow came towards them, Orlis pacing rapidly through the barn.

"Miach was disturbed. There was something else going on here, but he would not tell me what. He was too disturbed for this to be a simple farmer." Orlis was as serious as Arrow had ever seen him, face pinched.

"Is he sending someone?"

"One of the Queen's cadres will be here soon. We are asked to wait." Orlis was still serious.

Soon. That suggested that they may have been on their way already. Arrow tilted her head. "What is it?"

"He did not seem particularly surprised by the death. He was more concerned by the *rallestran*."

Rallestran who had been confined to a barn with open doors. Voracious eaters who had not eaten the corpse laid out before them, Arrow thought, and opened her senses a fraction, seeking active magic.

"Something is wrong," Kester repeated Arrow's earlier words.

"No more active magic. There was a containment around the body," she told them, sight overlaid. "We should search before the White Guard arrive," she suggested, glancing around the barn. This single building was large and would take a while to go through.

"We are not splitting up," Kester vetoed the idea before she had even voiced it. "Can you record the scene?"

"Of course."

Glad to have something simple, and constructive, to do, Arrow spoke the necessary words and felt the pull of magic as the spell activated, preserving the details around them. Walking slowly, she made her way along the centre of the barn, traces of her spell cascading around her, committing everything to memory.

There were no more apparent surprises in that barn. They walked through the other two barns with similar results. Hundreds upon hundreds of drying flowers in the second, and in the last, noticeably cooler than the other two, great, shallow troughs of water, full of cut flowers with the slight trace of a preservation spell running through them.

"There are a lot of flowers," Arrow remarked as they came out of the final barn into sunlight.

"It is a flower farm." Orlis shrugged.

"I mean, there are fields full of flowers which look ready to be cut, and barns full of flowers."

"Full stock," Kester agreed, looking around. "There is no cart to take the deliveries to the Palace."

"The lanes around are too narrow for any large carriage," Orlis said.

"Was Gilean here?" Arrow asked.

"There is no trace of him."

They turned and looked at the residence, with its closed doors. Arrow opened her senses again, examining the building in second sight. Absolutely ordinary. There were the usual ward spells she would expect in any Erith building, well crafted and settled into the fabric of the place. The wards were dormant telling Arrow that no living creature was inside.

Casting her attention wider she looked across at the half dozen cows, who were watching the trio with idle interest, chewing perhaps on grass or perhaps on whatever feed had been left for them. There was nothing remarkable about the creatures, either.

She came back to the first world to find that Kester and Orlis had moved towards the cows, checking their condition and exchanging cryptic comments she did not understand. She had had no notion that either of them knew anything about animal welfare but from the confident, calm way they moved among the large, docile creatures she realised that they were both familiar with caring for animals.

She stood in her borrowed clothes and felt the same sense of displacement she had at the Palace the day before. As out of place here, in the midst of the Erith, as she ever had been in the Taellaneth or the human world. The magical training she had received, so grudgingly, was the least part of what she needed to know to survive the Erith. All her years of service to the Taellan had not prepared her for being among the Erith as an almost free agent. Sighing, she wondered if she looked as awkward as she felt.

The tug of another set of wards pulled her attention away. She moved around the side of the residence as one of their horses made a low sound and saw a cadre of White Guard approaching at a steady, ground-covering run.

By the time the cadre had reached her, Kester and Orlis were beside her again. The leader of the cadre exchanged easy, friendly greetings with Kester then Orlis, and turned to her.

"And you must be Lady Arrow. Miach speaks highly of you. I am Elias." A high ranked warrior, with braids as complex as Miach's, and the Queen's symbol woven in. Second cadre to Miach's, if she had to guess. Which meant that Miach had sent people he trusted, and a far more senior cadre than was warranted, to investigate this site.

"Honoured to meet you, *svegraen*." Arrow made a shallow bow on instinct, unable to escape her training.

"Miach says there has been trouble?" Elias looked past them and his eyes widened, taking in the charred remains. "An understatement as usual." He turned and gave low-voiced orders to his cadre which had them spreading out and moving forward to search the open barn.

"The body is in there." Kester inclined his head towards the barn. "We turned it to make identification but have not otherwise touched it. There were no obvious signs that anyone else had been there. The *rallestran* were also in the barn."

"And had not touched the body?" Elias' gaze was sharp.

"There was a containment spell," Arrow said.

"Could you tell the maker?"

"No one that I know."

"There must be hundreds," Elias said, almost to himself, going past them to look at the charred mass. "Killed cleanly," he added, tone approving. Arrow's fingers clenched around the flask in her pocket, swallowing against more nausea. The warrior glanced up, trace of amber in his eyes. "You are every bit as powerful as Miach said. I did not believe it," he added, candidly, "as no one has wielded that kind of power since Serran."

Arrow shifted awkwardly under the intense scrutiny, finding nothing to say in response, hoping that he would not start discussing her relatives with the same casual ease as Miach had used, and then wondering just how many people at the Palace knew her history.

"You made good time," Kester commented. Arrow's attention caught. She had not missed that detail, but was slightly surprised Kester voiced it. Elias was not deceived by the mild tone either, a brief smile crossing his face.

"We were on our way. The farm's delivery cart is at the Palace. With the cart horse but without the farmer, or its contents."

"And Miach sent you?"

"He could not come himself." Elias' face closed, friendliness vanishing behind a mask.

"The farmer was not just producing flowers," Arrow told him. It was not a question and the warrior simply looked back at her, unblinking. "There is mercat among the crop."

Kester and Orlis hissed in surprise even as Elias' face tightened further.

"Not many people know that," the warrior told her, easy manner entirely gone, light catching the hard planes of his face and glitter of amber in his eyes. Not as powerful as Miach. Plenty skilled enough to kill her, though. Warriors were trained to act against mages as well as protect them. A chill ran through her. This was a warrior who had dedicated his life to his Queen's service and would kill in her service without a second thought.

"It has many uses," she said, fingers clenching in her pockets again. Many uses, many of them as close to illicit as any plant could come. A powerful plant, it was used in some advanced magic to add potency to healing potions. All Academy students in the higher cycles were required to study it. Distilled a particular way, a method that was forbidden, it made Erith susceptible to suggestion. A lesser known effect, and one of the good reasons to keep such a plant, was its use in aiding the frailty that came with age. Arrow's stomach twisted. There were very few good reasons why the Queen's own guard were keeping such a close watch on a farmer producing mercat so near to the Palace. The Queen and her Consort had been in power for many years, and had neither of them been young when they were chosen for the roles.

"Where is Noverian?" she asked.

Elias' expression froze. Noverian was considerably older than his *vetrai*.

"You need to ask Miach."

"What is it?" Orlis asked, frowning in puzzlement.

"And Her Majesty?" Arrow faced the leader of the Queen's second cadre with a straight back, hoping she did not betray her racing pulse and twisting stomach. She remembered the delicate Erith woman who had seemed far smaller than she had expected.

"Ask Miach." Elias sighed, showing his own age. "It is not for me to speak."

"What is going on?" Orlis demanded.

"Later, mageling." Kester's voice was sharp.

"Whoever was here did not leave any trace beyond the dead body and containment spell," Arrow told the warrior, conscious of the warrior's cadre returning and forming a loose ring around them. There were no weapons shown, but the subtle tension in Kester showed he had spotted the possible threat, too.

"The knife is unmarked and not traceable," one of the cadre put in. "Close quarters, stabbed head on. A single, clean strike. He knew his attacker."

"And there is no trace of mercat in any of the barns," the leader of the junior third spoke up. Arrow thought it was interesting that they had checked. Her own, internal, review of the recordings she had taken confirmed the warrior's statement.

"So how did you know?" Elias turned back to Arrow.

"It is growing in the fields. I thought it was odd that there were two shades of purple in some of the fields, and the farmer had a petal clutched in one hand," she answered.

"And why are you here at all?"

"We are trying to trace Gilean vo Presien," she answered before Orlis could speak. "I have a commission from Preceptor Evellan for such."

"And we are providing escort," Kester added, before Elias could ask.

"Show me." Elias held out a hand. Arrow pulled the document from an inner pocket, glad she had not trusted it to her bag. The warrior read it in silence, amber flaring as he tested the parchment with his senses. "Copied at the Archives," he noted, and the note of approval was back in his voice. "Very wise." He handed it back to her. "Gilean is not here, then?"

"No. And does not appear to ever have been. At least not recently."

"Why did you think he was?"

"People reported him travelling in this direction, and he mentioned this place in a half-written letter in his rooms," Orlis put in, as sober as Arrow had ever seen him.

"Gilean has not been seen for days," Elias began, interrupted by one of his cadre who made some hand signal Arrow could not follow. Elias stepped aside from the group, holding out his hand, taking the small communicator disk the other warrior handed him, the speaker at the other side of the link hidden from Arrow's view.

The conversation was brief and, by Elias' tone, urgent. Arrow could not hear the words, judging by the indrawn breaths from Kester and Orlis that the news was extraordinary. Elias stalked back to them, face pinched.

"There has been another death at the Palace. I am sorry, Arrow."

"Why?" She blinked, wondering what required his expression of regret to her. "Who has died?"

"Seggerat vo Regersfel arrived last night and was found dead in his bed this morning."

"Impossible. Seggerat would not allow himself to die in his sleep," Arrow replied immediately and saw by the gleam in Elias' eyes that he perfectly understood her.

"Miach is worried. Asks that you return at once."

"Of course."

"We need to remain here. Travel with all speed."

Kester exchanged farewells with the warriors and before Arrow quite knew what was happening she was back on her horse and riding after Orlis' back along the narrow grassy lanes away from the farm, requiring all her energy to stay on the horse and having none to spare to consider that her second grandfather was now dead.

CHAPTER THIRTEEN

T he journey back to the Palace took a mere fraction of the time that it had to leave and passed in a blur for Arrow, the Erith horses proving they were equal to every legend told about them.

They gave the horses back into the horsemasters' care then made their way to the Palace, Arrow still light-headed and breathless from the pace and yet another rapid transition, stumbling a little in Kester and Orlis' wake as they strode through the Palace gardens to a side door for the main building.

Miach met them at the doors, shadows under his eyes suggesting that he had not slept for several days, face tight with displeasure or anger or possibly both. Arrow ducked her head rather than meet his eyes. There were too many secrets here and she had the feeling she would be uncovering more and more.

"He is still in the House rooms," Miach told them, not bothering with a greeting. "Word is spreading, and the House are not happy."

"You preserved the scene?" Kester asked, voice clipped.

"Naturally."

They did not speak again until they had gone along a seemingly endless succession of wide, high-ceilinged corridors and up two shallow flights of stairs. Arrow was hopelessly lost, something that was becoming familiar in the Palace, the mental map she had started to prepare having no reference point on this route. Every corridor was as finely decorated as the last, with handwoven rugs underfoot and priceless art treasures along the walls and in specially designed niches. She was breathing hard, struggling to keep up with the others' pace, the shadows of bruises across her body aching as more of her energy was spent in moving.

"House Regersfel's rooms take up one corner of the building." Miach checked his headlong stride as they came to the top of what seemed to be the last flight of stairs, pausing to cast a glance back over them. Arrow drew in a much-needed breath, paying attention, trying to understand what he was and was not saying. "They are neighbours with House Falsen and House Sovernis."

"Were any of the other Houses in residence?" Kester seemed familiar with arrangements which had Arrow's mind spinning. Houses had their own rooms in the main Palace building? Or perhaps just the oldest, more powerful Houses. It might explain why such a large building was required. There were at least twenty major Houses, and dozens more minor ones.

"Not that we are aware." Miach's jaw flexed, betraying anger. Arrow wondered who was guarding the Queen with the second cadre absent, inspecting the farm, and the Queen's first guard here.

They moved along yet another wide and beautifully decorated corridor at a carefully sedate pace, almost elaborately so. Putting on a performance, Arrow understood at once, her suspicion confirmed as they turned a corner and a babble of noise, angry voices raised, greeted them. The corridor ahead was full of House Regersfel retainers, many of whom Arrow recognised, and a White Guard cadre she also knew. Kallish nuin Falsen remained impassive under the loud threats from one of the senior House retainers, folding her arms across her chest and staring the man down. The warrior knew they were there, the briefest look up missed by the angry House retainers.

"No." A voice she knew all too well. Eshan nuin Regersfel was here. Naturally. And not happy to see her. It was very familiar even in this unfamiliar place. "No. A million times no."

Whatever further protest Eshan was going to make was drowned out as other retainers turned their anger on Miach.

"This is an outrage! Seggerat deserves the utmost respect!"

"You have no right to keep us from our residence!"

The outcry continued for some moments before Eshan shoved his way to the front.

"You cannot bring it here. It is an abomination."

"Ladies. Sirs." Miach's voice, laced with power, cut through the babble. "I remind you that you are here, we are all here, at the Queen's grace. She has charged me to learn the truth of this death and to use all available resources to do so."

"It is a violation to bring it here." Eshan spluttered the words, normally pale skin mottled red, lips trembling with the force of his feelings.

"The Lady Arrow has a commission from Preceptor Evellan and the Queen's own command," Kester said mildly.

Eshan's mouth dropped and his lips moved soundlessly for several moments.

"You ... you are part of this, my lord?"

"Eshan," Kester said, "stand aside. We want to find out what happened here as badly as you."

Eshan did not in fact step aside, but allowed himself to be gently steered out of the way by Kester. Arrow and Orlis slipped past, Arrow's ears burning at the narrowed glares she received from the rest of the House's retainers and a few comments, muttered loudly enough to carry to even her dull hearing.

"*Svegraen.*" She greeted the cadre.

"Mage. It seems you have been having adventures without us." Kallish's mouth twitched in what would have been a smile in less solemn circumstances. "Nothing has been disturbed, Miach."

"Good. Arrow, do you want to go in alone?"

"Yes, thank you."

"Second door on the left," Miach told her.

One of Kallish's cadre held the door open for her and she stepped from the crowded corridor with its bitter anger into the hushed, refined quiet of a House.

The Palace disappeared and House Regersfel took its place, the Palace's masterful ward spells replaced by layers of wards with the unmistakable signature of the House's ward crafter. She was in an entranceway designed to impress any visitors, the furnishings so similar to the manor at the Taellaneth that she stopped in her tracks, displaced again, looking reflexively to her right, expecting Eshan to arrive, pinch-faced and irritated by her presence in his master's residence.

Not a sound met her waiting ears. A blink and she remembered where she was. Another blink, a moment's pause, and she could see the changes. This entrance was different to the Taellaneth manor in shape and layout. The manor house was larger, with a stone floor. Here the stone floor was replaced by a handwoven rug she hesitated to step on. Even with the housekeeping spells active on it, it was ancient, a prized object of the House. The walls carried carefully displayed parchments, shimmering faintly with preservation spells. Proclamations, declarations of gratitude from past monarchs for good deeds by the House. There were a half dozen here, and more at the manor. All originals. And none from the current Queen, for that would be in bad taste, in Erith terms.

Still off balance, she looked around the square hallway and its many doors and felt lost. Each door was the same as the next, all closed. Silently thanking Miach, she moved to the second on the left, the door almost hidden in a deep recess that she suspected would be heavily warded during the occupant's sleep. She paused to put on her gloves before she touched the door handle.

Stepping into Seggerat's sleeping place felt like the violation that Eshan had claimed, her human made boots sinking into softness, the room one that no one outside the House was ever meant to see. She paused, considering taking her boots off, all too easily picturing both Eshan and Seggerat's disgust. But the one was dead and the other had no power to order her. So, she forced herself a step forward, apprehension crawling up her spine. She had never seen Seggerat in anything less than formal dress, prepared for the outside world, her meetings with him almost always in public spaces or, on rare occasions, his study at the manor house.

The hushed quiet of the bedchamber and the sweet smell of Erith death in the air sent another prickle along her spine, her wards rising in response, sheen of silver casting some light in the shadowed room. The room was easily as big as the hallway outside, walls covered in rich red brocade fabric, matched by the drapes around an enormous four poster bed that dominated the room, dark wood adding to the gloom. The only light was a sliver of daylight getting in where one of the heavy velvet curtains had been pulled back a fraction, giving her just enough to see by.

The bed, almost as big as Arrow's entire residence at the Taellaneth, was covered with a patterned quilt in stylised patterns of leaves and flowers, its rippled surface flat across the bed except for the slender length at one side.

He was so small, Arrow thought, from her position by the door. So much smaller than he had seemed in life, with his will and intelligence dominating every space he was in.

In this refined, quiet space he was reduced to a slight dent under the quilted cover, his own stillness a reflection of the room.

She forced herself to move forward, to close the door behind her and approach the bed. On the stand beside his head there was a carafe of water, an empty glass that looked untouched, a glass lantern with the end of a candle inside, long since died out, and a small portrait in a wooden frame.

Careful not to disturb anything, Arrow bent and looked at the portrait, a sharp pain striking her chest as she recognised the subject. Alisemea. It was possible that Seggerat had kept a portrait of his long-dead child next to him at all times. Arrow doubted it. In the same way she doubted that Seggerat had died in his sleep. Someone had placed the portrait there. As someone had placed a book in the library that also connected to Alisemea.

She turned, finally, to Seggerat himself. He was paler than normal, and too frail, the skin of his face sinking across his bones, showing the shape of his skull in sharp relief, defined lines of his features the product of centuries of a pure Erith bloodline, untainted by any other race.

She found her hands clenched into fists and loosened them with conscious effort, drawing a slow breath in. Calm was surprisingly difficult to find. Seggerat had been everything but warm to her in life and yet her chest ached with the knowledge that her last direct living relative was dead.

Grandfather.

The word, never spoken aloud, sounded strange in her mind, a clumsy set of sounds like her first attempts to learn the common language. She tried it again.

Grandfather.

No better. Worse, in fact, as the word had acquired hard edges which hurt.

It did not suit the unyielding face Seggerat had presented to her. She knew that he had other grandchildren, products of children from his second *vetrai*. She wondered if he had ever been kind or generous to them, and could not picture it.

The hurt made her draw a sharp breath before she packed it away, suppressed the ache and disciplined her mind, years of practice at the Academy coming to her aid. There was work to do. Finding out how he had died.

Even assuming a work-like front she could not bring herself to touch his remains, calling power instead, gently folding the quilt down to find him lying perfectly straight on his back, arms folded across his chest, soft white of his fine lawn nightgown smooth and undisturbed. There had been no obvious violence in this death. Second sight did not show her any active spells around his body, though she was troubled by his posture. Laid out for the funeral rites, even his hair smooth.

There was the faintest trace of disturbance in the air around him, the slightest trace of something or someone else, too faint for her to follow, even fully into the second world. The disturbance led away from the body, to a corner of the room that held the discreet, hidden door to the servants' passageway. There the disturbance pooled, as though whoever had created it had stood, waiting. For what, she did not yet know. Marking the location in her mind, she turned back to look at the room from this angle. The whole room was clearly visible, including the two other doors, one to the hallway and one that probably led to a dressing room. A good place to lie in wait if you knew that there were no servants due.

The edges of her vision blurred, normally a sign she had pushed herself too hard. Not today. Her power had recovered from the *rallestran* and was vivid inside her, eager for use. She tried another breath and coughed, lungs not working properly, coughed again. Her wards flared in alarm and she moved, stumbling towards the door to the hallway. Lungs burning, she fell to her hands and knees, effort of breathing loud and harsh in her ears as she crawled, shaking with effort, towards the door, vision fading as she went.

The last thing she saw before she lost consciousness was the door opening and a pair of polished boots coming towards her.

"You do get into trouble without me," Kallish said cheerfully.

"H-how-" Arrow choked, coughed, and breathed, a great, heaving breath that wheezed into her starved body. She was sitting propped up against a wall in the entrance hall, grateful thanks of various monarchs for House Regersfel's service above her head.

"Wanted to escape the crowd," the warrior said, no guilt in the admission, "and thought there might be something interesting where you were. What happened?"

Arrow breathed a moment more, ache easing from her lungs, thinking about what she had found.

"Someone changed the air in that room," she concluded. "There was no active spellwork around the bed or the body. But there was a disturbance in the air, and ..." Her voice failed into more coughing. Kallish handed her a flask, the ritual becoming familiar. She still had Kester's flask in her pocket, she remembered, but accepted Kallish's offering. Arrow sipped the Erith tea for a moment. "Passive spell," she continued, "which I could not identify. It was not battle magic."

"Changed the air." Kallish sat back on her heels, head tilted, apparently deep in thought. "Someone has an interest in history."

"Pardon?"

"Some time ago there was a series of unexplained deaths in the heartland. A number of very prominent people died apparently in their sleep. No one could work out why until-" Kallish stiffened, amber flaring in her eyes. "Until the Lady Teresea was called to the scene and saw the trace of magic."

"A reader would have spotted it," Arrow agreed, trying a deep breath. When she did not immediately begin coughing again, she decided she could stand. Kallish rose with her.

"A disturbance you said?"

"Yes. Someone else was in the room. They left almost no trace."

"Can you follow them?"

"I can try. I am not sure-"

"Good. Xeveran." Kallish did not raise her voice much but a moment later Xeveran put his head round the door to the hallway, the babble of noise confirming that none of the House had left, Eshan's complaining tone cutting through the rest as he continued to protest that the abomination had been allowed inside.

"Kallish?"

"You are in charge here until I get back." Kallish's lips twitched as Xeveran made a very unprofessional grimace before ducking back into the corridor. "Come on, then."

"Should we tell Miach?" Arrow hesitated.

"And share the fun? No." Kallish turned to the door as it opened again and Kester and Orlis slipped through, closing the door firmly behind them.

"You found something?" Kester asked.

"A disturbance." Kallish's eyes gleamed. "There was someone else in the room. We are going to follow."

"We will come, too." Orlis lifted his chin.

"Stay out of the way, then," Kallish ordered, and nodded her head to Arrow. "Lead on."

"Be careful crossing the bedroom. Try not to breathe," Arrow warned them, taking a deep breath herself before opening the door to the bedroom and walking through, not pausing to look at Seggerat's body, reaching the servants' door and opening it with little fuss to reveal a spotless, gloomy corridor beyond, wide enough for a servant and tray to pass through, but not for two people to comfortably walk side by side.

"A servant?" Orlis sounded sceptical.

"Hush, young thing," Kallish reprimanded from just behind Arrow's shoulder.

Arrow ignored them as best she could, sliding back into the second world, finding that slight disturbance and following it.

The trail took them a good distance, as far as she could tell, blind to the first world, having to stop several times as the faint thread dissipated amongst other, far stronger traces. Genuine servants, going about their business. The thread was faint enough that she would normally have believed it several months old, and yet it crossed over the more vivid traces of the servants, telling her it was very recent.

Finally there was a solid door in front of her, Palace wards bright in the second world, and another small pause in the trail, showing whoever it was had waited here a moment before going through the door.

Arrow put her hand out and pushed open the door, stepping through into blindness, the brilliance and complexity of the spellwork in this new place over-whelming her fully-opened second sight.

A moment later and the world shifted and spun as something in the first world knocked her aside.

She slid along a polished surface, scrabbling her way back into the first world even as she tried to stop her movement and her wards flared around her.

The first world was shadowed and full of the sound of steel on steel. Swords. Fighting. She managed to get her knees under her and kept low, trying to see through the gloom. Night time. No magic involved. She whispered the necessary spell to enhance her vision and found Kallish and Kester facing off against a dozen opponents in a uniform she recognised, Orlis hovering behind them, calling mage fire to his hands.

"Hold!" she called, coming to her feet. "Stand down! We are sent by Miach."

The White Guard cadre who had been attacking Kallish and Kester stopped at once, backing away from the bared steel. Arrow murmured another spell, harder without chalk, and threw sparks of light up into the air.

They were in the ruined library, all the bookshelves now on the floor, deserted apart from the alert cadre and Arrow's group.

"How did you get here?" The leader demanded.

"Attacking without warning?" Kallish snapped back, sword still out. "Not the usual way."

"Nothing is usual at the moment, *svegraen*." The leader sighed, and sheathed his sword. His cadre followed suit, Kallish and Kester also putting away their weapons. Behind them Orlis lowered his hands, the small spark of mage fire he had been building dying out.

"We were following the trail of someone who was in Seggerat vo Regersfel's room when he died," Arrow told them. "He came in here."

"Impossible. This place has been under guard the whole time, and apart from you there has been no one else inside."

"Then he must have hidden from you, because his trail comes through here."

"Can you find it again?" Kallish asked.

"No. There is too much active spellwork in here." Arrow looked around, remembering the wonder of her first sight of this library, perhaps gone forever. "If we can find where he left I might be able to trace it."

"There has been no one through here," the leader insisted again.

"Then perhaps he is still here?" Kallish suggested.

The leader swore, sending a third to guard the main doors with a quick gesture. "Then let us search."

Arrow was getting familiar with the routine of White Guard searching, careful to keep behind Kallish and Kester as they and the other two thirds of the cadre made their way through the library, past its many bookcases and the ruin that was the site of Lady Teresea's death. Nothing. Also becoming familiar.

Every warrior was frustrated and worn by the time they were finished searching and had confirmed that there was, indeed, nothing to find. No hidden magician or assassin ready to leap out and attack them.

Head aching from use of magic, her second sight as sharpened as she could make it, Arrow had no explanation as to why she could not find any further trace of whoever had stood in Seggerat's room then moved directly through the servants' corridors to the library. Whoever it was must have watched Seggerat die, she realised, skin crawling. Watched the struggle for air, the fight for life even as the spell deprived his body of what it needed. If he had suffocated the way she had, he would not have died in that resting pose. The killer had stood, protected from his own spell, watched Seggerat die, and then arranged his body to be found.

And, according to Kallish, the killer had done this before. Arrow had never heard of the other deaths but the Erith did not like to discuss their failures. Her jaw clenched. The Erith had failed to catch a killer, the deaths stopping only when Lady Teresea had been brought in and confirmed that spellwork had indeed been used. Now Teresea was dead and the killer was back. There had been too many deaths. No more, Arrow decided. Not if she could help it.

It was deep into the night when they finished, another cadre appearing to take over watch and surprised to find additional people in the library. The leader of the library cadre left to report to Miach, and Arrow suggested that they return to Seggerat's rooms.

Kallish gave her a long, hard look and suggested that they rest instead, and resume in the morning. To Arrow's surprise, Orlis agreed, deep shadows under his eyes, his skin chalky with fatigue.

CHAPTER FOURTEEN

— · —

S he walked with Orlis back to the magician's dormitory.

Orlis' shoulders were slumped and his face, seen in the fading light, was pinched, shadows under his eyes showing how worn he had become. He was too quiet, barely saying a word in the entire walk. There had been no trace of Gilean at all through the day and no further word. Just more questions. More death. And a near-miss, White Guard fighting each other in the library.

Arrow would have tried to speak to him, form a plan of what to do next, what questions remained unasked, but she had worries of her own. She had been unable to trace Seggerat's killer. And had nearly fallen victim to the same trap. Kallish had rescued her. Again. The fading bruises across her back twinged, healing disrupted by the events of the day, reminding her of a more direct attack. The Palace was as safe as the Taellaneth, it seemed. There had been no time to ask Kallish, or indeed Miach, for body armour. Even now, with Orlis for company, she was conscious of all the places a potential attacker could hide around them and all the places about her person where a physical weapon could strike. Even with the dormitory's wards around her, bitter experience told her that she would need to keep candles burning overnight, and bar the door and window, or she would not sleep.

As well as the physical danger, the day had hurt in other ways. She could still hear Eshan's voice railing against the abomination, other House retainers gathered around him, some silent, some murmuring agreement, staring at her with hard, angry eyes. They were shocked and grieving, and it was nothing new, but it still stung.

She shivered lightly, trying to find something positive for her mind to work on. Orlis had proposed they each bathe before discussing matters further. A hot bath was still a rare luxury and one she could look forward to with simple pleasure.

"I wonder what they want." Orlis' voice broke her gloomy thoughts.

She blinked, seeing a small group of Erith ahead of them, dressed in the plain, discreet clothes of high-ranking servants. They also, she saw as they drew closer, wore the Queen's emblem, the frivolous knot of bright fabric that every Erith would recognise.

"Good day to you." A small Erith man, his head barely reaching Arrow's shoulder, stepped forward and made a brisk bow. "We are sent to ready you for the reception tonight."

"Ready?"

"Reception?"

Orlis and Arrow's questions came out on top of each other.

"Your presence is requested and required. Both of you. Her Majesty is hosting a reception in honour of Seggerat vo Regersfel."

"There was no mention of this," Arrow began, then saw Orlis' sideways glance. Her brows drew together. "Was there?"

"There was some talk. I assumed it would not include us." Orlis' nose wrinkled in distaste. "I hate these things. So formal."

"Your attendance has been personally requested," the servant told Orlis, mouth twitching in a poorly hidden smile.

"Curse it, Thoris, you know I hate these things."

"As does our lady. And yet ..." Thoris left the words hanging and turned to Arrow, making another shallow bow. "We anticipated that you would not have formal clothing for such an event. We are here to assist you prepare."

Blinking, Arrow looked past him and saw that most of the half dozen servants gathered behind him were carrying large, plain cloth sacks carefully draped over their arms and shoulders, the last carrying a pair of heavy-looking leather satchels.

She had no time to think before Thoris competently took her under his care, ushering her into the magician's building, ignoring the cascade of amber wards. He had organised a bath for her, giving her some privacy to bathe. The servants then produced a riot of colour from the plain sacks they had carried. Clothing, as vivid and rich as anything the Taellan wore, and far more opulent than anything Arrow had worn before.

In short order she found herself dressed for a formal evening amongst the Erith in brighter colours than she had ever worn among them. Wide-legged trousers and a narrow-sleeved undertunic made of deep, vivid blue silk that felt like water against her skin covered with a knee-length brocade overtunic of rich red stitched with silver, a colour rarely worn by the Erith. They had even brought different footwear for her, lightweight slippers in the same blue as the trousers. Having dressed her head to toe, the servants performed a final miracle, managing to tame her hair, using a lightly fragranced oil to coax the unmanageable tangle into smooth curls that fell halfway down her back.

There were no mirrors in the room for her to see if she looked as different as she felt, or on the path that Thoris led her on back to the Palace, through another set of double doors guarded by warriors. He left her at the bottom of a wide set of stairs, leading up to a double height open doorway from which came the sound of conversation.

She stood at the foot of those stairs, unable to make her feet move for a moment, everything around her unfamiliar, and nothing familiar about her person apart from the mage sword strapped across her back and the *kri-syang* along her forearm. Not the things for a formal reception, Thoris had pointed out, but she would not leave either behind. The sword was concealed by a minor glamour, drawing sharp-eyed glances from the White Guard at the doors, but she was as entitled to her sword as they were to their weapons and they let her pass.

The stairs were directly ahead of her, lit by glimmerlights at floor level, casting the rest of the entranceway into shadow. In the shadows Arrow could feel eyes watching and looked across, wary, to see the familiar spark of amber battle wards and points of White Guard weaponry. Another cadre. Miach was being very careful.

She made herself take the first step and the one after it, and kept moving.

The stairs split at a half landing, one branch going left and one right, and she took the right hand fork, following the turn to come to the next floor of the Palace where the shadows were replaced by brighter lights and the muted roar of conversation, more people speaking together than she had ever heard before. The doorway framed a room full of finely dressed Erith, the glitter of jewels making her glad for the first time of Thoris' intervention.

She caught sight of an Erith lady nearby and stepped back automatically to let the other past, pausing as the other Erith copied her movement and then freezing in her steps, realising she had seen her own reflection in a floor-to-ceiling mirror next to the open door. An Erith looked back at her, tall and slender, clothed as a lady might be, who did not like the fuss of skirts around her. Thoris and his fellows had worked a miracle on her, she thought, stripping away all that was familiar. She stared at her reflection with wide, startled eyes. Her skin gleamed slightly from the bathing oil and her hair, usually a snarled mess, lay in demure curls. The dim lighting in the hallway added angles to her apparently human face, casting her Erith heritage to the fore for the first time.

Her heart thudded, silver growing in her eyes as she stared. The reflection was that of a stranger. A servant playing dress up. Apart from the silver, she did not know herself.

"There you are." Orlis came up the steps and paused, foot missing the last step so he stumbled. "Well, you look different."

"As do you." She turned from her reflection to assess the changes. The journeyman's plain, serviceable travel clothing had been replaced by a gentleman's attire, narrow, dark trousers, a pure white shirt and a knee-length coat of deepest blue. His unruly hair had been smoothed and tied back into a neat knot, red eyes flickering with amber as he looked past her to the room. Like her, he now looked more Erith than not. Sometime since she had last seen him he had found time to eat, the pallor of his skin gone along with the shadows under his eyes. She found her own stomach hollow and wished there had been time for her to eat, too. Her earlier headache from magic use was still there, faint and persistent.

"I hate these things," he said. "Shall we go?"

"I assume so." She walked with him to the door, finding Miach just inside.

"Good, you are here, and I see Thoris found you. The lady would like to speak with you later, but for now you should mingle."

The better part of the warrior's attention was elsewhere, eyes on the crowded room, words spilling faster than normal. Even warned by the roar of conversation, Arrow's breath caught at the sea of Erith in the room. Dozens of extraordinarily beautiful people, dressed in their finery, eyes sharp even as their lips smiled.

"Mingle, he says," Orlis grumbled, heading into the room, Arrow following in his wake, anchored to something familiar in a sea of strange faces, her stomach twisting as more than one Erith twitched their skirts or robes to move out of her way. Her earlier speculation that those at the Palace did not know who she was faded with each twitch.

Orlis led them to a relatively quiet spot by the wall, putting his back to the wall as if it were his last defence, tucking his hands into his pockets and glowering at everyone nearby. Their small spot of calm grew as people edged away from his temper, giving Arrow a chance to assess the room. A vast room, high ceiling overhead painted with images from Erith history and myth, walls plain by contrast, drawing attention upwards, and to one end of the room where there was a raised dais and a pair of ornate chairs, one slightly larger than the other. Searching her mind for knowledge of the Palace, Arrow guessed this must be the Queen's Receiving Room. It was larger than she had imagined, air scented with a gentle green scent she remembered from the Queen's rooms.

Next to her Orlis made a huffing sound worthy of a shifkin.

"Stop sulking," Arrow told him, speaking as softly as she could. "You are drawing more attention."

"I am?" He straightened a little, expression lightening a fraction. "Standing about for hours is not my idea of fun."

Arrow bit her lip against an unexpected laugh. "Try standing through a Taellan meeting. They talked about crops for half a day once."

"Really? What on earth did they find to say for that long?"

"Something very important, I am sure." Arrow was distracted in turn, seeing a few familiar faces in the crowd. Many of the Taellan were here. Naturally. Gret vo Regresan glimpsed her through the crowd, expression frozen before he recognised her, his face tightening as he turned away, nearly bumping into the person next to him. Diannea vel Sovernis was also present, in close conversation with a lord from another House who looked faintly familiar.

Closer to her the crowd parted a moment and a middle-height Erith dressed in floor-length, elaborate robes came towards her. He made a shallow bow as he stopped, closer than she was comfortable with, the full folds of his robes brushing the slightly flared panels of her overtunic.

"And how are you enjoying your stay at the Palace, Lady Arrow?"

"It has been most interesting, my lord," she answered, making her own bow, as shallow as his own. There was very little amber in his light brown eyes, blond hair plaited behind his ears, falling halfway down his back. The older style cued her to his age; apart from the very young and the very old, it was nearly impossible to tell an Erith's age.

"And now you are hiding?" he asked, waving his hand to indicate her position at the wall, large square-cut ruby in his signet ring flashing as it caught the light. "So far away from everyone else."

"By no means," she began, wishing she knew who this man was.

"Oh, excellent." He had his hand under her elbow before she could react, her personal wards flaring and damped down with an effort in this crowd, steering her away from Orlis and the wall and into the room, towards a small group of four Erith who were apparently engaged in serious conversation.

All conversation ceased as her escort drew her closer and her stomach tightened again as she saw that one of the four was Priath. His presence was somehow dimmed in this room, perhaps with so many other forceful personalities pressing around.

"Good evening to you. You look quite the lady. Who would have imagined it?" The words were light, the tone was not. The other three Erith with him gave small, nervous laughs. Arrow made a polite bow, Court manners coming to her rescue.

"I do not imagine you have had much chance to attend such events." Another of the three spoke, taking his cue from his master. They might all be wearing rich clothing, but the relationship was clear.

"Not much, no," she agreed. If they thought to goad her, they were likely to be disappointed. She had survived having the spoiled offspring of Erith nobility as her classmates at the Academy. Her classmates had teased her, humiliated her on a near daily basis when she had worn the collar and broken her bones more than once. The silver power inside stretched lazily, reminding her of what she carried. What none of them could take away.

"Perhaps you served at some?" another asked.

"That was not my duty."

"Oh, do tell, what was your duty?"

"The Taellan required my service and my silence. My lord. My lords." She made another shallow bow, deciding she should leave before they pressed her harder on matters she was not permitted to discuss.

"There you are." Kester's voice had never been so welcome. "Gentlemen." His voice was mild. He put a hand under Arrow's elbow and gently steered her away, dropping his hand when she tensed.

"You are keeping dangerous company," he told her, walking with her back towards where Orlis was still standing, expression once again thunderous.

Arrow bit her lip to hold in hasty words. Priath and his cronies could try to provoke her and she felt mildly unsettled. Kester scolded her and she wanted to scream at him.

"That man is awful," Orlis said as soon as they were in earshot. "And your eyes flared, Arrow. You should be more careful."

"Thank you." The words were very precise, measured just so, delivered in an apparently meek voice. She should not scream at Orlis, she reminded herself. It was likely he meant well, and venting her temper would only draw more attention. She lowered her eyes, called on some calm and settled herself again.

"She does clean up well, though," Orlis added, "yes?" He tilted his head to Kester.

The warrior looked at Arrow, expression unreadable, and made a small bow. "You do look well," he agreed.

Arrow bit her lip, turning her attention elsewhere. Well. The small point of hurt in her chest burrowed deeper. It did not matter. None of it mattered. She was here at the Queen's own command. A command she could not politely decline within the Palace. This evening would be over soon enough and she could continue on her way, find Gilean and then go back to the quiet solitude of her workspace, to the easy demands of the 'kin, who were straightforward in whatever they asked of her, and to the plans for her future. Travel. Seeing things she had only read about, for the human world had its own wonders. There would be no need to think of this warrior, too close to her side, who had kissed her and shouted at her and whose entire behaviour she could not understand. And no need at all to consider why the compliment, a polite response to Orlis' prompting, had stung so badly. She did not need compliments. She had survived without them.

"Abomination!"

The hated word twisted the sting inside her. From reluctant compliment to enthusiastic insult in a few heartbeats. The word had been shouted, so that those gathered around could not fail to hear it. Her spine stiffened, wards stirring in response to her alarm, the sword at her back awake. There was no physical threat, though.

Eshan weaved through the crowd towards her, more dishevelled than she had ever seen him, his over robe sliding off one shoulder, shaking hand pointing towards her.

"You killed him! Killed him!"

Arrow held her ground, lifting her chin a fraction at the wild accusation. She could not run from it, as that would seem an admission of guilt. Of all the things the Chief Scribe had accused her of, she thought bitterly, this public accusation was groundless.

Abomination. A blight among the Erith. Ungrateful. All those other claims, repeated over the years, were truth. She was not grateful to the Erith for her life, no matter how much Eshan wanted her to be.

He lunged forward, pointing fingers clenching into a fist, and was blocked by a uniformed warrior, Kallish easily holding the Chief Scribe at arm's length.

"You are drunk," Kallish said in disgust, nose wrinkling. "Come, I will see you to your rest."

"Abomination, I say. Should have been killed at birth."

"Away, now." Kallish's tone flattened. The rest of her third gathered around her, forcibly escorting the furious scribe away, the crowd rippling to give them room, a murmur of conversation following.

"You should come to these events more often," Orlis said, suddenly cheerful, "this is the most fun I have had in years."

"I am so glad you are enjoying yourself," Arrow answered, not looking at him. Voice calm. A small wonder in the evening. She could still manage outward calm. Not looking at anyone, that hated word ringing in her head. Abomination.

The silver was restless inside her, wanting out, wanting to be used, responding to the anger that she had kept contained for years and now struggled to hold in. *Let us show them,* the power seemed to say. *Let us show them exactly what an abomination can do.*

She lowered her eyes to hide the silver, taking a slow, deep breath, reminding herself that it did not matter. She had a job to do, and when that was done she could leave and never return.

The murmur rising in the crowd continued and she could hear that word repeated. Seggerat's description of her before she had been old enough to understand what it meant, the elder reluctant to be in the same room as she was, let alone look at her.

The murmur died a fraction and the crowd parted. Arrow felt her skin prickling, wards wanting to rise again in response to her continued unease. She could try to tell herself that it did not matter, but she did not believe that. Not entirely. She was tired of the stares, of the displacement, of being the unwelcome figure in the room. She wanted out.

A more welcome figure strode through the slight gap in the crowd and made a shallow bow. Miach. Fully armed, dress uniform bearing the faint traces of previous wars.

"The lady would speak with you, if you will come with me."

For a moment she was tempted to refuse, to walk away, out of this room, out of the Palace, and keep going until she was back in the workspace with its familiar scents and the reassuring hum of her own wards around her. She could bar the door and set the wards to stun anyone who tried to enter, or worse. There was a tight knot of anger and hurt constricting her breathing and her feet twitched in their flimsy slippers. And yet she could hardly refuse the Queen's summons, even as an exile. Miach would stop her, for one thing, which would draw much more attention than she had at present. So, she straightened a fraction and inclined her head to the warrior.

"Of course." Somehow her voice was still calm and even.

Arrow left Orlis and Kester without a backward glance, wondering what they would find to entertain them when she was absent.

There was a tightly gathered knot of bright colours at the other side of the room, a chattering, laughing cluster of Erith who fell silent as Miach brought her into their midst.

In the heart of the group was the Queen. Transformed from the delicate lady Arrow had met, she stood straight, eyes clear and bright, dressed to outshine everyone else in a floor length dress of bright amber, sparkling with diamonds. She was accompanied by three Erith ladies whose clothing was less elaborate but equally finely made.

"There you are. How lovely. Do excuse us." The Queen turned a small smile on the crowd around them which melted away at once, leaving Arrow in a small space of quiet with the Queen, her three ladies and Miach, who remained beside her.

"Your majesty." Arrow made a bow. War mage to monarch. Not as low as some of the still-watching crowd thought she should bow, judging by the slight intake of breath. The Queen, however, gave her a warmer smile.

"I see that Priath lost no time in seeking you out," the Queen said directly. Arrow blinked, startled at the frank speaking. The Queen's eyes dipped down a moment then back up. Arrow followed her glance and found that she was standing in a spell circle marked on the floor. All the other courtiers were outside the circle, which was active with runes for confusion and silence. Their conversation would not be overheard.

Arrow's spine prickled, hairs raising at the back of her neck and she had to consciously suppress her wards from rising, reminded that she was in the Palace, heart of Erith politics.

"That is so," she answered the Queen at last.

"What did he want?"

"I believe he wanted to remind me that I do not belong." The words were out before she had a chance to think.

"That is not true." The Queen's face softened, trace of her age showing. "I decide who is welcome here, not Priath." She watched Arrow for a moment, eyes sharp. "And we have much more unpleasant matters to discuss. Seggerat's death."

"Murder," Miach put in.

"Magic was used. The same person who killed Teresea?"

"There was no complete trace, but possibly." Too many questions.

"No proof?"

"Nothing more than a feeling. The spellwork in Seggerat's room was finely done. It almost caught me," she admitted, cheeks burning as she did so. "And the mage fire used to cut down the bookcase in the library was also finely done." She hesitated, prompted to continue by a lifted brow from the Queen. "In time I may be able to identify the magic user." She would not dignify the murderer by calling him a mage or magician.

"In time?" Miach prompted. Arrow wanted to shift under his gaze but there were too many eyes around them.

"As I become more familiar with the Palace, and the heartland's magic, it is a little easier to sort through the traces."

Both seemed to understand her perfectly, even with a lifetime spent in the heartland.

"But for now, with Teresea dead, there are no readers here to follow the trace or confirm the identity." The Queen sighed, her age showing again for a moment.

Arrow stayed silent, having no words of comfort to offer.

"There is more," Miach said. "There is more than one person involved in this."

"What do you mean?"

"There was more than one person in the library. I do not know enough to follow them yet, but definitely more than one." Arrow paused, wondering if she should tell the Queen about her own attack.

"More than one person is involved," Miach confirmed.

"Seggerat's funeral rites are being read tomorrow." The Queen was not ignoring Miach. Her mind had moved to something else, some plan Arrow could not see. "Will you be there?"

"I had not planned to do so." Arrow could only imagine the horror in the House if she turned up.

"Then, will you go back to the House's rooms and see what more you can learn? This needs to stop." The Queen's voice hardened, brittle steel imperfectly concealing pain. "There have been too many deaths."

"I will do my best to find out what has happened." Arrow promised, body moving in a reflexive bow, too many years as the Taellan's servant making the habit ingrained.

"I understand that the House does not recognise you." The Queen might be hurt, but she was dangerous, too, for Arrow's peace of mind.

"I am not Named." And wanted, badly, to be elsewhere. There were too many people here, watching for her mistakes, her lack of grace, waiting for her to fail.

"Nonsense." The brisk response was unexpected.

Arrow blinked again, chest tightening with the old shame. "Seggerat told me so several times. And that my lineage is struck."

There was a sharp gasp from the ladies gathered and she felt Miach's attention sharpen on her. Without a Name, without her lineage, she had no status at all among the Erith. She could defeat a hundred *surjusi* and it would make no difference.

"Cunning old devil." The Queen's voice was laden with emotion Arrow could only begin to guess at. Sadness. Admiration. Bitter hurt. "This is a conversation for another time, I feel. We have talked too long." The Queen's eyes went past Arrow to survey the room. "I understand that Evellan has commissioned you to find Gilean, and I want you to find what you can about these deaths. You may draw on all the resources here to do so. Miach will see to it that there is no interference."

"Kallish nuin Falsen has offered her services and that of her cadre," Miach said. Arrow was somehow not surprised.

"Yes, she would. Young rebel." The Queen's voice held a fond note and Arrow nearly choked at the description of Kallish. One she would never have come up with herself, but which, oddly, fit. "We will speak again." The Queen smiled at Arrow, a warmer smile than before, and placed a hand on her cheek. "Good hunting, mage."

"And to you." Arrow bowed once more as the Queen and her ladies swept past, breaking the spell of the circle and being swallowed by the crowd in moments.

"On Kallish's recommendation, we have moved you into one of the annexes rather than leaving you in the magician's dormitory," Miach told her, voice low, "so make sure you leave with some of her cadre." He paused. "She seems to think that you attract trouble." Even without looking at him she could hear the laughter in his voice. Colour washed over her face, tips of her ears prickling under her hair. Fortunately, Miach did not seem to expect a reply.

CHAPTER FIFTEEN

———— ፨ ————

Before Arrow could find anything else to say, Miach had ducked back into the crowd on some errand of his own, leaving her alone. But only for a moment. Before she had done more than take a step she was surrounded by richly dressed Erith. Far from reviling her, they were now openly curious. She was showered with invitations. Come and talk with them. Walk with them the next day. Visit with them and take tea. Take a stroll around the Queen's garden. She recognised a few faces as among those who had twitched their clothing out of the way when she first entered the room. It seemed the Queen's attention still had power in the Palace and was noticed. Arrow had no appetite or time for the courtiers' games. She made a shallow bow, drawing a few frowns, then excused herself with no promises made.

She had memorised where the main doors were and headed in that direction. The Queen had spoken with her. It seemed that there was nothing more for her to do.

She had taken only a few paces before a warrior appeared beside her. Xeveran.

"Good evening, *svegraen*."

"Good evening, mage. We cannot leave quite yet. The Queen will make a speech, and then we can leave. Kallish is watching Orlis. This way."

He steered her gently away from the path to the doors, the presence of a fully armed warrior parting the crowds, and back to the patch of wall where Orlis' mood seemed to have improved dramatically. The improvement in his temper was perhaps due to the fact that he seemed to have found a pair of Palace servants who were carrying trays laden with food, small bites of the best that the Palace kitchens had to offer. He was making his way through the food on the trays, talking animatedly with Kester, who was watching the crowd with most of his attention, answering Orlis absently as Arrow and Xeveran arrived. Kallish was standing at parade rest a few paces away, her presence, like Xeveran's, ensuring the crowds stayed back.

Before Orlis could ask any of the dozen or so questions she could see bubbling on his lips, the whole room fell silent at some invisible signal. Arrow turned to find that the Queen had ascended the dais at the end of the room, her ladies and Miach, with his third, gathered around her.

Arrow was not quite sure what the Queen said, the monarch's voice carried through the room by a gentle spell which must be woven into the dais, as her attention was snagged by several clusters of the gathered nobility. Priath, a pair of lords she did not know, a cluster of ladies and lords most of whom were strangers, and a few other individuals scattered around.

She had no idea why those individuals attracted her attention. It was as though someone had marked them, telling her to look at them, to see how they were behaving, who they were talking to.

And then the Queen's speech ended and the bubble was broken, the crowd becoming a crowd again, with no one person standing out. Arrow blinked, found one side of her face felt warm and put a hand to her cheek where the Queen had touched it. The faintest trace of spellwork met her fingers. Subtle enough that her wards had not reacted and she had not spotted it until now.

Arrow's heart thumped, throat tightening. The Queen was far more than she appeared, like many Erith. Somehow the Queen suspected that she herself was in danger and had just pointed out the likeliest suspects to Arrow. And only Arrow. She remembered the reading stand behind the Queen's shoulder when they had talked, sitting next to the unlit fire. The volume had been open at the illustration of a plant with purple flowers. Mercat. Arrow's skin prickled. Would she have spotted the mercat in the flower fields if the Queen had not left that clue for her? She liked to think so, as it was an anomaly, but the Queen had not been sure. The Queen was sure of one thing, though, and that was that she was in danger.

"We need to talk," she said to Kallish. "Now."

"Bring the cadre," Kallish told Xeveran. "This way."

Silently blessing Kallish for not questioning her, or insisting they stay longer, Arrow walked with her escort through the doors and down the stairs. Kallish turned them along a corridor inside the Palace, one Arrow did not recognise.

"We have the smallest annex."

"The entire building?" Arrow's voice squeaked.

"It is not a big building," the warrior sounded amused, "and far easier to defend if we are the only ones there. You are coming with us, young thing." The warrior reached out and snagged Orlis' sleeve when he would have sidled away.

"But I only had a bite earlier. There was no dinner. And Gilean's rooms ..."

"Food will be provided. Your belongings have been moved. There is a watch on Gilean's rooms."

"Am I included?" Kester asked from somewhere behind Arrow. He sounded amused.

"If you wish to be." Kallish sounded tense and Arrow realised that she was keeping a close watch on their surroundings.

"Trouble, *svegraen*?" she asked, voice as low as she could make it.

Before Kallish could answer, a blur of dark rushed out of one of the side corridors and hit Arrow side-on, tumbling her to the ground. She raised an arm as her wards flared. Something cold sliced through her wards and into her skin. She twisted, trying to get away, hearing a cry of alarm over her head, the sound of rapidly approaching feet, a shout of anger she thought might be Kester, the bright amber of Orlis' power, the sound of Kallish's weapons striking something.

She huddled on the ground, frozen, unable to move, wards in tatters about her, the cold sting of whatever had sliced through her defences and skin growing, creeping up her arm. Poison. She had been poisoned. Something on the blade.

Her mind scattered, thoughts going adrift until she forced them back. Her second sight would not work properly, but ahead of her she could see a tell-tale dark fissure that would take her into shadows. She managed to get her feet under her, arm clutched to her side, and spoke the necessary word to open the door. Heard and felt Kallish's anger, then the warrior grabbed her arm. Arrow was already moving forward, and stumbled, falling into the shadows, taking Kallish with her.

"Where are we? What is this place?"

"This is the shadows," Arrow answered, and straightened, surprised. Her mind was clearer here. She quickly glanced around. No immediate threat. Kallish was on guard, weapons ready, eyes skimming their surroundings.

"Why are we here?"

"The blade was poisoned." Arrow looked down at her arm, the cloth neatly cut, the flesh of her arm opened to bone along her forearm, blood flowing freely. The numb sensation was receding. "And I saw the shadows so I came here. It seems to have helped."

"Poison? What sort?"

"I do not know. Something that interfered with my magic and made me freeze."

"Sounds like a pure dose of mercat."

Mercat again, Arrow thought, mind beginning to fade at the edges. There was an easy cure for mercat poisoning, if only she could remember what it was.

"This will hurt," the warrior warned before shoving her blade into Arrow's arm.

Arrow screamed, falling to her knees. That was it. The cure. Put a steel weapon into the wound and use power to draw the poison out. It hurt.

She was drenched in sweat and shivering in pain when Kallish was finally satisfied. The warrior drew her weapon back and flicked the blade. The poison, pure darkness even in this place of shadows and colour, slid off onto the ground.

"All out." Kallish produced a cloth from one of her pockets and quickly bound the wound. "Can you stand? I do not know how to get back."

"Yes," Arrow answered automatically. One did not show weakness among the Erith. She tried to stand. Kallish put a hand under her elbow, helping her up. "This way." She found the doorway still open and stumbled back through it.

They came back to the first world to find the cadre on alert, more than one weapon turned to them before the warriors recognised them.

"The mage is wounded. To the annex. Now, and quickly."

Arrow was gathered up, off her feet as easily as she would carry her satchel. Undurat, she thought. Second in Kallish's third, a giant Erith who had carried her before. Careful as he was, her arm bumped against his coat, every nerve in her arm set alight, and a whimper escaped her throat before she could check it.

"Sorry."

"No time. Go." Kallish's voice snapped.

She was jostled, bumped against an armoured shoulder, sensation of air past her face and the jolt of Undurat's pace telling her they were running. Warriors rarely ran. Her mind dissolved again, hissing in pain as the rapid movement jostled the wound. Not quite as bad as Kallish removing the poison, the pain was clouding her mind, thoughts scattering, eyes not working properly.

There was a loud bang. A door opening, thumping against a wall. Rapid orders given in a breathless voice that did not sound like Kallish's normal, cool tones. A flare of amber, battle wards raised. And stillness. Finally.

Undurat put her down on something firm, her head on something soft. Everything was blurry. She blinked rapidly, trying to see, and realised her face was wet. She was crying. Stupid tears.

"Let me see." Orlis' voice was soft. Someone moved her arm and she made a low, moaning sound. "Did you get all the poison out, Kallish?"

"Yes, young thing. Mercat."

"There is something else wrong, then. She should be more alert."

"Another poison?"

"Possibly. I will need to test her blood."

"There is plenty of it."

"Lights at all times and line of sight watch." Kallish's voice was moving away as she issued orders.

"Who was it with the knife?" Arrow asked, fragmented parts of her mind coming together for that one, essential question.

"A null."

"Null." She turned the word over in her mind, brow creasing. "No. Do not know."

"A null is someone with no magic who has the ability to cut through any magic," Orlis explained. He sounded tense. She wished she could see him, but her eyes would not clear.

"Not Erith."

"No. Nulls are Erith. Very rare. Not as rare as you, but close." Kester was behind her now, his voice low, too.

"Not rare." She huffed a laugh and then hissed as it hurt. "Ache all over," she said, words as blurred as her sight.

"Definitely poison," Orlis said, a tremor to his voice. "What can you taste, Arrow?"

"Taste. Ugh. Bitter. Rotten."

"*Surrimok* venom." Orlis sounded reluctant. "Kallish, we need tea and a bucket. Lots of tea."

The rest of the night passed in a haze of misery as Erith tea was forced down her throat. Her stomach rebelled and she threw up into the bucket Orlis held. Then he forced more tea down her throat, Kester and Kallish helping hold her down when she struggled against the mage's hold. Her wards would not rise, her mind unable to form the simple commands that would set them up in her defence. More tea. And she threw up again. And they repeated the process. Over and over. Until her throat was raw and her every muscle ached and she never, ever, wanted to see or smell Erith tea again.

She had lost count of the repetitions, but the last dose of tea was still inside her and the others seemed happy. Her eyes were clearing slowly and she could make out a beautifully furnished room with pale wooden panels on the walls and light coming through the windows.

"Morning already."

"Nearly noon, actually." Orlis' face appeared in front of her. He looked as ill as she felt, skin pale and drawn, deep circles under his eyes. "You are past the worst but you should sleep the rest of the day. I healed your arm when the poison was out."

"You need rest too," she told him, thinking that sleep was an excellent idea.

"Is she awake?" Kester asked from a short distance away.

"Yes." Orlis rose and stretched, joints popping. He yawned and scrubbed his hand through his hair, destroying the last of the style he had worn the night before.

"Kallish said this might help." Kester held out a cup to Arrow. She struggled to sit up and took it, sniffing cautiously. Erith tea. Her insides twisted.

"Ugh." She held it as far away as she could. "No more tea. Please."

"It will soothe your stomach."

The pair of them were dark shadows looming over her and her heart thudded, fright taking over. They might force more tea into her as they had so often during the night, hazy memories of the long, awful night too fresh in her mind. The Erith had her as helpless as she ever had been wearing a collar. She had no strength to fight them. Her wards flared silver, brilliant in the sunshine. They took a step back, exchanging frowns.

"Please," she repeated, turning her head away, ashamed of her fear and the weakness that meant her hands were shaking.

The room was so still she could hear her own breathing, harsh and rapid. She could not look at them, holding the cup away from her with both hands, more tears falling. Her wards died as she called them back.

"I will find something else," Kester said, taking the cup gently from her, careful not to touch her. He left the room with rapid, tense strides. Orlis sighed, settling beside her.

She was on a long bench, she realised. Long enough for Undurat to lie on with his head and feet supported.

"We did not know if you would live," Orlis told her, then shocked her speechless by folding her into a warm hug, familiar scent of burnt amber enveloping her. She returned the hug awkwardly, patting his shoulder. He held her shoulders for a moment, red eyes bloodshot as he stared at her. "Do not go anywhere without an escort. There will be a warrior in the room with you when you sleep."

"A null." She remembered that from the night before. "That was the one who attacked me before?"

"We think so." He shivered. "Elias' cadre are tracing all the known nulls."

"Elias?"

"The attack was in the Queen's house," Orlis' mouth twisted, corners pulling down, "and she is not happy. The attacker meant to kill you this time."

"Yes. Two poisons. Seems overkill." She drew her feet up onto the bench, rested her head on her knees, the residual ache from the poison seeping away. "And you saved my life again. Thank you."

"Not alone. Kallish and Kester were here all night, too. Kallish made the cadre take turns to rest. She is consulting Miach at present."

"Here. This might be better." Kester advanced, holding a different cup. She took it gingerly, sniffed, and felt her mouth curve up. Mint. Fresh, untainted. Her stomach eased just at the scent.

"Thank you."

She drank the whole cup in quick, greedy gulps.

"Sleep," Orlis reminded her, taking the cup. "The first door on the right."

"Come, I will show you." Kester offered a hand as she got off the bench. She shook her head, preferring to stand under her own power, only to clutch at his arm when her knees wobbled. "Not many people survive *surrimok* venom poisoning."

"Yes. Thank you."

"You are the one who survived." The tone was weighted with a feeling she had no name for, his arm steady as he walked her, slowly, the short distance out of the room and to the first door on the right where a pair of warriors waited. They opened the door and her entire focus became the bed waiting for her, piled high with blankets.

She thought she managed a farewell to Kester, stumbling forward and collapsing onto the covers, sinking into the never ending softness with a sigh.

At the edge of her hearing she heard a low voiced conversation.

"Should we try to put her under the covers?"

"Not a good idea. Trained war mage. Put a blanket over her."

A light, soft warmness covered her from chin to toes and she slid into blissful sleep.

The room was full of sunshine when she woke, and a pair of warriors who carefully searched the bathing room before leaving her there alone to wash and change, finding the clothes Orlis had provided at the Academy, so long ago, cleaned and waiting for her along with her bag, its wards undisturbed, all the contents in order. The bright clothes she had worn since the reception were gathered by one of the warriors.

The warriors then escorted her from her room to the first room, where Kallish, Kester and Orlis were settled around a large table, remnants of a meal before them, a few used plates at other chairs suggesting that the warriors were taking it in turns to eat.

"How do you feel?" Orlis asked.

"A little sore. And hungry."

"Undurat, ask the kitchens for more. And more mint tea," Kallish instructed. The giant warrior padded silently away, leaving Kallish's dark eyes assessing Arrow as she sat next to Orlis, opposite the warriors. "You seem better."

"Yes. Thank you. Thank you all."

She had nearly died. Again. It was a tiresome habit. And they had rescued her again. Which was a wonderful gift.

She sipped the mint tea Kester handed across the table to her, stomach growling.

"How long was I asleep?"

"Nearly a full day."

She paused before taking her next sip. That made it the second day since the reception. Whatever momentum there had been in the investigation had faded. She could only hope they could recover it. Despite the rest, she still felt heavy, as though she had not slept nearly long enough. A sensation she was very familiar with. "What news?"

"None of the nulls could have attacked you. Elias is certain, and Miach vouches for him."

"They are the Queen's own guard," Kallish scolded Orlis.

"And only interested in protecting the Queen. What about Teresea? What about the farmer? What about Arrow?"

"So, if not a null, then who?" Arrow's head pounded with the brewing argument and she reached into a pocket, looking for a healing potion she thought she had put there. Instead of the potion her fingers closed around a folded cloth. Curious, she brought it out of her pocket and unfolded it, finding the tiny scrap of cloth from the library.

"What is that?"

"I had forgotten it. When Teresea died, there was someone else there. He left this behind."

"What an odd thing." Orlis' eyes flared amber as he looked at it. "So dull in first sight and so vivid in second."

"I know." Arrow was distracted as Undurat returned and put a tray piled high with food in front of her. She thanked him, meekly taking a plate and a few items from the tray under his stern gaze. He seemed satisfied, his attention caught instead by the scrap of cloth.

"An invisibility cloak," he said. "I have not seen one for years."

"A what?" Arrow stared, sure she had misheard. Such things were legend among humans. The Erith did not believe in fairy tales.

The giant blushed, and sat on one of the chairs at Kallish's gesture.

"That is the common name. It is ..." he paused to find the right words, "woven by the same temples as make the war mages cloaks. On one of the islands in House Nostren territory. Or so legend says."

"I have never heard of such temples." Orlis' curiosity was alive again. As was Arrow's.

"War mages cloaks are woven elsewhere?" She had always assumed that the Academy was responsible for producing the cloaks, or the war mages themselves.

"Yes," Kallish's face tightened, eyes not quite meeting Arrow's, "and gifted where the temples deemed appropriate. You are not the first graduate without a cloak."

Before Arrow could give voice to the many questions that raised, Kallish turned to Orlis, giving him more information to answer the questions burning in his eyes.

"No one knows where the temples actually are. Rumour says that they were destroyed a long time ago, during the last mass incursion." Kallish's attention was sharp on the scrap of cloth, at odds with the sorrow in her voice. "But another story goes that a previous Consort decided they had insulted her and insisted they were pulled down stone by stone."

"We believe that the cloth is no longer made," Undurat added, "but it was supposed to work a bit like the shadow realm."

"All colours at once." Arrow nodded, picking the scrap up and turning it over, seeing the colours flare in second sight while they remained dull in first sight. "A very clever disguise."

"Unless you use magic. Then it is blinding."

"How many people go about using their second sight all the time?" Arrow turned to Orlis. "I only found this because I was examining the spells in second sight. If I had been in the first world I may have missed it."

"The cloth was supposed to go through wards," Undurat added, helping himself to some items from Arrow's tray.

"Like a null." Kester was the first one to say it, Arrow too busy eating under Kallish's stern gaze.

"So the attacker could be anyone," Kallish finished the thought, clearly displeased. Her head tilted, attention caught elsewhere and a moment later Arrow heard a brisk knock at the outside door. Surprised, she twisted in her chair, just able to glimpse the edge of the door, closed in defiance of Erith customs, the small entranceway windowless and dark. Xeveran's third flowed through the room to take up position around the space before Xeveran himself opened the door. It opened so that Arrow could not see the gap, just the slice of light that cut through the entrance hall followed by another shadow entering the building, Xeveran closing the door quickly, the building's wards flexing in readiness for the next visitor.

"Come and sit." Kallish waved to a chair. Miach came into the room and took a chair in silence. He was still pristine in his clothing, dress uniform telling Arrow that he may not have slept since the Queen's reception. The shadows under his eyes and pale undertone to his skin added weight to her guess.

Undurat rose without complaint and disappeared into the building again.

"What have you learned?" Kester asked, not giving Miach a chance to settle.

"Too little. There has been no poison blade found, and no trace of anyone in the corridor when you were attacked."

"There were more attackers?" Arrow had not spotted anyone else.

"A few." Kallish dismissed Arrow's concern with a wave of her hand. "Unskilled and mostly untrained. They were no difficulty."

"And not traced." Miach scowled. "The ward keepers say there was nothing there before you came along. They insist that the attackers were invisible."

The others' eyes all turned to the small scrap of cloth as Undurat came back with another tray laden with food, and a pot of Erith tea. Even catching the scent made Arrow's stomach twist and she picked up her own cup in haste, inhaling the mint.

Miach, naturally, demanded to know what the cloth was and Undurat and Kallish repeated their explanation.

"I know this cloth. There is very little left and mostly kept tightly guarded in Houses. Not something to be used lightly."

"And yet someone is using it."

"Yes, young thing." Miach sighed, scrubbed a hand across his face, shoulders slumped. "And we cannot trace them."

"Not normally, no," Arrow said slowly, idea forming.

"Not without escort, mage," Kallish said firmly.

Arrow sighed, about to protest, when the muscles along her arm cramped from holding the cup, not fully healed from the knife wound, and she had to put her cup down. She inclined her head instead. "I do not know how many I can take. We will have to experiment a little."

"Arrow, I have not slept for three days. Explain." Miach's tone was forced patience, the promise of violence barely hidden.

"Arrow is a shadow-walker," Orlis said, normal good mood restored, "and if this cloth is like shadows then-"

"You should be able to trace these attackers in the shadow world," Miach finished, expression lightening a fraction for the first time since he had sat down. He reached for a cup and a plate.

"You will need armour," Kallish said, tone making it an order.

"Yes. I have been meaning to ask." Arrow felt her mouth twitch in an unexpected smile at Kallish's sour look. She could almost hear the lecture that ran behind the warrior's eyes before Kallish simply shook her head, glanced across the room to Xeveran and lifted a brow. He ducked out of the room at once, not needing any words. Arrow held in a sigh, the healing wound on her arm stinging. An armoured coat would have stopped the blade. She knew she needed one so it was foolish to resent having to wear one.

"There was another disturbance earlier," Kester said, "not far from here." Arrow trusted his word. She had slept through the whole thing.

"Evellan and Seivella," Miach answered, putting his fork down for a moment, all lightness gone.

"Here? Why?"

"They claim they were summoned by the lady to explain their actions." Miach was staring into nothing, eyes flat. "And that they arrived only this morning."

"Claim?" Kallish picked up the word.

"The lady has sent no such instruction. None of her cadres recall it."

Arrow drew a breath in, considering the implications of that. There was no way, given what she knew of Evellan and Seivella, that they would both, voluntarily, leave the Academy together and come to the Palace. Nor would they make up such a tale. Someone was sending orders in the Queen's name. And not just minor orders. Summoning the head of the Academy and his deputy was a bold move.

"Is the Academy guarded? And the Taellaneth?" she asked.

"Yes and yes. Whintnath has closed the gates. At both sides. And the wards are up." Miach was grim.

It would need every Teaching Master and Mistress, and several of the senior students, to maintain the Taellaneth's wards, crafted into the great wooden walls. The White Guard stationed there would normally assist, but would be too busy with additional patrols. The Taellaneth was a defined space, with clear boundaries, but it was a big area.

"How did they get here? The mirror needs both ends," Orlis said, cutting across Arrow's thoughts.

"The portal mages had instructions to assist."

"In the Queen's name, too?" Kester's normally golden skin was a shade paler, perfectly understanding the implications, along with everyone else at the table.

"That is treason," Orlis murmured.

Unless you had no allegiance to the Queen, Arrow thought, stomach twisting again, and there was only one person in the whole of the Palace that applied to. UnNamed and with no House claiming her, she was an obvious suspect.

"She believes she is in danger," Arrow told them, catching the attention of the entire group. The weight of the stares made her continue. "At her toast to Seggerat she showed me a number of different people. Possible suspects." She touched her cheek, where the Queen had put her hand.

There was a pause around the table as the others considered that.

"People often forget she is a skilled mage," Miach murmured, mouth thin, "and also a stupidly stubborn female. She has said nothing to me."

"One of her favourites was killed. Seggerat died. The farmer who supplied her mercat is dead. And where is Noverian?" Arrow asked, more bluntly than she had intended.

Miach lifted his head, eyes black shot with amber as he stared at her, face set. A powerful mage in his own right, and with the Queen's authority to act in the Palace and across all Erith territory. In the hard lines of his face, Arrow saw the determination that had kept him at the Queen's side for decades, defeating her enemies with the cutting intelligence she could see in his eyes. A chill worked its way through her body but she did not back down. She was no reader, to see the truth of matters, but she had an instinct that the answer to that question was as important as knowing what had happened to Gilean.

"Noverian's people are not talking," the Queen's guard said at length, finishing the last of his tea in one swallow.

"He has not been seen for days," Orlis said, "although no one is sure when he was last seen or where."

"He is not behind this." Miach's voice was heavy. "He and the lady respect each other too much."

"I did not say he was." Arrow leant forward, catching his attention again. "He may be in danger. Along with the Queen."

"Proof? Evidence?" Miach was bitter. "I have nothing to force his people to open his rooms to me. And the lady will not hear of it."

"We can ..." Arrow began, then hesitated. Miach was loyal to his Queen and she had been on the verge of suggesting something he might regard as treason and try to prevent. "We will search for these attackers," she finished instead. He tilted his head, eyes gleaming.

"That would be a help."

"May I speak with Evellan and Seivella?" she asked as he rose from the table.

"They are in the dungeons under guard. No visitors may enter." The gleam was still in his eyes, though.

"I understand. I hope that they are being cared for."

"Healers have attended them but they are generally left alone."

"I see."

Kallish rose and walked Miach to the door, exchanging a few quiet words as they went. Arrow pulled the tray of food towards her and ate rapidly. There would be no more rest for a while and magic use required a great deal of energy, even with the vast power she carried.

"Armour," Kallish said flatly when she returned, eyes on Arrow.

"Yes, *svegraen*," Arrow said meekly, between mouthfuls of food.

"And at least a full third."

"I will try." Arrow glanced at her now-empty plate, remembering the amount of power required to enter and leave the shadow realm. "Can we bring food?"

"You want to stop for a snack? Gilean is in danger." Orlis' hair was on end again, worry making his tone sharp.

"I know," Arrow answered softly at the same time as Kester spoke.

"The mage knows what she is about. And Gilean's absence concerns us all."

"I need my bag." Arrow ducked away from Orlis' eyes and left the room on quick strides.

CHAPTER SIXTEEN

— · —

Xeveran held an armoured coat for her and helped her shrug into it, ensuring the fastenings were done. The warriors had somehow found a better fit than the one she had borrowed before. The one that had saved her life, deflecting a bullet just enough to injure rather than kill. She might be tall as an Erith, but she was not as broad as the warriors who wore these coats. It was still heavy and unwieldly, but more fitted around her body so it did not hamper her as much. She put the satchel over her shoulder. Kallish's third were ready, their own coats fastened to the throat, weapons prominent.

"You are in charge until I return," Kallish told Xeveran.

"Lights and line of sight at all times, yes," Xeveran replied, accepting his command and stood back to let Kallish's third gather around Arrow.

"I do not know if this will work," Arrow told them, drawing a deep, steadying breath. Her stomach was fluttering with nerves, the food she had consumed settling uneasily.

"We will try and see," Kallish said implacably, waiting.

"Very well. *Svegraen*," Arrow turned to Xeveran, "solid objects are impassable in the shadow realm. That means that if we succeed we will need to leave through the door."

Xeveran considered the closed front door for a moment.

"So, we should not immediately panic at the door opening and closing by itself." He nodded, accepting the situation with a calm that Arrow envied.

She gathered her power, and opened her second sight. The powerful ward spells in the building flared to life before her eyes, testament to the Palace ward keepers' skill, leaving little room for shadows. She blinked, her eyes adjusting to the brilliance. There was a fissure there, a slender gap. She spoke the command for it to open and hesitated. The shadow world was still new to her. There had been little time for experimenting, even with the more relaxed life in the human world. She could see the first world shapes of Kallish's third round her, patiently waiting. They would not be able to see the fissure, she realised. Still, she hesitated another moment before holding out a hand, the Erith's disdain for her too ingrained. "I think you may need to touch me, *svegraen*, for this to work."

Less than a breath later, five hands landed on her, three on her arm and one on each shoulder. The lack of hesitation and the unfamiliar sensation of others' hands on her, not in pain or threat, made her pause again, nerves overwhelming for a moment.

She took another breath, conscious that all the warriors would be able to sense her tension, and not wanting to explain it, then forced her feet to move. One step forward. The five hands tightened slightly but stayed with her. Another step and another and they were through the fissure and into shadows, the first and second worlds disappearing.

Kallish's third murmured uneasily at the new sights around them.

"This is the shadow realm," Arrow told them unnecessarily. Five pairs of eyes turned to her, curious and attentive. She could not remember being the subject of such polite and close attention before and had to clear her throat to loosen her voice before going on. "Things do not work the same here. We can move much more quickly and each step will carry us further. Second sight is not reliable. And wounds here will translate to the first world." She paused, trying to think what else was important. "And you use more energy here than in the first world."

"And we cannot go through solid objects," Undurat added. "Can we harm beings in the first world?" His eyes were on a nearby shadow in the first world that Arrow thought was Xeveran.

"Unlikely," Kallish put in, "or the rogue would have killed us all without showing himself."

"You can touch solid objects. But not damage them. I have ... tried to damage solid objects from the shadows," Arrow admitted, heat rising across her face as the warriors turned their attention to her. "I do not recommend it." She could still feel the echo of recoil through her arm from trying to punch a wall. "The first world objects seem impenetrable from the shadows."

"But things in the shadows can be harmed, yes?" Kallish was watching her surroundings, the shapes of Erith in the first world and the slightly darker shapes that were the room's furniture.

Arrow nodded once in reply. Kallish thought a moment more before tilting her head back to Arrow.

"Head for Noverian's rooms. We should be able to slip past the guard."

"Without opening a door?" Arrow asked, sceptical.

"The guards go in and out," Kallish explained patiently, "and will not be looking for something in this realm."

"Alright." Arrow took a step forward, pausing when she realised that all five warriors were still touching her. "I do not think you need to hold on to me here. Just for entering and leaving."

"No?" Kallish's eyes gleamed and she took a few steps away, lifting higher from the ground than normal. "This will take a little adjustment."

"Perhaps outside, where there is more room?"

The warriors agreed and they slipped through the building's door with little fuss, heading to one of the many garden spaces that were scattered between Palace buildings. Once there, the warriors went through a series of drills that had Arrow's heart thudding, throat tight with nerves as they ran, jumped, wrestled and went through weapons drills with bare steel, all at a much faster pace than she was used to seeing. One of Undurat's jumps took him level with the upper storey windows of one of the buildings in the first world and so, of course, all the warriors had to try and go higher.

Arrow stayed on the ground, testing her sight instead. The lines of power of second sight were there but made little sense to her eyes. Perhaps with more practice she could make sense of them. At least she could see the shapes of things in the first world, and avoid walking into walls. Or bumping against people. She wondered what it would feel like, in the first world, to encounter someone in the shadow world, or if anyone in the first world would realise they were being watched. Kallish would help her experiment, she was quite sure, and also quite sure that this was not the time or place.

The jump competition seemed to be over, Undurat the absolute champion.

"Which way, *svegraen*?" Arrow asked. Kallish pointed out a direction and the group fell in together.

Arrow found herself surrounded by the warriors as they walked, struggling a little to keep up with their pace and glad that, for the first time in what seemed an age, her ribs were not cracked, broken or bruised.

They arrived at the building with the Queen's rooms and went around to another entrance, passing numerous shadows that were Erith in the first world. Whatever wards were in place in the first world did not appear in the shadows.

Unlike the doors to the Queen's private chambers, this set of doors were open, in Erith tradition, and they went up a wide flight of stairs to a set of double doors with a pair of Erith outside. Arrow was getting better at interpreting the glimpses of the first world from this realm and thought that the pair were White Guard.

"Now we wait," Kallish said as quietly as possible.

It did not seem long before the doors opened, a new pair of Erith emerging. The doors were left open while the new and old pairs stood together. Doubtless exchanging information, Arrow thought, as Kallish grabbed her shoulder and moved her forward through the open doors, the other warriors following.

Arrow noted that Kallish seemed familiar with the layout of Noverian's rooms as the warrior guided her through a series of large chambers, all with their doors open, until they came to another, closed door.

"Noverian's chamber. We may find information here." Kallish's voice was a bare sound.

After checking that there were no Erith in the first world, Undurat opened the door and the group filed in. The room was empty.

"We need to explore in the first world," Kallish said, lifting a brow at Arrow.

"Yes. Of course." Arrow held out her arm and five hands took hold of her again. She found a fissure, with a little effort, and spoke the word for opening, stepping through.

Coming back into the first world was a heavy drag, the weight of the hands trying to pull her back into the shadows, but she set her jaw and took the few, necessary steps to come out of the shadows.

Once out, all the warriors with her, her knees gave out and she collapsed onto a handmade, priceless floor covering.

"You are bleeding," Kallish noted, kneeling in front of her.

"I am?" Arrow touched under her nose, following Kallish's gaze, and found she was indeed bleeding.

She glanced up and found that the warriors were standing still, breathing heavily as though from a long, hard run.

"The shadow world requires a great deal of energy, it seems," Kallish observed. "Good thing you suggested we bring some food."

Arrow pulled a plain cloth from her bag and blotted her nose while the warriors rummaged in the small packs each of them carried, which she had not noticed before, producing enough food for them all, and, for Arrow, a small flask of mint tea while they shared a larger flask of Erith tea.

Arrow stayed on the ground until her legs felt less hollow and shaky, then rose, looking around for the first time, shivering lightly as she considered just where they were and what might happen if they were discovered.

Noverian's bedchamber was twice as large and even more opulent than Seggerat's, decorated in shades of blue from the deep midnight of the ceiling above to the pale froth of the cushions on a large chaise by the window. A window which looked out onto the Queen's favourite garden. By Arrow's estimation, the entire third could have lain side by side on the bed without touching. It was a room fit for a King, and she wondered, briefly, what the Queen's chamber was like.

"Are we on the floor above the Queen's chambers?" Arrow asked, trying to remember how many stairs they had climbed.

"Yes. There is a set of stairs down to her chambers from the corner, there," Kallish nodded. "Heavily warded, keyed only to a few people." Arrow's face must have betrayed her surprise at the warrior's knowledge as Kallish's mouth tilted in a smile. "A great many years ago, I was a junior cadet assigned to Miach. Before he had his own cadre."

"He must have been in the Queen's service a long time," Arrow said unguardedly.

"Yes."

"No one has been in here for a while," Undurat commented, catching Arrow's attention. He was right. The air in the room smelled slightly stale, and there was a fine film of dust on the low dresser against one wall. Dust that would never have been permitted in the Taellaneth.

"So, Noverian is not here," Kallish concluded, "and has not been for some time. A week?"

"Longer," Undurat concluded, "judging by the dust."

"How long is it since he was seen in public?" Arrow asked.

"Miach said ten days."

"That would fit," Undurat agreed.

"And his guards have been concealing his absence." Kallish's face and voice were grim. Arrow swallowed, looking around the room. She could not think of a good reason why warriors sworn to protect the Consort would have hidden his absence.

"Mercat," she said suddenly.

"What?"

"The farmer who died was growing mercat. With enough mercat, a skilled magician might be able to stop the guards from realising that Noverian is missing."

"Really?" Kallish's disbelief was clear.

"It would require a whole field of the stuff," Undurat added. "The warriors who guard the Consort and Queen are not chosen lightly."

"I know." Arrow shook her head, unable to explain why she was so certain. She turned her attention back to the room. "Nothing has been disturbed. He either went willingly, or was taken elsewhere."

"We need to go through the rest of the rooms." Kallish turned to the door.

"How? The guards are there. Do we want them to find us?"

Kallish's face took on an irritated expression more suited to Orlis than a senior warrior.

"We cannot see into the first world from the shadows?" One of Kallish's third asked, the most junior, Arrow thought.

"I could try making an opening," Arrow speculated aloud, then nearly choked on inappropriate laughter, imagining the six of them going from room to room, peering through a slit from the shadow realm like children behind a curtain. From the twitch of Kallish's mouth she had caught the humour in the situation as well.

"The guards should patrol the other rooms regularly. All the doors were open," Kallish noted.

"Let me look around here for a moment," Arrow suggested, not quite ready to leave.

"Do you see something?"

"I am not sure." Arrow dropped into second sight, the effort a tiny one compared to entering and leaving the shadow realm, and looked around the room again. "Battle wards!"

Erith amber rose around them immediately, the third on alert and closing around her.

"What?"

"There is a spell trap here. We are lucky not to have triggered it." Arrow was still in the second world.

"In Noverian's chamber?" Kallish hissed.

"Yes. It is over the dresser." The dusty dresser, sitting innocuously in the first world, tempting any casual passer-by to investigate the anomaly of dust in the Palace.

"Dangerous?"

"It will eliminate this floor of the building, I believe."

"Battle magic."

"Yes."

"Can you unravel it?"

"Yes. But it will take energy."

"We have more food, and some potions from Orlis." Kallish's voice, even in the second world, was dry. If Arrow had not known the warrior she would have missed the humour. Even faced with a spell trap, the warriors around her held firm and thought clearly.

"Please keep watch."

"Mage."

Arrow dropped her awareness of the first world entirely, examining the spell trap more closely. The knot of magic was not by any magician she knew, but it was clean magic, purely Erith in origin, and far less masterful than the spells prepared by the rogue she had defeated in the Taellaneth. She thought it might be the same magic user who had used mage fire to bring the bookcase down on Teresea. The same one who had killed Seggerat, and other Erith before. The thought of him so close to the Consort and Queen, and going where he pleased in the Palace, twisted her insides.

It still took some time to unravel the spell, the various strands of magic falling away to leave the second world safe again.

She came back to the first world to find that the third had not moved, battle wards still shimmering in the air, all the warriors alert.

"It is done." She took a step towards the dresser, wobbled, and was held up by one of the warrior's hands under her arm. "I think," she said, and had to pause for a breath, words jumbled, "this may be the same as before."

"The same magic user who killed Teresea?" Kallish seemed to catch her meaning, jaw tight. Arrow jerked her chin once and wished she had not, lightheaded for a moment.

"Is it safe to open?" Undurat asked.

"Yes." Her face warmed as she leant into the hand supporting her, waiting for her knees to function again.

At some unseen signal, a pair of warriors went forward and opened the dresser. It was a huge piece of furniture, appearing small only next to the size of the room, with a solid wooden top and a series of carved wooden doors and drawers along the front. The warriors quickly and thoroughly searched all the drawers and cupboards, coming back to Kallish with a small fabric pouch that smelled vaguely familiar.

"Some kind of herb?" Kallish sniffed at the open end of the pouch, nose wrinkling.

"Mercat," Arrow told her. She lifted a shoulder when Kallish turned to stare at her, and straightened away from the warrior who had been propping her up with a murmured thanks. "The Academy requires its students to be able to identify herbs and plants that we may use."

"Mercat again." Kallish's fingers tightened around the pouch for a moment before she handed it back to the warrior who had found it. He returned it to its hiding place, at the back corner of one of the drawers. "Setting a spell trap to protect mercat seems ..." The warrior waved a hand, searching for the right word.

"Overkill," Arrow agreed. It was a human term that did not adapt particularly well to Erith, but Kallish accepted it.

A soft sound from the other side of the closed door had them all looking around, the warriors going completely still with the sort of attention Arrow had seen from the shifkin more than once. She kept herself as motionless as possible, hoping her breathing was not too loud.

Kallish signalled and Undurat crept across to the door on completely silent feet, an impressive achievement for so large a person. He listened intently for a few moments, then came back.

"Patrol," he said as quietly as he could.

"We should leave." Kallish's voice was equally quiet and she turned an expectant look to Arrow.

Finding the entrance to the shadow realm was easier, because she had not closed the opening behind her. Five hands descended on her and she stepped through into shadows, feeling a dragging exhaustion, stumbling a little when they were through.

"We will return to the annex. Go to Evellan and Seivella tomorrow," Kallish ordered.

"Give me a potion. We should go now. The longer we leave it ..." Arrow did not finish the sentence but by the expressions around her, she did not need to. One of the warriors handed her a vial that bore the unmistakable trace of Orlis' healing magic and she swallowed the dose in one gulp.

"The dungeons are this way."

The dungeons were too well guarded, with barred doors, to permit the warriors through, even in the shadow realm. They returned reluctantly to the annex, where Kester was professionally reviewing his weapons, an impressive array of them laid out on the dining table, and Orlis was pacing the length of the building, his hair even more tangled than before. Orlis whirled on them as soon as they reappeared, demanding answers.

Pleading genuine tiredness, and wanting some quiet, Arrow left Kallish and the others to tell Orlis and Kester what they had found. The presence of two warriors in her room almost made her turn back. She had forgotten Kallish's edict. She lay down, intending to feign sleep for a while so she could think, only to wake hours later to find the warriors still on alert, and a tray, piled high with food, balanced on a stool near the door.

Not surprised to find she was hungry after the walk in shadows, Arrow finished the food, then took the tray through to the dining room, wondering who else was awake.

Kester was settled at the table, still, with only a few weapons left in front of him. He rose as she came in and she stopped in confusion, wondering if she had interrupted some warrior ritual. One of the warriors from the junior third approached her and took the tray away.

"Wine?" Kester gestured to a small tray at the end of the table which held an opaque glass bottle, a pitcher of what she assumed was water and several glasses. There was a glass on the table near his chair, half-full of deep red liquid that she could not smell over the weapons oil.

"I do not think I have had wine before." Arrow's brow creased as she tried to remember.

"Another time, then. Water?"

"Thank you."

She settled on the other side of the table, her back to the door, slight itch between her shoulder blades even with the obvious presence of so many warriors, and watched as he poured a glass of water and placed it near her, before going back to his place and continuing his weapons maintenance. He was using some kind of oil on a slender, lethal looking dagger. The scent was so familiar that Arrow found her shoulders relaxing.

"Is Orlis asleep?"

"Finally, yes." Kester's mouth tightened. "He was beginning to slur his words. Kallish thought she might have to knock him out."

"Difficult to do to a trained mage," Arrow observed, sipping the water. The last remnants of sleep were fading, and a new bit of information was calling for attention in her mind. While she had been sleeping, the book that Evellan had left for her, the only written information that the Erith had about shadow-walkers, had opened itself. She could usually keep it hidden when she was awake but it had found its way into her dreams more than once.

"Kallish knows the guards who will be at the dungeons tomorrow. They might give her access."

Kester's words faded as the bit of knowledge roared to the forefront of her mind. Arrow froze, glass held part way to her mouth, eyes flaring silver as the pages of the book fluttered inside, turning her stomach and the food that had been settled so happily moments before. She hated that book, even as she valued the information.

"Arrow?"

Kester's voice brought her back to the here and now. She had the impression it was not the first time he had called her name.

"Yes?"

"Are you alright? You were not yourself for a moment."

"Evellan's damned book," she told him, too annoyed to be polite, and took a hasty gulp from her glass. The bright cold of the water calmed her temper a little. Kester had been with her when she had found the book, so he needed no more than that to understand her.

"More new lessons?"

"It chooses the worst times." She scrubbed her face with her hands and rested her forehead on her palms, elbows on the table.

"What is it this time?"

"A way into the dungeons. I think." She closed her eyes and reviewed the information again. A way to use magic in the shadow realm, to open locks, and cast a quick glamour to hide the opening of the door. It should work.

"Not alone." The tone was flat, determined. It mirrored the tone that Kallish used often, drawing a smile from Arrow as she lowered her hands, coming back to the here and now.

"It uses a lot of energy to take people with me," she began her objection.

"I will come with you." He was looking directly at her, eyes flecked with amber. She took a breath in, surprise and discomfort warring for attention, and found her lungs full of cardamom and weapons oil. The familiarity of the scents distracted her. At least she told herself that was the reason she agreed. The fury he had shown in the workspace was gone, as if it had never happened, replaced by something she did not yet understand, something that she wanted to understand and run away from at the same time.

She ducked away from the difficult tangle running through her and instead checked her pockets quickly and found that she had a few pieces of chalk, and a vial of Orlis' healing potion. It would need to do. If they delayed, Kallish would demand they wait until morning and try her method.

Kester had all his weapons stowed again and was standing next to her when she looked up, his face unreadable, hair bound back in warrior's braids.

Arrow held out her arm and to her surprise and further discomfort, he took her hand. There was nothing personal in the touch, it was a simple handclasp, but the sensation of roughened, warm skin against hers threw her off balance for a moment before she could focus again and remember what it was she was supposed to be doing.

The fissure from earlier was clear in her sight and she took Kester through much more easily than the five warriors from earlier.

CHAPTER SEVENTEEN

— • —

A lthough it was deep into the night, the shadow realm was still bright to her eyes, all colours and all seasons present at once. Kester had instinctively let her go when they stepped through, hands going to weapons hilts as he turned in a slow circle, making sure they were alone, then leading them out of the annex into the night.

"Do you know the way to the dungeons?" Arrow thought to ask, feeling foolish for the question as soon as she voiced it.

"This way." He indicated with one hand, other hand staying on a weapon hilt, and walked with her, testing his balance and strides as Arrow repeated the information she had given the warriors earlier. There was no time for jumping this time, though she could not help wondering whether Kester could match Undurat's leaps.

This late into the night there were few people around, so they made their way easily around the Palace buildings to a heavy door that was solid and real in the shadow realm, and somewhere Arrow was sure she had never been before. And would not be able to find again in daylight, in the first world. She was thoroughly lost.

"Through here, then there are stairs down and a metal door at the bottom, and another metal door further in which leads to the dungeons themselves. There are guards at each one," Kester told her. She must have shown surprise for he smiled a little. "All White Guard spend some time at the Palace, and we all have to take turns guarding the dungeons. Even when they are empty, which they often are."

"Even the Queen's own guard?" Arrow asked, curious.

"The more junior of them, yes. I do not think Miach has guarded the dungeons in my lifetime."

"This is a new spell," Arrow warned him, approaching the heavy door, "and you will need to stay close to me in order for the glamour to hide us."

"Very well."

He was close enough that she caught another scent under the weapons oil and cardamom. Citrus sharp and sweet. Distracted, she took another breath before opening her second sight and her mind to the book. The spell was waiting for her when she looked and moments later the door lock clicked open, a wave of shadow surrounding them as Arrow opened the door and they slipped inside.

Even in the shadow realm, the steps inside were worn from centuries of use, the first damaged things that Arrow had seen in the entire Palace, and she was careful where she put her feet as they descended, the shapes of four Erith in the first world ahead of them.

The spell modified itself, which made her grit her teeth before sketching the necessary runes in the air, rather than speaking the spell, so that the glamour came first, then the door unlocked and they slipped through again, with no disturbance in the first world, the guards continuing their vigil.

The final door was as easy as the first and they were through, walking down a short, low-ceilinged corridor that opened out to a larger space, reflections of containment wards shining amber and green and crimson in the shadows. There were three other people present in the first world, all behind the containment wards.

"We are in the dungeons. There are no guards here overnight," Kester told her.

Arrow made another opening and stepped through into the first world, Kester holding her shoulder this time.

She had to blink several times when she was back in the first world, thinking she was blind but then realising that it was simply dark, the only light provided by faint glimmerlights at the entrance to the corridor. The air was cold, scented with earth, stone and water.

She and Kester were standing on a rough stone floor in a large, low-ceilinged space which had been divided by metal bars to create cages. There were small niches set into the earth at the back of each cell to afford the prisoners limited privacy, but otherwise the entire room was open to view from the central space.

"Arrow! Kester!" The voice, low and astonished, came from the cell to her right. She turned, saw nothing, and muttered a curse against her impure Erith heritage that left her senses so dull, then a quick spell to enhance her sight.

Evellan was more dishevelled than she had ever seen him, dressed in plain, dark clothing, hair tangled, his ever-present shadows coiling restlessly. He also looked ill, his face hollow, lines around his mouth and dark circles under his eyes, his body slightly hunched over as he came towards them.

"Lord Evellan." She took a step towards his cell, pausing when she realised that there was someone in the cell beside his, lying on a low bench in the niche at the back.

"Took you long enough to find us." Seivella rose to her feet and came forward, standing beside Evellan, each about a pace inside their respective cages. The wards on the cages stirred, amber rising, reacting to the proximity, but remained passive. Arrow wondered how long it had taken the pair to work out how close they could get to the bars without alerting the guards.

"You have only been here a day." Kester's voice was cool, perhaps resenting the criticism.

"Have you found Gilean yet?" Evellan asked, voice urgent.

"No."

"There has been rather a lot going on," Kester added, voice still chilly.

"Why? What has happened that was more important than finding Gilean?" Evellan snapped. Kester took a step forward and the wards on the cage brightened, reacting to his presence.

"Lady Teresea and Seggerat are dead," Arrow said plainly.

The exclamations of surprise were loud enough that Arrow thought the guards would hear. Evidently, Seivella and Evellan realised that, too, quietening their voices. After a quick look into second sight, Arrow realised that a confusion spell would not work here as there were counter measures woven into the wards on the cages.

So she told them as quietly and quickly as she could about the events in the Palace and at the farm, Kester adding a comment now and then. Evellan was experienced enough in receiving bad news that he remained silent, Seivella biting her lip, hard, in several places to hold in an exclamation.

Before they could begin to ask any of the dozen or so questions brewing, she held up a hand, palm out, cutting them off.

"And now I think you should tell us why you are here, and still contained."

"The second part is easy to answer." Seivella held out her wrist, showing a thick silver cuff with runes carved on it. Evellan raised his hand, showing a similar bracelet. "They have suppressed our magic."

Arrow spared a glance at the devices. Old, strong magic had been crafted into the silver bearing the familiar traces of the Palace ward keepers. "And why are you here?"

"Ask the White Guard. They brought us." Seivella folded her arms across her middle, scowling. "In the middle of the night without any courtesy."

"Orders from the Queen," Evellan put in. Anger brightened his eyes, mouth a thin line.

"Not from the Queen," Kester contradicted. "Miach is sure of it."

"And Miach knows everything, does he?" Evellan spat back. Not just angry, Arrow realised, he was furious.

"The Queen is aware there is something going on," she said. "But I do not think she is talking to anyone." She had mentioned the mercat in her summary.

"That sounds like her." Seivella's voice was coated with bitterness. "Always plotting and planning and the rest of us have to scramble to keep up. And she is ruthless."

"Whoever is behind the deaths is trying to eliminate everyone they think can stop them. Teresea. Seggerat. Arrow." Kester was giving Seivella a hard stare.

"Me?" Arrow's voice squeaked.

"Your abilities are known," Evellan's voice softened, "among certain circles."

"You have been gossipping about me?" Arrow was not sure how she felt about that. Angry. Embarrassed. And also curious as to why the elite among the Erith would find her, an exile, worthy of discussion. Her curiosity was quickly answered, Evellan tilting his chin towards her.

"There has not been a single shadow-walker for centuries. Very few Erith alive remember the last one."

"No-one knows what you can do," Seivella said bluntly, "and they are worried."

"The Erith have always been worried about me," Arrow answered back, eyes shimmering silver, reflecting her temper. "It is why they had me collared and oath-bound for years."

Evellan's colour rose, eyes dropping, unable to hold her stare. Seivella glared back, cheeks flushed but defiant.

"And why are the Erith so interested in me now? I am exiled."

Evellan lifted a brow, wry twist pulling his mouth, and she had to concede he had a point. She might be exiled, but she was standing in the Erith heartland.

"We might not fully understand what you can do, but we know your abilities are special." Seivella's voice was unexpectedly gentle.

"The Erith are keeping track of me so they can use me in future," Arrow concluded, hugging her arms around her middle. She straightened her spine, power rising so her eyes flared silver. "I am not going to be used again."

"We do not have time for this now." Seivella's voice had hardened again, a tone Arrow was familiar with.

"I suppose we should get you out," Kester put in. He sounded reluctant. Arrow had been so intent on the Preceptor and his deputy that she had almost forgotten him. She glanced across and saw the set line of his jaw, amber flare in his eyes.

"That would be helpful," Seivella agreed.

"Unwise. Our captors put us here for a reason, and they may be working for the Queen," Evellan objected.

"You are half-dead, old man," Seivella snapped at him.

"The Queen did not put you here," Arrow disagreed, opening her sight again to examine the cages. She wrinkled her nose. "The wards and spells on these cages are strong. It will take time to unravel them."

"They are guarded against a magical attack," Seivella told her, irritated. "Not that we could form a magical attack with these things on." She shook her wrist.

"Well, perhaps picking the lock would work." Kester stepped forward, wary of the flare of amber. He hesitated a moment, then put his hand to his chest, where the White Guard wore their medallions, and spoke a word. The amber wards died at once. A White Guard password, Arrow realised, curiosity prickling, watching as he reached into an inside pocket and produced a small leather wrap which opened to reveal a set of finely-crafted metal tools that were completely unfamiliar to her.

"Lock-picks?" Seivella's voice had lost its harsh edge. "When did the White Guard adopt breaking-in as an acceptable battle tactic?"

"We use whatever means required," Kester answered absently, most of his attention on the lock of Evellan's cage.

The lock gave with a quiet click and the door swung open.

As Evellan stepped out, a flicker of movement at the edge of her sight caught Arrow's attention. She turned in time to see one of the shadows in the room moving, forming into a too-familiar, dark-clad shape. Her wards flared in response to her alarm as she faced her attacker, battle wards blazing in the first world.

The attacker cut through her wards with the same ease as before, aiming a bladed weapon at her. She darted to one side, stumbling on an uneven patch of floor, catching herself against the bars of a nearby cage, the prison's wards flaring in alarm.

The magical alarm was joined a moment later by the sound of steel on steel as Kester knocked the attacker's weapon aside with his own blade.

"Get behind me," he snapped to Arrow.

"He has a null cloak," she told him as she scrambled to move out of his way, stepping behind him. The armoured coat she was wearing, hampering her movements, would provide some defence, but she had nothing to combat the clothing the attacker wore.

"You were warned to leave." The attacker spat the words, voice low, then lunged forwards, blade extended. Kester slapped it aside. Safe for a moment, Arrow opened her senses, trying to see the attacker properly. The clothing he wore, however it was made, made him blurred in second sight, distorting her senses as it reminded her of the shadow realm, all colours blended together to a bland darkness in the first world.

The clothing disguised his outline as well as his presence to her senses, but the cloth could be torn, she knew, from the tiny scrap she had found in the library. Arrow stayed behind Kester as the pair circled, waiting for a chance.

He lunged past Kester again, blade deflected by a White Guard weapon, and Arrow seized her chance, stepping forward and grabbing a handful of what she thought might be a sleeve. He swore, words she had rarely heard, and pulled back. Between them, the cloth tore with a sharp rending, Arrow left holding half of a sleeve, the attacker's forearm and hand exposed. Ghost white Erith skin, with a vicious looking scar across the back of one hand. He growled something that might have been a curse, drew another knife from somewhere and lunged forward again. The flat of Kester's blade slapped against his wrist and his hand opened, blade clattering to the floor.

"Let me out!" Seivella called from her cell.

The attacker darted one way, Kester following, only for the attacker to immediately go the other way. Arrow opened her mouth to cry a warning, realising that it was not needed as Kester's second blade blocked the attacker's move.

Behind the attacker, the short corridor to the dungeon's entrance brightened.

"Guards on their way," she warned Kester.

"Naturally." He did not sound out of breath, feet sure and quick as he stayed between the attacker and Arrow. "Can you make an opening? Evellan, get back in your cell for the moment, Arrow and I will hide."

To Arrow's surprise, the Preceptor did as he was asked, even pulling the door shut behind him. Arrow followed the movement and saw Kester's lock-picks on the ground in front of the cell door. She ducked down, picked them up, and opened her sight to find the fissure that she had created to get them here.

The heavy sounds of footsteps on the stairs signalled the arrival of the White Guard. The attacker made a low, furious sound worthy of a shifkin.

"This is not over yet, *Arwmverishan*." Definitely Erith. No other race could produce such venom with one word. There was absolute conviction in those words, a promise that sent a tremor through Arrow before the anonymous Erith darted away from Kester, heading for the corridor and escape, and Kester let him go, turning back towards Arrow.

"Now."

"Here." Arrow grabbed his wrist, as he was still holding weapons, and pulled him into the fissure with her, not a moment too soon as the dungeon area was abruptly flooded with White Guard, armed and alert.

From the shadow realm, Arrow could not clearly make out what was happening but the newcomers took a long time to go around the cells, checking there was no one else there. They must have seen the dark-clothed attacker but did not pursue him, staying in the dungeon.

In the shadows, Arrow stood next to Kester by the back wall of the dungeon, trying to keep her breathing calm and even. He seemed to have realised that they could not talk, putting away his weapons and lockpicks before standing still, a White Guard on watch, observing the shapes in the first world. The only sign he had been in a battle the slightly stronger scent of cardamom twinned with a stronger hint of the citrus she had smelled earlier. A combination that should not have worked, teasing Arrow's nose.

The overlay of cardamom, which had long been a favourite of hers, mingled with the memory of the attacker's words in a bittersweet tangle. Yet another Erith wanted her dead. It was no surprise. And it still stung. After the quiet acceptance of Miach and the Queen's guard, the warmth the Queen had displayed, and the discovery, which she still found hard to believe, that there were mixed-race Erith living in the heartlands, the reminder of how despised she truly was had stung more than usual. Her eyes prickled. Stupid eyes. She blinked, clearing them. It was not the time or place for silly emotion. Back in the workspace the shifkin had provided, warded and alone, she could be emotional as much as she liked, or so she told herself.

After what seemed a very long time, the shapes in the first world disappeared back along the corridor. Evellan and Seivella were each at the back of their cells, keeping still.

"There are three people in the cells," Arrow remembered, seeing the third tucked away at the back of one of the cells opposite Evellan and Seivella. None of the guards appeared to have gone near the other prisoner, although they had gone into Evellan and Seivella's cells.

"We should check," he agreed, "once we are back."

"Of course." She opened the fissure again. He put his hand on her shoulder and they stepped through, Arrow's body heavier as she came back to the first world again.

"I think you saved our lives," Evellan said by way of a greeting. "None of the guards seemed surprised to see the attacker."

"He just ran past them." Seivella's voice was bitter again. "Get us out of here. Now."

"I will." Kester picked the locks quickly, with no interruptions this time.

While he was working on that, Arrow turned her attention to the other prisoner. Even with her sight enhanced, she could barely make out a bundle of cloth that might have been a person at the very back of the last cell next to the wall.

"What are you looking at?" Seivella was beside her, free of her cage. "Here," she held out her wrist with the cuff, "get this off."

"That will take time," Arrow replied absently, the better part of her attention on the person in the other cell.

"There is nothing there," Seivella snapped, temper fraying.

"Can you open the door?" Arrow asked Kester. He was frowning slightly, too, staring at the same spot as Arrow had been.

"It does not look as though there is anything there," he objected.

"Arrow, we do not have time. There is nothing there. Let us go." Evellan's voice was impatient.

"In a moment," she promised, opening her second sight and drawing in a sharp breath. No wonder they could not see anything and all wanted to leave. There was a powerful keep-away spell set around the other prisoner, and if Arrow had not already seen through it in the shadow world, she did not think she would have noticed the extra spell work amongst all the wards in the dungeons.

"*Svegraen*," Arrow spoke to Kester, silver brightening her own eyes, adding a touch of power to her voice, just enough to call his attention, "will you open this door for me?"

"Of course, mage."

Kester opened the door, clearly still puzzled by why she wanted into an unoccupied cell. She called a little more power and sent a spark of light into the cell ahead of her, just enough to prove, to her own eyes at least, that there was someone in there.

As she walked forward a fizz of magic against her skin told her she had stepped through the threshold of the concealment spell, the trace of magic tantalisingly familiar. The same magic user who had created the slender blade of mage fire that had killed Teresea.

With the breaking of the concealment came sounds of disbelief behind her.

"There was someone there all along?" Evellan sounded disturbed. "How did we not see that?"

"Concealment spell," Arrow told him briefly, over her shoulder, all her attention on the figure lying on the bench. A male, she thought, lying on his side with his back towards her. Alive, as his body was shifting slightly as his ribcage moved, faint rasp of breathing carrying to her over the soft sounds of her own footfalls.

"He may be dangerous," Kester said just by her ear.

She jumped, letting out an undignified squeak of surprise. She had not heard him move.

Perhaps woken by Arrow's cry, the prisoner stirred. He tensed, then slowly turned onto his back, then sat up, feet moving to the floor, movements careful.

An elderly Erith male, his now-tangled and filthy hair pure white, pale eyes carrying the faintest trace of amber, he stared up at them with no recognition in his face, not making any further move.

"Noverian," Kester hissed, astonished.

"Who is that?" the Erith male asked, eyes staring straight ahead. Not pale eyes, Arrow realised, but blind eyes. She had never heard that the Consort was blind, but trusted Kester to know him.

"Kester," he answered, "with Arrow, Evellan and Seivella."

"Arrow? Oh, yes." The male's head tilted. "Alisemea's child. How do you do, child?"

"Well enough, my lord," Arrow answered. In the midst of the shock of finding the Consort here, her mind tried to remember what the proper address was for the Consort and failed to provide an answer. She hoped she had been polite enough.

"We should go." Seivella hissed from a short distance behind them.

"Yes," Kester agreed, going forward to Noverian. "Can you stand? Walk?"

"I am ... not sure. They have not fed me for days."

"And injured you before then." Kester's voice was grim and Arrow realised that the Consort's clothing might be dark now, but had not all started off that way. His sleeves were mismatched, one paler than the other. Kester got Noverian's uninjured arm across his shoulders and lifted the Consort to his feet, an involuntary noise from Noverian betraying how badly he was hurt. Seen upright, the Consort was a middle-height Erith male, once broad shouldered, now dangerously thin.

"We need to go back the way we came." Arrow's legs were heavy as she followed Kester and the Consort out of the cell. She looked at the four other people she needed to take with her through the shadows and realised she did not have the energy. A quick search of her pockets and she found a healing potion, hesitating a moment before swallowing it herself.

"That would have helped Noverian," Seivella hissed at her, "or Evellan. What were you thinking?"

"Travelling the shadow realm takes a lot of energy," Kester answered unexpectedly, "particularly with more people. Are you ready?" This last was directed at Arrow. She pulled the cell door closed behind them, and after a moment's thought, put a spark of her own power into the concealment spell, reviving it.

She moved towards the centre of the dungeon and stepped on something metal that clattered, unnaturally loudly, against the floor. The attacker's knife. Its blade glistened oddly to her sight.

"The guards are coming back," Kester said urgently.

"Go. Take Noverian and go," Evellan urged, "he is more important."

"But-"

"Go," Seivella agreed grimly, moving forward with Evellan to stand shoulder to shoulder, facing the corridor. Their cell doors were still open, the knife at their feet.

"We will come back for you as soon as we can," Arrow promised. Kester grabbed her shoulder, put Noverian's limp hand on her arm, and she opened the fissure, dragging them through with an effort that made her gasp.

Safe in the shadows, she closed the fissure and glanced back to find four guards surrounding Evellan and Seivella. It looked like the Academy masters were being attacked. She made a low noise in her throat, stepping forward, held back by Kester's grip on her shoulder.

"Noverian first. They are both tougher than they look." His voice was the lowest whisper he could manage.

Arrow knew he was right, but had to force herself to stay still while one of the masters, Seivella she thought, was beaten to the ground, landing next to a small mass of tangled spellwork that she thought might be the knife. One of the guards picked up the knife. There was a short discussion, evident by the positioning of the guards' bodies, before Evellan and Seivella were gathered up and put back in their cells. Two guards remained. Two left, heading up the stairs.

Kester nudged Arrow forward, eyes intent on the departing guards. A useful diversion, Arrow realised, as they would be opening the doors anyway. She made herself move forward.

They made it out of the dungeons with less fuss than they had entered, travelling back to the annex as swiftly as possible, arriving back in the first world to find every one of Kallish's cadre on high alert, Orlis with battle magic to his hands, cries of discovery and alarm following their arrival as Arrow collapsed onto the floor, Noverian only remaining half-upright with Kester's help.

———*ell*———

Amid the babble of questions that followed their arrival, Noverian was settled on the chaise which Arrow had recently used, and the entire junior third were sent to the kitchens.

Arrow lay on the floor for a few moments, letting the fuss happen above her, watching as Orlis changed seamlessly from battle magic to healing magic, kneeling by the Consort, face reflecting his concern.

"Are you alright?" Kallish asked.

Arrow blinked, looking up at the cadre leader. She judged that if she said she was alright, there would be an almighty lecture. If she said she was not alright, there would still be the lecture. She sat up carefully, head spinning slightly, and nodded once.

"At least you took Kester with you," Kallish said, startling Arrow into looking up again. The warrior's mouth twitched in a tiny smile. "And are not injured. This time."

"This time," Arrow agreed, getting to her feet, and promptly making her way over to the dining table, settling on a chair. Her whole body was weak, legs trembling. "I do not think I will be going into the shadows again for a while." She rested her head on her hands, elbows on the table, hoping that the world would settle down and stop spinning.

"Perhaps this is the after effect of two doses of poison?" Kallish asked. Her voice was politely enquiring, the bite in the words only evident from the glint in her eyes when Arrow glanced up.

After that quick glance, Arrow stayed silent. The warriors settled to guarding the room, a pair at each entrance, and two more behind Noverian.

"He has been badly beaten," Orlis said, sitting back on his heels. He was chalk-white, whatever benefit he might have had from sleep washed away, blue-tinged circles under his eyes. "And malnourished. Some broth, if there is any available."

"Where did you find him?" Kallish wanted to know.

"In the dungeons. Behind a concealment spell." Kester's voice was grim. "He said he had not been fed for days."

"He can hear you." Noverian's voice was thready. Arrow lifted her head in surprise. She had thought he would be asleep under Orlis' healing magic.

"Highness." Kallish took a step towards him and made a low bow.

Noverian managed to sit up and open his eyes. He looked worse in the better light of the annex, Arrow noted, with the clear trace of old bruises across his face, crusted blood on one sleeve. He was breathing too fast, still, chest rising and falling under filthy clothing. Clothing that had once been as fine as any courtier would wear.

"How is Frey?" he asked, staring ahead with his sightless eyes.

"She seems well," Kester answered.

"Seems?"

"She attended the reception for Seggerat the other night and spent some time talking with various courtiers and paid tribute to Seggerat. Beyond that she has not been seen in public for some time." Kester's tone was matter of fact, a warrior delivering a report.

"Seggerat is dead? How?"

"Murdered." Arrow matched Kester's matter of fact tone, ignoring the startled gasp from a few of the warriors, watching Noverian's face. She had a notion that the Erith Consort was tougher than they were giving him credit for. He had been at the centre of Court politics as long as the Queen, after all. Her guess was proved as he closed his eyes, murmuring a quiet blessing, then opened his eyes again, expression determined.

"Who?"

"We are trying to find out. Among other things." Arrow felt her shoulders slump. Gilean's disappearance. Teresea's death. The mysterious attacker with his null clothing. Seggerat's death from a previously used spell. She sat back in her chair and became aware of the weight of one pocket. The null clothing, that she had managed to tear off.

She pulled the sleeve out into the light. In the first world it was bland, easily overlooked. There was a pale shirtsleeve underneath.

"You took that from the attacker?" Kallish crossed to her with quick strides. "Did you see him?"

"Very little. A hand and forearm. Pale skin. And a scar across the back of his hand." Arrow demonstrated on her own hand. "The right hand. His clothing was finely made." After a lifetime among the Erith, who valued appearance, she had noticed the quality of his clothing as automatically as she checked her own wards.

"How many Erith are scarred?" Kester asked. It was not an idle question, Arrow knew. Erith healed quickly and well, and even if they did not, Erith healers could cure almost anything without leaving a trace. Any Erith who bore scars might do so by choice, or because they had been gravely injured far from care. Or because they had been damaged by magic. She straightened in her chair at that thought.

"It could have been a burn from mage fire."

"That narrows the possibilities." Kallish looked grim. "I have sent for Miach. He will know candidates."

"Miach? Here?" Kester objected.

"Not my guards?" Noverian asked, puzzled frown crossing his brow. Orlis had come back to his side with a shallow bowl of broth. Somehow the Consort maintained his dignity, half-lying on a chaise being fed broth like an invalid.

"Your guards did not notice your absence," Kallish answered. Noverian paused in drinking the broth, then nodded once, accepting Kallish's judgement.

CHAPTER EIGHTEEN

The wards of the building flared, bringing Arrow to her feet and weapons out into the hands of every warrior. Moments later the front door shook with a series of heavy knocks.

Without waiting for orders, Xeveran and his third went to the door, Kallish's third closing around Noverian, the final third staying back, spread out in the room, every warrior on high alert.

Arrow murmured the spell for mage fire, calling crackling silver power to her hands and found Kester nearby, blades ready.

After the briefest look outside, Xeveran sheathed his sword, waved his third to one side, and opened the door, standing silhouetted against the early morning light, vulnerable to whoever was outside.

"About time. What in hells is going on?" Elias stamped through the door, not waiting for an invitation. He was alone, dressed for combat, a longbow slung across his body, quiver of arrows at his shoulder. "Those on watch are talking nonsense and I cannot ..." His words died as he glanced into the dining room. He swallowed whatever he had been about to say and made a bow. "Highness, we have been concerned about you."

"What is happening?" Noverian asked, worry in his voice.

"The Palace watch will not let me through. The doors are shut." Elias' tone was grim. The leader of the Queen's second cadre had been banned from the building. Arrow's fingers twitched even as she drew the mage fire back into herself. But Elias was not done yet. "The dungeon guard are claiming that Evellan and Seivella tried to escape to assassinate the Queen. Something about a poisoned knife. Why are they here? Why are they locked up?"

"That is not good," Kallish commented.

Arrow took a step forward, drawing Elias' attention.

"Have you just returned from the farm?"

"Yes. It took an age to go through everything and then there was nothing of interest there." The warrior sounded thoroughly disgusted. "I sent the others to rest while I reported to Miach. Or tried to. No one would answer a straight question. What has happened?"

"Seggerat was murdered," Arrow began. Elias made an impatient noise.

"I know that. The cunning fox would never allow himself to die in his sleep. What else?"

"Evellan and Seivella were summoned in the Queen's name, then taken to the dungeons when they got here. Again in the Queen's name."

"The lady would not order that," Elias said definitely, with no hesitation.

"Well, they seem to believe it is possible." Arrow's voice held a snap she heard too late.

"You have spoken with them?"

"Yes."

"How did you get past the guards?" Elias asked, curious.

"Another time." Arrow waved the question aside. "We were attacked in the dungeons. The attacker dropped a knife and fled past the guards. We found the Consort in a cell in the dungeon."

Elias had moved to stand inside the room as she spoke, mouth half-open, face reflecting his shock.

"The lord was in the dungeon?" His voice was high with disbelief.

"Yes." Noverian stirred, sitting up straighter. "It was most uncomfortable. Elias, where is Frey?"

"I do not know. I could not get through the Palace." Elias' astonishment was replaced by concern.

"We need to find her." Noverian tried to get up, held back by Orlis' hand on his shoulder.

"My lord, you need to rest," the journeyman said firmly.

"Let us go. Elias, can you get your cadre?" Kallish asked.

"In moments," he confirmed.

"Do so. Quickly." Kallish turned her back on him, taking his compliance for granted, and hesitated for a heartbeat before issuing orders to her own cadre. Xeveran's third and the junior third would remain with Noverian and Orlis in the annex, on high alert. She and her third would go with Arrow and Kester, and Elias' cadre, to the Palace to see what was going on.

"I can call another cadre," Elias offered.

Kallish considered the offer a moment.

"No," Arrow said, surprising everyone, including herself. Instinct had made her speak, her mind catching up a moment later with the reasons. "The Consort's guards did not notice he was missing and the dungeon guards let the attacker past, then accused Evellan and Seivella of plotting murder."

"Agreed."

Arrangements made, Kallish led her group to the front door and out into the morning, tensing a moment as she spied a cadre of White Guard coming towards the building at a full sprint.

"Elias' cadre," she told Arrow as she relaxed, then shot a hard look at Arrow.

"I know. Stay within your guard. I am getting very tired of people trying to kill me." Arrow sighed and checked that her coat was fastened, wishing she had time to get some more supplies from her bag. She had a few bits of chalk in her pockets but nothing else. Even as she thought that a gentle pulse of magic at her back reminded her of the sword she carried. As they walked towards the Palace buildings, she wondered when she had grown so used to the sword's presence that she no longer noticed it moment-to-moment. Wondered, too, if a sword made to cut through spirit could harm an attacker cloaked in null cloth.

Elias had been telling the truth. The Palace doors were shut, a third of White Guard barring the way, visibly tense as they saw a full cadre and another third approaching.

"The Palace is in lockdown," the third's leader said. Not high enough ranked to stand against either Elias or Kallish on any other day, Arrow saw, the braids on his sleeves barely enough to lead the third. She gave him credit for following orders, though.

Kallish opened her mouth to argue and Arrow remembered that she carried one more item that might be of use. She opened her coat, to Kallish's protest, and dug out the parchment that the Preceptor had written for her, holding it open in front of her like a weapon.

"I have orders to pursue enquiries and you are impeding my investigation. Stand aside."

To her surprise, it worked. The warrior's face paled as he read the brief lines scrawled across the parchment and he swiftly stepped aside, drawing his third with him.

With the doors closed behind them, Elias took the lead, heading for the main part of the Palace.

"The Queen's rooms are the other way," Kallish pointed out.

"The lady is this way," Elias countered, and kept walking.

The Palace was unsettled, the wards restless, making Arrow twitch in response, her wards shimmering for a moment before she reasserted control. The Palace itself was not a threat. But something was. The power that the Palace ward keepers had so carefully crafted and built into the building's fabric over centuries contained battle magic that was waking in response to a perceived threat. Ancient defences, including finely-crafted constructs of battle magic, hovered at the edges of Arrow's second sight, ready to be deployed.

"The Palace is awake," she told her companions.

"Too early for most courtiers," Elias objected.

"The Palace, not its inhabitants," she clarified, looking about as they walked. Elias shot a glance at her over his shoulder, brows lowered in a frown.

"The Palace defences have not woken for centuries."

"They are awake now. There is a threat somewhere."

"They only respond to threats against the monarch." Elias quickened his pace as he spoke, his cadre moving with him as one. Arrow stretched her legs to keep up, hoping that they did not start running.

They rounded a corner and a familiar set of stairs rose over their heads, leading to the open, and unguarded, doors to the Receiving Room where Seggerat's reception had been held. Elias took the stairs three at a time with his cadre. Undurat simply put an arm around Arrow's waist and carried her up with the rest of the warriors, setting her down at the top. She thought for a moment that she should be embarrassed, or perhaps annoyed, at being carried, but it meant that she was not out of breath and had arrived at the same time as the others.

The Receiving Room was much larger than Arrow remembered, no longer crowded with finely dressed Erith. There was a tight knot of Erith at the far end, around the raised dais, Miach and his entire cadre gathered close around the Queen and her ladies. In the middle of the room was a third of warriors, two Erith kneeling before them. Evellan and Seivella. A slender object lay on the floor between the kneeling magicians and the dais. The knife. To Arrow's surprise there were also several courtiers scattered about the room, perhaps those who had not been to bed yet and were curious as to what was happening.

"Majesty, they were trying to escape." The guard's tone was not one Arrow thought many people used when talking to their monarch, carrying exasperation.

"Who was?"

The Queen's voice, a little slurred, had Arrow whipping her head back from her casual inspection of the room, cursing her inferior eyesight. The lady might be apparently awake, settled on a throne-like chair, but that voice had not belonged to the keen mind that Arrow had met before. From the tension in Miach and his cadre, and the slight intakes of breath Arrow could hear around her, it had taken others by surprise as well.

Only the lady herself seemed oblivious, blinking slowly as she looked around the room, not focusing on anything in particular.

Elias brought their group to a halt a short distance behind the guards, too far for Arrow's eyes but clearly not for the Erith. She checked an impulse to move further forward even as Kallish moved slightly, the warrior shifting her weight towards Arrow, making it clear they were to stay where they were. There must be some protocol in play, Arrow realised.

"Majesty." The guard's tone was perilously close to a snap, a tone no Erith should take with their monarch. Miach took one measured pace forward and even at the distance, Arrow could see the amber in his eyes. The guard ducked his head, heat rising up his neck, visible between his collar and carefully braided hair.

"Explain the situation, please." Miach was drawing attention away from the Queen, Arrow thought, as the Queen's ladies fluttered around her, bright coloured gowns oddly fitting for the room but jarring against the bound prisoners. One of the ladies offered the Queen a glass of what looked like tea.

"The mages Evellan and Seivella were under watch," the guard began, checking as Miach subtly moved his weight forward, amber still prominent in his eyes. He cleared his throat and improved his tone to something approaching a subordinate reporting to his superior before continuing. "By order of Her Majesty, waiting for further orders. There was a disturbance in the night and when we went to investigate we found the mages out of their cells and a poisoned knife on the ground."

"The mages were still cuffed when you found them?" Miach asked.

"Yes, *svegraen*."

"And the cell wards were intact?"

"Yes, *svegraen*."

"Then how did the mages get out of the cells? And where did the knife come from? Surely they were searched when they were put into the cells?" The icy tone reminded Arrow forcibly of Seggerat, carrying the same weight of authority and expectation of response.

"I cannot explain it," the guard sounded like he was speaking through gritted teeth, "but the knife was there and the mages were out of their cells."

"Did I order them imprisoned?" The Queen's voice was still blurred. She was resting against the back of her chair, head slightly to one side as though it were too heavy for her neck. She was holding the glass of tea, untouched, in front of her.

"Our orders came from you, majesty." The guard made a sorry attempt at a bow, so evidently lacking respect that several warriors around Arrow tensed again and Miach's jaw twitched.

Arrow did not have much attention to spare for the warriors, eyes keen on the Erith's monarch as she, finally, seemed to remember that she held a drink. Second sight did not reveal any unclean magic around the Queen. There was next to no magic around her, in fact. The slightest shade of a personal defensive ward, and nothing more. Arrow frowned, focusing her sight further. The Queen was a powerful mage in her own right, and her personal wards should be blazing in second sight, like the haze around Miach.

She came back to the first world at the slight, unchecked murmur of sound that rippled around the room.

The Queen had finished her tea and was transformed by it. She sat up perfectly straight, spots of high colour rising in her face. Fury or embarrassment. Arrow could not tell from this distance.

"What is the meaning of this?" she hissed. Anger, then. On the dais, Arrow saw the lady who had handed the drink to the Queen start, eyes widening in surprise. A few other ladies also twitched. Arrow took careful note of the one who did not.

"Majesty?" The guard did not bow, drawing a sharp, amber-flecked glare from his Queen.

"Why are Evellan and Seivella here, and in such a condition?"

"You ordered their imprisonment, majesty. They were plotting to kill you."

"Ridiculous. I did no such thing, and nor did they," she contradicted flatly. "Release them at once."

"Majesty," the guard began his protest.

"At once, I said. Miach." The Queen merely tilted her head to him and he stepped off the dais, striding forward with purpose, the rest of his cadre staying in place.

With the Queen's first guard coming towards him, face set, the guard decided to comply, rapidly moving to take the cuffs from Evellan and Seivella. Neither magician rose to their feet, the way they were huddled close to the ground making Arrow think they were both badly injured. They were also still surrounded by the guards from the dungeons, Miach pausing in his forward momentum as the magicians were released.

Elias finally moved forward, his cadre fanning out around him until they surrounded the dungeon guards and the magicians. As they moved, Miach made a hand gesture to one of his cadre, who slipped out the back of the room. Going for healers, Arrow would guess.

"Elias, what brings you here?" the Queen asked, voice sharp.

"The Palace is awake, my lady," he told her.

Like Elias earlier, the Queen did not understand, issuing a short laugh with no humour in it. "Nonsense. None of the layabouts will be up this early." She frowned, then, taking in the handful of courtiers around the room, eyes lingering on the faces turned towards her.

Miach had understood, though, and stepped back to the Queen's side, battle wards rising from his cadre at his command. The Queen shot an irritated glare at the head of her guard.

"I have been woken up with fantastical stories of assassination plots, and now battle magic in my Hall. What is going on, Miach?"

"Nothing good, my lady. We should get you to safety."

"This is my home, Miach. All of it."

"My lady." He turned to her and made a low speech, mostly too quiet for Arrow's blunt hearing to catch, apart from a few words here and there, including Gilean. When he was done, the Queen sat back in her chair, chin lifted, holding his eyes. Judging him.

"Let Gilean speak for himself," she answered, voice carrying.

"Gilean is not here, majesty," Miach said quietly.

"Nonsense." The Queen spoke with the same certainty as she had refuted the charge that she had ordered Evellan and Seivella imprisoned. Arrow's attention sharpened, wondering if the Queen had seen Gilean more recently than anyone else. Or what the Queen might know. From the way she was looking around the room, it seemed possible that the Queen believed that Gilean was in the room. Arrow sucked in a breath, finally thinking to use her second sight on the rest of the room. A few of the Erith inside were wearing camouflage spells, thick enough that she could not trace their true shape. One of them might be Gilean. Or he might not be here at all.

After some further conversation on the dais, the Queen rose, steady and sure, and came down the dais steps, moving towards Evellan and Seivella with single-minded purpose, her ladies and warriors around her.

"Do you mean me harm, old friends?" she asked bluntly.

"No, majesty." They answered in chorus, voices both weaker than Arrow had ever heard them.

"See that they are taken to their usual rooms and tended by healers." The Queen's orders were directed to Elias, who bowed at once, acknowledging the command. Miach's face was grim, snagging Arrow's attention away from the

Queen. Perhaps the Queen's first guard had believed in the plot, perhaps he did not think that Evellan and Seivella, so recently implicated in a critical threat to all Erith, should be allowed to roam free or, perhaps, with the Palace waking in response to a threat against the monarch, Miach simply did not want to lose any of his resources, Elias' cadre as valuable as Miach's own. Whatever the reason, Miach did not contradict his lady.

Evellan and Seivella were taken into the care of Elias' cadre and left the room far less violently than they had entered, Arrow was sure. The Queen was staring at the dungeon guard, eyes partly unfocused, the same unfocused look that mages had when staring into the second world, but when she spoke it was apparently unrelated.

"Arrow, have you made progress?"

"Very little, your majesty."

The Queen's gaze, now sharp, fell on Arrow's face, mouth tightening in displeasure.

"There is too much mystery here," she said, eyes flickering with amber. Not as strongly as they should, Arrow thought, dismayed. Whatever had been in the tea had revived the Erith's monarch, but not enough. She was still ill under the stimulant, the pallor of her skin imperfectly disguised by cosmetics, even this early in the day, and despite her inferior eyesight, Arrow could see fine lines fanning out around the Queen's eyes and mouth that Arrow did not think had been there before.

"Majesty." Arrow took a step forward and made a small bow, Erith Court gesture familiar to all around her. "You have given me a task. Will you trust me to see to it? It is early still and there is a long day ahead."

"Work fast," the Queen commanded and swept from the room in the midst of her ladies and guards. The last Arrow could hear was a sharp-toned comment, directed at Miach. "Stop hovering like an old woman. I can manage perfectly well."

Even with the audience around them, Arrow could not help the frown that gathered on her brow. The wards of the Palace shifted, visible even in first sight. There was something very wrong, the Palace's magic sensing a growing threat, not a lessening one. She turned to her companions to find similarly grim expressions on their faces and was glad that Noverian and Orlis were safely within the annex.

"We should go," she murmured, seeing the interested gazes from the courtiers around the room.

Kallish agreed with a sharp jerk of her chin and the group closed in, ready to move.

The courtiers were leaving the room, too, the air filled with quiet whispering as they talked about what they had just seen, more than one casting a quick, apprehensive glance back to the empty dais. The Queen had been monarch for a long time, even as Erith measured time. Everyone knew that her reign would come to an end at some point, but Erith were long-lived and she had seemed, until now, healthy in public.

"The lady is not well," Kallish murmured in Arrow's ear as they left the room.

Arrow did not answer, attention caught by one of the courtiers who had moved a little way along the corridor, on his own, and now turned back, tipping his head at Arrow in a familiar gesture, flare of amber in his eyes too strong for a simple courtier. Without thinking, Arrow set off down the corridor, her companions close around her.

"What?" Kester asked, voice tense.

"I think that may be Gilean," she told him, mentally reviewing her defences and checking her coat was fastened. "Or a trap," she added.

Kallish made a noise that sounded suspiciously like a choked laugh.

Before Arrow had time to glare at the warrior, they had arrived at a turn in the corridor. The courtier was standing around the corner, in a seeming dead end to the corridor, with a large painting hanging on the wall behind him. The painting was a pastoral scene with cows in the foreground. Cows.

"Red spotted cows," Arrow said, anger flaring. "Curse it, Gilean, what is going on?"

"You are not very respectful of your elders," the courtier answered, camouflage spell sliding away to reveal Gilean, hollow-cheeked, hair lank around his head.

"I find very few of my elders deserving of respect," she snapped back, temper still high.

"Indeed." The mage's voice was full of laughter. He gestured to one of the walls. "Shall we?"

"Indeed." She clenched her jaw and followed him as he drew a quick spell on the wall's surface, lifting the camouflage spell on it to reveal a plain wooden door bristling with wards. The wards peeled back at his touch, allowing them through.

The room inside was windowless but not airless, low-ceilinged enough that Undurat's head nearly brushed the bare plaster, lit with a few glimmerlights that brightened as Gilean entered.

A mage's workroom, Arrow saw, with a simple cot bed in one corner and a long workbench covered in bits of parchment, chalk, a burner, pots for stirring spells, a scattering of herbs and all manner of other items that she knew were used in spell making.

"You have been busy, mage," Kallish commented, eyes taking in everything around her, including the fact that there was only one door. Undurat moved at Kallish's gesture to stand with his back to the door.

Gilean laughed, a bitter sound that Arrow thought could easily have come from her own mouth.

"Not busy enough. The Queen is still dying, and Noverian is missing."

"Dying?" Kester picked up the word.

"Yes." Gilean sighed, body slumping against the workbench. He lifted a hand to move a pot out of the way of his elbow, fingers trembling.

"Do we have tea, *svegraen*, and perhaps some food?" Arrow asked. She recognised the signs of over-use of magic and not enough food. In disguise and probably wary of discovery, Gilean had been burning through his resources.

Kallish shot Arrow a hard look, but her cadre provided a flask of tea and a few paper-wrapped packets of food for the war mage. Gilean took the supplies gratefully, biting into the food, finishing it all in quick bites, the hollows of his face filling out as he ate.

"The Queen is dying," Kester prompted once the food was gone.

"Yes." Gilean closed his eyes a moment, and they were full of amber and the unashamed sheen of tears when he opened them again. "Someone is managing to poison her."

"She is protected," Kallish objected.

"Even so. She is being poisoned."

"We saw," Arrow said softly, remembering the hazy confusion the Queen had shown before her tea was provided, the fine lines on her face. "I thought she was taking mercat," she added and saw Gilean's face tighten. "You knew."

"I recommended it. Small doses, just enough to help with ... well, none of us are getting younger." He was furious as well as grieving, Arrow saw.

"What poison?" Arrow asked, glancing at the scattered items on the workbench.

"I do not know. I have been trying to find out."

"What works badly with mercat?" Arrow asked, a long-ago lesson from the Potions Master calling for her attention.

"Not much." Gilean dragged a hand through his tangled hair. "I have tried them all. None of them fit."

"What if she was taking far more mercat than is good for her. And something else, something very simple," Arrow suggested, mind working in quick spirals.

"She would not take more," Gilean objected.

Kallish made a rude sound, expressing her disbelief, drawing a scowl from the war mage. The warrior was unimpressed.

"Noverian's guards were high on the stuff, and influenced not to notice he was missing. And the dungeon guard were influenced by something. There is far more mercat about than you realise, mage."

"Was missing?" Gilean caught those words.

"We have him," Arrow confirmed.

"That is good to hear." The mild words were a cover. Gilean slumped back against the bench again, tension fading from his body as he scrubbed his hands across his face, rubbing away dampness.

Arrow's anger spiked irrationally. He seemed to believe the worst was over. The shifting tension in the Palace around them, which she could sense as an uneasy drift against her skin, told her otherwise. They could not afford to relax.

"You were attacked in your rooms. Orlis is worried." She watched his face tighten, tension returning to his shoulders.

"Could not be helped." Gilean's voice was tight and he would not meet her eyes. "Some damned Erith got right through my wards. I barely got away."

"And then hid," Kallish pointed out.

"Operational prudence," the war mage spat back.

"We have encountered this attacker." Arrow drew Gilean's attention away from the scowling warrior. "He keeps trying to kill me."

"Shadow-walker. Yes. He would." Gilean's mouth twisted in what might have been a smile.

"Explain." Silver flared in the small room, Arrow's wards reacting to her temper. She was in no mind to be patient.

"You need to work things out for yourself, young thing," he countered, amber-pointed gaze steady on her face.

"I have been beaten up, nearly died in Seggerat's rooms, stabbed with a poisoned blade and attacked without provocation. And no one is willing to answer even the simplest question. I am losing patience." The silver in Arrow's eyes grew.

"Good. Take that temper and use it," Gilean recommended, a genuine smile on his face. He shoved limp hair back from his face. "There are plenty of secrets to discover."

"I am sick of secrets. And deception."

"Your feelings are irrelevant," Gilean answered.

Arrow's wards shivered in the gloom. Her feelings had been irrelevant for most of her life, constrained by the Erith's demands then the oath spells. She was no longer a puppet. She opened her mouth to make a hasty reply, then checked. A war mage she hardly knew was being rude. Deliberately so. He had found a weak spot and was pressing, hard. Trying to make her lose her temper. Trying to make her back away.

"So what are you hiding?" She murmured, half to herself, and saw the truth of that in Gilean's response. His head snapped back as though struck, and his eyes dropped from hers.

"Find out for yourself."

"We could ask." Kallish's offer was unexpected. She was staring at Gilean with narrowed eyes, considering.

"He is weak," Undurat agreed calmly from his post by the door.

"I am still a war mage," Gilean hissed.

"Barely." Arrow sniffed, catching the game. She folded her arms, a deliberate provocation as it told Gilean she did not see him as a threat, unable to use her hands for spell casting.

"Barely a challenge," Kester added, moving oh-so-casually to stand just behind Gilean's shoulder, within easy reach. They were cousins, Arrow remembered. A long-lived race like the Erith had many complicated family ties, and she thought that Gilean and Kester were far more distantly related than Kester had been to Teresea. Still, they were distant family. Gilean shot a sour look at his cousin but his wards stayed dormant.

The mage glared at Arrow.

"Find out for yourself."

"I am, mage. I am asking you." She caught his eyes with hers, silver brilliant in the darkened room.

"The Queen is dying," he said at length, words slow and reluctant.

"You said that already," Kallish pointed out, drawing a short, wicked looking blade from somewhere about her person and beginning to play with it, tossing it in the air and catching it, blade reflecting the silver of Arrow's magic.

"No," Arrow shook her head, "not now. Before. You mean the Queen was dying before. She was already dying. And Noverian knew," Arrow added, sucking in a much-needed breath, the Consort's odd persistence in asking after the Queen making sense.

"Of course he did." Gilean's voice was a growl. "They have been inseparable since they met."

"Poison or natural?"

"Impossible to tell."

"So that is why you came to see Evellan."

"None of the Queen's ladies seemed worried."

"Well, one of them was not surprised this morning," Arrow countered, brain busy. She had only the faintest idea how Erith monarchs were chosen. There was no line of succession, and the monarchs were notoriously reluctant to nominate heirs or successors while they were alive for fear of a coup attempt.

"There has been no Challenge," Kester noted, "so clearly the Court does not suspect."

"After this morning, they will." Gilean was bitter, and grieving. One of the Queen's favourites, Arrow knew.

"And there is no heir named," Kallish added, sheathing her knife.

"Quite. It will be chaos." Kester took a step away from Gilean, looking like he wanted to pace but not having room to do so.

"But the Queen and Consort both knew," Arrow pressed, "so they have had time to make plans. Perhaps not name an heir, but do something."

"They have," Gilean confirmed, shrugging, "but they have not confided their plans to me."

"To anyone else?"

"Teresea or Seggerat would be the most obvious candidates," Kallish put in. "The lady had a clear way of seeing, and Seggerat was one of the few Taellan with no ambition for the throne."

"Or Eimille vel Falsen."

"True," Kester agreed with Arrow, "but they are not close. Eimille carries out her duties, but prefers to spend time within her House."

"We need to speak with Noverian," Arrow concluded. "Gilean, you will come with us."

"Will I?" His brow lifted, humour lighting his face.

"There is a faceless killer who can break through wards running about the Palace. Yes, you will come with us. If I could figure out that you were in the hall, others will, too."

Gilean heaved a sigh worthy of a fifth cycle student asked to repeat his rune work, but he pulled his disguise around him again, gathered a few items from about the room, and they left, sealing the room behind them.

CHAPTER NINETEEN

— • —

The day was still young, Arrow realised, as they made their way through the Palace. Early enough that very few people were about, so there were few witnesses to the odd grouping of warriors, mage and courtier as they headed for the annex.

They had reached one of the main corridors, walking at a steady pace used by White Guard and servants among the Erith which allowed them to travel quickly but not draw undue attention, everyone in the group silent and focused. With years of practice, Arrow kept pace with the others easily but Gilean was struggling, his breathing harsh and rapid with exertion. Arrow turned her head slightly to make sure his glamour was covering his exhaustion.

An unseen blow knocked her off her feet, flat onto the thick carpeting, a wave of magic reverberating through her, more powerful than anything she had ever felt. Battle magic. Wards. Ancient spells come to life. All in a maelstrom that swept onward. The thump of magic coursed through the building as a wave, rattling the doors, shaking the floors. In its wake alarms blared, deafening, and magical constructs asleep for centuries now crawled out of their hiding places, down the walls, tails lashing, hissing their fury. Before Arrow had time to raise her wards, a wash of the sweet, unmistakable scent of Erith death followed the wave of magic through the building. Not just any Erith.

"The Queen is dead."

She was not sure who spoke. Or how she had heard it, skull ringing with the alarms. A dissonant chorus of brass that set her teeth on edge. She managed to get her knees under her, limbs shaking with the aftermath and shock, and looked around.

Her companions were on their knees as well, expressions pinched with pain and grief, more than a few noses bleeding.

She drew a deep, harsh breath, heart sore as Erith death coated her lungs again. She would never get used to that scent. The Queen. Dead. All that clever scheming, the warmth that had led an elderly monarch to take time to speak to a young half-breed about her mother, the iron will that had held power for so long. Gone.

As she gathered herself to stand she was knocked flat again by a wordless shriek that cracked the air, sending amber lightning in great sheets throughout the corridor. The cry drilled through her skull. Eyes blurred. Chest ached. Lungs burned. Agony and fury and grief. Not hers. She clutched her hands to her ears in an effort to block out the noise but it continued, a great wave of anguish that seemed to never end. Pure amber. Bottomless. The heartland, she realised. The land itself was mourning in one unending wail of loss and fury.

She was shaking with the force of it. No. Not her. Everything. The ground was trembling. The delicately crafted ceiling above, a masterpiece of Erith craftsmanship, was shaking, great cracks appearing. The walls shook, paintings falling to the unsteady ground, tapestries following in piles of richly coloured fabric. Plaster came off the walls, the bricks of the building coming apart, clouds of dust rising.

Bright lines of spellwork shone through the dust and chaos, the Palace's ward spells trying to hold the building together and repair the damage even as the heartland tried to tear everything apart. The heartland, the source of the spells' power, was winning.

Arrow struggled to one knee, coughing as she breathed in dust. Her hands were shaking as she drew her *kri-syang*, spilling the necessary drops of blood onto the carpet, setting a connection to the heartland.

She was immediately blind. All senses gone for a few, terrible heartbeats. No sound. No taste. No sensation against her skin. The heartland was vast, her mind unable to comprehend just how big.

Then pain. Of course. Lungs burning with effort. Heart thudding. Skin crawling with fine rivers of prickling discomfort. Her whole body straining with effort to hold itself together and obey her will to hold the connection to the heartland.

Perhaps the most stupid thing she had ever done.

But.

There.

In the blankness. A listening. A feeling of attention directed to her.

"Stop." Arrow knew that was her voice as she hurt from the effort of forcing air through her lungs and making her lips move. But it was a bare whisper. "You will kill everyone. Destroy everything."

Somehow she was heard. The pressure eased and the next breath hurt less.

The pressure rose again, holding her down, the heartland's grief coursing through her with a burn hotter than mage fire. She screamed, no sound emerging, and huddled into herself, waiting for the end. Stupid. To try and communicate with the heartland.

She was blind, still, but breathing, still. Surprise had her straightening up. Limbs intact. Another surprise. The heartland's grief was still there, wearing a great hole in her chest. But it was listening.

"Someone did this." She felt her lips crack as she spoke. "I will find out who." The promise was for the heartland, ready to destroy everything as its monarch had died. It was for the elderly Erith who had been clever and kind and cunning and died too soon. And it was for herself. Sick of more death. Sick of Erith politics. She wanted a quiet life. The workspace. The shifkin's easy requests. The lure of travel to places she wanted to go to but had never seen before.

There was a pause, Arrow concentrating on breathing, then the pressure eased slightly and a gentle brush, carrying the scent of burnt amber, against her cheek. Offer accepted.

The blankness lifted, eyes watering as blinding light stabbed them. For a moment all she could see were shapes that made no sense, colours blurring together, ears assaulted with a cacophony of sound. Training asserted itself, a deep breath drawn in, the basic checks that every Erith would know. Wards. Breath. Sight. Sound.

The Palace had stopped falling apart. The ground was still. The walls holding, just, exposed bricks held together by spellwork, a sheen of amber coating the damaged areas. Ceiling plaster, centuries of dust normally hidden from view, lay in thick piles across the priceless carpets, daylight shining through new holes in the roof.

Around her, White Guard were gaining their feet, far more slowly than she had ever seen them move, faces pale and strained, a few with nosebleeds, hands less steady than normal as they checked their weapons. Kester was helping Gilean to kneel, the war mage looking too fragile in the chaos.

A low growl close enough that she could almost feel the warm breath on her face had her heart racing again. One of the Palace constructs was approaching the group. A great cat, beast made entirely of intricate spellwork that she would have admired in other circumstances. It walked on four giant paws, lengthy claws sliding out and retracting with every pace, leaving no tracks in the dust and chaos of the floor, brilliant, striped amber and black of its hide glinting in the morning light, blazing green eyes assessing its prey as it moved, white teeth bared in a low, menacing snarl, tufted tip of its long tail flicking from side to side.

Kallish faced it, putting her hand to her chest, where her medallion would sit, and speaking a word. The beast paused, shook its head, and gave another low growl before continuing. Kallish said another word. And another. And the beast kept stalking them.

"Someone has changed the passwords," Gilean breathed, his voice faint, a tremor clear to Arrow's ears. "This is not good."

In the distance more screaming started, accompanied by more snarls. Erith screams.

"Can you stop it?" Kallish asked, eyes flicking towards Arrow but otherwise not moving. The other warriors were also unnaturally still, attention all on the construct.

"I can try." Arrow managed to sit up, drawing the beast's attention. The second world was blinding with the complexity of the construct's spells, the spells holding the Palace together and the defences of the Palace alight and active. She set her jaw and focused on the construct. Beautifully crafted spellwork, a mastery she knew would take decades to achieve. And a clumsy bit of spellwork tied around the construct's legs, reminding her of a collar. A later addition that stood out. Not the Palace ward keepers' work. Too hasty, and far less refined. And unskilled. No master magician had done this, just an apprentice believing his own skills greater than they were.

It was a matter of moments to rip out the added spells.

"Try now," Arrow told Kallish.

Kallish repeated her password and the beast stopped, settling down, a low purr emerging from its constructed chest.

"Someone did change the password," Arrow said grimly, getting to her feet. "It was clumsy work, done singly."

"And on more than one," Kallish said, head tilted to hear better. Around the corner ahead of them were more screams of agony, shouts of pain and anger, the low, tense growl of a construct.

The warriors had their weapons ready and moved forward without the need for spoken commands, Arrow following, trusting Gilean to manage his own feet.

They rounded the corner into a scene of carnage. The air was saturated with the scent of Erith death, several bodies lying too still on the priceless Palace carpet amid more ceiling plaster and dust. Blood sprayed the walls and the damaged ceiling, high above, two constructs turning on anything that moved. The few Erith left alive were huddled together, trying to remain as still as possible.

"Mage," Kallish ordered. The warriors formed a kneeling wall in front of Arrow, weapons out. There was no time for her to consider the implications. She slid into second sight. The same clumsy spellwork had been used here.

Before she could act, the construct she had healed sprang over her head in an easy leap, landing on one of the altered creatures. Even in the second world her ears filled with the quiet, deadly snarls of two predators fighting.

With no time for finesse she ripped out the spells.

"Now," she told Kallish and came back to the first world to see all three constructs crouch down in front of the cadre leader, low purrs acknowledging the correct passwords. Two of the constructs were blood-spattered, the third unscathed.

The warriors rose to their feet, Arrow's mouth dry as she considered that, once again, they had put their lives between her and danger, expecting and trusting her to deal with the magical threat. It was how mages and warriors had worked together for years. But it was not something she was used to, feeling the weight of their trust heavy on her shoulders.

"We need to make a sweep," Kallish said, grim as she looked around the corridor, took in the damage that the two constructs had done.

"This is on the way to the library." Arrow recognised the corridor, some instinct prompting her to move that way. "We should check there first."

Kallish gave her a hard look but agreed, sending the constructs out ahead, the small group following. The wounded courtiers pled for aid as they passed.

"Get to the healers," Kallish told them, "you can all walk."

Arrow had never heard the cadre leader sound so bleak, and wondered if she, too, was fighting the pain of the Queen's death, the heavy scent of death seeping into every pore, coating her lungs, making it hard to walk forward.

They left the courtiers huddled in distress. Kallish had been right, though, none were gravely wounded.

The great doors of the library were torn open, a pair of altered constructs pacing in front of the door, tails lashing, baring their teeth as the group approached.

Arrow ripped the spells out in a heartbeat or two and the constructs joined their brethren, rubbing faces together, purrs rising in the quiet air.

Inside the library it seemed still and quiet, somewhat shadowed for morning.

Kallish gave a series of quiet commands to the constructs, Palace training clearly still fresh in her mind, and the five bounded away, spreading out through the library as the warriors followed. Gilean was just behind Arrow, wearing his own face, which sat oddly above the fine courtier's clothes. Perhaps he had no energy for the glamour, she wondered, seeing his face hollow again. His breath was still rapid.

"Stay by the door," Arrow suggested. His eyes flared a moment then he shook his head, irritated with himself.

"I am too weak," he agreed.

"*Svegraen*, is there more food for the mage?" Arrow asked. Kallish shot an irritated look over her shoulder, doubtless wondering if this was the right time for snacks. The warrior assessed Gilean's state and jerked her chin at one of her third. More food was provided, along with a small vial of healing potion.

The warriors pulled the damaged doors back together, blocking that exit, and left Gilean there to recover, the rest of them moving forward into the vast space. It was too dark. Arrow looked up at the domed ceiling and saw that someone had painted a new design. It looked like a child's painting, hasty brush lines in vivid paint colours, but it was in fact a series of runes.

"Stop."

The warriors halted at once, following the direction of her gaze.

"What is that?"

"An amplification spell."

"That is forbidden," Kester pointed out.

"I do not think this person cares," Kallish answered.

Arrow took note of the extent of the spell and began a careful circle around it on the floor, drawing a little of her own power with her. Amplification spells were not all forbidden, just those requiring a sacrifice. And this one required a sacrifice. She could trace the runes designed to draw power from whatever creature was to be used.

The spell work was oddly crude, like the alterations of the constructs. Perhaps because a paintbrush was harder to use than chalk, but Arrow did not think so. The spell crafter had definitely undertaken some training but had not completed their studies. Or perhaps they had been denied access to the Academy. Or were too old to have gone through the Academy's programme.

"Do you recognise the mage?" Kallish asked.

"No. Quite untrained. The work is primitive." She wrinkled her nose in distaste. So much ignorance. Paired with enough power to do serious harm. There was a reason the Erith had an Academy. "Not a graduate."

"Homeschooled." Gilean's voice made Arrow jump. He was looking better and was following them in their slow circle of the spell. Arrow glanced back to the door to find he had left it guarded with a fierce offensive ward that crackled in her second sight.

"Who?" Arrow asked.

"No one I know," he answered, tilting his head back to look at the spells again. "How did they get up there?"

"Levitation spells," Arrow answered dryly. They were in the library that until recently had held floating shelves.

Gilean made a noise, acknowledging her point, then blinked and looked around the room. "What happened here?"

"The Lady Teresea was killed. Over there." Kallish pointed.

"Someone used a very fine blade of mage fire to cut through one of the levitation spells and brought a bookshelf down on her. After they had hit her over the head," Arrow clarified.

"I am sorry," Gilean said softly, directing his words to Kester. The Taellan's face was grim, shadows under his eyes. There had been too much death, Arrow thought.

"The same person?" Kallish wanted to know.

"Definitely not. The mage fire was delicate. This is ... not."

They had nearly completed a complete circuit of the spell, a thread of Arrow's power following them, nearly invisible in the first world, Gilean and the warriors careful to stay outside the slender line.

The centre of the circle, on the floor, was a jumble of bookshelves and shadow. Arrow could not see into it and, from the others' frowns, they could not either. A magic shadow. It could conceal a cadre of White Guard, a rogue magician or two, or nothing at all. Arrow did not think it was nothing.

The deep pools of dark elsewhere in the room held no threats, rippling with movement as the constructs paced, tireless, in search of hidden prey.

"Is the magician here?" Kallish wondered as they reached their starting point.

Arrow shook her head for an answer, unable to tell, focusing instead on drawing the ends of her power together to complete a circuit that flared once in the first world.

"The spell is contained. We should investigate," she told them. She opened her second sight a fraction, overlaying onto first sight and, seeing no immediate threat in the circle, stepped over the line and into the influence of the amplification spell.

As soon as she stepped over the threshold she knew she had made a mistake. An all-too-familiar form rushed out of the shadows, knife raised. Dark cloth, bright knife blade. Soundless and quick. She thought she made a sound of alarm, tripping over something on the floor as she tried to move away from the attacker.

She hit the floor with a thump, hard edges biting into her leg and hip. Books. Pages skidded away under her feet as she scrambled to rise, one handed, calling mage fire to the other hand. Silver snapped around her as her wards rose, useless against the null.

Kester joined her, blades ready, as a third of White Guard piled onto the attacker, pinning him to the ground, tearing at the null clothing he wore until it was in shreds around him, useless, threads gathered by one of Kallish's cadre. Stripped of his disguise, the attacker was revealed to the uncertain light.

A tall Erith male, face unfamiliar to Arrow, wriggled under the warriors' hold, teeth bared as he spat a stream of curses at them. Older, somehow, than Arrow had expected, he had the same ghost white skin and pitch black hair as many within the Regersfel House.

Even as she thought that, one of the warriors made a low sound of discovery and named him. "Learvis nuin Regersfel. Sell sword."

Arrow's attention caught on the venom in the warrior's tone. Sell swords, those who would sell their services to whoever would pay, were rare among the Erith, most Erith staying loyal to their Houses.

"Regersfel?" Kester asked. "Well, that explains a few things."

"Does it?" Arrow asked.

"Why he might want you dead," Kester said, as though that should explain matters. Arrow felt a frown gather on her face. She was missing something. There was no time to ask about it now.

"Although it does not explain how a Regersfel got hold of null clothing," Kallish observed, straightening as her warriors tied up their captive so securely they had to help him to his feet.

At full height, he was a head taller than Arrow, deep blue eyes glaring at her with barely a fleck of amber in their depth.

"You should be dead," he told Arrow, voice low and vibrating with anger and disgust. "Abomination." He spat in her direction, her wards flaring at once. Freed of the null clothing, he could not harm her. Not physically at least. She tried to keep her face calm.

"I do not think it was your idea to kill me, though," she said, taking her cues from his clothing, which was fine, but old and worn, repaired rather than replaced. Adopted into the House, not part of the inner circle. A sell sword. Almost as embarrassing as she was. Not favoured.

"I was happy to do it," he replied, baring his teeth again.

"No doubt." Arrow ducked her head away from the hate in his gaze. There were more important things to focus on. She picked up one of the scraps of cloth. "This did not come from the House. Where did you get it?"

He gave a sharp, sarcastic bark of laughter. "Why should I tell you?"

"You will tell us," Kallish said, silky smooth.

Before she could go on, the silver containment circle flared.

"There is someone else in here." Arrow dropped the cloth and called mage fire again. The warriors dropped their captive back to the ground with no ceremony and Arrow could not help a sympathetic wince at the sound of pain he made, hitting the scattered books at full force.

Battle wards rose around the small group, Gilean coming to stand at Arrow's shoulder.

Across the other side of the circle a figure detached from the shadows and ran for the silver shimmer of the line, covered in a heavy cloak that disguised their shape. The figure hit the circle at a full run and Arrow hissed, going to her knees with the pressure of another magician's power against her own, the scrape of pain passing quickly as the other simply kept going, running for the edge of the library.

Arrow expected the warriors to give chase but she had forgotten about the constructs. Kallish had not, issuing a quick series of shouted commands that had the constructs converging on the running figure, bringing him to the ground, cloak ripped from him as he fell to reveal a familiar face.

"Queris vo Lianen," Kallish said, grim, and stalked out of the circle, careful to step over Arrow's power rather than through it on her way towards the prone lord. Undurat gathered their other prisoner, simply lifting him over the circle, dropping him on the floor beyond it and then dragging him by his collar across the polished wooden floor of the library, not caring if he bumped against furniture or fallen books on the way, the others following.

"What did you hope to gain?" Arrow asked, crouching between two of the constructs to get a better look at the lord. Far from the polished courtier she had seen before, he was in disarray, hair tangled, eyes red-rimmed as though from lack of sleep, or perhaps grief for the Queen's passing, his lips trembling slightly as he stared back at her. His personal wards were disrupted but she could easily trace the same clumsy hand that had drawn the spells on the library ceiling and tampered with the constructs.

"Take your power. Take the throne." His voice quivered, tongue darting out to lick his lips, pale amber growing in his eyes as he stared back at her. "Frey's mind was gone. No fit monarch. I was next. It should have been me. Unstoppable."

Arrow drew a breath and stood up so fast she was lightheaded for a moment, glancing back at the amplification spell drawn across the library's ceiling.

"Kill me in the circle. And draw my power." She was freezing inside her clothes. If the warriors had not been with her, he could have succeeded. She had nothing to combat the null clothing. No defence against physical confrontation. Unlike the oath-spells she had carried for so long, her cooperation was not required for this spell. Between them, Learvis and Queris could easily have held her down, sent her blood across the remnants of the library, drawing her power out.

She looked down at the Queen's cousin, the feverish glint in his eyes and wondered how he had hidden his ambition for so long. Even as she thought the question, she had her answer. This was the Palace. The Erith Court. Wearing a mask was second nature. Everyone did so. So, Queris vo Lianen had played the part of a dutiful cousin, eccentric but harmless, and studied forbidden magic in his spare time. Not very advanced studies, judging by the crudeness of his efforts, but effective. She wondered if he had practised on anyone else first, unwelcome memories rising up of the rogue magician Nuallan, who had perfected his bloody craft over decades. She did not think Queris was as ruthless as Nuallan, though, and was thankful for it. If Nuallan had been given access to a null, she would not have been able to stop him.

And still, there were pieces that did not make sense.

"If you wanted to bring me here and kill me," she turned to Learvis, "why did you warn me away the first time?"

"Interfering bitch." His eyes glittered with fury as he stared up at her from the ground.

"Warn her?" Queris tried to sit up, movement checked almost at once as the constructs growled. The lord had not lost his voice, though. "You said she escaped. You were supposed to bring her to me!"

Arrow tilted her head, considering Learvis. She remembered the tiny scrap of cloth, evidence that he had been there at Teresea's death. Had perhaps held the lady so that someone else could deliver the fatal blow.

"But you did not expect Lady Teresea to have a knife, did you?" she murmured, mostly to herself, and saw by the tightening of his face that she had guessed right.

"Stupid bitch," he said.

"You were there when she died. With her killer. So, who else are you working for, Learvis?"

His face paled to chalk, ghost-white, eyes widening in fear, and he shook his head, unwilling to even open his lips to refuse her question.

She gathered some power, reviewing the truth spells she knew, and did not get a chance to use any.

The library doors exploded inwards in a thump of magic that had all of them huddling down for a moment, wards not proof against the backlash of power and rain of splinters that soared through the vast room. Gilean made a small sound of pain, the protections he had woven on the door ripped apart by whoever was coming inside.

Miach and his cadre, faces pale and strained, marched inside and stopped short at once, staring at the spell crafted across the ceiling, the silver containment circle, then across to the group, at the constructs guarding the lord on the ground, the tied up Regersfel scion and Gilean vo Presien, wobbling slightly on his feet.

"I look forward to the explanation." Miach's voice was hoarse, grief and exhaustion warring. "But for now, we need your help, Arrow."

"Of course. What is required?"

"The Queen is dead." Miach had to pause, voice choking. "And Noverian is missing. We searched his chambers. We need your help to find him."

"Noverian is Regent until a new monarch is appointed," Kallish explained quietly.

"Do you have more guards available?" Arrow asked. Miach's eyes narrowed in suspicion but he nodded. "These two need guarding."

Miach lifted a brow and Kallish provided the briefest, barest, explanation Arrow had ever been privileged to hear. It said something for Miach's many years as the Queen's first guard that he accepted the blunt explanation with barely a blink, issuing a few terse orders to the junior third in his cadre which had them running out the door at a full sprint.

"There are bodies in the Palace. Many bodies." Miach's voice caught.

"Lord Lianen changed the constructs to respond to him," Arrow told him, moving a few paces towards him, concern growing. "Are there more constructs still attacking?"

"No." The warrior's shoulders slumped. "We managed to defeat the other two."

At cost, Arrow guessed, seeing the ripped uniforms and blood spattered across the cadre. Not the warriors' blood. More Erith had died, though. The scent of the Queen's death was strongest in the air, but far from alone.

"I see you found Gilean," Miach said.

"She did," Gilean confirmed. He was still pale, and too thin.

Nothing more was said for a moment.

"How did she die?" Kallish asked, coming to stand beside Arrow.

"Another glass of tea. She had a seizure." Miach closed his eyes briefly, a pair of tears sliding down his face through blood spatter. "Gone in a moment, before anyone could even send for the healer."

"Are her ladies under guard?" Arrow asked. She might not know the name, but she remembered the face of the one who had not looked surprised at the tea's effect on her Queen. Poisoned by one of those closest to her, despite her fabled sharp mind, the same mind eroded by mercat. No fit end for a monarch who had ruled her people with a ferocious intellect and abundance of personal charm.

"In the dungeons," Miach answered, tipping his head to her, a glint of approval in his eyes. "Elias is on watch with his cadre. Her rooms are under watch by the third cadre." Miach's face hardened as he looked down at Queris. "And this one has questions to answer."

"Not about the Queen, though," Arrow told him. Miach's brow lifted, face still tight, skin pale. Decades of service. Many times Arrow's life. The echo of the heartland's grief, muted but still present, shone in Miach's eyes as he stared at her.

She blinked, finding her own eyes hot. "He thought her mind had gone. Not that it was done to her." She glanced aside at the constructs, tamed under the White Guard's command and her throat tightened. "But he should answer for the deaths caused by tampering with the constructs' spells."

Miach's chin dipped, acknowledging. She thought of the dungeons and the questions that Miach, and other White Guard, would want answered. The Queen's cousin was about to discover just how privileged his life had been.

Running footsteps at the door drew their attention as the junior third returned, breathing hard, two more cadre of guard following in their wake, the new warriors pristine and alert compared to Miach and his cadre.

"Thornis, take these two prisoners in hand. Separately. And be careful with them. Gea, with me."

Orders given, the cadres moved to obey without question. Arrow wondered if they were usually so quick to follow Miach's commands, out of years of habit, or if everyone was still shocked by the Queen's death.

"Arrow?" Miach looked to her for direction.

"The annex." She did not look at him, heading for the door.

"He is in the annex?" Miach hissed in her ear, catching up with her.

"Not here," Arrow answered. "We need to get to the annex," she amended, glancing across at Gilean, "and regroup."

Miach made a low sound impressively close to a shifkin's growl of anger and stalked beside her, tense and angry, all the way to the annex.

Noverian was still on the chaise, looking healthier than he had been when they had left earlier, apart from the steady stream of tears down his face. Orlis was huddled on the ground beside the Consort, half-dozing, paler and more tangled than ever. He looked up the moment the group came through the door, eyes unerringly going to Gilean.

"So, you are alright, then," the journeyman said, and closed his eyes again, body relaxing.

"He is nearly done," Noverian said softly, brushing tears from his face, and sitting up fully.

"Highness." Miach, his cadre and the new cadre knelt as one.

Arrow found a spot at the edge of the room crowded with White Guard and slumped against the wall. No one had tried to kill her for a while, the attacker who could break through her wards was in custody, and she was surrounded by warriors. She thought it was safe to relax for a moment. Just a moment to catch her breath and steady herself.

A few moments was all she needed to realise that the talking would go on all night, and that none of it involved her. She straightened slightly, intending to slip out of the room, and found Kallish beside her.

"The spells in the library need taking down," Arrow murmured, as quietly as she could manage. They might be crudely drawn, but the forbidden magic cast across the library's ceiling could still be used.

"Very well. Xeveran." The one word was all that was needed to attach Xeveran and his third to her.

They made it out of the talking room and into the entrance to the building before Arrow's stomach rumbled, loudly enough that the warriors around her heard, lips twitching.

"We will need-"

"Food. We have supplies," Xeveran confirmed as he escorted her out of the building. He sounded more cheerful than Arrow had ever known him. He must have seen the surprise on her face. "Things happen around you, mage, and it has been a very trying afternoon staying still."

CHAPTER TWENTY

C leansing the library of the spells had taken far less time than putting them up, Arrow was sure, but it was still late into the night when she finished, the library as safe as she could make it. The work had been uneventful, much to Xeveran's obvious disappointment. He and his third had to content themselves with playing with the constructs still padding around the room. Arrow found herself distracted more than once by warriors throwing balls of ripped parchment for the constructs to chase. They were a rare sight, Xeveran told her, and many of the White Guard had only seen them in training. The cadre that had been assigned to guard the library had been entirely superseded by the constructs and it would take the Palace ward keepers themselves to put them back to rest. When the ward keepers had time. They were busy shoring up the Palace's structural spells, making hasty repairs to the building to keep it in more or less one piece until proper repairs could be made. No one was feeling any great sense of urgency, though, with the scent of death in every part of the building and outdoors, and the heartland's grief an ever-present ache.

Returning to the annex they found the main room still full of people talking, the tantalising scent of food curling out, overriding the scent of death. Dusty and tired, she did not want to step into a room full of high-ranking Erith, but Xeveran steered her that way.

Apart from Xeveran's third, who still looked a little battle worn, the other warriors had managed to somehow rejuvenate in the hours they had been away. Uniforms were crisp, faces unlined, eyes keen. Alert and ready for action. Gilean and Orlis were nowhere to be seen which meant, Arrow hoped, that they were resting. Noverian was seated at the head of the table, holding court with quiet grace, listening to the various pieces of information he was being given by the warriors.

The jarring note in the room, for Arrow, was Kester. Dressed as a lord again, in understated finery, he was standing near Noverian, listening to the update Miach was providing, face grave.

They glanced up as Arrow came across, and Miach held a chair for her, a few places down from Noverian and far higher than she had title to at any Erith table. She hesitated, but the growl of her stomach brought her to the offered place. Undurat had apparently been assigned to her care as he immediately brought her a plate of food and a tall beaker of what she hoped was plain water and not cooled Erith tea.

"The Palace is quiet, everyone in mourning," Undurat murmured, setting a plate in front of her. "The Taellan session is about to start."

Arrow paused, hand partway towards her mouth, and set the food down.

The Taellan did hold sessions mid-of-night when the occasion required, and if ever there was a need it was now. The Queen's death was a gaping hole in the Erith government, the uneasy balance shattered. The Palace might be in shock just now, but the Erith would be demanding answers soon. And guidance.

And yet.

Seggerat was dead. With that, Eshan lost his place as Chief Scribe. Between them they had held an iron grip on the Taellan and its proceedings for far longer than Arrow had been alive. Which left the question.

"Who called the session?"

"I do not know." The warrior straightened, brow creasing as he looked across at Kester. "*Svegraen?*"

Arrow watched as comprehension flickered across Kester's face.

"Unclear. The request was passed by Palace messengers. Miach?"

"The messengers did not know who called the meeting." Miach was frowning now, too, concerned.

"Another trap?" Kester's eyes gleamed. Arrow was certain that under the fine clothing there was body armour and an array of weapons. Still, the Taellan normally met in private, with no guards in the room.

"A meeting would be an ideal opportunity to strike," she said, getting up from her chair. Her knees shook a little, body heavy with the aftermath of using magic.

"Sit. Eat." Undurat put a hand on her shoulder, pressing her back down again, a casual gesture he would have used with any warrior under his care. She did not so much sit as fall back into the chair, face warming again.

"Miach has selected the cadre to guard the room," Kester told her, eyes meeting hers across the table, "and meetings are always warded."

Uncomfortable under the steady stare, which felt too intimate for the setting, Arrow dropped her gaze, staying silent as the warriors and Noverian completed arrangements over her head, starting to eat at Undurat's prompt.

She glanced up again as a third of White Guard left with Kester in their midst, an odd, dull pain in her chest along with a shimmer of apprehension. It felt wrong that he was going into almost certain danger, leaving her behind. That sense of wrongness bothered her. They had no claim on each other. None at all. And yet he had stood by her in danger many times. Perhaps that was why it felt wrong he was facing danger without her.

He glanced back at the doorway, a quick look she did not think anyone else noticed, and she ducked her head back to her plate, caught staring like an ill-mannered child.

"Here." Undurat was back at her side with another plate of food. She had not realised she had finished the first one.

"I do not think I have ever seen anyone eat so much," Noverian said in wonder.

Arrow froze, conscious of the stares from around the room. She had never worried about what she ate before, as it was usually barely enough to replace the power she used. Now her fingers clenched on the utensil, misaligned bones making her grip slightly awkward, and stared down at the plate of some of the finest food the Erith had to offer, and wondered if she should eat it.

"You have not worked with many mages," Kallish said easily, settling into a chair nearer Noverian, at Arrow's side, and nudging Arrow with her elbow. "They need at least as much food as a warrior, often more."

"Power use drains us." Gilean's voice drew everyone's attention to the door. Not resting, then. He had bathed since Arrow had last seen him, clothed again as a war mage with his light-absorbing cloak around him. Yet he did not look healthy, the bones of his face standing out in sharp relief, hands skeletal as he grasped the back of a chair before taking his place opposite Kallish. "And I would wager that Arrow has used a lot of power."

Noverian digested the polite rebukes in silence, pale eyes wandering across the room. Arrow's attention snagged again, distracting her from yet another plate of food even as Gilean inhaled his first plate and started on his second.

Noverian had been blind in the dungeon. She was sure of that. Covering it well in public, as any Court-dwelling Erith would. But he had commented on the sight of her food and, as the Consort's eyes drifted around the room, she wondered. It was one thing to use low-level spells to make up for a loss of sight. There were plenty of Erith who had done so, many of them accomplished magicians. This seemed different.

Orlis stumbled into the room, hair in rough knots around his head, and took his place beside Gilean. He looked marginally better rested than she felt, a touch of colour back in his face, the deep hollows under his eyes gone.

Watching under her lashes, Arrow saw a quiet glance between Noverian and Orlis and wondered just how much healing the Consort had required. And how Orlis had managed to restore the Consort's sight. And whether Orlis knew he had done so.

"Does the Taellan know you are alive, my lord?" she asked, sitting back.

"Not yet," he answered, ghost of a smile crossing his face.

"We need to draw the conspirators out." From the expression on Kallish's face, she was looking forward to it.

"When you have eaten, we should go."

"Go?" Arrow swallowed, hard.

"We are going to surprise the Taellan," Miach confirmed. Unlike Kallish, he was sombre, eyes still shadowed. If Arrow had to guess, she would say that surprising the Taellan had not been Miach's idea. Noverian or Kallish, more likely. And the Consort impatient enough that she could not delay for another, badly needed, plate of food.

Still, she had consumed enough to function, and had functioned on far less. Energy was creeping back into her body. She rose, ready to go, tracking Noverian's eyes as they lifted to the point above her shoulder.

"A war mage's sword. Carried by a shadow-walker." The Consort rose, a faint smile on his lips. "Truly a momentous day."

Arrow watched his back as he left the room in the midst of Miach's cadre.

"What is going on, *svegraen*?" she asked Kallish.

"I am not quite sure." The warrior rose, checking her weaponry with swift, professional attention. "Shall we go and find out?" That gleam was back in Kallish's eyes.

Gilean waved a hand from the other side of the table.

"We will follow in a moment." He glanced at Orlis, who was unusually silent. "Or perhaps longer."

"Not too long, old man, or you will miss the fun," Kallish warned, striding towards the door with a distinct spring in her stride. Arrow shook her head slightly, falling in with Kallish's third and the junior third as they followed. Xeveran and his third remained standing around the room. Waiting for Gilean, she assumed.

───ℓℓ───

Outside the bite of an early spring night made its way through layers of clothing, the sky above the Palace buildings full of the bright points of stars. Even though she had seen the stars here before, Arrow still found herself trying to make sense of the patterns. They were far, far from the Taellaneth, from Lix, and from everything that she knew.

A curl of magic, a tendril of the heartland's vast power, coiled around her, providing a touch of warmth as it lazily wandered through her. The vast spirit of the Erith lands lay just at the edge of her senses, quiet after the furious grief of the Queen's passing, the thrum of sadness still carried in the ever-present scent of death. Yet under that was the fresh scent of growing and spring, the promise of continuity. Arrow nearly stumbled again, wondering just how many monarchs the land had seen pass, and what secrets it could share if it had a mind to do so. The curl of magic lingered a moment more, a gentle stroke of warm, brilliant amber against her cheek, before it left her, whole in her own skin, her own familiar silver power content inside, the newly familiar shape of the sword's spells at her back.

She had been distracted for the entire journey across the Palace grounds, the warriors keeping the group outside the buildings, cloaked in shadows, no alarms raised by the presence of White Guard within the Palace, Noverian concealed beneath a billowing, dark cloak that Arrow thought simply drew more attention.

They were ascending the shallow steps to a grand entranceway that Arrow was sure she had not seen before, a pair of enormous wooden doors, as tall as a two storey building, standing open in traditional Erith welcome under a sweeping arch of pale stone. There were warriors inside, a full cadre with one third on each side of the entranceway, the final third standing in front of a slightly smaller set of doors that were firmly closed.

The cadre came on alert as they entered, weapons raised even against their own kind, until Noverian stepped forward and, with a move that looked very practised to Arrow's eyes, flung the cloak to one side. She tracked its movement as it slid across the stone floor to a heap against the wall. Lighter than wool. Silk, perhaps. The Consort had a flair for the dramatic. No one would make a silk cloak for any practical purpose. Too fine to provide any decent warmth. But it had billowed quite nicely as they had walked.

No one else had paid any attention to the cloak.

"Highness." One of the warriors near the door gasped and knelt on the same breath, bowing his head. The others followed suit until Noverian stood, with only Miach close to him, the Consort's face unreadable as he looked around.

"The Taellan is in session?"

"Yes, my lord." The warriors rose in a single move. Arrow could not see who had spoken, the entranceway lit only by a few glimmerlights, making it difficult to see.

"Open the door."

"We have orders, my lord."

Noverian did not bother arguing, just looked at Miach who in turn glanced at Arrow. She called some power and went forward, Kallish and her third flowing around her as though they did this every day, until she reached the doors. The warding spell bore all the marks of the Palace ward keepers, immaculate spellwork shining in her second sight. She broke it with a spoken spell, the echo of the break carrying into second sight, taking an alert to the ward keepers. Whatever was left of the Palace guard, after Miach putting so many cadres to work, would arrive soon. It was not subtle, but, with that pile of silk and unnecessary drama lying next to the wall, she did not think that Noverian wanted subtle. She put a hand on the unwarded doors and pushed, power behind her move, so that the doors swung open silently, moving out of the way so that Noverian could make the grand entrance he was no doubt planning.

The room inside was the most ornate that she had seen in the entire Palace, including the Receiving Room, glimmerlights reflecting from gilding on the domed ceiling above, mirrorglass panels in the walls reflecting back images of the faces of the Taellan, startled by the intrusion, most rising to their feet from around an oval table, the chair at the head of the table, where Seggerat would normally sit, empty, a thick band of purple silk draped across it in memory of his death.

The room's atmosphere vibrated with the force of the argument the Taellan had been having. Arrow knew them well enough to recognise the signs. A flushed face here, tight mouth there, hands clenched together in sleeves at another chair.

Apart from Kester, who surely must have been expecting them, the only person who did not seem shocked was Eimille vel Falsen. The eldest among them, the lady had not risen from her seat as the doors opened, simply turning her head to see who was coming into the private meeting. Recognising Noverian, her eyes widened a fraction, and she rose then, taking a step towards the Consort.

"Old friend." Her voice, warmer than Arrow had ever heard it, cut through the babble from the other Taellan, silencing them all. "One bright moment in these dark times. It is so good to see you."

"And you, Emmy." Noverian's mouth relaxed into a smile and he tipped his head in her direction, eyes travelling around the room, face tightening again to a closed, unreadable expression as he examined the Taellan.

Arrow's mind caught on the nickname, an oddly childish one for the dignified lady that she had always known, but she followed the direction of Noverian's glance and saw the bows from the Taellan, some considerably slower than others. She took note of the ones who were slow, and was confident that Miach and Kallish were doing the same.

"What is it doing here?" Gret vo Regresan. Predictably. Not even respect for the Consort overriding his fury at Arrow's presence. "It nearly killed my son!" His voice echoed from the mirrorglass panels.

For a moment the world slowed and Arrow realised, once again, far too late, how vulnerable she was. In the middle of Erith lands, in the Palace no less, surrounded by the most powerful Erith alive. With Evellan's order to find Gilean fulfilled, some could argue she had no good reason to be here. Her throat closed, pulse racing. Inside, the silver power coiled, ready to be used. The shadows were only a few moments' work away. She gave a quick glance to either side, judging how close Kallish and her third were, dismay twisting her stomach as she realised how thoroughly she was pinned. It was doubtful she could make the shadows before one of them got hold of her. All it would take would be an order from Miach or Noverian. Her mouth was dry, body tense.

"Your son was a willing host for a *surjusi*, as I recall," Noverian's voice, calm and sure, cut through Arrow's panic, "and in more danger from that than the Lady Arrow's blade."

The constriction on her chest eased and she could breathe again. She looked across to Noverian, standing only a few paces away, the Consort's gaze hard on Gret's face.

"Lady Arrow." Gret sneered, the force of his disgust a familiar jibe. Arrow was disappointed in herself at how much it still hurt, after years of his disdain.

"The only shadow-walker alive," Eimille said, her voice returned to the dispassionate, cool tone Arrow was more familiar with. The lady glanced back at her fellow Taellan, face hidden from Arrow. Whatever Gret saw made him clamp his jaw shut in fury.

"Will you sit?" Eimille turned back to Noverian, gesturing to the table. Apart from Seggerat's empty chair, there were two other empty chairs in the room. Both gilded to match the room, one slightly larger than the other. Monarch and Consort. In the centre of their council, on either side of the table.

Noverian's formal expression slipped as he let out a long breath, grief and resignation combined. He moved slowly around the table, reluctance obvious, to the larger of the chairs, and took his seat. In the Queen's chair. The Taellan bowed as one, more than the few faces pale, and more than a few tears showing. Arrow felt an answering stab of pain in her own chest. The Queen was dead. Until the Erith chose their new monarch, by whatever tortuous process they had devised, the Consort was acting Regent for the Erith people.

A small hand gesture from Noverian, and Miach's cadre spread themselves about the room. No longer the Queen's guard, Arrow realised for the first time. Until the Regent gave other orders, or the new monarch did, Miach was the first guard for the Palace, his assignment to protect whoever was the reigning monarch, so Noverian was now his responsibility as much as the Queen had been.

Kallish's touch on her arm nearly made her jump. The warrior gestured back towards the wall and, grateful to be out of the centre of attention, Arrow went with the third to stand in a servants' alcove, feeling oddly displaced and oddly at home at the same time. Waiting in a servant's place for the Taellan to require her attention was so familiar that she automatically adjusted her posture to fit, straightening up, folding her hands behind her back, her body remembering how to be still and wait with no need of prompting from her mind.

The room doors were still open, but no one moved to close them, which was just as well as moments later the pounding of running feet drew closer and closer and two full cadre of White Guard ran into the room, weapons ready.

Miach's cadre, who had surely been expecting the others, sprang forward to form a guard behind Noverian. Most of the Taellan sprang to their feet, cries of surprise and outrage rising along with demands for answers from the newly arrived White Guard.

And in the midst of the confusion, too many White Guard milling around the room, the Taellan not keeping still, Arrow, quiet and still in her position at the side of the room, saw the flicker of bared steel where it should not be.

Without thinking, she rushed forward, perhaps making a sound of alarm, Kallish and Undurat on either side, cries of alarm filling the room, turning to shrieks as fully half of the newly arrived warriors peeled back their uniforms to reveal brilliant scarlet under-tunics and attacked the other warriors with no warning.

The room was full of the sounds of battle, weapons clashing, the cut-off cries of pain from warriors as strikes hit home, screams from the Taellan as the attacking warriors bore down on them, more than one of the lords and ladies of the Erith taking refuge under the table.

The knife that Arrow had seen had vanished in the confusion.

Miach's cadre had dragged Noverian bodily back from the table and were surrounding him in an impenetrable wall, battle wards raised, not making a move to help the other warriors or the Taellan, their duty clear.

"Do something," Kallish hissed in Arrow's ear. Her third were around Arrow, weapons up, trying to hold their position. Protecting a war mage. Giving her room and space to work.

Arrow shook herself out of her shock, trying to make out the pattern of the battle, hands automatically drawing runes for mage fire. She forced herself to stop. Mage fire was lethal, and she could not be sure of hitting the attackers. Something less than lethal.

"Be ready," she told Kallish who nodded grimly, and signalled to her third.

Gathering all her power together, Arrow knelt and put one hand on the floor. No blood required for this, she spoke a quick holding spell.

"Jump!" she told Kallish. To her surprise, the third obeyed, leaping off the ground. She poured her power into the hold spell, sending it out across the room, clutching at all the feet and limbs on the floor. By the time the third landed on the ground again, the spell had taken hold, freezing everyone else in place.

"It will not last for long," she warned the third. They wasted no time, finding restraints from somewhere and gathering up as many of the red-fronted attackers as they could.

The hold spell had only frozen people in place, not stopped their mouths, and as the five warriors moved around the room, the air was full of curses and fury from both sides, Miach's voice penetrating the air demanding release, along with fury from the Taellan who had ducked under the table, now unable to move at all, and Gret demanding Arrow's head at once.

Arrow ignored them all, eyes scanning the room for that knife she had seen. Slender and lethal, it had not been wielded by White Guard. One of the Taellan, apart from Kester, standing calmly with both blades still ready, was armed. She moved forward, going towards the table, power lessened but still strong, even as the hold spell began to wear off. A few feet twitched. Noverian, surrounded by warriors, had not received as full dose of the spell as others, and worked his way out from his protection, much to Miach's fury, the cadre leader grasping the Consort's sleeve. Noverian shook him off, stepped out of the circle of the warriors' protection, eyes wide as he took in the carnage of the room, the red-fronted warriors who had attacked. And among the Taellan a richly-clothed noble lunged forward, flicker of steel visible.

Arrow cried a warning, sending a shock of power across the room. Noverian gasped, stumbled back. The soft-clothed body hit the ground under Arrow's power, knife clattering to the floor, even as Miach shook off the hold spell, grabbed Noverian back and moved, blade sure and swift, and parted head from body of the attacker.

Arrow was almost on them when a familiar head, separated from its body, rolled almost to her feet. Diannea vel Sovernis.

Noverian stumbled again and Arrow cursed, looking for the knife. Poison. It had to be.

"What poison?" Miach demanded, furious, face white, harsh lines forming around his mouth and eyes.

Kallish knelt by the knife on the floor.

"Smells like *surrimok*."

"Where is Orlis?" Miach demanded.

"A moment." Arrow pulled a communicator disk from her pocket, glad she had thought to bring one, only to hear more footsteps at the door. Gilean and Orlis, surrounded by Xeveran and his third, arrived, whatever argument they had been having vanishing as they saw the room.

Arrow stepped out of the way, back against the wall as Miach and Kallish's cadres, along with the loyal warriors, tied up the crimson-fronted traitors, tended to various wounds, coaxed the shaking Taellan from underneath the table, settled some of the more frightened of the Taellan at the table, all the while keeping an eye on Orlis who was using every scrap of power he had to keep Noverian alive, Gilean assisting, their differences put aside.

Eventually the room was quieter and calm, a pair of dark-robed magicians arriving as the hush fell, expressions stern at first, changing swiftly to shock and then concern as they saw the Consort lying on the floor, two mages pouring power into him.

"What has happened?" the smaller magician asked. "The room's wards are down." Palace ward keepers, Arrow realised, from the subtle design on their robes. She tried not to move, to avoid drawing any attention.

"Too much to tell just now." Whatever rest and energy Miach had recouped was long gone. The first guard looked exhausted, the rest of his third gathered close around him. One monarch lost on his watch, Arrow realised, and he thought he might lose another within a day. Not a happy thought for someone who had served the Erith monarchy for his whole life.

The room was crowded already, even more so as Evellan and Seivella arrived moments after the ward keepers. Unlike the ward keepers, they assessed the room with sharp, intent gazes before turning to Noverian and going forward side by side, offering their help. Even injured, they were both skilled magicians, and Orlis accepted their aid with a grateful glance up and tip of his head.

The White Guard separated out a pair of the disloyal warriors to keep in the room, sending the remainder off in charge of Gea's cadre. Diannea vel Sovernis' sightless eyes were still staring at the domed ceiling, expression caught in horror as she had witnessed her own death in Miach's blade coming towards her.

Arrow could not help wonder what had prompted the lady's defection, to attempt to kill the Consort. The House might be known for its hot-headed young, but the elders were normally more even tempered. And she had risked her entire House, not just her own life, on this terrible gamble.

"Will you examine her?" Kallish asked quietly, coming to stand beside Arrow. "We need to know if there are any clues."

Arrow's stomach twisted at the thought of going near the headless body, the thick spray of blood making a large pool that everyone was trying to avoid, sweet scent of death choking her lungs.

"Here?"

"We cannot wait." Kallish was grim, eyes flicking to Noverian. Still breathing, but his face was pale and dewed with sweat, and the magicians around him were fading. There might soon be another death. And then there would be more chaos, allowing the conspirators to get away or hide. The lady Sovernis had not been working alone. *Surrimok* poison was rare, and not from her lands.

"Yes." Arrow agreed, hunted through her pockets and found her gloves, walking with Kallish until she could kneel beside the body, avoiding the blood pool and avoiding looking too closely at the severed neck.

Diannea vel Sovernis had been a middle-height Erith lady, dressed richly as befit her station and her House, favouring the looser style of draped clothing of her region rather than the corsets and full skirts of Eimille vel Falsen, House Falsen's lands in a cooler climate.

Arrow began with the lady's arms, finding a concealed sheath for the knife along one arm, and an odd marking just above her wrist on the other arm. Kallish examined the mark but declared it unfamiliar, calling Undurat and Xeveran over to look as well.

As more gathered around the body, the Taellan began to stir, angry murmurs from a few, with phrases such as "lack of dignity" and "respect for the dead" clear to Arrow. It was only a matter of time before Gret vo Regresan, who had not been one of those under the table, surged to his feet and demanded her removal.

Near her, Kallish stiffened and turned her head towards the Taellan, eyes narrowing. Arrow could not see her full expression, but the Taellan stilled, some of their faces paling a fraction.

"This woman does not deserve our respect," Kallish told them, words clipped, "having tried to kill the Consort."

The Taellan subsided into silence again, a few mutinous expressions that would have looked quite appropriate on youngsters. Standing among them, Kester bit his lip to hide a smile, eyes glinting before Arrow ducked her head back to her work.

She moved to the lady's torso, pausing at once with a small, surprised noise.

"She is wearing body armour."

"Indeed?" Kallish was still grim.

"The House is known for its weapons," Xeveran commented, crouched on the other side of the body. "Can you undo her tunic so we can see the make?"

It was a sensible idea, even if Arrow's being revolted at the thought of stripping the lady in such a public setting. She checked for the clothes fastening and shook her head.

"It fastens at the back. We will need to move her."

"Anything else you can learn?" Xeveran accepted her assessment.

Arrow moved around the body, finding a slender knife tucked into the lady's boot, and a hard weight in a pouch at the lady's waist which turned out to be a clouded glass jar that she opened carefully, taking one small sniff before closing it rapidly.

"*Surrimok* poison," Kallish said, nose wrinkling. Arrow handed the jar to Kallish, not wanting to hold it anymore.

Preliminary search done, Arrow opened her second sight, not expecting to find anything. Any magic the lady had carried should have gone with her death. And yet the body glowed faintly with spellwork.

"Someone had woven a spell across the lady," she told Kallish, tracing the lines of the spell in second sight.

"To what purpose?"

"Unclear. I do not recognise the spell."

"The mage?"

"I do not know." Arrow frowned. There was something faintly familiar about the spellwork, but she could not be certain. Too many impressions from the last few days crowded her head. "Maybe someone who was in the library. But not the one who used mage fire in the library."

"Can you trace them?"

"Him," Arrow said definitely, enhancing her sight with a quick spell, the lines clear before her eyes. "Someone I have met in the Palace. Not very familiar, though."

"So none of the Taellan. Not Miach's cadre. Not mine. Elias? His cadre?"

Arrow could not see Kallish's face from the second world, could only judge how tense and concerned the warrior was by the brittle quality to her voice. Distantly she heard some gasps from the Taellan and an indrawn breath she thought she recognised as Gret vo Regresan about to launch into a tirade.

"Quiet." The one word was flat, full of command. Kester.

"Not Elias or his cadre," Arrow confirmed.

"Good."

"One of the courtiers, then," Kester suggested, tone reflective.

"Most likely."

"What do you need to find him?" Miach's voice, harsh and flat.

Arrow tipped her head, considering the information in the spellwork. She now had different examples of the magician's work.

"Assuming he has made his own ward spells. I would need to be in the same room as him."

"Everyone makes their own ward spells," Miach said.

"Not necessarily," Arrow countered, looking again at the spells overlaying Diannea vel Sovernis. "I think this may be a form of warding."

"Not there to influence the lady?"

"No, *svegraen*." Arrow came back into the first world and looked up to meet Miach's eyes. "As far as I can tell she acted in her own mind."

Miach was tired and worn enough that he could not hide his reaction to that, a drain of colour from his face, mouth pinching in pain.

"But not alone," Kallish reminded them, rising, along with her warriors, to face Miach.

The pain in the senior warrior's face lessened as he thought for a moment.

Arrow rose to her feet as well, removing her gloves and tucking them away while she thought. Her eyes turned to the two red-fronted warriors tied up and under guard and she took a step towards them before she was really sure what she was doing. The impulse seemed a good one, so she kept going.

"May I see his wrists, *svegraen*?" she asked the nearest warrior on guard. He lifted a brow, the only sign of surprise, but obliged, kneeling by the prisoner and pulling his sleeves back from his wrists. The same mark that Diannea vel Sovernis had on her wrist was on the inside of the prisoner's wrist, the prisoner himself struggling to break free from his ties as it was discovered.

"That would have to hurt," Kallish observed, once more at Arrow's shoulder.

"A test of loyalty, I imagine." Arrow's eyes lingered on the mark exposed to the light and flinched internally, imagining the pain of such a wound. Erith did not scar easily, and despite many efforts by younger Erith, could not tattoo their skin, so anything that could cause so small and so deep a mark must have been excruciatingly painful, the wound deliberately kept from healing until the mark had taken.

"A brand." Miach's voice had lifted. Something concrete to hunt for.

"We cannot ask the entire Palace to strip," Kallish said, although it sounded as if she were seriously considering making the demand.

"No." Miach sounded equally intrigued by the idea. "But we can offer a blessing."

"Sneaky." Kallish approved, dark eyes reflecting satisfaction as she turned to the senior. "Both wrists, though."

"A blessing?" Arrow asked.

"A gift from the Consort, a remembrance of his *vetrai*," Miach explained, then continued at Arrow's evident confusion, "usually a piece of ribbon tied around a wrist, gifted at a funeral rite."

"Ah." Arrow blinked, processing that idea. It had merit. She had never been to a funeral rite, so had no idea how common such a thing might be or whether the Erith would find it suspicious that the Consort suddenly wished to revive an old custom. But there was one possible flaw. "Could the mark be concealed with cosmetics?"

"Possibly." The hope died in Miach's face.

"We can find the mage who put the spell on the lady Sovernis," Arrow reminded him, wanting to offer some comfort. The confident, calm warrior who had met her in the mirror relay room not that many days before was entirely gone, and she did not like the change.

"He will live."

Orlis' voice, quiet and hoarse, cut the tension in the room. Everyone, even the prisoners, sagged in relief, all eyes turning to Noverian. The Consort was lying on his side, evidence of his sickness and the poison all around him, pungent odour almost overriding the scent of death. His too-thin shoulders and rib cage rose and fell with deep breathing, but it was steady and sure.

"Back to the annex," Kallish suggested. "Xeveran, we need a litter for the Consort."

Xeveran had his third organised in moments, tearing down an old and probably priceless tapestry from the walls in the entrance and, using White Guard spears, extended to their furthest reach, quickly made it into a makeshift litter.

Watching the quiet, efficient progress, Arrow's eyes drifted to the ward keepers, standing in stunned silence inside the doors. They bore all the appearance of not wanting to be there at all, to witness such things, at the same time as taking everything in, eyes darting about the room.

Another impulse had her moving across the room to them. It could take her days to search the Palace for the magician. The ward keepers lived here, and had to be familiar with its residents. Especially the ones who could craft such fine magic.

"Sirs."

Two pairs of amber-flecked eyes turned to her.

"There is an additional ward spell on the lady Sovernis. Can you tell its maker?"

"Perhaps."

"Possibly."

Arrow waited while they exchanged glances, each swallowing, hard, perhaps realising just how deep a conspiracy they were on the edges of. The taller, more junior, nodded once and focused his gaze on the lady's body, avoiding her detached head.

"Priath," he said definitely after a moment. "Unquestionably. He has grown far more accomplished than I had realised."

"We keep an eye on him," the senior added, seemingly reluctant to speak so freely, "as he has several times attempted to cross our wards."

"Attempted?"

"Does it matter?" Miach's eyes were bright. He had a target for his rage and grief.

"I think it does. Sirs?"

"In the last few weeks he has tried to reach the dungeons, the Queen's chambers and the Consort's rooms more than once."

"He has long wanted power," Kallish said, quickly checking her weaponry, words directed to Miach. "Send Elias with the Consort. We will come with you for Priath."

"Careful," Arrow warned, "he has been concealing his skill. And will not be alone."

"That is why you will come with us."

"It does not fit," Kester objected. He had somehow detached himself from the listening Taellan and stood next to Miach. "He has wanted to be part of the Taellan, not sit on the throne."

"We will ask him when we find him," Kallish promised, and strode away, issuing orders as though she, not Miach, were in charge.

Miach was standing perfectly still, arrested expression on his face, even as his cadre prepared for battle.

"No. He does not want the crown," he said after a pause. "He would rather sit in the shadows behind the crown."

Arrow nodded. That fit with her own observations of the man.

"And do his work through others," she added, "so very little is actually done by him."

"He still needs found." Kallish was not going to be diverted.

"And we need to talk to the ladies." The ladies in waiting even now kept in the dungeon.

"We need you for Priath," Kallish objected.

Arrangements made, the group dispersed. The Taellan were left, still in a state of shock with one of their number dead on the floor, under watch of their cadre. Elias' cadre escorted Noverian, Orlis, Gilean, Evellan and Seivella back to the annex along with the Palace ward keepers, who promised to reinforce the building's defences so that even a shadow-walker could not get through, with a knowing look in Arrow's direction. Arrow took note of, and filed away for the future, the confidence they had that they could block a shadow-walker.

Miach and Kallish's cadres, with Arrow and Kester, headed through the Palace, the Erith going at a fast enough pace to draw the swift attention of every Erith they passed. The entire Palace would be ablaze with gossip within a very short space of time, Arrow knew. She also knew that it could not be helped. They could not give Priath any warning.

_____ ele _____

In the end, her attendance was not required. They found Priath sitting in his own rooms, casually sipping Erith tea, waiting for them. He was pale, jaw set and determined, but not surprised to find two cadre of furious warriors seeking his immediate arrest. That alone set everyone on high alert.

Searching Priath and his rooms took the rest of the day and uncovered nothing, even when Miach, furious, made the lord strip and checked his entire person for marks, finding nothing. Arrow used her second sight and even stepped into shadows, outside Priath's presence, to see what they had missed. She gained a headache and a nosebleed but no new information. Whatever the lord had done, he had concealed it well. Their only evidence of his involvement was the additional ward spell on Diannea, which Arrow could confirm was his work. Evidence that he had conspired with Diannea, at least, and she had brought a knife meant for Noverian. Perhaps enough for a conviction of attempted murder. Not nearly enough to satisfy Miach.

Miach's original impulse was to send the lord to the dungeons, checked only when Kallish reminded him that the dungeons would be quite full by now, and it might not be a good idea to put all the conspirators in the same place. Instead, another cadre of White Guard and a pair of war mages that Arrow did not know, were assigned first watch over the lord.

They left the lord's rooms in the mid of night, all weary to the bone, Arrow feeling hollow and light-headed from magic use and hunger.

"The lady's rooms?" she asked, annoyed with herself for not thinking of it earlier.

"Under guard, along with her House. The C ... the Regent will need to decide how that will be dealt with." Miach ran a hand through his hair, smoothing back wisps that were coming free from his braids. He looked around the group. "We all need some rest."

"The annex has room," Kallish offered. She was less weary, but even her normally pristine appearance was rumpled.

"Yes."

So they made their way back to the annex and found it crowded but, as Kallish had said, with room. Particularly as none of the White Guard minded sleeping on bed rolls on whatever patch of floor they could find.

CHAPTER TWENTY-ONE

Everyone else was busy with something or other. The entire Palace was drawing breath. Emergency repairs were being carried out, injuries healed and preparations underway for the Queen's funeral rites the following day. The Erith believed in releasing their dead as soon as possible.

And after the funeral rites there would be more ceremony, which seemed to require as much preparation as the funeral. Apparently Noverian was required to take public oaths as Regent, and the former Consort seemed at least as concerned about his outfit for the occasion as he was about the ceremony itself. He had what appeared to be the entire household of Palace servants bustling about, searching for the perfect shade of red for a suit for the occasion. There had been at least four dozen bolts of cloth brought for his inspection before he, with apparent reluctance, settled on one, and then began a similar painstaking process of discussing the shape of the outfit.

For all the attention to his wardrobe, he still looked frail, requiring close attendance from both Orlis and Gilean. Evellan and Seivella had collapsed and were under careful watch of the Palace healers.

Miach was re-ordering the White Guard. Those at the Palace at least. Arrow could foresee some fiery discussions with Lord Whintnath ahead, the head of the White Guard still at the Taellaneth, maintaining the Taellaneth's borders.

And in the middle of all the activity and bustle there was nothing, for the moment, that Arrow could do. There would be no more investigations today. Her eyes were blurred from the different shades of cloth. Gilean was found. Priath was under watch. The null was under watch. She was as safe as she could be among the Erith.

And she had the sense of a small, and fast-closing, opportunity to explore the heartland. To take a pause of her own, see what she could before she was sent into exile once more.

There were questions to be answered. There was a murderer still on the loose. But today was not a day for pursuing that.

She set off with no particular direction in mind, taking in everything around her, trying to store up the memories and impressions in case she did not return.

Her feet were sore and her mind swirling with images before the day was half done. As the afternoon faded, she found herself drawn, on impulse, outside the main Palace buildings, past workmen assessing the damage the heartland had caused, along a remarkably plain path that led her to the oldest parts of the Palace. No longer inhabited, the windows blank, no movement or lights inside despite the gathering night. At another time the empty spaces might have felt threatening, and yet she was quite sure that there was no threat in the quiet buildings around her, a warm coil of the heartland's magic, a feather-light touch on her shoulder, next to her sword hilt, urging her onward.

The oldest buildings of the Palace, perhaps the oldest buildings the Erith had, were arranged in a great circle around a tree so ancient that it hurt Arrow's eyes to look at it, and she had to shut down her second sight completely. Still her feet took her forward.

She stopped, breathing too fast and chest tight. The heart of the Erith. The great tree, more magic than bark and branch, the roots of it stretching deep into the ground, too deep and too far for her senses to follow. Its branches shivered in a light breeze showing the first buds of spring, the fully open leaves of summer, the golds of autumn and the bare branches of winter. Everything cast in vibrant, abundant life. The brighter, daylight twin to the shadow world. And she should not be here. Years of derision and contempt from the Erith rose up in her memory. *Arwmverishan*. Abomination. The unwanted, unNamed creature.

She was about to move, letting her feet take her away, when the tendril of the heartland's magic pressed, ever so slightly, on her shoulder.

The heartland wanted her to stay. The understanding came without words, in the coil of magic around her, and the loneliness in that wordless request closed her throat and she had to swallow before she could answer.

"For a bit. Alright."

The weight of the heartland's presence pressed her feet into the soil, sent her leaning back against the thick trunk of the tree, sheltered and protected by its branches and leaves. Nothing could touch her. No one could hurt her. No one could harm her. It was the safest she had ever felt in her life. The sheer scale of the presence made her believe it. The heartland's protection was huge and sincere.

The heartland wanted her here. Her. Here. In the midst of the astonishing beauty of the Erith lands. Where there was magic visible in the air. Where there were wonders she had only read about waiting to be seen.

A great part of her wanted to stay. The little she had seen beyond the Palace was beautiful. And there were others out there, mixed race like her. People who might understand the difficulties of not being pure Erith but living among the people.

And there were Erith who would accept her without name calling. The Queen herself had shown kindness, and her first guard had shown her a portrait of her mother. Not all Erith despised her.

But.

"I cannot stay."

The pressure did not ease, a soundless plea coursing through her, catching the breath in her throat.

"I am not welcome here. A half-breed. Nameless. No House." Her chest hurt saying the words. However true they were, it still hurt.

A swell of emotion washed over her from the second world, the heartland's anger and determination.

"I would like to come and visit again. Explore a little more. Hopefully without anyone trying to kill me." The humour fell flat, even to her own ears. The pressure in her chest eased as the heartland considered it, then gentled to another feather-light caress, this one on her left cheek, high on the cheekbone. A brief kiss which carried the heat of summer, the crisp green of spring, the chill bite of winter and the rich shades of autumn. A wish of safety. A sense, grafted into her very bones, that here was somewhere she was and would always be welcome.

Whatever had held her against the tree was gone and she stepped out of its shade, not surprised to find more tears on her face. The heartland's presence contained everything that was Erith. All the beauty, the pride, the arrogance, the savagery, the artistry, and the love they were capable of, the dark and the light all mixed together, the light out of reach for Arrow.

She walked through the spaces between silent, unoccupied buildings until she heard voices. A number of the Palace inhabitants had gathered, the heady scent of food carrying in the light breeze. Not wanting company, she skirted around the noise, finding a place in shadow to observe one of the gatherings. They were courtiers, brightly dressed but less merry than they would normally be, exchanging soft words. A remembrance for their Queen, perhaps.

From this distance none of the Erith's darkness was visible, only the beauty, each one as striking as the next, voices a soothing melody as she could not hear the individual words, the bright array of colours somehow pleasing to her eyes. Her chest hurt again. She had seen so little of the Palace, of the heartland, or everything that was most of her heritage, and after the brief glimpse she was to be excluded again, a Nameless outcast. It should not hurt so much. The heartland, and the Palace, held no safety. Not for her. And there was nothing to hold her here, not really. Her eyes, disobeying her mind, searched the crowd for Orlis, or Gilean, or Kallish, or Kester. Perhaps especially Kester, an odd sense that she may not see him again taking hold.

And why would they see each other again, she asked herself, adopting a stern tone. An exile and a Taellan. There was no common ground. They had fought together, yes, and he had sought to offer her something that she still did not understand. But beyond that. Nothing. She had more in common with Kallish, more shared experience, and an oddly keen understanding of the older Erith's quirks, like her love of human technology that sat oddly with her pristine appearance as the most proper of White Guard.

She should leave. Go back to the Taellaneth and then to the workspace. Things were much simpler there.

Yet there was something, like a loose thread, that kept trying to get her attention. Miach thought that he had all the conspirators gathered. All dead or under guard. Priath and Learvis still to be questioned, answers not yet complete. Knowing that, she still had the strong sense that her tasks were not yet done. Something had been overlooked. It seemed all too neat. It made no sense that Priath had acted all on his own, or that he had done anything directly at all. He preferred manipulation to action. Queris vo Lianen's desperate bid for power made sense and fit with his character. Priath's apparent actions did not. Neither did Diannea vel Sovernis' attempt to kill the former Consort. And Learvis had not named Priath as his co-conspirator in Teresea's death. Teresea's killer was the dangerous one, identity not yet revealed.

Her eyes shimmered silver in the dark. There was something she had missed. She needed information.

—*ell*—

The library was, not surprisingly, empty and still at this hour, between midnight and dawn, so Arrow had the place to herself as she searched the records cards for the correct index. The constructs had not bothered her, purring contentedly as they recognised her and let her past. Their unceasing vigilance meant she was confident of not being disturbed.

"What are you looking for?"

Kester's voice, soft as it was, startled her enough into an undignified start and squeak of surprise. She glanced over her shoulder to find him standing outside the reach of her wards, dressed as a warrior once more. Keeping one finger on the record she had found, she turned more fully to scowl.

"I was trying to be discreet."

Something crossed Kester's face as he looked at her. Surprise. Recognition. The tiniest hint of a smile. Amused at her annoyance, perhaps. Whatever it was, the expression was gone before she could trace it, and he answered her question.

"You were. Kallish is quite upset you managed to persuade the door guards to let you out earlier. The only reason she is not here is because it would create more fuss."

Arrow's irritation spiked. It had been a risk, going back to the annex for some food before coming here. But she could not remember the way back to the magicians' dormitories, and their refectory, and had not wanted to draw more attention. So, it was really her own fault that Kallish had noticed her absence.

Not really pacified, Arrow shrugged a shoulder and turned back to the parchment. She pulled her wards closer, though, allowing him to approach.

"Palace ward keepers?" Kester read over her shoulder. "What is it?"

"Something," she told him, voice clipped. She had enhanced her sight and had thought that her wards, as well as the pacing constructs, would prevent anyone sneaking up on her. Kester's arrival, unheard and blind to her wards, put that in doubt. And the constructs would not stop a warrior.

"Perhaps I can help." He did not seem dismayed by her tone or the shoulder she had turned towards him, voice mild.

"Were you part of the Palace guard for long?"

"No. Only for my training."

"Good. Here." She handed the record she had found over to him and watched as he read the list of entries. Palace ward keepers, apprentices and novices, a complete record dating back centuries. Far down the list, script so old it had faded with time despite the preservation spells, were two names close together.

"Priath and Noverian were novice ward keepers together," Kester said, sounding faintly puzzled. "It is not that unusual. A lot of Erith take the tests. Particularly high ranking Erith who are not heirs to their Houses. It is a respected profession."

Arrow blew out a breath, wondering how much of her suspicions to share. Suspicions that would not let her rest, despite her fatigue.

"Priath is entirely too confident," she told him bluntly, "for someone who supposedly murdered one of the Queen's favourites."

"I thought so, but why is this important? Priath and Noverian were novices along with several others."

"All the others either progressed in their studies or withdrew through lack of aptitude." Arrow pointed to the brief notes next to each name, which set out what had happened to the novice. "There are no such notes next to Priath or Noverian's name."

"And?"

"They did not fail." Arrow knew she sounded exasperated and could not help it. She knew it was a tenuous link, but it made sense. At least in her own mind.

"And?" Kester repeated. She looked across, silver bright in her eyes.

"They chose not to continue as ward keepers once they had reached the stage in their training where the oaths are required. Or were required. Novices take oaths now, too. Ward keepers are mages trained to excellence in one thing and one thing only. They are not harmless." She clamped her jaw shut before she could say more, having to trust in his intelligence enough that he would be able to follow her reasoning.

It seemed he did. With her enhanced sight she saw him pale.

"So, Noverian and Priath have the knowledge of a junior ward master and none of the oaths."

"Quite."

"Priath is dangerous. But Noverian?"

"Priath is the one people know about. He is very dangerous," Arrow agreed, "but prefers to stay just out of the light. He likes people to know he is dangerous and to fear him." Arrow thought of the chill that ran through her the first time she had encountered the lord. He exuded far more menace than Seggerat ever had. And yet her conclusion was that Seggerat had been far more dangerous, with a brilliant mind honed and kept sharp over many years as head of the Taellan. "Noverian, on the other hand, has spent a lifetime in Court and apparently done very little with it."

"He was devoted to the Queen."

"That may have been true once," Arrow said, turning away to close the records.

"He is Regent. This ..."

"Yes. Now do you see why I came alone?"

"Clever little thing." A quiet voice, one they both knew, spoke from the shadows. Arrow bit back a curse. She had not set perimeter wards, not wanting to draw more attention. Which meant that, as with Kester, there had been no warning of the newcomer's arrival. And, like Kester, the constructs had not seen him as a threat.

Noverian stepped out of the shadows, fully restored to health, pale eyes gleaming with amber power to rival Evellan's. He was not alone. There were shapes moving with him in the shadows. Warriors. White Guard with red ribbon on their uniforms. Red again. The red of his coronation suit.

Kester muttered something under his breath. A curse Arrow was not familiar with, anatomically highly unlikely. He drew his blades, amber of his wards flaring.

"Ward keeper, remember?" Arrow said softly, her own wards kept dim with effort. There was threat in the shadows. Instead of her wards, she gathered a few spells of battle magic, fingers twitching as she drew the necessary runes in the air. Much harder than with chalk, or even spoken words. At least they did not have the null anymore. Although, in the right circumstances, a ward keeper could be nearly as deadly as the null.

Whilst she frantically tried to remember the supposed skills of a ward keeper and work out how they might harm her, she also took stock of the former Consort. The spare frame, ribs showing and face gaunt, was gone, along with any sign of the *surrimok* poisoning. She shivered lightly, remembering how drained Orlis was and wondered just how much of his power Noverian had taken. And not just Orlis. Gilean, Evellan and Seivella had helped with his healing. Some of the primary threats to the former Consort, all dealt with in one go. Apart from her. She was fatigued, but not drained. With the Consort's access to Erith secrets, it was likely that Noverian knew as much about her as Evellan did. Dangerous for her and for Kester as the little she knew of the Consort could be summed up in the ward keepers' records and her own observations. Still, that gave her an opening to try to draw him out.

"How long were you poisoning the Queen?" she asked, moving to keep him in sight. The others with him she assessed quickly. No serious power among them. From Kester's wary stance, they were probably skilled warriors. Genuine White Guard, then, suborned to the Consort's will.

"Clever little thing," he said again, an odd hunger crossing his face. "Would not have been needed if she had just died when she was supposed to."

"The Queen's riding accident. That was two years ago. You have been planning this for two years?" Kester's voice was clipped, lip curling in distaste.

"Oh, longer."

"Longer," Arrow said at the same time. The details of the Queen's accident had not been widely known and she had only heard about it through a casual mention at one of the Taellan's meetings. A horse from the Royal stables had apparently taken fright at something, as horses did from time to time, and the Queen had nearly, oh so nearly, fallen to her death down a steep ravine. The Taellan had been disturbed, but not suspicious. The Queen's love of dangerous riding was well known, and some had even suggested that it was only a matter of time before an accident like that had occurred.

But if the incident had been planned, that took a considerable amount of patience and time. Time to prepare the horse, time to select a route, time to persuade, without seeming to, the Queen to ride along that route, on that horse, at a time when the horse could reliably be spooked. Judging by the satisfaction in Noverian's face, Arrow thought he had been planning to kill his *vetrai* for several years before the riding accident, and perhaps even decades. Whatever affection that had once been between Queen and Consort was long gone, at least on his side. Replaced by what she had not quite figured out yet. Resentment, certainly. And the disappearing affection had apparently unearthed Noverian's long-suppressed ambition.

"You have never shown any interest in ruling," Kester objected, the thought so close to Arrow's own that she glanced aside, finding his gaze intent on the former Consort, his jaw set in anger.

"She would not let me." The venom in his voice made Arrow want to take a step back. Whereas Priath was cold in his calculations, always assessing where his best interests lay, Noverian's ambition burned unchecked.

"Let you? You were full grown when she ascended the throne. If it was not to your liking, you had time enough to change matters." The scorn in Kester's voice was too sharp to just be about Noverian. Kester had lost his own House as part of the negotiations that had seen his only sister wed to Juinis vo Halsfeld. Arrow had often wondered just how the younger brother felt about the loss of his House, and what kind of a sister would insist such a bargain was made.

"So, when Gilean suggested mercat to help her age well you supported her. Like a good *vetrai*." Arrow had not realised she was capable of that much sarcastic bite to her voice. The tiny smirk on Noverian's face told her she had hit the mark. There would be nothing suspicious, nothing at all, in a Consort supporting his Queen in looking after her health. "And then, what, you added more and more to her dose?"

"Clever." Noverian's voice held a bite now, too.

"She trusted you," Kester said, voice rough.

"And your guards," Arrow said, sorrow making her voice hoarse, "you poisoned them, too. They did not even realise you had gone."

"Her guards." Noverian sneered, amber in his eyes flaring. Far more powerful than anyone had thought he was, Arrow realised. And judging by the fine, subtle wards around him, far more skilled than anyone had realised, either. He may not have the title of ward keeper, but the detail of the spells she could see, gleaming in second sight, demonstrated the skill required.

"You set up the disguise around yourself in the prison," she realised finally. The work had not borne Priath's signature and none of the other conspirators they had met had the skill necessary. And with that realisation, everything else fell into place in a sickening sequence.

"You killed Teresea." The words were bitter on her tongue. How could she have missed that. The same magical signature in the dungeons, and at Teresea's death. And others. "And Seggerat." Her stomach twisted. "And all those people who died, all those years ago. Killed in their sleep like Seggerat. Did Teresea guess? Is that why she had to die?"

"Clever little thing." It was not an admission, but the glee on his face was enough, for Arrow at least.

"And what about Diannea? Did you try and recruit her?" Even as she spoke the question her stomach turned.

"Priath's whore." The contempt in his voice chilled her again.

"Priath's?" Kester's voice was tight. "But surely Priath was conspiring with you. Why would his lady try to kill you?"

Noverian's laugh carried through the still air of the library. Arrow never wanted to hear that sound again. It crawled over her senses, a whisper in the dark when the room was empty.

"We needed a distraction. Besides, he was growing tired of her. Stupid female thought she had some claim on him."

Arrow remembered the severed head on the meeting room floor, the sightless eyes, and felt nothing but pity for the woman, used and disgraced in a conspiracy for power.

"Head of her House. Taellan in her own right." Kester was furious, white-lipped, eyes shimmering amber. "How much mercat did Priath need to turn her mind?"

Noverian laughed again, the sound carrying a trace of chalk scraping on slate. Arrow's skin prickled. He looked sane. But clearly was not. The glee in his face showed her how much he had enjoyed the deaths, the conspiracy.

And it would have been so easy for Priath to drug his lover. A toast. A shared glass, Priath careful not to drink. A gift of food. Arrow's mind turned on a dozen different ways, chilled again as she thought of Priath whispering his desires into the lady's ear, Diannea unable to resist. Arrow knew what it was like to have no control over her actions as the oath-spells had not permitted disobedience. She did not wish it on anyone.

She discovered she did not want to think of that any more, burn of anger chasing away the cold.

"Did you also beat yourself up and starve yourself?" A seemingly perfect alibi. The Regent could not have been slipping around the Palace killing people if he was weak and half-dead in the dungeons.

"Do not be foolish. I allowed myself to be taken. Queris' little plot was an amusing diversion, and it meant I had a ringside seat for your reunion with Evellan."

There. In the midst of the finely crafted wards, something that Arrow could use. A tiny flaw. Her eyes narrowed, silver glinting. If only there was a way she could keep Noverian distracted.

"So you suggested that they imprison you in the Queen's dungeon?" Kester prompted, taking a step forward, drawing Noverian's attention. Arrow wondered what it was about evil men that led them to be so garrulous. Nuallan had been the same. Or perhaps it was just Erith nobility. Most of the Taellan could talk for hours about the most inconsequential matters.

"Where else were they going to keep me? And Queris liked the irony of it, or so he said. Have you killed him yet?"

"He is taken care of," Kester said ambiguously, taking another step towards the lord. "Along with Learvis." Noverian's sneer showed his opinion of the sell sword.

"Sneaky little runt. He was quite fascinated by you," Noverian told Arrow. "Brought me little things he thought you would enjoy."

Arrow's skin crawled. The book, *On the Capture of Mages*. Alisemea's book. And her portrait, beside Seggerat's bed. She had known that they were put there to draw attention, but the thought that Learvis and Noverian had discussed them had her swallowing hard against nausea.

"I assume the sell sword is dead?" Noverian asked, voice a light conversational tone.

"He is taken care of," Kester repeated, holding his ground. Arrow used the cover of his shoulder to sketch a hasty spell, pouring power into the shapes. An unravelling of sorts.

The spell bit and for a moment she thought it had succeeded, Noverian becoming utterly still, eyes blank with the intense focus of a magician looking into the second world. Then his lips curved in a smile Arrow hoped never to see again, and his eyes, full of amber power, met hers.

"You are not skilled enough for such work. Come here." A sinuous thread of power, a pre-prepared spell triggered by an apparently casual gesture of his hand, wrapped itself around her wards, biting into the spells with the tearing agony of another magician's power against her own. Pain blinded her for a moment, white and searing, her own wards used against her, knotted into the entrapment spell, dragging her towards Noverian, who was watching her with the same contempt she used to see on Seggerat's face. The comparison made her shiver lightly.

But Noverian had forgotten something that Seggerat never would. Arrow had been under the absolute control of the Taellan for many years. She had learned to survive, to keep secrets hidden and to mask her own power despite the oath spells in her blood. The hasty spell she had released fizzed out, its work done, and her wards followed, vanishing like smoke. No Erith would voluntarily drop their wards, the last line of defence for some against an attacker. Unlike most Erith, Arrow knew that wards were not secure. She had taken a bullet despite her wards, saved only by the armoured coat she had been wearing, and in the past several days at the Palace, an attacker in null clothing had sliced through her wards more than once. Being without wards was not terrifying to her. Losing control of her own body was. Her deepest fear brought to pass, had Noverian known it, by anchoring into her wards. Dropping her defences was the less terrifying option.

Noverian's hold on her slipped away and she stepped sideways, away from Kester, and released the second spell she had prepared, a slender thread of power that eased into the spaces between his wards. There was no point in directly challenging wards made by a ward keeper, but she could break them or bypass them and so she did.

"What are you doing? You should not be able to do that!" His confidence wavered. "Stop that." He was arrogant enough that he thought his command should be enough. Used to power all these years, no matter how bitterly he may have resented the greater power wielded by his *vetrai*.

"What are you doing, Arrow?" Kester asked, interested.

"The problem with being very good at something is you tend to rely on that as your only defence," Arrow answered obliquely.

"I am not just very good," Noverian snapped back, some of his confidence returning, his wards flaring in the first world as he poured more power into them, "I am the best."

"I doubt that. Your formal training did not progress beyond the novice stage of the ward keepers' programme. Your work is good, but I have seen far better in the walls and fabric of the Palace."

A lash of amber power streamed out from Noverian, barbed hooks visible even in the first world, seeking something to latch on to, finding nothing, Arrow's wards still down.

"How do you fight a ward keeper, little thing?" he sneered, apparently not realising that his attack had failed.

"You do not. You fight the one hiding behind the wards," she answered. Then she spoke a final command, the silver strands of her power that had laced through his, in the gaps between his spellwork, tightened at once and the lord found himself held, trapped within his own wards, the spells losing their flexibility, Arrow's power filling all the tiny gaps and crevices. He uttered a roar of pain and fury, another magician's power laced with his, eyes widening slightly as he spied something behind Arrow and Kester.

Arrow did not turn. Only foolish people turned away from as potent a threat as Noverian, even though he was held. Kester glanced over his shoulder instead, moving smoothly, guarding Arrow's back.

"Miach." Noverian's voice was a low growl, coated with venom, "Kill these traitors."

"No."

Arrow had never heard so much emotion in one word before. Miach sounded lost, defeated. Heart-sick.

"I command you. As Regent ..."

"As one who has confessed to poisoning our Queen, you have no standing as Regent," Miach corrected, still sounding defeated.

"I did no such thing."

"We heard everything," Miach countered. Arrow risked a glance across. The first guard tipped his head to one side. The shadows of the library had not just concealed Noverian's men, Arrow saw. Miach's cadre were there along with Gilean vo Presien, looking as heart-sick as Miach sounded, shoulders slumped.

"You nearly killed Orlis." Gilean's voice was harsh with emotion far darker than Miach's. The war mage stepped forward, one hand lifted, brilliant power lighting his eyes.

"No!" Arrow tried to intervene, sensing as soon as she moved that it was too late.

Gilean's power, strong and sure, blasted into Noverian, lifting the former Consort from his feet and sending him across the room into the nearest bookshelf, the wooden structure shattering with the force of the impact. Gilean's power coated Noverian, battle magic unrelenting.

Arrow screamed, caught between Noverian's wards and Gilean's fury, dual scrape of other powers against her unwarded senses sending her to her knees, sight fading to black as she fought the magical backlash.

"You will kill her, too, you fool!" Kester's shout hurt her too-sensitive ears.

"He needs to die."

"Then kill him. But only him."

"I do not have the right," Miach said, sadness carrying to Arrow even over the assault of magic. Something about his sadness, Gilean's determination and

Kester's cool sense allowed her to gather some of her will together and resurrect her wards, the most basic protections, around her. The agony of other magic lessened and she straightened slightly from her huddle on the floor.

Still blind in the first world, all she could be sure of was the sound of fighting, steel on steel, a confusion of shouted commands, pleas and fury and the gathering of Noverian's power as her hold on him lessened. He was far more powerful than Miach or Gilean knew, a gathering of rage in second sight. Before she knew what she was about, the hilt of her sword, a war mage's spirit sword solid and real in the first world, was in her hand and she was stepping forward, feet following a pattern she did not know, arm moving in one, smooth movement. There was a moment of resistance to her blade and then nothing, her body clenched with a further, tearing pain as Noverian's wards expired with his life, freeing her magic, followed by the unmistakable sweet scent of Erith death.

Her sight returned and she had to blink several times, thinking she was imagining things. The library was brightly lit, almost as if by daylight. Underneath the perfect ceiling was chaos. Bookshelves broken, their contents scattered, the one that Noverian had collided with fragmented, and liberally coated with his blood, Noverian himself lying in an unnatural shape in the midst of the wreckage, head cleanly parted from his body, eyes now permanently sightless turned up to the ceiling.

Noverian's warriors were dead. Miach and his cadre had given no quarter, simply slaughtered their former comrades. The cadre were grim-faced, jaws set, glitter of too much emotion in their eyes. Kester was supporting Gilean to a nearby stool, the war mage pale and shaking with the aftermath of effort.

The grey weight of the dead pressed on Arrow and she sank to her knees, shoulders bowed, stomach hollow with loss. Not the sharp stab of grief at the loss of someone she had known, but the simple, profound sense of absence that followed every death.

Even as she stayed huddled on the floor, a tendril of warm power, the endless, bottomless well that was the Erith heartland, wound itself around her in the gentlest of hugs in the second world. The constriction of her chest eased and she could breathe again, eyes clearing although there was still damp on her face.

"Are you alright?" Kester was crouching in front of her, eyes intent.

"Yes." She immediately gave lie to that as she tried to stand and wavered on her feet, held up by his hand under her elbow.

"Death sickness," Gilean commented, voice harsh. "Part of the burden of being a shadow-walker." He gave a sort of laugh at Arrow's expression. "No, other Erith do not feel the loss the same way you do. We mourn those we have loved, but we do not miss those we have killed." His breathing was harsh. "But the shadows contain everything."

Arrow thought about that for a while. It felt right. The shadows contained every potential colour, every potential season all at once. It made sense that the loss of life would be felt in those shadows, no matter who had died.

"You killed the Regent." Miach was not condemning her. The sadness in his voice and face made her own eyes fill. If ever there was a warrior who had lived their duty, it was Miach. And two monarchs were dead on his watch in less than a day.

"I had orders." Arrow's voice was hoarse. She glanced at her sword, clean and showing no sign of the Regent's blood, and sheathed it before she reached into her pocket, pulled out Evellan's orders, now tattered from so much careless handling.

Miach read the orders, mouth tightening.

"To seek justice for Gilean."

"Justice as I judged it," Arrow pointed out. She was no lawyer, but had stood through enough of the Taellan's meetings to know how Erith law worked. "Both Gilean and Orlis nearly lost their lives to this. And I made a promise to your lady." Her throat closed a moment, a wave of unexpected grief reminding her of that most difficult Erith. "To find out what happened to Gilean. What happened to Teresea. And to see that it was put right. And I made a promise to the heartland." Her voice stopped for a moment, the echo of the heartland's grief coursing through her. "The heartland loves its monarchs." The echoes of the promises she had made was in her voice, the thread of power reflecting a magician's oath.

"She told me." Miach's jaw clenched as though he, too, had his own moment of sorrow. He handed the parchment back to Arrow. "And I say that you have fulfilled your oaths and your orders."

To her surprise, his mouth then curved up in a smile. A genuine expression with no shadows in it.

"And perhaps something good has come of this. You have been talking with the heartland." His words made no sense, his eyes straying to the left side of her face. She remembered the heartland's caress earlier and put her hand up to her skin instinctively, feeling nothing. "The heartland marks those it favours," he continued, pulling, of all things, a small mirror out of one pocket and handing it to her. "It favours very, very few."

She turned the small piece of mirror to her face and went still at what she found. High on her cheekbone, towards the outside corner of her eye, where no one could fail to miss it, was the faintest outline of a curling leaf, the Erith's symbol for the heartland. She touched her skin again, feeling nothing on the surface, and rubbed the mark. It did not move or fade, or redden along with the rest of her skin, remaining pale and distinct.

"I do not understand." Far from being favoured, she felt used. The casual marking by the heartland stung. Another loss of control of her body, something else done to her without her consent.

"No, you would not," Miach said, sad, taking his mirror back. He paused a moment, as though gathering his thoughts. "You did not notice the same mark on the Queen? Or Teresea?"

"No." Arrow's face formed a scowl without her permission, and she glared at the warrior. She should have noticed such a distinctive mark, she realised.

"The heartland marks those it favours," he said again, one hand lifting to indicate her cheek. "Many Erith spend their lives seeking communication with our heartland. She is an extraordinary gift to the Erith, yet she speaks to very few. And fewer still earn her favour. To be marked by the heartland is something very special indeed."

"More special than being a shadow-walker?" Arrow's tone was nasty. Spiteful. She could not help it. So many lies. So much information withheld.

"Not quite." There was a note in his voice that suggested he understood at least part of her anger. "A shadow-walker is something almost unique. We know of none other alive. There are, though, a few of the heartland's favoured alive. Perhaps it would help to meet them?"

Arrow drew a breath to answer and Gilean moved behind Miach's shoulder. A small motion, just enough to send a ripple through his cloak and catch Arrow's attention. And so she did not shout at the first guard. Instead she bit her lip, hard, until she could manage some courtesy, and saw by the returning shadows on Miach's face that he knew his offer had not been appreciated.

"I am needed elsewhere, *svegraen*," she managed to say, her voice a reasonable tone.

"We will have a relay set for you tomorrow. After ..." He closed his lips together, jaw tight.

After the Queen's funeral rites. Which Noverian was to have presided over, a last act of a faithful Consort, before he took oath as Regent.

"Well, at least we will not have to look at that red suit again." Arrow heard her voice say, her unedited thought let loose without permission. Noverian's suit for his oath taking, the work of a dozen harassed tailors.

Miach's lips twitched and he laughed, a fresh, welcome sound, eyes dancing.

"Indeed. Perhaps we can burn it instead?" Gilean suggested.

CHAPTER TWENTY-TWO

M emory of that red suit burning merrily in the annex fireplace was small comfort the next morning as Arrow accompanied the procession to the Erith's graveyard. The most sacred space the Erith had, the place was a waking nightmare. *Vicandula* stretched as far as the eye could see, each grave plant in its own spot, often with a small plaque beside it recording the name and House, and the worthy deeds, of the Erith whose soul stone had been raised in that spot.

Arrow's eyes were burning as she kept the steady, even pace with everyone else. The Queen's body was being carried far ahead of her, Miach's cadre bearing their mistress to her final rest, no one disputing their right to do so when the full details of Noverian's treachery had become clear.

The difficult morning followed a seemingly endless night. Defeating Noverian, as hard at that had been, had only been the start of it. There had been no rest for anyone after that.

There was a first round of questions for the conspirators still alive to provide answers. Queris was finding the dungeons even more uncomfortable than Arrow had imagined he would, and after so short a time. The ladies had been questioned, most set free. The one who had given poison to the Queen was dead. Miach had been in no mood to give quarter.

Priath turned a sickly shade when Miach told him what Noverian had revealed. And yet, Priath was too cunning to admit to anything, still settled in silence. Not forgotten. Never forgotten, but set aside, now in the dungeons with Queris for company. It was its own form of punishment, for the two thoroughly disliked each other. And they were guarded, for now, by a trio of constructs. Mercat would not work on the constructs, and any attempt to interfere with the constructs' delicate magic, now that the creatures were active, would result in a swift, painful death.

The questions were not done. Had barely begun. And Miach was facing a hard, uncomfortable truth. Not everyone who had followed him had been coerced. There were likely to be more Erith who, like Priath, wanted more influence. The Queen had never been one for sharing power. Not even with her Consort, to whom she had apparently been quite devoted until the moment of her death.

Evellan and Seivella still had questions to answer about their involvement with Nuallan, but so far Lord Whintnath and the remains of the Taellan had accepted the magicians' assurances that they had never acted to harm the Erith, only to try and stop Nuallan. Restored to health, with the weight of treachery and death around them, no one could doubt either of their sincere grief and the sense of loss they still felt for the young man that Nuallan had been before the incursion so long ago.

The Palace ward keepers had swept the entire complex overnight, no easy feat, and had found several more constructs and defences that had been tampered with and had declared those areas out of bounds to everyone apart from their number. There had been no arguments, not even from the remaining Taellan, who normally hated their freedom being constrained. It would take some time to dismantle all the harm.

The Library remained closed. It might never re-open, Miach had told Arrow in a rare moment of candour. Too much blood had been spilled. Arrow felt sorrow at the loss of something so unique, even though she had only seen it already damaged, and could understand the outrage being expressed by a number of Houses at the loss. That outrage was met, measure for measure, by the quiet, unyielding grief of the families of those who had lost their lives.

And so everyone who could walk, the entire Palace from the most junior servant to the highest ranked member of the nobility, were here in the Palace's vast graveyard to bid farewell to Freyella.

For the first time in her life, Arrow felt she was simply one of the crowd among the Erith. Everyone else was caught up in their own concerns.

Arrow had been offered a place with Orlis and Gilean, both looking healthier even if Orlis was still furious, further ahead in the procession along with Kallish and her cadre, and had declined, preferring to stay within the crowds. Too many people knew her face already, and there were too many of House Regersfel around, many of whom were of the same mind as Seggerat and Eshan, that she should never have been allowed to live.

As it was, she was somehow surrounded by junior White Guard, a few wearing the mark of the Queen's own guard. Miach's doing, along with Kallish, she suspected.

The funeral rites passed without incident for Arrow and no one around her commented on the tears that ran freely down her face, their own tears flowing as Miach spoke the necessary words and the Queen's body disappeared forever, her *vicandula* springing up, larger than the others nearby.

There was food and drink afterwards, a custom which was apparently shared by Erith and humans alike, with solemn toasts to the Queen's memory. There was no mention of Noverian, whose body was already interred, along with the very few Erith whose crimes were judged serious enough that their souls remained inside flesh and bone. There was no mention of any of the events of the past few days.

Arrow stayed as long as she thought was polite. Miach had arranged for a mirror relay to be set up for her as soon as the rites were concluded. She had her satchel with her and nothing else to pack. The heartland's grief still ran through her, wanting her to stay. Arrow was in no mind to listen. The heartland had marked her without consent. However prized such a thing was among the Erith, Arrow could not move past her anger. Not yet. Perhaps in time she would come to accept it. Perhaps not. Until then, perhaps she could find a way to conceal it. If spells would not work, the human world contained a wide array of cosmetics she could try.

It was a petty grievance on this day, she knew. The Erith's Queen was dead. The entire Palace mourned. The heartland mourned. The sweet scent of death was everywhere, hurting her chest and closing her throat.

Time to be gone. Everyone she knew, everyone familiar to her, were caught up in their own concerns. She was alone among the biggest crowd of Erith she had ever seen, wandering aimlessly as the day turned to afternoon. She found herself at the edge of the crowds eventually, glad of the space. Time to leave. She slipped away, making her way along a quiet corridor.

It was probably rude to go without saying goodbye. That did trouble her. She hesitated in her stride, wondering if she should go back. Bid farewell to those she knew. Gilean. Orlis. Kester. Kallish. Miach. The thought of going back into the crowds, with the unfamiliar faces and glittering array of finery, held her to her course. Time to go.

"Lady Arrow." The voice, female and unknown, startled her.

Her wards flared for a moment as she turned, an instinctive reaction.

One of the Queen's former ladies stood perfectly still just outside the reach of her wards, eyes wide and flecked with pale amber as she took in the silver flare. Dressed in the traditional purple of mourning, the lady looked pale, smudges under her eyes, her hands tight around an ornate scroll held before her. One of the Queen's ladies, released from prison after close questioning. Not a conspirator.

"My lady," Arrow answered, calling her defences back, "my apologies. You startled me."

"I did not mean to. You looked far away."

"What can I do for you, my lady?"

"Frey was ..." The lady's voice choked. The shortened name and obvious grief were clear signs of genuine affection from this lady. "Well, towards the end she was often incoherent, but she insisted that I take this into keeping and pass this to you if ... if she could not."

"Do you believe she knew what was being done to her?"

"She knew something was wrong, certainly. But she would not have known who to trust. Not with one of us poisoning her." The lady closed her eyes, and a bright trace of tears coursed down her cheek. "She was old, yes, and perhaps it was her time. But it was cruel."

"Yes." Arrow agreed. Cruel was exactly the right word for what had been done, the Queen's famously sharp mind eroded by drugs while the lady herself was aware that something was wrong, not knowing who to trust, knowing that someone close to her was responsible.

"Yes." The lady echoed, then held out the scroll. "She wanted you to have this. I believed she hoped to speak with you again before you left. Alisemea was one of her favourites. And mine." The sorrow in the lady's voice drew an answering ache from Arrow, even though Alisemea was simply a name, and a painted face.

"What is this?" Arrow did not take the thing offered, staring at it with suspicion. It looked perilously like a Naming scroll, only far more elaborate than anything she had ever seen before. There had been some in the Archives, ancestries of long dead magicians whose lineage was of particular interest. With no scroll of her own, Arrow had spent time studying those scrolls, learning the importance of lineage to the Erith.

"It is your Naming scroll."

"That is impossible." Arrow dismissed the idea with a half-laugh, bitterness clear to her ears. "Seggerat told me, many times, that I was not Named."

The lady's expression, sorrow and sympathy mixed together, held back more words and whatever additional bitterness and scorn Arrow had in her.

"You never knew her, but there is no possibility in this world or the next that Alisemea vel Regersfel would allow her child into the world unNamed. She wanted a child. She wanted you, very badly. There were baby clothes made, a crib for you, and your Naming scroll prepared long before you were born, the scroll waiting only for your Name."

Arrow felt as though her entire body had frozen. It had never occurred to her that Seggerat had lied, she realised. Not with the scorn and disgust heaped upon her by many other Erith. Many of the Taellan in particular. Seggerat's cronies. With the command, given almost at the start of her service under oath, to never speak of her lineage, she had never been able to ask about her family, however curious she may have been. And with the passing of years it had not occurred to her to wonder what say, if any, her birth mother might have had in whether she was Named, and, more than that, whether she was even wanted.

The thought of a young Erith lady preparing for a birth of a mixed-breed child with hope and anticipation had never crossed Arrow's mind. A crib. Clothes.

That spoke of an expectant mother with hopes and dreams for her child. Antic-ipation of what the child might be.

The great, yawning void that had opened up inside her when the Queen had told stories of her mother was abruptly less empty. She had not been an unwanted child, considered shameful by her mother.

"I am sorry to cause you distress, but not sorry to tell you these things," the lady added.

Arrow became aware of tears on her face and wiped them away, wiping her hands on her clothing before she carefully accepted the scroll. The magic bound into the parchment resonated against her skin. It was hers. A drop of her blood would have been bound into it, so it could be no one else's scroll.

"I have a Name." The words were awkward in her mouth. The idea was mo-mentous. To be Named was to have standing amongst the Erith. To be recognised by their laws. To be counted as something. Not an it anymore, but she.

"Mealla vel Liathius."

The Name rang through her entire being, holding her still again. It was too much to comprehend. A Name. And not of the Regersfel House, either. For her paternal grandfather. A sign that, whatever else might be true, Alisemea had not been ashamed of her connection with House Liathius.

Arrow wiped away more tears.

"I am sorry. I do not even know your name."

"I am Raselle, of the House Presien. Yes, Gilean is my cousin. Distantly. And I am also, somewhat removed, your aunt."

"My lady," Arrow began, but had no more words, throat closing in.

"I would like to get to know you a little," the lady continued. Not just a lady or any Erith. A relative. Arrow's mind spun at the idea. A relative, of an old and respected House, who wished to claim kinship with her. It was extraordinary.

"I ..."

"You must go, I know. The mirror relay will not be held forever. Come back, though. Soon." The lady reached forward and touched her fingers, warm and soft, to Arrow's wrist, a small gesture to her, but one which further unbalanced Arrow's world. Among the Erith she could count on her fingers the number of

people who had voluntarily touched her skin without intending to cause harm.
Nassaran. Vailla. Hustrai. Orlis. Kallish. Kester. And now Raselle.

elle

The Naming scroll tucked into her bag, heavily warded, her mind still struggling to pull together all the various strands, she made her way between the silent
buildings, now and then catching echoes of spells at the edges of her first sight.
Part of her wanted to stop and look and examine the ward masters' craft or just
marvel for a few more moments at the Palace itself. There had been so little time
to simply look around since she had been here. The greater part of her, though,
wanted to get to the mirror relay and be away before any more revelations could
be made.

She had thought she might become lost again, in the maze of Palace buildings,
but she could feel the mirror relay ahead of her, or perhaps she was being guided
by the heartland which had, reluctantly, accepted her wish to leave.

The Naming scroll seemed to weigh her down, potent evidence of Seggerat's
lies. And others, too. How many of the Taellan had known she was Named? How
many of the Erith who had bullied her at the Academy? Evellan? Seivella? Eshan?

Eshan must have known. He had been privy to all Seggerat's affairs for so
long, and had been a retainer in the House when Alisemea was alive. Knowing
that Arrow was a full member of the House and not just adopted in, as he was,
explained some of his resentment. Still, she could not find any forgiveness for him.

And the others. So many others. Those who had known, those who had suspected, and those who were too far removed that they had no actual knowledge.
All conspiring, to various degrees, by their silence to keep Seggerat's version of
events true. An unNamed, bastard offspring, unwanted and discarded. The story
woven by Seggerat required that she be grateful that the Erith had taken her in and
trained her. Of all the things they had asked of her, she had most comprehensively
failed to raise any gratitude for their care.

For access to magic, yes. For access to the world of spells, the lines of power, the wonder in everyday objects. That, she was grateful for. No human magician could have trained her as well as the Academy, and the 'kin did not use magic in that way, so the only place she could have learned was among the Erith. Magic had been her captor, the oath spells woven into her blood keeping her tied to the Erith for so long. Magic was also her escape. The lines of a well-crafted spell. The harnessing of power few Erith could master so well. Knowing there was something worthy about her, even if it was simply her skill in magic.

But everything else had been a lie. Not unwanted. Not unNamed.

Fury sparked her to a faster pace, human-made boots striking Erith gravel with clipped, hasty strides. She barely saw the path ahead of her, stung to her core. Anger and the heart-deep sting of lost trust. Everything she had been told about her life was false. There was no abandonment by her parents. She was not unwanted. And she had two Houses she could claim access to and shelter from. Two of the oldest Houses among the Erith. Liathius House had faded over her life, its most famous son long gone, no other blood relative prepared to keep the House alive. But the Regersfel House would have to admit her. With the potent evidence of her lineage, they would not risk the social ruin of failing to support her.

A laugh, a bitter sound she had not heard from her mouth before, choked her throat. Social ruin. There was something deeply unsettling about the new knowledge that House Regersfel would have to take her in, that failing to take her in might cost them the respect of the other Houses. Even if she had only been an unwanted mixed-breed, she had seen every day in the Palace that there were mixed-blood people living among the Erith, some enjoying positions of responsibility.

No wonder Seggerat had banned her from the heartland. Even constrained by the oath spells, unable to act, she would have realised in moments that there were other people like her in the world. Other people who did not meet Seggerat's high standard of purity.

And she was not just a mixed breed. She was a shadow-walker, something the Erith needed. A hard smile lifted the corners of her mouth. They might need her. She was certain she did not need them. Not anymore. There was the workspace waiting for her. And work. And a half-packed travel bag with maps and plans and a world to explore.

"Arrow!"

Miach's voice. From the slightly exasperated tone, not the first time he had called her. She had been so angry she had forgotten the most basic rule among the Erith, to always be alert for danger. Earlier, she would not have believed Miach would harm her. For a moment, she wondered, not trusting her own judgement.

To her surprise, he was alone, the purple armband the only sign of mourning, everything else about him as pristine as usual, even the shadows of tiredness gone from under his eyes.

"You were leaving without saying goodbye?"

Something in his voice stopped the bitter words at the tip of her tongue. She swallowed, looked again, and felt an unwelcome prickle of shame. He may appear pristine, but there was a tightness to his mouth and a depth to his eyes that had not been there when she had first met him. Decades of close watch and protection for his monarch and he had lost her, and her Consort, within a day of each other. He deserved better from her than for her to run away.

"It seemed easier." She hesitated. "I did not mean to be rude." That was true enough. And she still wanted to move, to leave as soon as she could. She needed a period of calm and quiet. She needed a space of her own. The quiet of the borrowed workspace called to her, the clear requests of the shifkin nation that were easy to understand, easy to follow, and did not carry with them any of the tangled politics of the Erith. That was what she needed. Her feet moved, wanting to go. Even the nausea of the mirror relay did not make her hesitate.

His mouth twitched in a smile, with little humour in it.

"I can understand that. The last few days have been ..." He closed his mouth firmly, jaw set. "But the relay will be kept ready for another half day."

"I ..." Her throat closed over. So much she could say, so much she wanted to say, and in the middle of it a wordless scream that she wanted to let out.

"Something has happened," he guessed, voice sharpening, "another threat?"

Her laugh was more like a sob.

"No. No threat. I just …" She could not speak more, waved her hand in a meaningless gesture, and drew a breath in. "This is not my home, *svegraen*. I was here at the Preceptor and then the Queen's request. Both expired. I should leave."

"The exile." His expression changed to comprehension. That was not quite what she had meant, but she did not correct him. "The Taellan have not yet had time to reverse that, and there are those who would still do you harm. Very well. Let me escort you to the relay."

"That is very kind," she began, and he cut her off with a hand wave.

"It is the least I can offer. I hope that, when the exile is reversed, you will visit again."

"Perhaps," she answered, not looking at him. Part of her ached with longing. There was something in the heartland that called her, perhaps just the echo of all that power and magic, just beyond her skin. Perhaps the greater part of her that was Erith recognised its homeland. And there was a vast world to explore here. The wonders of the Erith lands, the beauty of the wild, so unlike the shifkin's home, everything that was Erith and everything that had been denied her until now.

Another part of her, in war with the first, wanted quiet and safety. There was beauty here, but also danger. And people who wanted to use her for their own ends. Even the heartland itself had marked her without her consent. Being used, her own wishes not consulted, was something she was heartily sick of, after fifteen years' service to the Taellan. She had barely begun to explore what might be possible outside the Erith's service. There was a whole world she did not know. The heartland might tempt her, but there were also vast spaces of shifkin lands, stretches of human-claimed lands and even neutral territories that all had their own wonders.

She found she could manage basic manners, though, as well as her unruly thoughts, although much of that was probably due to Miach's easy presence, undemanding as he escorted her to the mirror room and bade her health before she left the heartland.

CHAPTER TWENTY-THREE

The workspace was blissfully quiet, the building around it free of any other people. The wards around the building were settled, dormant but ready to warn her if anything approached.

She had managed to get out of the Taellaneth more or less under her own power, the nausea of the mirror relay countered by a healing potion from her bag. The entire Taellaneth had been quiet, the faintest echo of the heartland's grief carrying through the scented air.

Now she was back to safety. No one had tried to harm her for days. The slight shift and creak of the building around her was familiar, the workspace full of the pungent scent of a new coffee blend she had decided to try.

There was another set of ceramic pots in boxes under the workbench. The Prime felt that having a cleansing spell to get rid of *surjusi* taint was worth the expense of more pots. Arrow had not dared use any of the pots yet, deciding instead to review her notes from her previous efforts. She had the ingredients set out across the bench along with her meticulous notes of the quantities used in her previous attempts. Somewhere in the measures and the notes she hoped to find the answer that would let her capture the fresh green scent and bind it to a stable cleansing spell.

It would not be that day. Despite the peace, the quiet and the solitude, she was finding it difficult to concentrate. Her fingers kept straying to the mark on her cheekbone, which she could not feel at all but which was visible in the mirror, and stood out in second sight like a signal fire when she had checked. The basic cosmetics she had tried had not hidden the mark. Her eyes kept straying to the other workbench. Hidden from sight was a backpack ready to go.

She had returned from the heartland to find a letter from the muster's lawyers, paper heavy enough to be used as Erith parchment, advising her that she had a share of reward money. It had taken several times reading through the letter before she had remembered the stolen goods she and Tamara had found by accident when chasing the human. So many days before. Apparently whatever had been in the crates had been hugely valuable, and the shifkin had decided to gift Arrow a share of the reward. She had been shocked at the sum provided. An enormous amount of money. More than enough for her to travel. Perhaps enough to buy her own residence in Lix. A modest one. But she had no desire to tie herself to one place just yet. The shifkin understood. At least, Zachary did, and his word was what mattered.

So, she had finished packing her bag. Basic clothing and equipment that she could carry with her. And tucked inside that, heavily warded, was the Naming scroll.

She was not quite ready to travel, wanting to finish this last task for the 'kin, and had hidden the scroll away in the hopes that, out of sight, she could focus on the task. It was not working.

Even as she sighed and turned toward the scroll, the flex of the building's wards, announcing a visitor, called for her attention.

She arrived at the front door of the building moments after the quiet knock, the camera view, inside the door, and the building's wards, identifying Kester vo Halsfeld. She hesitated a moment before opening the door, an odd, uncomfortable fluttering in her stomach. She had not said goodbye before leaving the heartland, which was probably rude, and after the happenings in the heartland, she was not sure what he might have to say to her.

He was dressed in his preferred day wear, a near approximation of a warrior's day uniform, braids replaced by leaf patterns woven into the fabric, and carried a large, plain cardboard box under one arm. The box made her blink as it was clearly of human make, and went oddly with the Erith clothing.

"Good day, *svegraen*." Her greeting sounded odd, too, even though Erith manners dictated that it was for her to speak first as the prospective host.

"Good day, Lady Arrow." The word might be solemn, but there was a hint of humour about his mouth and eyes that somehow made her relax.

"Would you like to come in?"

"Thank you."

Not knowing what else to do, she led him back to the workspace and self-consciously tidied her clumsy notes into a neat pile, not looking at the other workbench, not wanting a reminder of their previous, awkward encounter. If he remembered, he gave no sign, looking with interest at the large stack of papers and range of ingredients set out.

"An interesting project?"

"Indeed." She opened her mouth to say more and then closed it. The Prime would probably not want his business discussed with the Erith. Frowning slightly, she wondered if she should have put the papers away completely. Or not let Kester inside the building.

"The 'kin are keeping you busy." His tone and manner were perfectly relaxed, no sign that he had spotted anything odd with her.

"Would you like coffee?" There, that was safe. Or apparently not as he tensed slightly.

"Perhaps in a moment." He put the cardboard box on the now-bare workbench surface and she felt all the tension come back into her neck and shoulders, remembering another box. He looked down at the box as he arranged it carefully, parallel to the side of the bench, then looked up, amber bright in his eyes. "I began badly. It was not my intention to ..." he bit his lip, a sign of uncertainty that made Arrow tense further. "There are rules of conduct. No." He frowned into the distance, apparently trying to gather his thoughts, and Arrow gripped her hands together, hidden by the workbench surface, fingers sore with the force of her hold. "It would please me greatly to know you better," he said at length, eyes returning to her face, "and to see where that might lead us."

Arrow's mouth was half-open, no sound emerging.

"And as apology for my clumsy beginning, I have a gift for you. With no obligation," he added quickly. He gave the box a little push, across the bench, until it was closer to her.

Seizing the distraction, Arrow took her time opening the box, lifting the top from it, her fingers clumsy. A gift. Freely given. A rare thing, in her experience. She set the top of the box aside. There was fine white tissue paper inside and the unmistakable scent of leather. She peeled back the tissue paper and froze, fingers closing, tearing the paper.

A messenger bag. And not just any messenger bag. A replica of the one she had carried for so many years, the familiar weight at her side that she missed almost like a limb, the finely made Erith satchel no substitute.

She lifted her eyes up and found a faintly concerned expression on Kester's face.

"It is as close as I could find to the one you had," he explained, voice a fraction too fast, "and it seemed something that you treasured."

"Yes." Her throat closed again at the one word and she looked back down, one finger tracing the stitching on the front. She lifted it out from the paper, the rustle loud in the quiet space, and turned it over. New, but it felt absolutely familiar in her hands. Far more finely crafted than the one she had had, it would wear well. Her lips curved up into an involuntary smile, eyes filling with stupid moisture that she blinked quickly away. "Thank you."

Kester's answering smile made that uncomfortable fluttering start in her stomach again and she ducked her eyes away.

"If you have time," he began, sounding far less hesitant than before, "there is a new exhibition at the sculpture garden. Apparently some of the human artists are quite good."

"We will stand out a little," Arrow answered, wry humour coming to her rescue. She was in human clothing, and could pass for human, but there was no mistaking Kester for anything other than pure blood Erith.

"I have a glamour."

She looked up to find a tall human male before her, a subtle alteration of features that was still Kester, just altered enough to pass for human. It was not something he had casually come across. That had taken practice. He had taken time and effort to prepare for this visit, to consider how they might spend some time together.

She looked back down at the messenger bag, and the fluttering vanished into lightness.

Go into the human world with Kester. Explore the sculpture garden. Learn a little bit more about this warrior.

"I would like that."

THANK YOU

Thank you very much for reading *Betrayed*, The Taellaneth - Book 3. I hope that you enjoyed continuing Arrow's story.

It would be great, if you have five minutes, if you could leave an honest review at the store you got it from. Reviews are really helpful for other readers to decide whether the book is for them, and also help me get visibility for my books - thank you.

Arrow's story continues in *Tainted*, The Taellaneth - Book 4, also available on Amazon.

If you want to know what I'm working on and when the next book will be available, you can contact me and sign up for my newsletter at the website: www.taellaneth.com.

CHARACTER LIST

Note: to avoid spoilers, some names may have been omitted, and some details left out.

The Erith

Bea vel Nostren - member of the Taellan; head of her House

Diannea vel Sovernis - member of the Taellan; head of her House

Eimille vel Falsen - member of the Taellan; head of her House

Elias - White Guard; cadre leader; cadre is second cadre of the Queen's guard

Eshan nuin Regersfel - Chief Scribe to Taellan; adopted member of House Regersfel

Evellan - Preceptor, head of Academy

Freyella - Queen; vetrai to Noverian

Geran vo Sovernis - White Guard; member of House Sovernis

Gesser vo Regresan - assistant Teaching Master; son of Gret

Gilean vo Presien - war mage

Gret vo Regresan - member of the Taellan; head of his House

Hustrai - Teaching Master at Academy

Juinis vo Halsfeld - member of the Taellan; head of his House

Kallish nuin Falsen - White Guard; cadre leader; adopted member of House Falsen

Kester vo Halsfeld - member of the Taellan; brother-by-marriage to Juinis

Orlis - journeyman mage

Messian - Steward at Taellaneth

Miach - White Guard; cadre leader; first guard to the Queen and in charge of Palace security

Neith vo Sena - member of the Taellan; head of his House

Noverian - Consort; vetral to Freyella

Priath - courtier at Palace

Queris vo Lianen - courtier, resident at Palace; Queen's cousin

Seivella - Teaching Mistress at Academy; deputy to Preceptor

Seggerat vo Regersfel - elder of the Taellan; head of his House

Serran vo Liathius - powerful mage; founder of the Academy

Smaillis - Teaching Master at Academy

Undurat - White Guard, member of Kallish's third

Vailla vel Falsen - member of House Falsen

Whintnath - Commander of the White Guard

Xeveran - White Guard, leader of third in Kallish's cadre

The shifkin

Andrew Farraway - member of Farraway muster, Matthias' twin and Zachary's son

Con - member of Farraway muster

Marianne Stillwater - mate of Zachary Farraway

Matthias Farraway - shifkin enforcer; mate of Tamara, Andrew's twin and Zachary's son

Tamara - member of Farraway muster, mate of Matthias

Zachary Farraway - Prime of shifkin nation; mate of Marianne Stillwater, father to Andrew and Mathias

Others

Arrow - mixed-blood, Erith-trained magician

GLOSSARY

Erith words and phrases

Arwmverishan - abomination

Baelthras - six-legged predators

Brother by *vestrait* - Brother by marriage (not the same as brother-in-law) – applies to Kester who became Juinis' brother when Juinis wed Kester's sister

Cadre - a White Guard unit, made up of three thirds

Ethtar - curse word

Gehthras - ancient Erith word for "open"

Graduate - an Academy student who has completed all fifteen cycles; highest standing of Erith-trained magicians

High magic - any form of magic, generally human or Erith, which requires a spell to work it, whether written, spoken or drawn

mestera ovail - command from a war mage to White Guard to be ready

Natural magic - innate magic which can be used without a formal spell, e.g. shifkin ability to change form

Nuin - signifies someone adopted into a House, not part of the blood family, for example Eshan nuin Regersfel

Shadow-walker - rare type of Erith mage

Surjusi - unclean spirits, lethal to Erith

Surrimok - mountain-dwelling predator in mostly-human (or simian) shape; yellow eyes, hands and feet adapted for climbing, and long fur.

Svegraen - term of address and respect for a member or members of the White Guard; literal translation is "warrior"

Taellan - refers both to the group of ten high-ranking Erith who make up the council of government for the Erith, answerable only to the Queen and her Consort, and also to an individual member of the council

Third - a group of five warriors making up part of a cadre

Urjusi - unclean magic

vel / vo - female / male versions of signifier of high ranking member of a House, usually the blood family or their *vetrai* or *vetral*, for example Eimille vel Falsen and Seggerat vo Regersfel

Vestrai / Vestrait - married / marriage

Vestran - betrothed

Vetrai - wife

Vetral - husband

Vicandula - plant, also known as Erith gravestone

War mage - mage who has completed all fifteen cycles of the Academy and graduated in discipline of war mage; entitled to wear the cloak of a war mage; swear oaths to protect the Erith

White Guard - elite warriors, undergo rigorous training, rank depicted by braids on their uniforms

ALSO BY THE AUTHOR
(as at September 2022)

The Taellaneth series (complete)
Concealed, Book 1
Revealed, Book 2
Betrayed, Book 3
Tainted, Book 4
Cloaked, Book 5

Taellaneth Box Set (all five books in one e-book)
Taellaneth Complete Series (Books 1–5)

The Hundred series (complete)
The Gathering, Book 1
The Sundering, Book 2
The Reckoning, Book 3
The Rending, Book 4
The Searching, Book 5
The Rising, Book 6

Ageless Mysteries
Deadly Night, Book 1
False Dawn, Book 2
Morning Trap, Book 3

Assassin's Noon, Book 4
Flightless Afternoon, Book 5
Ascension Day, Book 6 (available October 2022)

ABOUT THE AUTHOR

Vanessa Nelson is a fantasy author who lives in Scotland, United Kingdom and spends her days juggling the demands of two spoiled cats, two giant dogs, a day job and her fictional characters.

As far as the cats are concerned, they should always come first. The older dog lets her know when he isn't getting enough attention by chewing up the house. The younger dog's favourite method of getting her attention is a gentle nudge with his head. At least, he would say it's gentle.

You can find out more information at the following places:

Website: www.taellaneth.com

Facebook: www.facebook.com/taellaneth

Printed in Great Britain
by Amazon

17454624R00164